KU-512-003

MURDER IMPERFECT

Aberdeenshire Library and Information Service
www.aberdeenshire.gov.uk/libraries
Renewals Hotline 01224 661511
Downloads available from
www.aberdeenshirelibraries.lib.overdrive.com

1 2 OCT 2012

2 5 MAR 2015

HEADQUARTERS

2 5 SEP 2015

25. NOV 15.

10. 01. 17.

13 Feb.

04. MAY 17.

HEADQUARTERS
1 9 JAN 2018

ABERDEENSHIRE
LIBRARIES

WITHDRAWN
FROM LIBRARY

ABERDEENSHIRE LIBRARIES
1920372

MURDER IMPERFECT

LESLEY COOKMAN

LARGE PRINT

Oxford

Copyright © Lesley Cookman, 2010

First published in Great Britain 2010
by
Accent Press Ltd.

Published in Large Print 2011 by ISIS Publishing Ltd.,
7 Centremead, Osney Mead, Oxford OX2 0ES
by arrangement with
Pollinger Limited

All rights reserved

The moral right of the author has been asserted

British Library Cataloguing in Publication Data
Cookman, Lesley.
    Murder imperfect.
    1. Sarjeant, Libby (Fictitious character) - - Fiction.
    2. Women private investigators - - England - - Kent
    - - Fiction.
    3. Gay men - - Crimes against - - Fiction.
    4. Actresses - - Fiction.
    5. Detective and mystery stories.
    6. Large type books.
    I. Title
    823.9'2–dc22

LP

ISBN 978–0–7531–8862–0 (hb)
ISBN 978–0–7531–8863–7 (pb)

Printed and bound in Great Britain by
T. J. International Ltd., Padstow, Cornwall

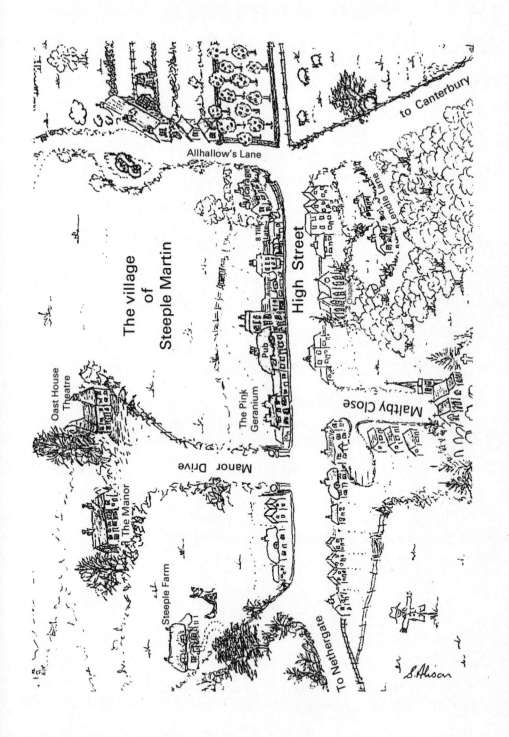

The village
of
Steeple Martin

Allhallow's Lane

to Canterbury

High Street

Vicarage

Lendle Lane

Chapel

Pub

Oast House
Theatre

The Pink
Geranium

Maltby Close

Manor Drive

Surgery

The Manor

Steeple Farm

To Nethergate

S. Alison

CHAPTER
ONE

The pantomime cow collapsed on top of the fairy at the very time Adam stepped off the ha-ha.

"He's moved back in again," Libby told her friend Fran on the phone. "I can't keep trailing backwards and forwards to the flat to look after him, and Harry certainly can't keep running up and down stairs."

"What did he do?" asked Fran.

"He wasn't looking where he was going and walked straight off the edge."

"Isn't it fenced?"

"Ha-has aren't fenced," scoffed Libby. "Don't you know that?"

"All right, all right. I'm not up on gardening terms. What does Ben say?"

"He's being very long-suffering about it," said Libby. "Lots of sighs."

"Oh dear. Still, it won't be for long, will it?"

"No, thank goodness. Meanwhile, Ben keeps taking himself off to Steeple Farm to do strange things with beams and floorboards, and I've got to take over the fairy as well as directing, which means we can both keep out of Ad's way in the evenings."

"Poor Adam!" laughed Fran.

"He is a bit grumpy," conceded Libby, "but with a bit of luck he'll get fed up and go back to his own flat."

"I thought you said he needed looking after?"

"He did, for the first couple of days, but he could move around the flat now, especially as it's all on one level. Here he has to come downstairs to the sitting room and kitchen. He demanded a television in his room the first few days. Cheek."

"So he's putting it on a bit?"

"Of course. Just like a man." Libby sighed. "Not like our poor fairy."

"What happened to her?"

"I told you, the cow fell on her. Broke her leg. She's furious."

"Won't she better in time for the run?"

Libby sighed again. "Plaster for at least six weeks, the hospital said. And as we open on the first Monday in January she'll have missed all the rehearsals."

"You've played the fairy before," consoled Fran. "You'll be fine."

"I'm too old," said Libby gloomily. "I'd rather be the witch."

She put the phone down and stared out of the window. December had started dripping wet. The tiny green opposite the house was almost a lake, and Romeo the Renault looked in imminent danger of sinking.

"Mu-um!"

Closing her eyes and breathing out heavily, Libby turned towards the stairs.

"What?"

"Any chance of some tea?"

2

"If you came down here you could get it yourself."

"Mum! I can't keep going up and down on my leg." Adam sounded indignant.

"You can get about on the level, though," said Libby. "All right. In a moment."

Muttering to herself, she went into the kitchen. Sidney, on the cane sofa in front of the unlit fire, put his ears back as she passed. The heavy kettle was already on the edge of the Rayburn waiting to be brought to a full boil, so she moved it and fetched the old brown teapot. Might as well make a proper pot and have one herself, she thought. It was mid-afternoon.

The tea made, she carried a mug up to Adam, who was lying on the bed in the spare room playing games on his laptop.

"Thanks, Mum." He grinned disarmingly. "You know you love me really."

"Don't bet on it." Libby sat on the side of the bed. "Wouldn't you be more comfortable in Harry's flat now? You'd be all on one level there."

Adam's face took on a pained expression. "I can't stand for long, Mum. What about meals?"

Libby sighed. "OK, OK, I know. But I can't keep running up and down like this, you know."

"Ben will be here, though, won't he?" said Adam hopefully.

"Not much," said Libby. "He's going to Steeple Farm to get it all finished off. They want to let it after Christmas."

"Good Christmas house, that," commented Adam. "You could have all of us there with no problem."

Libby looked at him with dislike. "I'm going downstairs," she said.

Of course, Adam was right. Steeple Farm was a large thatched farmhouse belonging to a member of Ben's family. Ben, her mostly significant other, was restoring it and had hoped to persuade Libby to move into it from her small cottage in the village, but Libby loved her cottage, she loved Allhallow's Lane and she loved being in the centre of Steeple Martin. So, for the moment, they were both squashed into Number 17, with the addition, currently, of Adam. Libby peered once more out of the window at the darkening sky and turned to the fireplace.

"A fire, Sidney," she said. "That's what we want. We need cheering up." Sidney's ears twitched again and his nose got pushed even more firmly under his tail. Libby creaked down on to her knees and began riddling the grate. She had just got her fingers suitably covered in coal dust and firelighter when her phone rang. Libby swore.

"What's the matter with you?" asked the voice on the other end.

"I'm lighting a fire."

"And it's annoying you?"

"No, you are, Harry. I'm covered in coal dust, and so is the phone now."

"Ring me back when you're clean, then," said Harry. "I want to have a chat."

Libby returned to the fire. Harry co-owned The Pink Geranium vegetarian restaurant in the village with his life partner Peter, who also happened to be Ben's

4

cousin. Libby had known Harry and Peter for several years; in fact it had been they who helped her find number 17 Allhallow's Lane in what they called 'The search for Bide-a-Wee'. Now Adam, Libby's youngest child, lived in the flat above The Pink Geranium, where he helped out in the evenings to augment his earnings as an assistant to a garden designer and landscaper.

Libby had listened to Harry's concerns over several matters in the last few years, from his last foray into heterosexuality to the arrangements for his civil partnership ceremony. He, in turn, had listened to more than his fair share of Libby's troubles and anxieties, most frequently her ambivalence in her relationship with Ben and her rather unwholesome interest in local murders. It occurred to her, rather shamefacedly, that Harry had been more of a support to her than she had to him, so she must make the time to listen properly and help in any way she could.

"But I can't do that!" she exclaimed down the phone ten minutes later, sitting on the cane sofa in front of a now nicely blazing fire.

"Why not?" said Harry. "You've peered into other people's private lives in the past — and without their permission, too. At least this time someone's asking you to do it."

"No, they aren't," said Libby, feeling hot and uncomfortable. "You're the one asking me to do it. This poor man wanted your help. You suggested me."

"I don't understand why you're so upset about it," said Harry. "All I'm asking you to do is look into some rather nasty letters Cy's had. And his panto gives you the perfect opportunity."

"Harry, I'm taking over the fairy here as well as directing," said Libby. "I can't possibly get involved with another panto."

There was a short silence. "Ah," said Harry.

"Look, I'm sorry," said Libby. "If you can tell me a bit more about it, I could p'raps ask Fran what she thinks?"

"I don't think he wants anyone else knowing," said Harry slowly, "but I suppose I could take you to meet him. How would that be?"

"Embarrassing," said Libby. "Couldn't you just tell me and see if I come up with anything?"

"I don't know all the background," said Harry, "but I suppose I could tell you what he told me."

"Go ahead, then." Libby settled back into the sofa.

"Face to face, Lib."

Libby sighed. "Come and have a cup of tea, then," she said, "or are you busy prepping up for this evening?"

"No, most of it's done. I'll pop round and then I can have a word with the invalid at the same time, can't I?"

"You can try and talk him into going back to the flat, too," said Libby. "I'll go and put the kettle back on."

"And I'll bring some of that carrot cake you like," said Harry. "See you in a minute."

Ten minutes later, Harry breezed into the sitting room shaking water from his navy pea coat and handing over a large greaseproof paper parcel.

"I'll dash up and say hello to old peg-leg first," he said, hanging his coat on the hook in the tiny vestibule. "Or he'll hear me and start shouting."

Libby put mugs, teapot, milk, and sugar and cake on a tray and carried them into the sitting room, where she switched on the two lamps either side of the fire and sat down, shifting Sidney out of the way. Harry appeared in the doorway and she waved him to the armchair.

"Now," she said, pouring tea into mugs. "Who is this Cy, and what is this all about? I'm warning you, I'm not ever getting involved in any more murders, so it had better not be that."

Harry raised his eyebrows.

"Not ever?" he said.

CHAPTER
TWO

"Cy is an old mate of mine from London days. He moved down to one of the Maidstone suburbs with his partner a few years ago, as he'd lived there when he was growing up." Harry sipped his tea and gazed into the fire.

"Yes?" said Libby after a moment. "And?"

Harry sighed. "Well, a few months ago he started getting anonymous letters."

"You said started. Has it gone on? How many?"

"I'm not sure but it must be about six, now."

"That's a lot." Libby frowned. "I assume he's been to the police?"

Harry shook his head. "He's aware of the attitude of most cops to this sort of thing."

"What sort of thing?"

"Us, stupid." Harry scowled at her. "Right bunch of homophobes, they are."

"Ian isn't," said Libby, taken aback and referring to Inspector Ian Connell, a mutual friend.

"He's different. And he wasn't sure at first, either." Harry shifted in his chair. "Anyway, it's what Cy thinks, so he hasn't told them."

"Is that what the letters are about, then?"

"Course it is."

"What do they say?" asked Libby. "And how are they written? Computer? Handwritten? The old cut and paste jobs?"

"Computer. I suppose the police could trace which printer was used, and probably what software from which PC, but that would hardly help, would it?" He sighed again. "Much easier when they cut words out of a newspaper and you just went round looking for papers with holes in."

"And what do they say?" prompted Libby.

"I've only seen the first one, but he says they're more or less the same. 'We don't want your sort round here, you filthy . . .' well, you know the sort of thing."

Libby nodded. "Nasty. But I don't know what you want me to do."

"I'm not sure either," said Harry. "I had thought if you could go over and give him a hand with his panto you could get talking to the friends and neighbours and see if you could spot any undercurrents. But if you've got to do ours . . ."

"'Fraid so," said Libby. "And I can't get out of it. We've only got three weeks left of rehearsal time, effectively, if you take out Christmas, and we're sold out for the entire run."

"Bloody silly, if you ask me," said Harry, "having a cow in another pantomime."

"We had to use the one we had made for *Jack and the Beanstalk* again, didn't we? What a waste if we hadn't."

"And I haven't even heard of the panto, either."

"Well, of course you haven't," said Libby reasonably. "It's a new one."

"Why did you choose one no one had heard of then?" asked Harry grumpily.

"I wanted to find one with a cow in it."

"And *Hey, Diddle, Diddle* has a cow, does it?"

Libby sighed. "Yes, Harry. The cow jumped over the moon, didn't she?"

"And how did she fall on the fairy? Don't tell me — she was jumping over the moon."

"Well, trying to, yes. The fairy puts a spell on her, you see."

"Bit dangerous, I'd have thought. Don't you go breaking any legs."

"Thank you for your concern," grinned Libby, "but I've changed that bit now." She put down her mug and cut herself a generous slice of cake. "So what do you want me to do now? Suggest something?"

"Have you *got* any suggestions?" Harry looked gloomy. "I promised I'd help, and that I knew someone else who could. I'm going to look a right arse if I don't."

"No, you won't. Why don't you just tell him I can't actually get involved, but I'd suggest he tells the police. If he really wants me to, I'll meet him, with you, perhaps, and he can show me the letters. They might give me some ideas."

Harry brightened. "Would you?"

"Of course I would. I still don't see what I can actually *do*, but it might help him a bit."

10

Harry leant over and kissed her cheek. "You're a champ, champ," he said. "I knew I could rely on you."

Libby laughed. "You knew you could persuade me, you mean."

"I knew you wouldn't be able to resist a mystery," Harry grinned back and stood up. "Right. I'm going to go and try my powers of persuasion on your offspring."

"To do what?"

"To come back to the flat and get out of your hair."

Adam appeared sheepishly in the kitchen some time later as Libby was about to dish up supper.

"I'll go back to the flat after supper, Mum."

Libby turned in surprise. "You don't have to, darling."

"Yes, I do. Harry put me right on a few things." Adam gave his mother a hug. "I take you a bit for granted, don't I?"

"Kids do that." She kissed his cheek. "Sit down and I'll dish up."

"Do you want a hand with your stuff?" Ben appeared in the kitchen doorway.

"Here's your hat, where's your hurry?" said Libby, raising her eyebrows at him.

"Not at all. He just won't be able to carry much." Ben avoided her eyes and sat opposite Adam.

"I'll drive you round in the car," said Libby, placing plates in front of them. "Much easier."

"And stop and have a drink with Harry, I suppose?" said Ben after Adam had left the table.

Libby stopped clearing plates. "I doubt it," she said. "But if I did, would it matter?"

Ben shrugged. "You seem to talk to him more than you do to me."

"Ben, you're not jealous, are you?"

Ben looked down at the table. "Yes, I suppose I am."

Libby snorted. "But Harry's gay and twenty years younger than I am!"

"I'm not jealous in that way, idiot," said Ben, and the mood lightened. "It's just — as I said — you seem to talk more to him than me."

"Harry's like a best girl friend," said Libby. "He gets jealous of Fran."

"Does he?" Ben looked interested. "I don't."

"Anyway," Libby picked up the plates again, "I won't have a drink because I'll have the car, so you can stop worrying."

"Why don't we both walk round with him and share the burden. Then we can both have a drink with Harry." Ben wrapped his arms round her waist.

"Good idea," said Libby. "And now let me go, or we'll never get there."

Adam seemed to have accumulated an awful lot of stuff in the few days he'd been staying at number 17, and Ben, Libby and Adam himself were quite heavily laden when they staggered up to the door of the flat over The Pink Geranium. Donna waved at them through the window of the restaurant.

"You go in and find Harry," said Libby. "We'll take your stuff upstairs. Then you won't have to keep going up and down."

Adam didn't argue, and, after another few minutes, Ben and Libby, having dumped the various bags on to the sagging couch in the front room of the flat, joined him on the sofa in the window of The Pink Geranium. On the table in front of him was a bottle of red wine and three glasses.

"Did Harry send this?" asked Libby, accepting a glass.

"No!" Adam was indignant. "I did. To say thank you for having me."

Ben patted him on the shoulder. "No worries. Any time."

Adam looked embarrassed. "Thanks, Ben."

They'd finished the bottle of wine by the time Harry appeared from the kitchen carrying another.

"That's me done," he said, pulling up a chair and pouring out more wine. "I take it you did want another one?"

"Er — thank you," said Libby.

"Well, now you're going to help me with my little problem, you deserve it." Harry lifted his glass to her.

"What problem?" Ben looked from one to the other. Adam groaned. Libby closed her eyes.

"Sorry, Lib." Harry pulled a face. "You haven't told them."

"Told us what?" said Ben and Adam together.

"Well, you see —" began Harry.

"Harry's asked me to see if I can help a friend of his who's been receiving anonymous letters," interrupted Libby. "There's not much I can do, but there's no way of me getting in to any trouble. Besides, Harry will be with me."

"Right." Ben looked doubtful.

"You say that every time, Ma," said Adam.

"Well, I don't get into trouble, do I?" said Libby.

"No, because there's usually somebody out there second guessing you and on hand to leap to the rescue," said Ben.

"Look," said Harry hastily, "if you don't want her to —"

"What?" snapped Libby.

"If I don't want her to she'll be all the more determined," said Ben with a rueful smile. Libby relaxed, but glared at Harry.

"I'll call you tomorrow," she said pointedly.

"Bloody hell, Lib," said Harry sleepily the next morning. "It's not nine o'clock yet!"

"I wanted to catch you before you went to work," said Libby. "Did I wake you?"

"Not exactly. Pete's just gone down to make coffee. What do you want?"

"I want to know when we're going to see this Cy person. I need to get my life in order."

There was the sound of Harry struggling to sit up. "Never. Your life's never in order."

Libby sighed. "Look, I've got Christmas to organise, a panto to direct and now the bloody fairy's lines to learn. If we're going to try and put your chum's mind at rest I need to do it soon."

"All right, all right. Ooh, ta, Pete." Libby heard a satisfied slurping sound. "Great coffee, Lib. Straight from Ethiopian Farmers."

14

"Good. Glad to hear you're supporting good causes. But what about Cy?"

"I'll ring him when I get up. He'll be at work, but I expect I can get him. And surely you know all the lines already? You've been rehearsing for weeks."

"I only know them vaguely," said Libby. "Will you ring me when you've spoken to him?"

"Yes, yes, yes. Now leave me alone. I need to commune with my inner soul."

"The coffee and Peter, you mean," said Libby. "OK, I'll go."

Libby went into the kitchen and put plates and mugs in the sink. Ben had gone off to the Manor to see if anything needed to be done on the estate, then he was going to Steeple Farm to carry on with the renovations, so she had the day to herself. After a bit of necessary housework, such as stripping Adam's bed, washing up and wiping Sidney's paw marks off every windowsill in the house, she planned to get on with her current painting, to be sold in Fran's husband's gallery in Nethergate. Her 'pretty peeps', as she called them in recognition of Ngaio Marsh's Troy, sold well to tourists during the summer season, being mainly of the bay and the town, several painted from Fran's front room window in Coastguard Cottage and others from a higher viewpoint, the top floor window in Peel House, where their mutual friends Jane and Terry lived.

After an hour or so painting, or staring, she thought she might have a cup of tea and a biscuit and start learning the fairy's lines. Wearing her director's hat, all she had to do today was take a rehearsal this evening, so the afternoon was free. With a bit of luck, if she didn't have to trek off to see Cy (and if he worked, how could she?) she could then light the fire and have a little doze on the sofa before cooking the evening meal.

She had just stuffed Adam's sheets into the washing machine when the phone rang and all the day's plans came crashing down.

"He's had another one, and something else has happened," said Harry. "He didn't go to work. He'd like to see us today."

"Something else?"

"He was beaten up."

CHAPTER
THREE

"Where was he beaten up?" Libby asked. They were in Harry's car on the M2 on the way to Maidstone, he having asked Donna, his efficient waitress, assistant chef and all round helpmate, to open up and do any prepping for lunch that was needed. Midweek there was little lunchtime trade, and Adam would help as far as his leg would allow him.

"He didn't say." Harry was uncharacteristically tight-lipped, and Libby thought she knew why. Over the past year, and particularly the last few months, more so-called 'gay-bashing' incidents had been reported in the media, including several resulting deaths. He and Peter had been lucky, but, since Libby had known them, Harry had toned down his very obviously camp manner and speech, which she had found endearing. Peter had always looked like an aloof aesthete and, as far as she knew, had never had any problems at work in London, but Harry had confided that with mainstream acceptance of homosexuality, and particularly since civil partnerships had become legal, gay people had become more visible in the community and easier to target.

"Also," he had continued, "a lot of wankers who used to be able to say what they like can't any more, so they're attacking us under cover. And people like Cy still don't like going to the police, so the rise in attacks is being under-reported."

Remembering this conversation now, Libby realised how close to Harry's heart this incident was. She felt a little upsurge of something like stage fright. What on earth could she do? Harry somehow thought she could help, but she knew she was a fraud. Someone who had got involved by accident in a few murder investigations in a sort of snowball effect, but who had no real expertise, or even deductive power. She wanted to stop the car, get out and run home. But Harry, and possibly Cy, were relying on her. She sighed.

They were driving down the hill towards the big M20 roundabout, now. Harry took the left-hand lane and plunged into suburban Maidstone. Eventually, they came to a an area Libby had never seen before; neat roads with grass verges, semi-detached mock Tudor houses, a few bungalows and neighbourhood watch posters in every window. Cul-de-sacs, crescents and closes abounded, and at the centre, a park. Only a small park, but there was a little pond, benches and a fenced play area. It was empty.

"This is it." Harry drew to a stop outside a bungalow at the crest of a slight hill. As Libby got out, she could look down over the rest of Maidstone and right across to the Weald. She walked round the car to join Harry.

"Very quiet," she commented. "Don't see it as a violent area."

"Hmm." Harry pushed open the little wrought-iron gate and led the way up the short path between laburnum bushes to the front door, hidden behind a glass porch. It opened before Harry had a chance to knock or ring the bell. He ushered her in in front of him.

"This is Libby, Cy. Lib, Cy."

In the darkness of the narrow hall, Libby looked up at the man before her. His face should have been handsome, under straight brown hair that flopped over his brow. But underneath that was a mass of blue, purple and yellow bruising. One eye was almost closed, and his lip swollen and crusted with blood. A long tramline of butterfly strips down one cheek led almost up to his eye, and Libby tried to control a shudder at what could have happened.

"Bloody hell, mate." Harry stepped up and enfolded the other man in a gentle hug. "What else did they do to you?"

"Ribs," said Cy in a muffled voice. "Come and see Col."

He led the way through to a large dining kitchen, which had obviously been knocked through. One end was pale wood and stainless steel, with more gadgets than Libby had ever seen, the other was solid, dark 1930s dining furniture, which looked as if it had come with the house. By the cooker, doing something elaborate with a huge coffee machine, stood a slight young man with wispy fair hair and an even wispier beard.

"Harry," he said, in a surprisingly deep voice. "And this must be Libby." He held out a hand.

"Hello," said Libby.

"Let's go into the front room, dears," he said. "Much more comfortable." He took Libby by the elbow and laid the other hand on Cy's arm, giving it a reassuring squeeze. "Come on, love."

The front room was a mixture of furniture of the same vintage as the dining suite and more modern pieces. A huge television dominated one corner. Colin deposited Libby and Harry on a sofa and gently settled Cy in one of the large armchairs.

"I'll get the coffee," he said, and bustled out.

Cy smiled — at least, Libby thought he did.

"Col's been wonderful," he said. "You'd think I'd just had major surgery, not just a kicking."

"Is that what it was?" Harry leant forward, elbows on knees.

Cy nodded and winced. "Down the road, near the park. Kids, I think. Someone came along and they made off."

"How did you get home? Who was the person who came along?"

"A friend. She lives over the road. She told me to sit still and ran up here to fetch Colin. Lucky he was here."

Harry turned to Libby. "Colin's cabin crew on long-haul flights, so he's often away for a week or more."

"Nice of her," said Libby.

"Yes." Cy tried another smile. "Her name's Sheila. She's in the panto society."

Colin entered with a tray on which were a large coffee pot, mugs in silver holders and a huge Victoria sandwich. He beamed at them and poured coffee.

"Cake, Libby?" he held out a plate enticingly. "Comfort food at a time like this, I always say."

"It looks gorgeous," said Libby. "Mine never turn out like that. I have to have Harry's."

"Oh, he's not bad." Colin winked at Harry. "Does a very nice carrot cake."

Harry snorted. "Colin grew up in his parents' bakery. Thinks he knows it all."

"Well," said Libby, through a mouthful of cake, "he does say you make a good carrot cake."

"Come on then," said Harry, when they'd all been served, Cy having been supplied with a straw for his coffee. "What happened last night and what's been happening recently?"

Cy had, apparently, been walking home from the station, from where he commuted to London almost every day. He had just rounded the corner of the park at the bottom of the road when he heard running footsteps and was grabbed from behind. He tried to call out, but his assailant or assailants started kicking him in the ribs and head. The attack didn't last long, as Sheila had turned up and frightened him, or them, away.

"And you can't imagine anything sillier than that," said Colin. "Sheila's about as frightening as an old cardi."

"Did she see them?" asked Libby.

"No, she says not," said Colin. "She had heels on and they must have heard her and scarpered. That end of the park is on a bend, so they'd only have to run round a bit further to be out of sight."

"Pity," said Harry. "So what did you do next?"

"Sheila came and got me, I jumped in the car and she insisted on coming with me, we drove down to where she'd left Cy propped up against the park railings and we got him into the back of the car. She's a good sort."

"Did you go to hospital?" asked Libby.

"He wouldn't have it." Colin frowned at Cy. "He said they'd have to report it to the police, and he didn't want that."

"You stupid old bastard," said Harry. "This is serious. You *have* to tell the police."

"That's what I said," said Colin, nodding furiously, "but then Sheila steps in and says it's all right, she knows how he feels, and she's a retired nurse, she'll see to him."

Libby raised her eyebrows. "A veritable angel, in fact."

"She's great, is Sheila," said Colin, and Cy nodded agreement, gingerly. "She popped in home, then came over here with her box of tricks and patched him up. She reckons he's got broken ribs, but they won't even x-ray those in hospital anymore, let alone strap them up, so all he's got to do is go careful. Not laugh too much." He reached over and patted Cy's arm. "Not that there's much chance of that these days, eh, lover?"

22

"So tell me about the letters," said Libby. "You think this is all connected?"

"Must be," said Cy, and nodded at Colin to carry on.

"Hurts him to talk you see," said Colin, offering the coffee pot again. "Well he started getting these letters some time ago. How long was it?" He looked at Cy. "Six months? I don't know if Harry's told you, but they were the 'we don't want your sort here' type of thing." Libby nodded. "Well, they got a bit worse, a bit more threatening with each one. Then we got another one yesterday morning before Cy went off to work. And this time it was different."

"How?" asked Harry.

"Hand delivered. The post doesn't get here till at least nine thirty. And then there was what it said." He looked across at Cy again. "Get out now, or we'll make you, more or less, only with very bad language."

"So it was actually threatening you with action?" said Libby.

"Not me, dear. Cy. None of them were addressed to me, only to him."

Startled, Libby looked at Harry. "I didn't realise," she said. "I assumed you were both being targeted."

Colin shook his head. "No. I don't know why. Both our names are on the deeds, we moved in at the same time, we both belong to the panto society, everyone who knows us, knows both of us, if you see what I mean. The only difference is that I'm away some of the time."

"Not the only difference," said Cy. "I come from here."

"You lived here when you were a child. It was back in the eighties."

"Were you born here?" asked Libby.

"Not in the house." Cy passed a hand over his face. "Sorry, difficult."

"But in Maidstone?" said Libby. Cy nodded.

"Josephine bought this house, well, her husband did, and left it to Cy."

"Josephine? That was your mum?" Harry asked Cy. Cy nodded again.

"So are there any people living here who lived here then?" asked Libby.

"A few. Lots dead." Cy took a sip of coffee through his straw. "Sheila wasn't here until a bit later."

Libby frowned. "Are you absolutely sure that these letters are threatening you because you're gay?"

Both Colin and Cy looked at her in amazement. "Well, of course! What else would it be?" said Colin.

"But you're both gay. You've just said yourself, both your names are on the deeds, everyone knows you both. So why only target one of you?"

CHAPTER
FOUR

Colin looked at Cy. "I did say, didn't I? Why just you?"

"Wondered." Cy nodded.

"So couldn't it be something else?" said Libby.

"There isn't anything else," said Colin sharply. "What would there be?"

"I've no idea." Libby shrugged. "It just seems odd."

"Cy's in a more — well — straight profession than Colin," said Harry. "That could be it."

"What do you do?"

"Sales," mumbled Cy.

"You're a salesman?" Libby's eyebrows disappeared into her hairline.

"He's a sales director," said Colin impatiently.

"Sales manager," corrected Cy.

"For a water cooler company," added Harry. "Quite small but they supply all the big city companies."

"Right." Libby looked pensive. "So is it a homophobic sort of business?"

Cy looked startled. "No idea."

"No jolly japing about gay people in the office banter?"

"Not heard any."

"Not many people in the office," put in Colin. "Lots in the distribution centre."

"Which is where? Not in the city, I assume."

"The other side of Maidstone, actually," said Colin.

"Really?"

"That's why Cy got the job. When we moved here. Seemed perfect."

"Did you move here first, or because of the job?" Libby was feeling confused.

"We decided to move in here when the then tenant's lease had expired," explained Colin, offering Libby another piece of sponge. "We'd let it ever since Josephine died. But we were both a bit fed up with London, and this is a bit nearer Gatwick for my job, and Cy could still commute to his job in London. Then we saw this job advertised as manager of the distribution centre."

"So you worked in Maidstone at first?" said Libby.

Cy nodded.

"Then he got promotion. So it was back up to London." Colin smiled across at Cy. "All the perks made up for it, though."

"Perks?" said Libby.

"Car, fares paid, you know, all the usual."

Libby, who didn't, nodded. "So could it be a jealousy motive, then?" she asked.

"Jealousy?" Cy frowned, as far as he was able.

"Somebody at the distribution depot who was passed over for promotion, maybe?"

Cy and Colin looked at each other. "We never thought of that," said Colin slowly.

"No, because you were only thinking of the gay aspect." Libby looked from one to the other. "Tell me, why did that worry you so much?"

Colin looked taken aback, but Cy's expression didn't change as far as she could see.

Harry sighed. "I did warn you she was a nosy old trout," he said. "But you thought she might help."

Cy tried to smile. "I don't mind," he mumbled. "Perhaps I'd better talk when I've healed up a bit."

"I can tell her," said Colin, sounding wounded. Cy leant over and squeezed his hand.

"I know."

"Panto," said Harry. "What are you doing about that? Libby's not only directing ours, she's now in it as well, owing to an unfortunate incident with the cow and the fairy."

Colin gave a hoot of laughter and clapped his hand over his mouth. Even Cy looked as though he would laugh if it didn't hurt.

"I'll talk to them tonight," said Colin. "I'm here for the next week, thank goodness, so I can help as much as possible. Cy can't go to rehearsals, of course."

Cy looked irritated, and it occurred to Libby that, good though Colin was, Cy was too independent to relish being nannied.

"Well, if there's anything I can do," she said, crossing her fingers, "give me a ring. Cy, when you can talk better, perhaps we can have that chat. There are a couple of things I'd like to ask."

"Nosy cow," said Harry affectionately, standing up. "We'll go now, Col. Thanks for the lovely cake and the coffee."

"Yes, thank you," said Libby. "I love the cake."

Colin saw them out to the car.

"Now you see why he wouldn't talk to the police," he said, holding the passenger door open for Libby.

"I'm not sure I do," said Libby.

"Well, for a start, would they have asked all those questions you did? No. They'd just treat it as a mugging and file it. And the letters. I don't think they'd even bother with those. We aren't living in an old Agatha Christie film."

"And she's not Miss Marple," said Harry, "or so she keeps telling us, but at least she can see possible other reasons for all of this, and might even take the time to look into it."

Colin bent down and kissed Libby's cheek. "Thanks, girl. It's made him happier, I can tell."

"So what did you think of them?" asked Harry, as he negotiated his way back towards Detling Hill.

"I liked them," said Libby, "even if I couldn't really tell with Cy the way he is. He's getting a bit fed up with Col mothering him, isn't he?"

"You noticed!" Harry slid his eyes sideways towards her. "Independent sod, is Cy."

"So he's been in business for a long time, has he?"

"Yes. Typical suit, shirt, tie, short back and sides type. Never let on that he was gay to anyone."

"Ah. That's what I thought," said Libby. "That's why I asked why it worried them."

"I don't think it worried Col," said Harry. "He works in an industry where it's been accepted."

Libby nodded. "Even before it was legal. There were always gay stewards. I remember a friend of mine who was cabin crew for British Airways saying a lot of them were, and there were a good few lesbians, too."

"Not a career I would have thought appealed to them," said Harry.

"You can get very close in a galley," said Libby. "My friend had an uncomfortable moment with a chief stewardess somewhere over New York."

Harry snorted.

"So was Cy worried when he worked in Maidstone that his fellow workers would find out about him? Living there and all?"

Harry frowned. "I don't know. The neighbours must know about them —"

"They admitted that," interrupted Libby. "Sheila obviously knows."

"So it follows that it wasn't impossible that someone at the distribution depot would find out. Perhaps that's why he opted for promotion."

"Apart from the rather more obvious advantages of more money, a car and everything else?"

"He's never been that interested in money, as far as I know," said Harry. "The house is mortgage-free, after all."

"Anyway, I shall wait and see until after Cy can talk to me. You see, it could be —"

"Anything," said Harry. "See? I knew you'd be hooked."

Back in Steeple Martin, Libby surveyed the ruins of her day. Learning the fairy's lines seemed to be a priority, after stuffing Adam's sheets into the tumble dryer. She found enough food in the fridge and freezer

29

to concoct some kind of meal for herself and Ben, decided two large pieces of Colin's cake had more than compensated for a missed lunch, and lit the fire. Sidney signalled his appreciation by coming to sit on her lap — with his back to her, of course — and she opened her copy of the script.

But *Hey, Diddle, Diddle* didn't hold her attention. For a start, her copy had been dismembered and put into a ring binder with lots of sheets of A4 for notes. Secondly, half the scribbled notes (her own) were on the actual script pages instead, and thirdly, her mind returned constantly to the attack on Cy and the anonymous letters. After a few minutes of trying desperately to concentrate on rhyming couplets, she gave up and let the ring binder slip to the floor. Sidney put his ears back.

First — why had Cy been the only one of the partners targeted by the anonymous letters? She had explained to Cy and Colin why she found this interesting — although that was not perhaps the right word — but they had not seemed to find this as surprising as she did. Yet Colin would have been the more obvious target on the surface, as he was, or appeared to be, the most blatantly gay of the two, and, as Harry had said, the industry in which he worked was well known for its acceptance of homosexuality. So why Cy? Who, apparently, never flaunted his sexuality and appeared to the general public as a perfectly normal business man.

When he and Colin had returned to Maidstone to live in his mother's bungalow, he had taken a job locally. Why hadn't the letters started then, if someone knew him or anything about him? And it would have been very easy to find out. The company would have had his details, although, of course, the Data Protection Act wouldn't have allowed just anybody to have access to those, but if someone at the company had taken a dislike to Cy, or had any suspicions of him, it would have been simple to follow him home and discover his living arrangements. Libby didn't think anyone would have been crass enough to question the neighbours, but it might be an idea to ask them as soon as Cy was able to tell her who knew them well enough.

Presumably the panto society did, and from the way Harry and Colin had spoken, that was comprised of very local people. Stranger and stranger. She frowned. Why on earth did Cy and Colin think the letters were about homosexuality? As far as she could see they almost certainly weren't.

And if they weren't, thought Libby, leaning her head back against the cushions, what was it about? That was the difficult part. Cy might be happy to have her poke about in the shallows of his homosexual life, but it was a different thing entirely to have her asking questions about the other areas. After all, there could be all sorts of secrets hidden, even criminal ones, given the nature of the letters.

She sighed and pushed Sidney off her lap. Tea was now necessary, as would have been, in the past, a conversation with Fran. But this time, no. She'd been entrusted with information that was not to be given to anyone, even the police, so she wouldn't tell Fran unless it became absolutely essential.

That was a thought, though. She moved the big kettle on to the Rayburn. If there was something criminal, or at the very least reprehensible, in Cy's past, it would explain his disinclination to go to the police, despite his protestations that the police were unsympathetic to homosexuals. And what about the attack? Why hadn't he reported that to the police?

She warmed the teapot and spooned in tea. Of course, there was a chance that his reasons were exactly what he said, the police were both dismissive and unhelpful towards crimes against homosexuals. Whether they truly were or not was another matter, but if Cy believed it that was all that mattered.

She went to the new laptop which sat on the table in the window in the sitting room. The laptop had replaced the desktop computer Ben had helped her buy a few years ago, and she found it much more comfortable to be able to sit on the sofa and wander across the internet than having to sit at the table. She fetched her tea and sat down.

A horrifying number of sites were thrown up when she entered 'gay bashing' into the search engine, but after refining it by several terms she came up with some reports that actually seemed relevant. One, in particular, was a BBC news report which covered the whole problem, and which Libby found quite sickening.

But it was the third item down which almost made her spill her tea.

'Gay man dies in unprovoked attack in Maidstone,' it read. And it was dated today.

CHAPTER
FIVE

Libby clicked on the link, her heart beating heavily. She knew logically, that this could not possibly be Cy, having left him alive less than two hours ago, but it was too uncomfortably close.

Sure enough, the link, to a local radio report, was about a death which had occurred the previous night. Libby's heart, which had began to slow to a normal rate, picked up again. When, the previous night? Where?

She reached for her mobile and sent Harry a text. Then, she picked out specifics of the report and put them into the search engine. Up came the same link she'd just used and one other, to a news blog.

"And how does he get his information?" muttered Libby to herself, then answered her own question by discovering that he was no amateur but the chief reporter on a local paper. The phone rang.

"Someone else was attacked in Maidstone last night," began Libby without preamble. "And he died."

"What?" Harry sounded confused. "What are you talking about?"

Libby explained.

"Fuck. Where was the attack? And why do you think it's linked?"

"It was on the other side of that park," said Libby, "and the guy was gay. Could they have been interrupted with Cy and just run off to take it out on someone else?"

"I suppose so," said Harry slowly, "but then it means it's random attacks on gay men. And you didn't think it was straightforward homophobia."

"I didn't think the letters were," said Libby. "But there's nothing to link them to the attack except the last one, is there?"

"And that's tenuous," said Harry. "So what happens now?"

"Could you let Colin know about this other attack? It might prompt him to take it to the police. If it is the whole gay community which is being threatened, they need to know."

"OK. It'll give me a chance to find out how they actually took our visit. You can never tell when people are just being polite, can you?"

"I wouldn't have thought our visit had much to do with politeness on either side," said Libby dryly, "but I see what you mean. Let me know."

The tea was almost cold, so she pushed Sidney aside once more and went to pour some more. She was aware that underneath the distress and discomfort of finding out about the attacks on both the un-named victim and on Cy, she was feeling very much more alive and alert than she had for months.

"You ghoul, you," she told herself as she sat down. "And you promised you wouldn't get involved again." She sighed. "The same as you do every time," she added to Sidney.

Libby sat in the auditorium of the Oast House theatre and surveyed the stage. Ensemble members — or chorus members, as she still called them — hovered around the edges giggling and whispering, two carpenters fiddled about with cut-out flats behind them, and Little Boy Blue scowled at the musical director.

"Where's Buttercup?" said Libby suddenly. Everyone stopped and looked round, startled.

"Freddy's here but Dean isn't," said a chorus member.

Libby sighed. "Well, where's Freddy, then?"

There was a muttered explanation from the chorus, and one of them detached herself and ran off stage.

"And where are the rest of them?" Libby asked of no one in particular. "It's bloody eight o'clock and we're supposed to have started at quarter to."

"They're amateurs, dear heart," said a voice behind her.

She looked up into Peter's amused face. "I know. And I have this conversation with you every time," she said. "I still can't get used to it."

"Look, the standard's going up every time," said Peter, climbing over the back of the seats and sitting down beside her. "There's nothing to worry about. Bob and Baz as the double act will do their own thing regardless and they've already got their own fan base, Tom is a great Dame and you'll be a perfect fairy."

"A bit different from Fairy Sugar Plum," said Libby gloomily.

"So make her funny. You know you like doing that sort of thing. Get someone to run you up a sort of sweetie-shop dame-like costume."

"Oh? Who, pray?" asked Libby. "Costume designers don't just turn up out of the blue, you know."

"Libby?" A young man with floppy dark hair ambled on to the stage.

"Oh, Freddy." Libby stood up. "Where's your front half?"

Freddy shrugged. "No idea, I'm afraid."

Libby ground her teeth silently. "Well you'll have to stand in for both halves tonight, then," she said. "Is there any other member of the cast here? We were supposed to be doing scenes three and four tonight, in case everybody's forgotten."

Peter patted her arm in sympathy as she sat down again. "Never mind, chuck," he whispered. "Be all right on the night."

Two hours later, Libby declaimed a speech from centre stage and then turned her back on the auditorium.

"Right," she said. "I shan't ask you to stay, but please could you try and learn your words, people? The dance numbers are coming on terrifically well, we don't want the dialogue sequences letting them down." She took a deep breath. "It's not long, and with a break for Christmas. Remember that."

The cast drifted off and Ben came down to where she stood. Once again cast as the King, he was also helping with set construction, so tended to be around for rehearsals, whichever part of the script was being rehearsed.

"Harry asked if we were going for a drink," he said.

Libby raised her eyebrows. "We usually do," she said.

"I think that was what he meant. He's hoping we'll go to the caff rather than the pub."

"Ah." Libby pulled a face. "His friend Cy, no doubt." She had told Ben about the visit to Maidstone that morning and about the news of the coincidental murder. He had not been overjoyed.

"I think so," said Ben now. "And I suppose you'd better listen, hadn't you?"

Libby peered round the auditorium. "Where's Pete?" she asked.

"He's gone. Harry called him, too."

"Oh, lordy, lordy," said Libby. "This doesn't bode well."

"No," said Ben, "it doesn't. But this time, you can't blame yourself. Whatever's happened."

There was a rowdy, ten-strong party in The Pink Geranium, but Peter was sitting on the sofa in the window with a bottle and glasses. He made a face as Libby and Ben came to join him.

"Bloody noisy lot," he said, pouring wine. "They were supposed to be gone by ten. Donna had to send the taxis away."

"Harry won't want to talk to us here, then," said Libby, accepting a glass. "Can it wait?"

"No idea. But you're right. He didn't want to talk in the pub, so it's unlikely that he'll be happy about this."

Adam appeared from the kitchen and nodded towards the yard. Ben got up and went to speak to him.

"He says to go up to the flat," he said returning to the sofa. "Bring the bottle."

Under the interested eyes of the party of diners, Adam led them through the kitchen and out into the yard.

"Door's open," he said, so they filed up the outside staircase and into Adam's tiny kitchen.

"Well!" said Libby, going through to the sitting room and pushing a bag off the sofa. "Very cloak and dagger."

"Hardly," said Peter, swinging a chair round to face her. "A lot of people saw us come up here."

"I know, I meant whatever he wants to *say*," said Libby.

Ben prowled round the room picking things up and putting them down.

"What's the matter?" Libby asked him. "You don't want to be here, do you?"

"No." Ben picked moodily at the edge of a crumpled magazine. "Harry's dragging you into something and it all sounds a bit — well — nasty."

"Gay bashing *is* nasty," said Libby.

"And is that all it is?" Ben came to sit beside her. "Are you sure?"

"It certainly looks like it now, doesn't it?" said Libby. "With this second murder and all."

"Second murder?" Peter said sharply.

"No, sorry." Libby frowned. "I meant second attack. First murder."

Peter frowned back at her. "So you think whoever it was meant to murder Cy?"

"Well, they murdered the other one, didn't they?" said Libby reasonably.

Footsteps could be heard running up the back stairs, and a moment later Harry, still in chef's trousers, arrived brandishing the usual bottle of red wine.

"Find the glasses, Lib," he said. "You know where they are."

Libby did as she was told and then sat back down on the sofa. "Come on, then, tell us what this is about," she said.

"I called Cy — well, Colin actually, because Cy isn't talking too well — and told him what you'd heard." He cocked an eyebrow. "And guess what? They'd heard too."

"Well, hardly surprising, I suppose," began Libby.

"No, petal. It was *how* they heard."

"From the radio? Television?" hazarded Ben.

"Another letter." Harry raised his glass. "Cheers."

Silence fell as they all looked at each other.

"What did it say?" asked Libby eventually.

"I quote," said Harry. "'You should have gone the same way. We're watching you.' Nice, eh?"

Libby shivered. "Lovely. So have they gone to the police now?"

"They hadn't when I called, but they have now. Colin said someone was going round to see them this evening."

"So what was so urgent about telling us tonight?" asked Ben.

Harry, Libby and Peter looked surprised.

"Because it's a serious development," said Libby.

"And there's even more of a threat," said Harry.

"And they're friends," said Peter.

Ben made a noise that sounded like 'hmph' and settled back into the sofa. Peter and Harry exchanged glances.

"What should we do?" asked Libby after a further short silence.

"Wait until after we hear from Cy and Colin in the morning," said Harry.

"Well, if the police are involved now, they won't need me — us — to investigate now, will they?"

"Especially as the murder is obviously connected to the attack on Cy," said Peter. "As long as they've shown the police the letter."

"I wonder what they think?" said Libby slowly. "That because the attackers were interrupted they just went off and killed someone else instead?"

"If it is gay bashing, why not?" said Harry.

"Because the letter doesn't seem to suggest that," said Libby. "Don't you agree, Pete? Ben?"

"I see what you mean," said Peter. Ben just shrugged and Libby heaved an exasperated sigh.

"Come on, then," she said, "let's go home."

"But we haven't finished the bottle yet," said Harry in surprise.

"I'd rather go, if you don't mind, Harry," said Ben, standing up. He clapped Peter on the shoulder and handed Libby her cape.

"Thanks," she said, and made a face at the others. "I'll talk to you in the morning," and followed Ben down the front stairs and out into the high street.

He stopped and turned to face her.

"I'm sorry, Lib," he said.

"I don't understand, Ben," she said, hugging her basket to her chest. "You were the one who said you thought I ought to listen."

He sighed. "I know. But that was because I thought it was urgent. It wasn't urgent at all. It was simply Harry doing theatrical flourishes. All he needed to do was give you a quick ring and say that Cy and Colin had been to the police and tell you about the new letter. That was all that was needed. There's no need whatsoever for you to go on investigating and we should all be heaving sighs of relief." He turned and began walking. "Instead of which Harry turns it into a drama."

Libby's mouth fell open. "But it *is* a drama!" she gasped, hurrying after him. "Cy's been beaten up, received threatening letters and now someone's been killed and it's linked to the attack on him." She shook her head in disbelief. "I can't think of anything much *more* dramatic."

"But not for you," said Ben. "Not this time." He stopped and turned to face her. "Please, Lib. Not this time."

CHAPTER
SIX

Harry was on the phone almost as soon as Ben had left Number 17 the following morning.

"I put my foot in it, didn't I?" he said.

"You somewhat over-dramatised," said Libby, "yes. Now he's saying he really doesn't want me to have anything to do with it all."

"No surprise there, then," said Harry with a sigh. "I suppose I can't blame him."

"Well, no," said Libby. "And now the police are involved I can't see that I can add anything."

"Mmm." Harry was obviously thinking. "I'll speak to him this morning and see how the land lies."

"It won't make any difference, Harry. I don't see how I can go interfering into a police investigation, especially after Ben has been so — so — well, definite."

"OK," said Harry with another sigh. "Apologise to him for me, will you?"

"No, you can do it," said Libby. "Take him to the pub."

"Oh, OK," Harry grumbled. "If Donna can cope at lunchtime. Is he at the Manor office?"

"I think so, but better try his mobile. He might have sloped off to Steeple Farm."

But whatever she might have said to Harry, or indeed to Ben, Libby was still intrigued. Certainly, with the discovery of the body on the other side of the park it looked as though Cy's and Colin's initial thoughts about the anonymous letters were correct, so why was something else niggling at the edges of her brain?

She abandoned the kitchen and booted up the laptop, tucking feet under dressing-gowned legs on the sofa. The local news sites all had accounts of the murder, and, to her surprise, it had also made the nationals. The redtops all screamed 'Gay Bashing Ends In Murder', as she would have expected, but from some of the other sites there was informed, or at least less sensational, comment. Nowhere was the victim named, and nowhere was Cy's attack mentioned, so either the police hadn't released that information, or Cy, despite having told Harry he had informed the police, hadn't. Chewing her lip, Libby tried a few more sites and eventually, to her surprise, came up with Cy's panto.

No wonder Harry had asked her to help, she thought with a grin. 'Cinderella,' read the item, 'a pantomime written by local actress Libby Sarjeant, performed by the Hop Hall Players.'

So why hadn't she known? If she could be bothered, she could look through the statements that came from her old society, who were at liberty to hire out her scripts for a small fee. They had all been written many years ago, and anything she wrote for the Oast House Theatre was not included. Besides, Peter wrote most of that, although *Hey, Diddle, Diddle* had been bought in, on the strict understanding that she, as the director, could change anything she wanted to. This usually happened with pantomime scripts, their authors being aware that being precious about one's gilded prose was just not an option.

Tucking her feet under her more securely, away from the suddenly playful Sidney, she typed in Hop Hall Players. Panto society, they'd said it was, but in fact it was a fully fledged amateur society with a very interesting history.

Started in the nineteen thirties by a group of hop pickers for their own entertainment on a large local farm, they had originally only performed musical and variety items, much as the concert parties of the era had done. During the war, when some of the regular East Enders had found homes in the area, hoping to avoid the bombs in London, they had got permission to perform in the oast house during the times that it wasn't in use. Eventually, after the war, more people had joined and a large shed once used for Salvation Army assemblies was commandeered to form a performance space. When the original farm had ceased hop production, the small society, by now calling themselves 'Hop Hall' had tried to buy it, but, as with so many oast houses, it had been sold and converted into a dwelling.

So the Hop Hall Players had continued to do what so many other societies throughout England had done, hired the village hall both for rehearsals and performances, and they were still doing it. They still appeared to be proud of their origins, however, and even boasted one or two venerable members who had been there during the war.

And what about Josephine, wondered Libby, looking up from the screen and giving Sidney an absent-minded stroke. Was she there then? Did she have anything to do with the Players? Colin had said Cy had grown up there, Josephine and her husband had bought the house, presumably when Cy was a child. So where had they been before then?

Working on the assumption that Cy was in his thirties, she supposed that Josephine had probably been born after the war, so wouldn't have been involved with the Hop Hall Players while they were still based at the hop farm. And anyway, she thought, standing up and tipping Sidney onto the floor, what had the hop farm got to do with anything anyway? She stomped upstairs to get dressed.

And what, she wondered later, while hunched over the heater in the conservatory, had made her wonder about the distant past in connection with Cy's beating? Well, with the letters, more obviously. And even more obviously, the fact that the Hop Hall Players had come up while she was searching for references to last night's murder. She sat up straight and nearly fell off the stool. Of course. It had been one of those research threads that leads somewhere else entirely, hadn't it? But what she had ignored was why the Hop Hall Players had come up in the first place.

In her haste to get back to the laptop, she knocked over the stool entirely, and had to stop and make sure the heater wasn't going to set fire to the conservatory.

The laptop was asleep by the fireside, its little light pulsing silently like a heartbeat. She opened it and backspaced until she reached the page which had first referred to the Hop Hall Players. And there it was.

'The police are not releasing the name of the victim, who was found at the entrance of Aird Park, opposite the Aird Memorial Hall, where the Hop Hall Players were rehearsing this year's pantomime.'

Were they? Cy hadn't been, neither had Colin or Sheila. Or had she? She had been walking home, so she could easily have been coming home from a rehearsal. So the second attack must have taken place after she'd passed the entrance of the park, but presumably, if the Hop Hall Players were anything like the Oast House company, there would still be people floating around for a good twenty minutes after rehearsal had finished. Had no one seen the body?

Or, thought Libby, striking the laptop with the flat of her hand in enthusiasm and losing the page, perhaps that's how it had been reported. By a member of the company. But in that case, why hadn't it been on the news yesterday morning before she and Harry had gone to see Cy? Why had no one heard anything?

She scowled at the screen and managed to get back the page she'd lost. It turned out to be yet another local news page, this time connected to a media company who also owned online television channels and free papers. She clicked the link to the TV channel and eventually found the report which had appeared on their morning bulletin with slightly more information than that which she had discovered yesterday afternoon.

It appeared now that the body had been just inside the park gates, which were closed, so was invisible to passers by, including all the members of the Hop Hall Players, until a late reveller, in the way of his kind, had needed a place of at least semi-concealment. The gates had not been locked, and his relief was somewhat tempered, not to say squashed, by the sight of a battered body lying among the rhododendrons.

So it had nothing whatsoever to do with the Hop Hall Players. Libby found herself slightly disappointed. It had been an intriguing thought, that whatever the reason for the anonymous letters and the beating, it had been hidden in a hop-picking past, as had the first murder Libby herself had been involved with. It just showed how ready she was to leap to conclusions which had no foundation. The original bull-in-a-china-shop, in fact, as her nearest and dearest frequently commented. And, in fact, it was nothing to do with her anyway. So why was she looking?

It was still raining. Libby put the laptop away and wondered what to do with the rest of the day. Yes, she could learn the fairy's lines. Yes, she could hoover the upstairs of the cottage. Yes, she could do some Christmas shopping. Her eyes swivelled to the laptop. Online. Or she could go and buy a Christmas Tree.

She drove through sheeting rain out of the village towards Canterbury and the Cattlegreen Nurseries. Nella and Joe had recently opened a farm shop in the village, where Nella mostly worked, while Joe still looked after the plants and a more extensive range of vegetables and groceries at the Nurseries, including a small Christmas Tree plantation. The 'boy', Owen, greeted her as she pulled up on the forecourt and hustled her inside.

"I'll get Dad," he said.

"Owen!" she called after him. "No, it's OK. I just want a tree. I'll go outside and find one, shall I?"

Owen turned back, looking doubtful. "It's very wet," he said.

"That's all right," said Libby. "I've got to choose one now, or the best ones will be gone, won't they? I'll soon get dry."

Followed by a dubious Owen in a waterproof hoodie, Libby led the way outside and to the back of the Nurseries' plot, where ranks of trees stood on a slight slope.

"Shall I tag one?" she asked. "I don't want to dig it up without your dad here."

"I said I'd get him." Owen looked resigned. "I'll go now."

"No, I meant it. Last year he let me tag it, and I came to collect it another day."

"Oh." Owen looked relieved. "Here, then." He pulled a white label attached to a red ribbon out of his pocket. "I'll go and tell him." He turned back to the building. Libby sighed. Owen was a sweet boy, but difficult.

She padded through the mud along lines of sparkling trees until she found one the right size and shape to fit the sitting room of Number 17. She tied the label where the star would eventually go, and realised she had nothing with which to write her name. Muttering under her breath, she pushed her way back towards the Nursery building.

"'Allo, Lib." Joe appeared before her. "I'll go and dig up that tree now. I bet you forgot to bring a pen, didn't you?"

Libby sighed and pushed wet hair out of her eyes. "Of course I did, Joe," she said. "Thanks. But I think I might have to leave it here for Ben to collect in the tank."

"He'll be coming to collect the one for the Manor, won't he?" said Joe. "I'll just put your name on it, then, and leave it here."

Libby made her sodden way back inside, where she found Owen, beaming and holding out a steaming mug.

"Tea?" she said, gratefully.

"Hot chocolate," said Owen proudly.

"Lovely," said Libby, taking hold of it in both hands and dripping into it.

"That's done, then, Lib," said Joe, coming in behind her. "That chocolate, Owen-boy? Enough for me?"

Still beaming, Owen disappeared into the back of the building.

"He's a lovely boy, Joe," said Libby.

"Aye. Better be kind and helpful than brainy, eh?" He went to the counter and ran a finger down a grubby price list. "You going to pay now? Or leave it for Ben?"

"I'll do it," said Libby. "I don't think it's fair to leave it to Ben."

"So, you going to move into Steeple Farm, then?" Joe punched keys on the till.

"No." Libby put her card on the counter. "Staying in Allhallow's Lane."

"Oh?" Joe's eyebrows went up as he pushed the card reader towards her. "More room at Steeple Farm, surely."

"There's only two of us, Joe," said Libby, keying in her number. "And the kids don't usually come down together."

"And your young'un's got that flat over Harry's place, hasn't he?"

"Yes. Helps out there, too."

Joe handed the card back. "Nice bloke, young Harry," he said. "Wasn't sure, meself, at first, but he's a good'un."

Libby put her head on one side and looked at him over the rim of her mug. "Weren't sure because he was gay?"

"Well, yeah." Joe looked away. "Not proud of it, but I know better now. Nella made me read a lot of stuff."

"Good for her." Libby smiled. "But do you think there are a lot of people round here who are still — well, *against* Harry and Peter? Or gay people in general?"

"Some of the old'uns, maybe. Some of the churchy folk." He shook his head. "Not many, though. Country folk don't mind much what other folks do. Mostly them from the town who do."

"Really?" Libby sipped her chocolate, which had mellowed from scalding to steaming.

"Yeah, from those estates and such. You know the sort."

Libby did. The macho types who thought the British Liberation Front was a good idea. Of course, they were the type who would be homophobic.

"And some of the old colonial types, too," she added.

"Eh?"

"From India. You know, the people who used to live abroad and think they ruled the world."

"Oh, ah!" Joe laughed. "Like old Colonel Feathers."

"Who?"

"Him who lived at the Old Hall. Thought we should all be like his servants back in India. His wife couldn't even wash a floor."

"Well, I don't suppose she ever had to," said Libby.

"My old ma taught her. She went up to clean for a few hours a week, did Ma." He shook his head and laughed again. "The stories she used to tell."

"And what about," mused Libby, still following her train of thought, "the nouveau riche?"

"The who?"

"People who've come up from nothing. You know — who own chains of second-hand car showrooms, or — or — oh, I don't know, betting shops."

"Oh, ah. Like them as live in the new houses out at Steeple Cross."

"I've been in one of those," said Libby, with a shudder.

"What was you doing? Catching a murderer?" said Joe, and laughed.

Libby scowled. Actually, she had been. Or rather, the police had been.

"Anyway, why are you so interested in people who don't like queers?" Joe took his own mug from Owen, who had reappeared.

"Oh, a friend who's been getting nasty letters," said Libby, finishing her drink.

"Not Harry or Peter?" Joe looked shocked.

"No, no. Just a friend."

"Cause trouble, those letters." Joe's expression had darkened. "We had an old maid in the village — ooh, years ago — who sent 'em. Course, we didn't know it was her. Another little old girl — friend of hers — killed herself. Then it all came out. Horrible."

"Goodness," said Libby. "I never knew that."

"Years before your time," said Joe. "Flo and Hetty'll remember."

"I bet they do," said Libby. "I'll ask them."

"And don't you go getting involved in anonymous letters," Joe called after her, as she went back to her car. "They're dangerous. Get people killed."

That's what I'm afraid of, thought Libby, as she drove away.

CHAPTER
SEVEN

"Do you remember some anonymous letters and someone committing suicide, Flo?"

Libby had decided to ask Flo Carpenter about Joe's story rather than Hetty, who might find it upsetting in view of some of the events in her family's recent history.

Flo waved at an armchair and blew cigarette smoke out of a corner of her mouth. The little sitting room was overheated and the blue smoke hung just beneath the standard lamp. Libby thought again about giving up smoking.

"Yeah, course. Old Amy Taylor, it was."

"Who was? The suicide?"

"Yeah. That Maud Burton wrote the letters. What d'yer want to know for?"

"Joe up at Cattlegreen was telling me this morning. He said it was horrible."

Flo nodded. "What you up at Cattlegreen for? He's got a shop here now, just round the corner from here."

Libby nodded. "I know. I was buying a tree."

"Christmas tree? You don't want to do that. Nice artificial one, that's what you want. Don't shed no needles." Flo held her hands out to her electric fire. "Like this, see? No coal, no dust."

"I know," said Libby. "I'm just a glutton for punishment. Anyway, you remember Amy Taylor and Maud Burton?"

"Told you I did. They was both church 'ens. Both fancied the vicar."

"Golly. Sounds like an old-fashioned detective story."

Flo cocked her head. "Well, you would think that," she said.

"Go on," said Libby. "When was this?"

"Back in the early sixties, must've been. Might 'ave even been in the fifties. Anyway, we 'ad a new vicar. Course, I wasn't living in the Close then, wasn't even built."

Maltby Close was the little lane that led to the church, and along which had been built tasteful retirement cottages attached to an original converted barn.

"Burton and Taylor, we called 'em," said Flo, gazing into her fire. "Always together. Then this new vicar come and off they went. Always tryin' to out-do each other. Bringin' 'im cakes, offerin' to do little jobs for him. Always hangin' around the church, doin' flowers, cleanin' the brass, that sort of thing. Then he finds out Amy plays the piano, and asks her up to some kind of party at the vicarage to play."

"And didn't he ask Maud?"

"No. And you can imagine what she thought of that. Anyway, it all calmed down, and then the letters started arrivin'."

"To Amy?"

"No, other people. My Frank, he got one, Hetty did, even Greg. The doctor — old Grimes, the churchwarden. Maud got one, too."

"And how did people know? They usually keep those sort of thing quiet."

"Well, the vicar got one, and he was so mad he stood up in the pulpit that Sunday and read it out. Then he said if anyone else had got them, they should come right out and say, so o' course, they did. And it was all round the village."

"And what about Amy?"

"Well, that was just it, you see. Old Maud didn't care about any of the others so she made stuff up, but there was one thing she did know about, and that was Amy's secret. So she sent her a letter after all the fuss about the others, threatening to tell. And Amy walked down to that old pond the other side of the village one night and drowned herself."

"And how did they find out? And what was her secret?" Libby was sitting on the edge of her chair by now.

"She left the letter in her little cottage and wrote underneath 'It's true'. And then o' course, the police had to look into it a bit, 'cause it was a death. And old Maud, she hadn't been careful, like. They found the writing paper and everything in her house. Then she breaks down and confesses to the vicar. Tells him it was all for him."

"But what was Amy's secret?" Libby leant further forward.

"You'll be off the edge o' that chair in a minute," said Flo. "Well, it was obvious, wasn't it? She'd had a baby in the war."

"Is that all?" Libby sat back. "So did Hetty."

"So did lots o' people," said Flo darkly, "but you didn't talk about it. People was still sent away in those days. Hetty went back to London, didn't she? Even in the sixties, girls were sent off to those terrible homes and had their babies taken away from them. Don't you remember?"

"I was a bit young, then," said Libby, apologetically. "I remember someone in my class having an abortion, though. It was a dreadful scandal."

"That was it, you see. It just wasn't done. Everyone *did* do it, o' course, but you mustn't get caught."

"So poor Amy had a baby. Did you ever find out who was the father? Or what happened to it?"

"They reckoned as it was a hopper."

"A *hop*-picker?" echoed Libby.

Flo nodded.

"They did cause trouble, didn't they?" Libby shook her head. "I mean, Hetty came back and married Greg, so everything was all right, but look at all the other stuff that happened."

Flo nodded again, looking inwards to her memories. "Oh, there was some 'andsome lads used to come down," she said slowly. "Just tryin' their luck, like. No papers, nothin'."

"No papers? I thought everyone had to have identity cards in the war?"

"You did. But there was ways of gettin' round it. And the farmers was often desperate for pickers, or for pole pullers. War, you see. All the boys were off fightin'."

"I thought it was mainly women and children doing the picking."

"Yeah. Mostly. And we used to get some o' them down, too. Women with no papers. Like they'd been bombed out and lost everything."

"Well, they could have, couldn't they?" said Libby.

"You 'ad to report it if you lost your card. But lots of 'em got away with it, for one reason or another. Didn't like the old man, or got fed up with the kids, or the mother-in-law."

"No!"

Flo shrugged. "It was different then. It was war. Nothin' was the same. People got off with each other just because they might never do it again." She shook her head. "That's what happened to Amy."

"It's awful." Libby looked at the glowing bars of the fire. "But you still haven't said what happened to the baby?"

Flo shrugged. "No one ever knew. Could'a been dead. I expect the police looked into it, but it never come out, if they did." She looked up at Libby. "And don't you go pokin' yer nose in, either!"

"Of course I won't," said Libby huffily. "No reason to."

"Then why was you curious? Why was you askin'?"

"I told you. Joe mentioned it this morning."

Flo eyed her shrewdly. "And why would Joe mention it? No reason it suddenly come out that I can think of."

Libby sighed. "It was anonymous letters," she said.

"You been gettin' 'em?"

"No, nothing like that, but a friend has."

"Oh?"

"Look, Flo, I can't tell you any more, but I was trying to find out what sort of person would send letters like that. Joe mentioned the story you've just told me, although he didn't know as much about it as you. He said I should ask either Hetty or you."

Flo still looked suspicious. "Why would you ask 'im?"

"Um," said Libby.

"Um yerself." Flo stood up. "Oh, well, if you won't tell me, you won't. But you did come 'ere askin'."

"Joe said he hadn't been sure about Harry," said Libby hastily. "Then he'd changed his mind."

Flo sat down again. "About *Harry*?"

"Being gay," said Libby.

"But 'e knew Peter. What's the difference?"

"I expect he didn't know Peter was gay. A lot of people didn't. Still don't."

Flo shrugged. "Can't tell their arse from their elbow, then. Bleedin' obvious."

"Yes, but everyone isn't as tolerant as you are, Flo," said Libby with a grin.

"Yer right there. Why, my Lenny could be right pig-'eaded about that stuff."

Libby's eyebrows rose. "But Peter's Lenny's nephew!" She was fond of Lenny.

"Never 'ad much to do with 'im, did 'e? Remember 'ow when we 'ad that business at the theatre, Hetty didn't want Len down 'ere?"

"Yes, but that was for an obvious reason. It's all cleared up, now."

"Yeah, but it meant for years Len didn't have anything to do with the family. I told you at the time."

"So did everyone," said Libby, "but he's all right with it now, isn't he?"

"Course 'e is." She stood up again. "You stayin' for a cuppa? He's gone down the shops. 'E'll be back in a minute."

"No, I won't, thanks Flo. I've got shopping of my own to do."

"Could'a done it up at Cattlegreen."

"I didn't think of it," said Libby. "I shall go to the butcher's and Nella's farm shop instead."

Lenny, Hetty's brother who now lived with Flo, his childhood sweetheart, appeared with a carrier bag and an umbrella as Libby was getting into Romeo.

"You didn't drive round 'ere!" he said, folding the umbrella. "Lost the use of yer legs, 'ave you?"

"She drove here from somewhere else, you nosy old blighter," said Flo from behind him. Libby gave them a wave and drove carefully down Maltby Close to the high street. Opposite, she could see Donna moving about inside The Pink Geranium, and Harry's tasteful Christmas decorations glinting as they twisted above her head.

She thought about parking and going in to see if Harry had heard anything more from Cy or Colin, but decided it might be tactless after he had promised to apologise to Ben for getting her involved. Then she realised that if he had managed to get hold of Ben, that's where he would be now, not to mention the fact that here she was, still getting herself involved with the story. With a tut of annoyance, she indicated, turned right and headed for home.

The heating had gone off and the house was cold. There was a forecast of snow for next week, she remembered, and hoped it wouldn't put everyone's Christmas plans on hold, or even disrupt panto rehearsals. She turned the heating on, turned up the thermostat and went to get kindling for the fire. Then remembered she'd been going to do some shopping. Sighing, she dumped the kindling on the hearth and went to put on her cape.

She opened the door straight on to Harry.

"Hello," she said, stepping back in surprise. "What are you doing here?"

"Fairly obviously, petal, I came to see you. Were you on your way out?"

"Fairly obviously," she repeated.

"Anywhere important?"

"Shopping, if you must know," said Libby. "Why?"

"Tell you what, then," said Harry, "you do your shopping and then come into the caff. I'll give you some lunch."

"I might have been doing supermarket shopping."

"No you weren't. You've got your basket with you. You don't take that to the supermarket."

"Curses," said Libby with a grimace. "Foiled again." She pulled the door shut behind her. "Come on then, off we go. Have you been to see Ben?"

"That's where I've come from," said Harry, as they set off down Allhallow's Lane. "Bloody cold, this walking, isn't it?"

"What did he say?"

"Not a lot, really." Harry turned up the collar of his pea jacket. "He didn't want to go for a drink, so I went up to the office. Het gave me some coffee."

"Is he mad with you? I couldn't get anything out of him last night except he didn't want me getting involved — *again*, as he put it."

"He says that every time," said Harry. "Mind you, so do the rest of us. But the other night he actually admitted that if he said he didn't want you to do something, that would make it certain that you would."

"But that was before he heard what you had to say last night. And I think he's realised, all over again, that he really has no sway over me at all. We aren't married, we have no children between us and he's living in my house." Libby kicked gloomily at a tussock of muddy grass at the edge of the path. "No wonder he wants to go and live in Steeple Farm."

"But he'd know you could still run back here if you got upset about anything. He's never going to be certain of you, Lib, you've got to face that."

Libby looked up at him. "I'd never thought of it like that before," she said. "How awful."

They turned right into the high street and Libby stopped outside Bob's butcher's shop. "I'm going in here," she said, "then I'm going to the farm shop. I'll come in after that."

"Don't be long," said Harry. "I have news."

Libby watched his tall figure striding away towards the restaurant and felt a shiver of apprehension in her stomach. For goodness' sake, what now?

CHAPTER
EIGHT

"Ok, what's the news?" Libby leant back in the sofa and folded her arms.

Harry beamed at her from across the coffee table. "Cy's panto is one of yours."

Libby cast her eyes to the ceiling. "Is that all? I already knew that."

"Oh." Harry looked surprised. "How?"

"I Googled it. First I found the Hop Hall Players, then that they were doing my Cinderella. I'm surprised I didn't already know, actually. My old society usually let me know if they've hired out a script."

"I should have thought of that," said Harry. "Here's Donna with the coffee." He took the cafetière and mugs and placed them on the table. "But that's not all."

"What, then? Come on, Harry, don't wind me up."

"Did you know the entrance to that park is right near to where the panto rehearsals are held?"

"Yes, I knew that too. I can research things on the computer, you know. I'm not a complete idiot."

Harry looked doubtful and she hit him with a menu.

"OK, well, it turns out the murdered bloke is also a member of Cy's group."

"No!" gasped Libby. "That's terrible!"

"Well, it pretty much rules out coincidence, doesn't it?" Harry pushed down the cafetière's plunger.

"So, I wonder if he was meant to be a warning to Cy?" Libby poured coffee. "But he can't have been. One or other of them was attacked straight after the other, by all accounts, and Cy's was only interrupted because that lady —"

"Sheila."

"Sheila — came along and disturbed them. So that note was an afterthought. Must have been."

Harry nodded. "Looks like it. Looks like it really is a hate campaign." He shivered. "Remind me never to go out after dark in Maidstone."

"Of course," said Libby slowly, "we do need to find out if the other person also received threatening letters."

Harry paused with his mug half way to his mouth. "Good God."

"Well, it's obvious, isn't it?" said Libby. "If it is a hate campaign against gays, they'll all be treated the same way."

"Unless they don't know where the other guy lives. Lived."

"We're still saying they. Do we know if it was more than one? I know Sheila didn't see anyone, and Cy said he thought it was, but surely it's only one person writing letters. Anyway, they'd have found out where he lived, if they'd taken the trouble to find out he was gay," said Libby. "And found out where he was likely to be. What was he in the panto?"

"He wasn't in it," said Harry. "He was something to do with costumes."

Libby rolled her eyes. "Couldn't have tried to be less stereotypical, I suppose?"

Harry grinned. "And Cy designed the sets."

"Oh, purleese! Did Colin do the wigs?"

"Colin's only there on and off, remember. I think that Sheila does the hair. Among other things."

Libby laughed. "Well, it must have made it easy to home in on his target, then."

"Him or them," said Harry. "Didn't he get the impression it was youngsters?"

"Did he?" Libby frowned. "I don't remember. So, a gang of young thugs. That's also a bit stereotypical." She looked up. "And I'll tell you what else, too."

She related her conversations with Joe and Flo and the story of Amy and Maud.

"It started because I asked Joe who he thought would be the type to write anonymous letters, you see. And he gave me some broad generalisations. And young thugs don't fit with any of them."

"But I bet the redtop reader with a chip on his shoulder does," said Harry.

"Who could possibly get hold of some young thugs and fire them up, you mean?" Libby nodded thoughtfully. "And do you suppose the police have thought of all this?"

"And more, I should imagine." Harry drained his mug. "I ought to get into the kitchen. Are you sure you don't want lunch?"

66

"Positive." Libby stood up. "I want to go home and do some Christmas shopping online. And I don't want to be too full to eat this evening and set Ben off again."

"How would that set him off?"

"He thinks I see too much of you. If I said I'd had lunch here . . ."

Harry grinned. "Poor old Ben."

"Not so much of the old," said Libby. "And now I've got to go back and start making sure he's a happy bunny this evening."

"Why this evening?"

"Rehearsal again."

"Well, he has to rehearse as well, doesn't he?"

"I know, but he's already at the sighing stage. You know: 'All you ever think about's the pantomime.' And now I'm the fairy as well it's even worse." She swung her cape round her shoulders. "Good job I don't have to get involved with Cy or his panto, really. I'd never have the time."

Harry opened the door for her. "Bet you still think about it, though," he said, with another grin. Libby made a face at him and went away feeling guilty.

She was surprised, sometime later, with the fire lit and a casserole simmering in the Rayburn, to receive a phone call from Colin.

"I hope you don't mind me ringing," he said, "but Cy still can't speak very clearly, and Harry was sure you wouldn't mind."

"No, of course not," said Libby, feeling slightly bewildered. "I heard about the other member of the society. Tragic."

"It was wasn't it? But at least we now feel those letters and the attack weren't personal. It's a weight off Cy's shoulders, I can tell you."

"And yours, I should imagine," said Libby.

"Well, of course, but it wasn't me who was getting the letters, or me that got beaten up. No, what we wanted to ask you was about the panto."

"Oh," said Libby.

"We didn't say anything the other day, and neither did you, but I suppose you know we're doing your 'Cinders'?"

"I do now," said Libby, amused. "I've just found out."

"Oh, you didn't know?" said Colin, sounding surprised.

"No. My old society hire out the scripts and sometimes forget to tell me."

"That's not right, dear. You need to be making money out of it. I shall get on to them."

"Thank you," said Libby meekly.

"Anyway, dear, what we wanted to ask you was this. Now I know how busy you are with your own, directing and being the fairy and all — Harry told us — but we wondered if you could find time to come and have a gander at ours? You see," he rushed on, giving her no chance to reply, "everyone's just shocked out of their boots about Cy and Patrick, and last night there was even talk of cancelling the whole thing."

"Patrick?"

"Yes, it was Patrick who was murdered."

"Oh, dear," said Libby, but Colin was already talking again.

"So Cy tried to make them see how much work had already been put in, and what a waste it would be. Well, I interpreted, obviously. Sheila backed us up, bless her, and then Cy had the idea that if you could come down and see a rehearsal and talk to them, it would be a bit of a boost." At last he fell silent.

"Right," said Libby slowly, after a moment.

"He didn't say anything then, of course, because if you couldn't come they would be even more let down. So what do you think?"

"Well," said Libby, and paused. "I could I suppose, but I wouldn't want to interfere with your production."

"No, no, we'd just like you to say if there are any — I don't know — hints or tips, I suppose, from when you did it. It would be such encouragement for them."

"Yes, I suppose it would, under the circumstances, but I'm not famous or anything, you know."

"You are in a way," said Colin. "But it would just be the thrill of the writer coming."

"When do you rehearse? I'm rehearsing at least three nights a week myself at the moment, actually four from next week."

"Oh, dear." Colin sounded mournful. "I don't suppose you'd fancy driving over here on a Sunday afternoon? Or do you rehearse then, too?"

"No to both questions," laughed Libby. "Sundays are sacrosanct. But if you're rehearsing tomorrow I could probably make it." If Ben doesn't get mad, she added to herself.

"Oh, that would be perfect! We've got a rehearsal tomorrow, and we called the whole cast and crew because of the situation. Oh, just wait until I tell Cy!"

"I'm glad you're pleased," said Libby, "but I will have to check with my partner in case he's already booked something in."

"Oh, of course," Colin said. "But otherwise, we'll expect you any time you like after eight, shall we? Do you know where we are?"

"Oh, yes," said Libby. "Right opposite where the other victim, Patrick, was found."

It wasn't until the end of rehearsal that evening that Libby felt able to broach the subject of the Hop Hall Players to Ben.

"Do you fancy going to see someone else's rehearsal tomorrow?" she said, linking her arm with his as they walked down The Manor drive towards the high street and the pub.

Ben hunched his shoulders inside his Barbour jacket. "In Maidstone, I presume?" he muttered.

Libby cleared her throat. "Yes."

Ben was silent for a moment, then, as they turned left into the high street said, "Why exactly? After what I said last night?"

Libby made a face at the pavement. "This is a morale-raising exercise, Ben. And they happen to be doing my Cinderella. It has been suggested that the author coming to talk to them might raise their spirits. They were beginning to lose the will to live, apparently."

"And that's all?"

"That's what Colin said when he rang earlier."

"Why didn't you *tell* me earlier, then?"

Libby sighed. "I knew how you'd take it."

He pulled his arm free and pushed open the door of the pub. "You won't need me there," he said.

"But I thought we could go for a drink, or even a meal, somewhere afterwards," said Libby, tagging behind him as he approached the bar. He ignored her and ordered drinks. Libby waited until her half of lager appeared on the counter, picked it up and moved over to a table where other members of the company were already seated.

"Had a row?" Peter was perched on a tall stool by a room divider. "Colin been on to you again, has he?"

"You know about it, obviously." Libby sipped lager.

Peter nodded. "He called Hal to get your number and ask if you'd mind."

"Well, I don't really, but Ben's sulking."

Peter looked over to where Ben had stopped to talk to some darts players. "I can see that."

"Pete, I know you all think I'm barmy chasing off and investigating things, but I have been *asked* into investigations, or Fran has, anyway. And this time it was Harry who asked me in. It really isn't my fault."

He patted her arm and slid off the stool. "I know, dear heart. Sit on here." He helped her up on to it. "So Ben doesn't want you going over to Maidstone?"

"I asked him to come with me," said Libby dolefully. "They only want me to talk to the cast about my own production. Just to cheer them up a bit."

"Make them more depressed, I should think," said Peter.

"Gee, thanks." Libby swallowed more lager. "Anyway, I thought if Ben came with me he might feel a bit better about it, and we could go somewhere for a drink on the way home."

"Getting out of our little cocoon here might help. It can be a bit stifling sometimes."

"You're all right," said Libby. "You go up to London on a regular basis."

"So could you. You don't have to stay down here, burying yourself in Kent."

"We're wandering from the point, here," said Libby sternly. "What do I do about Ben?"

"You've offered an olive branch, but from what I can gather, Lib, you don't really appreciate him telling you —"

"Asking me."

"All right, *asking* you what to do."

"In a way, I don't. Harry says he doesn't feel secure in our relationship, though, and I don't want him to feel like that. And I do go off on my own rather a lot."

"You're not joined at the hip. And you're doing the panto together. You're hardly ignoring him."

"You're being on my side," said Libby. "I thought you'd stick up for Ben. He *is* your cousin."

Peter made a face. "I know. But looking at the bigger picture, my sweet, it seems to me that the path of your true love has been remarkably rocky. And it's not our Ben who's been swerving off down the highways and byways, it's you."

72

Libby gasped. "I haven't! I haven't looked at another man —"

"I didn't mean that, you old trout. I meant you haven't really decided what you want, have you? Live with, live without. Move to Steeple Farm, don't move to Steeple Farm. Marry or not marry."

"That's never been an option," said Libby, colouring. "I've always said I didn't want to get married. And I knew Ben would be upset about not moving to Steeple Farm, which was why I shilly-shallied. He's really a much nicer person than I am, you know."

"I know he is," said Peter, and grinned at her affronted expression, "which is why I feel I ought to protect him from you. So go off and do what you want and he might come to his senses."

Libby looked at him uncertainly. "I'm not sure what you mean," she said, "but I *am* sure it's not very nice. Ben!" she turned as he came up to her side and dropped a kiss on her cheek. Peter sighed theatrically.

"What's up with you?" said Ben, putting his bitter on a shelf behind Libby.

"He's been telling me how I'm not good for you," said Libby, with more than a hint of malice. "Protecting you, he calls it."

"It's much too late for that." Ben grinned and gave his cousin a friendly punch on the arm. "I'm a lost cause." He turned to Libby. "And we're going for a jaunt to Maidstone tomorrow, aren't we?"

CHAPTER
NINE

Ben drove. He'd been perfectly happy about it, if not over-enthusiastic, but Libby was, in the vernacular, waiting for the other shoe to drop. She was silent all the way to Maidstone, only rousing herself to give Ben directions, as far as she could, to the Hop Hall's rehearsal space. The satnav had been unable to help on this point, as they hadn't been able to find a postcode for it.

It was quiet, only a striped police tape fluttering from the closed gates of the little park. There were no parking restrictions other than zig-zag lines outside the park, but opposite was a blessedly unlined roadway. Ben parked a little way down from what had been the village hall and was now the community centre, with modern extensions on both sides. Libby pushed open one half of the red-painted double doors and led the way inside.

About twenty people were dotted around the large, harshly lit space on linked plastic chairs. On the stage at the end, someone tinkled half-heartedly at an upright piano and two men stood deep in conversation in front of a half-painted flat. Colin, sitting on the edge of the stage talking to a large woman in red, saw them, waved and jumped down.

"Hi, Libby," he said, bustling up the centre aisle, "so glad you could come." He turned to Ben. "And this is your partner?"

"Yes, this is Ben," said Libby. "Ben, this is Colin. Where's Cy?"

Colin shook Ben's hand enthusiastically. Ben seemed amused.

"Just down here, dear." Colin led the way down the aisle to where Cy sat with an older woman in the front row. "Here they are, love," he announced, "and this is Libby's Ben." He waved a hand. "And this is our Sheila — who saved the day."

Sheila smiled nervously, and looked at Cy. Libby guessed she was at least twenty years older than she was — odd, because somehow she'd imagined her younger — her hair a sandy and white mixture in what looked like a corner shop hairdresser's shampoo and set. She wore a camel-coloured tailored coat and sturdy brown shoes and looked as though she would never in a million years go near anything to do with amateur dramatics.

"Hello, Sheila," said Libby. "We heard all about your bravery."

"Oh, I wasn't brave." Sheila's voice had a soft, whispery quality that made her difficult to hear. "I just happened to come along at the right time."

Right." Libby nodded. "And you didn't manage to see what the thugs looked like?"

"Libby." Ben spoke for the first time. "I'm sure Sheila's been asked that more than enough times."

"Sorry," said Libby. "It's just so awful, isn't it? You never think it could happen to anyone you know."

"Oh, I know," said Sheila in a stronger voice, nodding madly. "Especially in a nice quiet area like this."

"So, you've come to give us a pep talk, Libby?" Cy's speech was still muffled, but he tried to smile.

"Colin seemed to think it was a good idea," said Libby, wondering now if it was.

"Oh, we do," said Colin. "Tell you what, I'll stand up and introduce you, and then we can do a little bit of — what, Cy? First act? Then you can tell us what you think."

"Oh, I don't want to criticise," said Libby.

"No, no," said Colin, looking anxiously at Cy. "Just — um — what I said on the phone. You know."

"OK." Libby nodded. "All right with you, Cy?"

"Ask the director," mumbled Cy.

"Oh — yes." Colin looked puzzled. "Who?"

"I think he's joking," said Sheila, patting Cy's arm. "The producer's not here." She sniffed. "Never is. Cy's done most of it."

"Oh, I see." Libby wondered how good it was going to be under these circumstances. Worrying.

She needn't have worried. Colin made a moving little speech about the death of Patrick Stephens, the man who had been murdered, the attack on Cy and the morale of the panto, finishing with the rather standard trite message that Patrick would have wanted them to go on, as indeed did Cy, and it was up to them all to do the best they could.

A small chorus of women in their thirties and forties gathered on stage, apologising that the dancers trained separately so it wouldn't look as good as it would eventually, and the pianist, who turned out to be the musical director, struck up a lively opening number.

Cinders, Buttons and the Uglies came on in quick succession after the opening chorus and, apart from some very obvious blocking and rather more delivery problems, Libby was satisfied that the Hop Hall Players had at least a viable production on their hands. She made a few modest suggestions and asked all the principals about their own parts. It was Cinderella who surprised her.

"I don't think I'm going to be able to do it," she said, drooping her head. A very pretty head, too, thought Libby, and an acceptably pretty voice. Not that strong, but Cy, or the original producer, had been sensible enough not to give her difficult songs.

"Why do you say that?" asked Libby. "You look great and you sound great."

"This is Lisa Stephens, Libby," said Colin quietly. "Patrick's sister."

Silenced, Libby gaped in astonished embarrassment. Lisa Stephens lifted her head and gave her a half smile.

"You weren't to know. And Mum told me not to come tonight, but I wanted —" Her voice wobbled and suspended. Libby, horrified, put her hand over Lisa's and looked wildly round for support. It came, oddly, from Ben, who put his arm round the girl and led her away, surrounded by a twittering group of chorus members. A sulky young man watched from the back of the hall. Disgruntled boyfriend, thought Libby.

"Why didn't you tell me before?" she whispered to Colin and Cy. "And why on earth is she here?"

"You heard her," said Colin miserably. "She wanted to come. It was a sort of — I dunno — exorcism, if that's the right word."

"Bloody stupid idea, if you ask me," said Ben, returning to them. "And no, Lib, I'm not blaming you this time. You weren't here to question anyone and you didn't. But what the hell she thought she was doing —" He broke off and shook his head.

Libby nodded and looked at Cy. "Is there more to this than meets the eye?" she asked. "What did she think she could achieve by coming here tonight? She shouldn't even be *in* the production any more."

He sighed. "If you've finished here, come and have a drink."

Libby looked at Ben.

"OK," he said. "Where?"

"Ours," said Colin promptly. "Someone else can lock up here. Sheila, you coming?"

But Sheila shook her head, and gathering her camel coat round her tip-tapped purposefully over to the group surrounding Lisa. Elbowing the crowd unceremoniously aside, she took the girl by the arm and led her to the side of the room where coats hung on a rail. The disgruntled boyfriend hunched a shoulder and left.

"That's all right, then," said Colin gratefully, watching as Sheila helped Lisa into her coat. "Sheila'll take her home and check on her mum, too." He shook his head. "Poor bloody family. Lost their dad only last year."

"Oh, my God," whispered Libby. "Oh, Cy, this is so awful."

He attempted a smile and patted her arm. "I know." He stood up, wincing and holding his ribs. "Come on."

Ben drove them all round the park and up the little hill to the bungalow. Colin bustled ahead to open the door and turn all the lights on, while Cy offered to take coats. Ben waved him away and threw his and Libby's on to a chair in the front room. Colin appeared with a tray on which stood various bottles. Ben looked away.

"Got any coffee?" he said plaintively. "I'm driving."

"Oh, sorry, pet," said Colin. "I didn't think."

Ben didn't even wince at being called pet. Libby decided it must be long exposure to his cousin and Harry that had de-sensitised him.

When they had all been provided with their beverage of choice, Colin, at a nod from Cy, began to speak.

"It seems Patrick had been getting letters, too," he said.

"You were right," Ben said to Libby.

"How do you know?" she asked.

"Patrick showed his sister a couple. And Lisa had this mad idea that it was somebody in the society, so she wanted to see how everybody reacted when she came down."

Libby was dubious. "But everybody's reactions would be horror under the circumstances," she said. "It wouldn't show her anything. And her boyfriend obviously didn't like the idea."

"Boyfriend?" said Colin, frowning. "I didn't know she had one."

"There was this guy there who looked as though he was," said Libby. "I'm probably wrong. I can't think why someone didn't stop her coming down."

"I don't suppose she was thinking clearly," said Ben.

"Why did she think it was someone in the society?" asked Libby.

"The letters referred to it," said Cy. "You knew he did the costumes?"

Libby and Ben nodded.

"There was a rather explicit reference," said Colin delicately. "We had a couple, too, didn't we?" he looked at Cy. "Well, you did."

"So it does look like it's directed at your sexuality rather than anything else," mused Libby. "And I wonder if it's just people in the society? Any other members — er —"

"Gay?" supplied Cy. "Not that I know of, and I think I would."

"What did the police say?" asked Ben.

"Nothing much." Colin shrugged. "They wouldn't even tell us who the other man was at first. We heard on the TV."

"And you don't know of any incident in Patrick's life that would make an enemy of someone?" said Libby.

"Or why someone would choose to victimise his family?" Ben added.

80

Cy shrugged and winced again. Colin sighed and shook his head. "He was a nice boy," he said. "Younger than us, of course, only in his twenties, but clever. Very clever. Mind, his dad never really got used to the fact that he was gay. Accepted it on the surface, course, but a bit uncomfortable."

"It's that generation," muttered Cy.

"Looking at Lisa, I would say that her parents are — or were — our generation," said Ben, with a look at Libby, "and we're hardly like that."

Cy's highly coloured face developed an even deeper hue. "Sorry," he said.

Ben smiled grimly. "Doesn't matter. What *does* matter is the effect this bastard is having on everybody."

This has got him angry, thought Libby. I wonder what he'll say when we're alone?

"Well, yes," said Colin, looking uncomfortable.

"And to be honest," said Libby, thinking the conversation needed a slightly different direction, "I don't think my input did much to cheer things up. It all fell apart, rather, didn't it?"

"No," said Colin, "I don't think so, Cy, do you? They all seemed pleased with what you had to say."

"They did," said Cy. "It did help, Libby, and I know you thought Col's little speech was a bit tacky, but it's true. I want the panto to go on, and I know Paddy would have done, too."

"OK," said Libby. "I wish I could do more, but I'm a bit tied up with ours. Is there anything you'd like to ask me about it, though, while I'm here?"

There was, as it happened. Cy even fetched his copy of the script, and while he and Libby pored over it, Colin made Ben another cup of coffee.

"Cy called Patrick Paddy," said Ben, leaning against the work surface in the kitchen watching the kettle. "Are they an Irish family?"

"Gawd love you, no!" said Colin, fetching a fresh mug. "Mum and Dad both come from East End families who came down hopping. They were some of the first Hop Hall players."

"Can't be many of those left," said Ben.

"Sheila comes from one of those families, I think, and there are a couple of oldest inhabitants who were founder members."

"They must really be ancient," said Ben, accepting his coffee. "If they were old enough to be pickers when they began their plays, or whatever they were." Libby had given him a potted background to the case and characters as far as she knew it the previous night.

"I think they must have been teenagers then," said Colin, leading the way back to the front room. "I don't know much about them."

"I bet Libby would like to meet them," said Ben quietly, looking across to where his inamorata was gesticulating wildly over the script, Brillo-pad hair flying and whisky glass in grave danger of losing its contents.

"Really?" Colin gave him a quick look. "I suppose I could find out . . ."

"Don't worry," said Ben, going to sit down again, "she'll ask if she does."

82

"But I thought she wasn't going to get involved with our — er — well, with the — er —"

"Investigation?" Ben's smile was crooked. "If she gets any time off from her own panto, she'll be investigating, don't you worry. Even though the police are. She'll think she's got an angle they don't have."

"Harry said that." Colin nodded. "She'll look at things they would brush aside. But," he turned to look Ben full in the face, "I got the impression you weren't very happy with her getting involved?"

"I'm not," said Ben. "She's got herself into some sticky situations in the past, but it's part of her, and I have to accept that. Besides," he glanced across at Cy, "there are a few living casualties of this one, aren't there? Something needs to be done."

"And you think your Libby's the one to do it?"

"She'll give it a try, anyway," said Ben.

CHAPTER
TEN

"What did you think?" Libby slid her eyes sideways to Ben's profile as he manoeuvred away from the bungalow.

"About the pantomime?" He picked up speed and changed gear.

"Well, yes, but about Cy and Colin."

"And the case?"

"Well," said Libby, "you did seem to be showing a bit of interest."

"In Lisa. It got to me a bit." Ben swung the car round a corner and headed towards Detling Hill.

"Yes. Perhaps that's what gets to me, too."

After a few minutes, Ben sent her a quick glance. "Did you mean that? Is that really why you do it?"

"No," said Libby sadly. "It's usually because I'm asked, and I never see the bodies, or the people who are really upset, do I? I think if I did I'd probably be put off for ever."

"That's what I'll have to do then," said Ben with a grin. "Aversion therapy."

"But it does get to me," she continued. "The fallout gets to me. How many people murder affects. It's always staggering. I mean, look at all of us during *The Hop Pickers*. And Fran and her family when her auntie died."

"But after that you haven't actually been personally involved with anybody," said Ben. "It's when you see the effect, like Lisa. And Cy's face, I suppose."

"So you're a bit more sympathetic now?"

Ben didn't answer for several minutes. Libby knew better than to push it.

"I suppose I am, if you really can make a difference," he said eventually. Libby kept quiet. After a few more minutes he said, "I'll even help, if I can."

"Thank you, Ben," said Libby. "We'll talk about it tomorrow, shall we?"

He gave her a quick look and a smile. "Yes," he said. "We will."

Saturday dawned grey and chilly. The threat of snow was still occupying all the weather forecasts, but looked as though so far it was holding off. Libby and Ben were both due at the theatre for non-rehearsal-type panto duties. Ben was overseeing and contributing to construction of scenery, Libby was checking box office receipts and reviewing costumes. Which made her think of Patrick Stephens.

Peter was wandering around the backstage area when she went to look for Ben.

"What are you doing here?" she asked.

"I *am* a co-owner," he said amused. "And as far as I know, I'm script editor for *Hey Diddle Diddle*, too."

"I know, I know. But still, what are you doing here?"

"Just checking." He looked up into the flies. "Set's looking good. Ben's in the workshop if you were looking for him."

"Well, I was, but seeing as I've bumped into you, how much do you know about Cy's panto society?"

Peter looked surprised. "Hardly anything." he said. "You probably know more than I do. Why?"

"Did Harry tell you that the murder victim is — was — a member as well? He did costumes."

"Yes, Patrick Stephens. He was a friend of Cy's — and Colin's. He's actually an apprentice to a dress designer or something. Or was."

"They didn't tell me that," said Libby, disgruntled.

"Did they think it mattered?"

"I don't know. They knew about the family, but didn't seem as upset as you would think, if he was a friend. And Colin didn't say anything about it when he asked us over last night."

"Us?"

"Ben came with me." Libby smiled. "He's going to help."

"Help —" Peter frowned. "Do you mean he's going to help you investigate?" Libby nodded. "I don't believe it."

"Ask him," said Libby, as Ben approached in paint stained jeans and T-shirt.

"You're going to help her investigate?" Peter turned a puzzled look on his cousin.

"I haven't seen the fall out from a case as closely as this since —"

"*The Hop Pickers.* Yes, I know."

"Well, this time, I happen to agree with Libby that the police are unlikely to look further than the obvious,

86

which is the gay aspect. Libby thinks there might be something else."

"That's not quite true," said Libby. "I did think that, but since Patrick was murdered, and he'd been receiving letters too, I've rather changed my mind."

"He'd been receiving letters, too?" Peter frowned. "So why do you think it's something other than being gay, Ben?"

"Because they're both in the same group. We haven't heard of any other related crimes, have we?"

"No reason why we should," said Libby. "As I say repeatedly, the police don't tell outsiders anything."

"No, but when the murder was reported on television they might have said something like 'It is being linked to a similar case in —' well, I don't know, but a similar case."

"Have they linked Cy's attack and Patrick's murder now?" asked Peter.

"Oh, yes, because Cy and Colin showed them the note they got."

"And has there been anything else on the news?"

"Not on the radio," said Libby.

"Local radio?"

"No, national. I don't listen to local radio."

"Well, what about local? You've got a mate at Kent and Coast, haven't you?" said Peter.

"I wouldn't say a mate, exactly," said Libby. Campbell McLean was a reporter for Kent and Coast Television's news programmes and had helped and in turn been helped by Libby and Fran a couple of years ago.

"It's an idea, though, Lib," said Ben. "You could call him, couldn't you? He'd know if there was anything the police knew that they weren't letting out."

Libby looked at him pityingly. "Just think about what you just said."

"I — er — oh." Ben looked dashed.

"What he might know," continued Libby, "is the existence of any other crimes — murders or attacks — which are similar but haven't been linked by the police. In public."

"I expect that's what I meant," said Ben.

"I expect it is, too," said Peter, patting him on the back. "Come on, if you've finished here, let's go and have a drink."

Libby went and locked the big back doors to the theatre and the wardrobe store, while Ben attended to the workshop. Peter made sure the alarm was set and they left the building.

"Do you think," said Ben, looking back at the Oast House as they made their way down the drive, "that we ought to have other people on the theatre committee?"

"What more than us three?" Peter looked shocked.

"What made you think of that?" asked Libby.

"I suppose it was going to see that other lot last night," said Ben, turning up the collar of his jacket.

"Why?" Libby frowned. "They weren't that brilliant, and it didn't look as though they had a particularly active committee. Although I don't know how you could tell."

"It was just — oh, I don't know — they seemed a more community-based outfit than we are. Run by the people for the people sort of thing."

Peter and Libby both looked at him in surprise, then looked at each other.

"Do you know," said Peter slowly, "I've never thought of it like that."

"Me neither," said. Libby, "but to be honest, I'm not sure it would be the better for it."

"Why?" asked Ben.

"Well, don't forget I spent quite a few years with my old society, and the politics of the committee there were staggering. There were loads of rows, a concrete hierarchy and some very dodgy artistic decisions."

"No new writing," nodded Peter. "I remember."

"No hiring of professionals," said Ben.

"That was rescinded when they realised how much they could make on a one-nighter," said Libby, "and come to think of it . . ."

"Yes, yes, but not now, Lib," said Peter. "We need to talk about Ben's suggestion."

"Looks like the pub again, then," said Ben with a grin. "Goodness knows what we'd do without alcohol."

"If they had a down on new writing," said Peter, putting glasses on the table ten minutes later, "how come they let you write pantomimes?"

"I'm not sure," said Libby, slipping her cape off and holding her hands out to the fire. "I snuck in under the wire, somehow, and I saved them money. So I carried on doing it. But nice little Colin made me think last

89

night. He said I should be earning money from the scripts, and I'm not."

"What happens, then?" asked Peter.

"Oh, I let the old society hire them out. No one pays performing licence fees, but I'm not sure the society don't charge a hiring fee."

"Then it should be yours!" Ben said indignantly: "Don't tell me they don't pay you?"

"No." Libby shrugged. "I've never thought about it."

"In that case, you silly old trout," said Peter, "you get all the copies back from the old society and refuse them the right to hire any more. We'll do it. Or you will, but first of all you'll have to make sure that anyone who might have hired in the past knows that. Have you got a list of the people who used your scripts?"

"No," said Libby. "I don't always get told."

"That's ridiculous!" exploded Ben. "I shall be having words about this."

"Oh, who with?" Libby looked interested. "I didn't know you still had contacts over there."

"We both have," said Peter darkly. "Say no more and leave it to us. Now, back to the Oast House committee."

"Come to think of it," said Ben, calming down, "after that little bombshell, which should have been the business of a committee, I think I've changed my mind."

"Quite," said Peter, languidly crossing his legs. "We own the theatre — or the family does — we designed and converted it and we decide what's best for it."

"I didn't though," said Libby. "And I'm not family."

"You are almost," said Ben."

"And you directed the first play, asked in by me," said Peter. "And we made you a director of the company."

"We're not a charity, though, are we?" asked Libby.

Peter raised his brows. "No."

"What are we then? Shouldn't we be paying our actors if we're a proper theatre?"

"We own the building," said Ben. "We're directors of the Oast House Theatre Trust. Profits go back into the trust which pays for upkeep and any extra goes into The Manor's coffers. We all do it for nothing."

"Oh," said Libby. "So the company's a separate thing?"

"The actors, you mean? Not really. We ask them to come and play, they come and play. They don't pay a membership fee. If they're cast they become members of the company for the duration. That's all." Peter frowned over his beer. "Why are you suddenly so concerned?"

"I don't know. It was Ben asking about a committee. I've never thought very hard about it before."

"Well, don't think about it now. We're not going to have one. If we need advice about anything, we know people to ask. Which, by the way, was something I wanted to talk about." Peter looked from Ben to Libby and back.

"Advice?" echoed Libby. "From us?"

"Not exactly," said Peter. "I was thinking about new writing again. We haven't had any since — well, since —"

"*The Hop Pickers*. We know," said Libby.

"Well, how about you writing something? And I know I still tend to think of that play as a bad experience, but it did draw the village together."

"Me?" Libby was surprised. "But I don't . . ."

"Yes, you do," said Ben. "We've just been talking about it. You write panto."

"Different from plays." Libby looked at Peter. "Would you like another local story?" she asked. "Only I've recently heard about one."

Peter pulled at his top lip. "Only if you could be sure it wouldn't have any nasty ramifications," he said. "What is it?"

So Libby told them about Amy Taylor and Maud Burton.

"I don't know what happened after Amy's suicide except they found the letter paraphernalia at Maud's. I expect I could find out — Jane's paper's probably got back issues on fiche. Or computerised by now, I suppose."

"A bit sad, though," said Ben. "No happy ending."

"I could make one up," said Libby. "Have another character who's an onlooker, perhaps. Who marries the vicar in the end?"

"Have a look and see what you can find out," said Peter. "If it's real people we don't want to go treading on descendants' toes." He shuddered elegantly. "We've done that already."

Libby patted his hand. "We know," she said. "I'll have a look and see what comes up. We're in no hurry, are we?"

"In a way," she said to Ben as they walked home a little later, "it could fit in with finding out about Cy's background."

"Eh?" Ben looked at her, startled. "What do you mean?"

"Hop pickers," said Libby. "The Hop Hall Players were founded by hoppers."

Ben sighed in exasperation. "What on *earth* has that got to do with Cy? He's only about thirty-five, if that."

"But his mum Josephine might have been the daughter of hoppers."

"How do you make that out?" Ben shook his head at her. "You really are amazing. How on earth you've connected Cy to hop picking apart from the name of his drama society I just cannot fathom."

"No." Libby was downcast. "You're quite right. I don't know what I was thinking. And we don't really need to go into his past anyway, now, do we? Not now Patrick's been murdered."

"It's a strange way to put it," said Ben, as they arrived at number 17, "but no. Unless we can find a link between Cy and Patrick apart from the society, but basically it looks as though it's a gay-hate crime."

"By someone with a connection to the society, though," said Libby, tripping over the doorstep. "Why do I still do that?"

"Because you're careless," said Ben, pushing her ahead of him into the sitting room. "Put the kettle on."

"Yes, master." Libby threw him a dirty look and her cape on to a chair.

"Sorry." He grinned and gave her a hug as he put her gently aside and went into the kitchen himself.

Libby hung her cape up under the stairs and went to the fireplace.

"So what are we going to do about helping Cy?" she said, riddling the grate with the poker. "You said you wanted to help, but we haven't decided how."

"I don't know," said Ben. "You know more about these things then I do."

"Great," she said, sitting back on her heels and looking at him. "So you commit us to helping and then don't know what we're going to do."

"Hold on a minute," said Ben, crossing his arms and looking stern. "I said I'd help *you*. You were the one who committed to helping, when Harry asked you."

"Young whats'erface got to you. That's why you said you'd help."

"Lisa, yes. And, though I don't necessarily like you getting involved in these things, I can see that in this case you might look into different aspects of what's happened rather than the obvious, as the police will."

"Hmm," said Libby, returning to the grate and piling kindling on top of a firelighter. Ben looked at her bent head for a moment, then went to make the tea.

"You told me you suggested there was something else behind Cy's letters when you went over there with Harry." Ben brought in two steaming mugs.

"Yes," said Libby, heaving herself up and on to the cane sofa. "But as soon as we heard about Patrick that seemed unlikely."

"Then why were you trying to link him to hop picking?"

Libby looked confused. "I don't really know," she said. "It was just when I was researching the Hop Hall Players I wondered if his mum had anything to do with them as she and her husband bought Cy's bungalow quite near the Aird Memorial Hall."

Ben looked exasperated once more. "But that wasn't the original headquarters, you told me. And when she bought the bungalow, it was years and years after the hoppers had gone. And by the way, why do you always say 'Cy's Mum' not his parents?"

"Because that's what Cy and Colin said to me." Libby frowned. "I suppose it is a bit odd, isn't it? Perhaps Cy's dad died, or she was divorced."

"She died, didn't she?" said Ben. "She must have been very young."

"Sixty-ish?" suggested Libby. "That is young these days, isn't it? Anyway, I can't very well go asking Cy if there was something odd about his parentage, can I? Not unless I find something to point to it, and I can't see how I'm going to do that."

"No," said Ben. "Neither can I." He looked across at her and grinned. "Not easy, this detective work, is it?"

CHAPTER
ELEVEN

Later that evening, Libby phoned Cy, who passed her to Colin on the basis that he was more intelligible.

"Colin, Ben and I have been working all the way round this, and we can't seem to come up with anything that the police won't be looking into. The only link is the society, apart from them both being gay, so is there anyone there who is rabidly homophobic?"

"Not that Cy knows of," said Colin, "and anyway, I think that's the direction the police are looking in."

"Yes, they would be," sighed Libby. "How about Cy's background? I know we went into it a little bit the other day, but it's the only other thing I can think of."

"His background? Well, we told you we moved here after he got his promotion, didn't we? And this was his mum's house."

"Yes, you did, and that Josephine bought it — when? When Cy was a child? Did he live there?"

"Oh, yes. You lived here when you were little didn't you?" he called out. "Yes, he says. Him and his mum."

"You said the other day, Josephine and her husband. Wasn't he Cy's dad?"

There was slight movement at the other end of the line and when Colin spoke, it was obvious that he was trying to keep out of Cy's hearing.

"No," he said. "As far as I can make out, she was a single mum. They moved here when she got together with — well, Cy called him his dad, but he wasn't really. I never knew him. He died really young, in an accident, I think. It hit poor Jo hard. She was a lovely lady."

"So you knew her?"

"Oh, yes. She used to talk to me sometimes. We'd come and visit, and Cy would go off to do some little job or other for her, and she'd talk to me."

"So where had she come from? Maidstone?"

"She was a hopper's daughter," said Colin. Pause. "Hello? Libby? Are you still there?"

"Yes, I'm still here." Libby took a deep breath. "I was just surprised. I'd wondered, you see, because of being associated with the Hop Hall Players if she was, but . . ."

"Oh, no, dear, she wasn't. Nothing to do with them."

"Really? Why? Do you know?"

"Not absolutely," said Colin slowly. "But I do know she was adopted. Well, fostered, I think. Not completely sure."

"It does a bit. How much does Cy know?"

"Not much more than me, I think. He's never talked about it."

"Do you think he would?" asked Libby.

"I don't know, frankly. And what good would it do? It doesn't link up with dear old Paddy, does it?"

"It might, mightn't it?" said Libby. "Suppose there was someone who was around then who knew something about Josephine *and* Patrick's family."

"It sounds a bit far-fetched to me," said Colin, sounding dubious. "And don't forget, those letters were about being gay. They didn't say anything else."

"I wish you'd kept them," sighed Libby.

"That's what the police said."

"Well, it's the wording, you see," said Libby. "There's a lot to be said for actually reading the stuff yourself."

Colin sighed deeply. "Well, I'll ask him. After all, he did agree to let Harry ask you in to help, didn't he? And that's what you're trying to do."

"Exactly," said Libby. "But if he doesn't want to talk about it, well, probably best just to leave it to the police after all."

"I'll ask him. I'm off again on Monday, so I'll try and get him to ring you tomorrow. All right?"

"And that's where we'll have to leave it," said Libby to Ben after she'd put the phone down, "so in the meantime, I might as well see what I can find out about Burton and Taylor."

"And how will you do that?" Ben had appropriated the sofa and sat with his feet up, his book resting on top of Sidney, who adorned his stomach.

"Oh, lord, I don't know." Libby sat down in the armchair. "Parish records?"

"Local paper, I thought we said?"

"Jane, yes. Can't very well ring her this evening, though. I'll have to wait until Monday."

"Why?"

"Well, it's Saturday evening. She and Terry are probably out, or something."

"She and Terry don't go out. You know that. They're worse than we are. And having been married since the summer, the 'or something' is probably no more than a take-away and a DVD."

"They won't want that interrupted," said Libby. "No, I'll wait till tomorrow."

"There's a connection, here, isn't there?" Ben looked at her shrewdly and put his book down.

Libby fidgeted with the tassel on a cushion. "Just a coincidence, really," she said.

"What is? Come on, Lib. I know that look."

"Amy Taylor had a baby, apparently by a hopper." Libby gazed into the fire. "Coincidence, see?"

"Oho!" Ben swung his feet to the floor and upset Sidney. "And you've now got it into your head that Amy's baby was Cy's mum!"

Libby looked somewhat disconcerted.

"Go on, admit it," said Ben. "I bet that's what you thought."

"Not really," she said. "That would just be too much of a coincidence, wouldn't it?"

"Yes, it bloody well would," said Ben.

"But on the other hand," said Libby, "if I can find out what happened to Amy's baby, it might give me a clue as to how Josephine came to be fostered."

"You could always ask me, you know," said Ben. "I was around at the time."

Libby stared at him, open-mouthed.

"Hadn't that occurred to you? I know I was only young, but I remember Burton and Taylor, and the secrecy that surrounded everything. Believe it or not, I used to go to Sunday School and Amy Taylor taught there. That's how the vicar found out she could play the piano."

Libby found her voice. "Why haven't you told me any of this before?"

Ben shrugged. "Flo knew more about it than I did. So did Mum, I expect. Why didn't you ask her?"

"I thought it might upset her, after — well, you know."

"Yes, I suppose so," said Ben. "In fact, a lot of people might think that it was a bit too near the knuckle after what happened last time."

"I was thinking about that," said Libby. "And I know that because of the play it brought up a lot of memories that may have been best left unstirred, but despite what Peter thinks, it wasn't the play that caused the murder, was it?"

"No," conceded Ben. "And to be fair, the village enjoyed it."

"I think they quite enjoyed the murder, as well as the play. The only thing to worry about, then, is what Peter said. Are there any descendants still around? And what about the vicar? And all those other people Flo said got letters?"

Ben stood up. "Drink?" he suggested. When Libby nodded he went to pour two whiskies. "Well," he said, returning with glasses, "let's see. First of all, the vicar. It was the Reverend Greene —"

"No!" gasped Libby. "I don't believe it!"

"Absolutely true, honest. Harold Greene, I think his name was. Doctor Abercrombie, Albert Grimes, the churchwarden, who also worked for one of the outlying farms, mum and dad both got one, so did Flo's Frank Carpenter. So Susan and I are still around, as are mum and dad, so's Flo, Abercrombie's long gone, and his children never lived here, Greene was moved on after the statutory time, whatever that was, and as far as I know, neither Amy nor Maud herself had any relations around. They could have had, of course, I doubt if I would have known. Cousins, maybe? I don't know if either of them actually came from round here, or if they'd moved here from somewhere else."

"What about Grimes?" Libby sipped her whisky.

"Oh, yes, Grimes. He lived in that row of cottages just off New Barton Lane."

New Barton Lane was the effective continuation of Steeple Martin's high street, at the junction with Allhallow's Lane and the Canterbury Road.

"The ones that stand at right angles?" asked Libby. "Where the river runs by?"

To call the Wytch a river was rather aggrandising, but that was officially its name. It ran parallel with New Barton Lane and disappeared into a culvert at the junction with the high street. It reappeared further down, as the high street turned into the Nethergate Road, and sauntered off in the direction of Steeple Farm, running in a little valley alongside Steeple Lane.

"That's it," said Ben. "Although they've all been gentrified since his time, so there are twee little bridges across the river. And new bungalows beyond them."

"Don't sound so po-faced about them," said Libby, amused. "People have to live somewhere, and those new bungalows were built by old Mr Boncastle for his farm workers. They aren't second-homers, or anything like that."

Ben sighed. "No, I know. And Boncastle was a good man. Trouble is, his own home *has* now become a second home."

Libby reflected on this. New Farm was further along New Barton Lane, and its farmhouse had subsequently been sold to non-farming people, after the rest of the farmland had been sold off. New Farm bungalows had been sold to their occupants for a nominal sum, according to Mr Boncastle's will, to the annoyance of the new owners of New Farm, who had been hoping for a quick and easy profit from the five buildings.

"Anyway," continued Ben, "that was where Albert lived. I doubt if any of his children stayed around the village. There would have been nowhere for them to live in those days."

"Where did Maud and Amy live?"

"Amy lived somewhere off the Nethergate road," said Ben. "I'm not sure where Maud lived. Could have been in the high street, or maybe Lendle Lane. Not sure."

"Where's the pond that Amy drowned herself in?"

Ben looked startled. "Good lord," he said. "I'd forgotten about that."

102

"How could you? That was how she committed suicide."

"Yes, of course, but I just — well, I just hadn't thought . . ." Ben shook his head. "Actually, I'm not sure."

"That old pond the other side of the village, Flo said."

"Ah." Ben looked up. "The dew pond, it must have been. We always called it the dew pond, although I don't suppose it was. Too deep. We were forbidden to go there, although some of the village boys did go. They fished there, although I always thought there weren't any fish."

"OK, so it was the dewpond," said Libby, irritated. "But *where* is it?"

"Oh," said Ben. "Between the Nethergate road and Steeple Lane, in a dip."

"So it could be fed by the Wytch?" said Libby. "In that case it isn't a dewpond."

"I know," said Ben, now also irritated. "I only said we *called* it the dewpond. Why are you being so picky, anyway?"

"If I'm going to write a play about it, I need to know the facts," said Libby.

"But you haven't decided to write it yet. You were just asking if any of the descendants were likely to be offended or affected by it. Hadn't you better find that out first?"

Libby frowned. "You said I should ask you. That's how the conversation started."

"Oh yes." Ben finished his whisky. "Well, as I said, I shouldn't think so."

"But you don't really know," said Libby. "I'd better see if I can get into the electoral roll."

"I don't think it's that easy," said Ben. "Phone book would be easier."

"But that would be the whole of the Canterbury and District area," said Libby. "How could you narrow down Steeple Martin?"

"Post office!" Ben looked smug. "Ali and Ahmed will know."

"Which one's the postmaster?" asked Libby. "And besides, it's probably privileged information. I expect they can't tell you, like interfering with Her Majesty's Mail."

"But people go in there to ask all the time," said Ben. "Ahmed was only telling me a little while ago, he had an American come in and ask if someone lived here, and Ahmed was able to tell him."

"Oh?" Libby was interested. "Who was that?"

"Oh, I can't remember, but it was a descendant of someone who went to the States in the war."

"Ooh, a GI bride?"

Ben looked at her with distaste. "I've no idea."

"Oh. Well, anyway, it means they might know. Shall we go and ask them?"

"Monday you can," said Ben. "Not tonight and certainly not tomorrow. Even if they do open on Sundays, it isn't fair to start asking them to go the extra mile when they could be trying to relax. They take it in turns, don't they?"

104

"And they do actually close in the afternoon on Sunday," said Libby. "OK, I'll wait until Monday. That's two things to do on Monday. Phone Jane and ask the boys."

CHAPTER
TWELVE

In fact, Libby could not contain her soul in patience until Monday morning, but telephoned Jane Baker early Sunday evening and asked if there was any way of accessing the *Nethergate Mercury*'s back issues, and if, back in the nineteen fifties, they were part of the same group as the paper covering Steeples Martin, Mount and Cross.

"I think it was independent back then," said Jane, "but it would have reported anything major going on in any of the Steeples. Everything's on fiche at the library, of course, I'll have a look tomorrow, and let you know as soon as I can."

"Oh, thanks, Jane. I didn't like to disturb you last night, it being Saturday, although Ben said you wouldn't have minded."

"No, you should have done. We only had a take-away and a DVD. What is it you want, exactly?"

Libby smiled to herself at Ben's accurate description of the Bakers' night in. "There was an anonymous letter scandal, followed by a suicide. We were thinking of a local play about it."

"Sounds a bit grim," said Jane dubiously. "Would the villagers want to be reminded of that?"

"The more I think about it," said Libby honestly, "the less I think they would, but I've got interested, now."

"Come on, Libby," said Jane, in much the same tone that everyone else used, "you can't go solving fifty-year-old mysteries."

"Oh, it isn't a mystery," said Libby, "and I'm not trying to solve it. Although," she said after a pause, "there is one aspect . . ."

"There," said Jane in triumph. "I knew it!"

"And what aspect is that?" asked Ben, when Libby put the phone down.

"Oh, just the father of Amy's baby." Libby was nonchalant.

"Oh, yes? Still on that tack? Look, Libby, it won't be anything to do with Cy's mum, you know. For a start, Steeple Martin's a hell of a long way from Maidstone, and certainly was in the nineteen-forties. Their hoppers would have been local. Well, it said so on the site you found about them, didn't it?"

"But they travelled around. Some of the people Flo was telling me about who didn't have papers. They were itinerants."

"How do you know?"

"George Orwell wrote about them," said Libby, looking uncomfortable. "In *A Clergyman's Daughter*."

"And in his essay on hoppers, I know." Ben smiled. "I come from a hop-picking family, don't forget, but, Libby, he was talking about nineteen thirty-one. Not the war years."

"But Flo said a lot of people came down from London who'd deliberately lost their identity cards. People who abandoned their families, or criminals —"

"I'm sure they did, but why do you think there's any connection either with Amy or Cy's mum?"

"Because of what Flo said about the pickers. Farmers were willing to take on men without identity cards because there was such a shortage, and a lot of them must have been criminals, mustn't they? Or what we'd call draft-dodgers these days?"

"Do we? I thought that was an American term. Anyway, yes, I suppose you could be right, but it still doesn't link Cy's mum with Amy Taylor for goodness sake. Why should it? Besides, Amy's baby was born early in the war, if I remember rightly, whereas Cy's mum would have been born much nearer the end, wouldn't she?"

Libby looked crestfallen. "You're right. I'm putting two and two together and making five as usual."

Ben came over and put an arm around her shoulders. "And despite what I usually say, you're so frequently right!" He gave her a little shake. "Cheer up, kid! Tomorrow you can look up Jane's archives and have a good delve into the Burton and Taylor mystery."

"But, you know," said Libby, perching on the edge of the sofa, "I think maybe I won't write their story. It would make me uncomfortable."

"Because of what happened during *The Hop Pickers*?"

Libby nodded. "The more I've thought about it over the weekend, the more it seems like an intrusion."

"Into what, though? I thought we decided last night that there wasn't anybody left who might be affected by it."

"Oh, you never know," said Libby. "Look how many times over the last few years Fran and I have found things in the past that have a direct influence on what's happening now. I don't want to stir things up."

"But if you go rooting round to find out about it, you'll be stirring things up anyway."

"Not if all I do is look through archives," said Libby. "There won't be anyone to talk to, and to be honest, I don't know why I still want to."

"Because of the connection with the anonymous letters," said Ben. "That's how you first got to hear about Burton and Taylor."

"Oh, yes," said Libby, looking up. "Do you know, I'd forgotten about that for a moment."

"You hadn't forgotten Cy's mum, though. How could you have forgotten the anonymous letter connection?"

"Oh, bother." Libby frowned. "I don't know. Everything's got a bit dissociated now. Perhaps I'd better go to bed."

"What a good idea," said Ben, holding out a hand to pull her to her feet. "Shall I come too?"

On Monday morning Colin phoned.

"I'm sorry we didn't get in touch yesterday," he said. "Cy was in a bit of a state."

"Oh dear," said Libby. "Because of me wanting to talk to him?"

"No, no, dear. Because I'm off to work again. I'll only be away a week — well, less, actually — back on Saturday. He's worried about talking to people. I said he's much better than he was."

"So does he want to see me?"

"Oh, yes, dear. He'd welcome it. He's not going back to work, probably until after Christmas, so it would be nice for him to have someone to talk to, apart from Sheila, who's said she'll pop in from time to time."

"That's good of her," said Libby.

"Yes." Colin sighed. "She's a good soul, well, you saw, didn't you, but she's not exactly a laugh a minute."

Libby grinned. "I think I see what you mean," she said. "So when shall I come over?"

"Tomorrow? I'm off later today, so things will be a bit chaotic."

"Morning? About eleven?"

"Lovely, dear," said Colin. "I'll tell him, and I'll see you when I get back." He gave a little giggle. "We've got quite friendly all of a sudden, haven't we?"

It was some time later, while Libby was staring gloomily at a new painting in the conservatory, that Jane rang.

"We haven't got any copies here before about 1979, so I can't tell you anything about Amy, but I looked her up online and found a couple of reports on odd little sites. Shall I email the links? At least it'll give you a date, and you can go to the library and look it up."

"Brilliant, Jane! Why didn't I think of that?"

"I don't know. I thought you were an adept silver surfer these days."

"Oi! I'm not that old."

Jane laughed. "Ever young, that's you. I'll email these links now."

"OK, thanks, Jane. I hope you didn't have to go to much trouble."

"No trouble for my own personal matchmaker," said Jane. "Bring Ben over for supper soon."

"Just name the day," said Libby, being a willing guinea pig for Jane's new-found expertise in the cooking department.

When Jane's email came through, there were several links, and Libby beamed at the screen, thankful for the insight she had once shown in doing her bit to get Jane and her husband Terry together. It meant Jane was always willing to do a little light investigating for her.

There were several short reports of the finding of Amy's body, and a report of the coroner's inquest on a genealogy site. This raised Libby's hopes of finding living relatives, but the site only provided access to paid-up members. However, the report, whether verbatim or not, was interesting.

Amy Taylor's body had been found by a dog walker (inevitable, thought Libby) early on April 21st 1957, in a small pond on land owned by Frank Carpenter. (Flo didn't tell me that.) It was Easter Sunday. The dog walker, a Mr Elliott Brown, had recognised her and tried to pull her out, but, on realising she was dead, ran to the nearest house to raise the alarm. Luckily, according to the coroner, the owners were on the telephone.

Of course. Libby looked up at the window. Everybody didn't have a telephone in those days. Unthinkable now, but for a lot of people, giving someone a quick ring meant a trek to the nearest red telephone box with four old pennies. She wondered which house it was. It could easily have been Steeple Farm. Who was living there then? Millie would have been too young, certainly not married yet. She returned to the screen.

For some reason, the police had gone to the vicarage. Perhaps Mr Elliott Brown knew that Amy played for the Sunday School and the vicar would need to be told? Anyway, the vicar had been told and was asked for the names of any friends or family. The vicar, Reverend Greene, as Libby already knew, had been called to give evidence and confirmed that he had asked to inform Miss Maud Burton himself, as she was a close friend of Amy Taylor, and, indeed, they had both been on the parish council. And how did Miss Burton take the news? asked the coroner. Badly, Libby gathered, from the measured tones of the report.

The police, in the form of an Inspector Chadleigh, had then gone to Miss Taylor's home and found the anonymous letter with its handwritten comment. This was agreed upon as the motive for the suicide, but had prompted Inspector Chadleigh to ask for an adjournment as it had been decided that the letter and its author must be investigated. The Inspector was asked if any others had been received in the village, and he was able to confirm that he knew of at least three, the vicar, Doctor Abercrombie, who had attended the body as police surgeon and Miss Maud Burton. The inquest was adjourned.

Frustrated, Libby tried to find further links on the site, but was unable to. Then she remembered Jane's other links, and began to investigate them. Most, as she had already discovered, were merely short reports of Amy's death. Then she had a brainwave and Googled Maud Burton's name, linked with Amy Taylor's. Sure enough, up came three top results.

The first was taken from a contemporary newspaper report. The other two linked back to it, so Libby downloaded the PDF document and settled down to read.

The first page was the newspaper report, copied verbatim. Maud Burton, it said, had been found in possession of certain items connected to the writing and sending of anonymous letters, and had admitted sending them over a period of six weeks. It further stated that it was the opinion of the police that the letter received by Amy Taylor had been the cause of her suicide, and this evidence was presented at the resumed inquest, which concluded with a verdict of suicide when the balance of the mind was disturbed. The coroner finished up with a severe lecture on the irresponsibility and dangers of anonymous letters, but no mention was made of a punishment for Maud Burton.

Well, thought Libby, I don't suppose it was — what did they used to call it? — an arrestable offence. Unless it was libel — or was it slander? — no, libel was written, slander was spoken. Then the defamation laws would come into play, except that in the 1950s things were very different. But in Amy's own handwriting there was the evidence that Maud's accusation was true. Nothing was said about the contents, true or otherwise, of the letters received by the Reverend Greene, Doctor Abercrombie, Albert Grimes, Frank Carpenter and Hetty and Greg Wilde.

However, at the bottom of the newspaper report was a link to the next page, and surprisingly, more information. Libby checked the name of the website and saw that it belonged to a Kent local history society. Well, perhaps she could get in touch with them and ask for their sources. She reached for her cigarettes and carried on reading.

Perhaps it was not surprising, the writer continued, that Maud Burton left the village almost immediately. There had been an unpleasant scene after the resumed inquest, at which Maud Burton had been required to give evidence, and within twenty-four hours she had left her cottage, in Lendle Lane, Libby noted, and never been seen again. She was understood to have a sister in the neighbourhood, but no one had ever met her, or even knew her name.

Amy Taylor, on the other hand, came from a local family. She had been left her house by her mother, and had not only a brother and a sister, but an aunt and cousins within a few miles of Steeple Martin. The family had been devastated, as would be expected, but only the aunt, a Mrs Stephanie Brissac, had known anything of Amy's 'disgrace', and had refused to talk about it.

So, thought Libby, there might be Brissacs still living in the locality, and they might know something about it. She put the laptop on the table and went to fetch the telephone directory — then stopped.

What on earth was she doing? This was not the back story she was supposed to be researching — or only on a superficial level, anyway. And the fact that there might be relatives of the two women affected still living confirmed her opinion that it might be considered less than tactful to write a play about them. She shut the telephone book. That was that then. She would go no further with the story of Burton and Taylor.

CHAPTER
THIRTEEN

The skies were full of yellowish grey cloud as Libby drove to her appointment with Cy the following morning. Snow was coming, and she only hoped it would stay away until after she got home again.

Cy's face was still a riot of colour, but far less swollen than it had been last week.

"Not sure what exactly you want to know," he said, as he sat her down at the table in the big kitchen-diner.

"I still think there might be something behind all this — well, the letters, particularly — other than homophobia. It's not the average gay-bashing, is it?"

Cy turned an ironic gaze on her. "It felt like it," he said. "And I bet it did to Paddy, too."

"Oh, yes," said Libby, feeling immediate heat in her cheeks. "Sorry. I meant —"

"I know what you meant." Cy filled a mug with coffee and took it over to her. "Colin said you wanted know about Josephine."

"Is that what you called her?"

"Sometimes. She preferred it to 'Mum'. She was very glamorous."

"And she was a hopper? Or from hopper stock?"

"Well, it's a bit confused, actually," said Cy, filling his own mug and coming to sit at the table. "She was adopted, you see, when she was quite young. At least she thought she was adopted. It turned out, when her mother died, that she had never been formally adopted, so she'd been fostered. Her birth certificate still had a mother's name on it, but no father's name."

"Sounds like someone else I know of," said Libby. "In fact, more than one."

"Really?" Colin looked interested. "Mum never tried to find out anything else, but I was always curious."

"So all she knew was her mother's name? And what was that?"

"Cliona Masters." Cy pulled a face. "Sounded made-up to me."

"And Josephine didn't want to try and find her?"

"She said if her mother didn't want her, then she didn't want her mother."

"Yes, but things were so different, then, Cy. If girls had babies out of wedlock they were often taken away from them. Even up as far as the sixties."

"Must have happened loads of times in the war," said Cy. "The ones you knew about — were they in the war?"

"Yes, well, one was a local girl who I think went with a hopper, and the other was an East Ender. Ben's mother, actually."

"Ben? Ben was a hopping baby?"

"No, but his sister Susan was. His mum was lucky. Ben's father married her. She's a terrific woman."

"Still alive, then?"

"Oh, yes, very much alive. The other one isn't though. She committed suicide."

"Oh, bloody hell," said Cy.

"Yes. Not until years later when she thought it would all come out." Libby was suddenly struck by a thought. "I don't suppose that's what happened to your grandmother?"

"My —? Oh, Jo's mum. I don't know." He looked thoughtful. "I suppose it's possible. How would we find out?"

"Death certificate? Your mum wouldn't have that of course, but we know the name and the year your mum was born. When was she fostered?"

"When she was a baby. So 1945. How would we do it?"

"I think," said Libby screwing up her forehead, "that you can do it online, but you have to pay. Otherwise you have to go to the National Archives. You probably still have to pay."

"So all we'd have to go on was Cliona Masters, 1945. Sounds like an uphill job."

"They do it on those television programmes," said Libby.

"They have professional researchers to do it," said Cy, "not a couple of amateurs like us."

"But there are loads of online genealogy sites, and print magazines, too. It's one of the fastest-growing hobbies, apparently. We ought to be able to find someone to help."

Cy stood up. "But I'm not sure why we'd want to. More coffee?"

118

"No, thanks. I mustn't stay too long, I want to outrun the snow." She peered towards the window. "Don't know how long it'll hold off."

Cy refilled his own mug and came back to the table. "So now you know about Josephine, what else do you want to know? I can't see that there's anything there that would make someone hate me."

"No," agreed Libby. "Did Josephine have any brothers or sisters? Adopted or otherwise?"

Cy shook his head. "No. Her parents were quite old when they took her. Never been able to have any, so I understood."

"So I wonder where they got her from? Direct from her mother, do you think? Or from some sort of organisation?"

"I don't know. And I still don't know what it's got to do with Paddy or me."

"Tell me what you know about Paddy," said Libby. "Where did his family come from? Do you know?"

"Hoxton, I think," said Cy. "Then they settled here. Paddy's mum was born here, and was around Josephine's age. Bit younger maybe."

"And there's no other link between the two families?"

"None." Cy leant back in his chair. "So you see, I can't think of anything other than us being gay that links us together. If you want to keep looking for a sick homophobe who knows both of us, fine. That's what Harry said you could do, but don't go digging up our families for no reason."

"No." Libby swallowed. "OK. Perhaps I'd better keep out of the way."

Cy leant across and patted her arm. "No, you're all right. If you think you can get to the bottom of it all, especially for Paddy's sake, go ahead. I'm just saying, I can't see what our past history has to do with it. Much," he said, leaning back and looking thoughtful, "as I'd quite like to find out about old Cliona."

Libby watched him in silence for a moment. "Well, maybe we could find out a bit more about her as a separate project."

Cy looked back at her and smiled. "Harry said you were a nosy cow."

"He was right," said Libby ruefully. "Look, how am I going to find out if there are any mad gay-bashers in your circle, or in particular in the Hop Hall Players? We've done the meet-the-author thing, and it didn't help much except to upset poor Lisa. I can't offer to come and run rehearsals — not that you'd want me to — because of our own panto. And I have the feeling that this weather is going to have us all in a right state over the next few weeks, so I wouldn't want to be trying to get over here anyway."

"You're right." Cy sighed. "I'm just hoping Colin will be able to get back at the weekend. The airports are on alert, apparently."

"So actually best to leave it to the police for now?" said Libby after a moment. "Their golden hour went a long time ago, so I should think things will go quite slowly, especially if their resources are stretched by the weather."

"Don't keep harping on about the weather." Cy went to the window and looked up at the sky. "OK. But I've got a suggestion. Why don't you go and talk to Sheila? She's been around a lot longer than most of us. Tell her why you're asking, and that I don't mind."

"Didn't you or Colin say she came from a hopping family, too?"

"I think so." Cy looked doubtful. "Not sure. She, or her family, were in at the beginning of the Hop Hall Players, at any rate."

"She won't mind, will she?"

"Not if I ask her." Cy went to the phone. "Shall I call her now?"

"Will she be in? I don't want to be too much longer," said Libby. "I can always call her from home if she'd prefer."

"No, she — oh, Sheila? It's me. No, I'm fine, love. Colin went off this morning, back on Saturday, if the snow doesn't stop the flights. Yes, yes, I know. Now, listen, Sheila, you remember Libby who came over on Friday? Yes, that's the one. Well, you know I told you she was going to have a little look into my letters for me? No, love, this was before we knew about Patrick, or my accident. Anyway, I wondered if she could talk to you about the old days. No, nothing like that. We just wondered if there was any reason, you know, going back a bit, why Paddy and I should have been attacked. Yes, I know, and the police think it was gay-bashing, but there could be something else, couldn't there?" Cy turned to Libby and, raising his eyebrows, shook his head. "You know more about it than anyone, love,

121

don't you? That's why I suggested it. Oh, yes, it was me. Shall I? You sure? Yes, she's here now. Well, I will, if that's all right. She won't stay long, she wants to get home before it snows. Shall I come with her? No? Oh, OK. Yes, love, I'll talk to you later. And thank you."

He put the phone down and turned to Libby. "Well, she wasn't keen at first, but when I said I'd suggested it she changed her tune. She says to pop over now, if you like, and I'm not to come with you." He pulled another comic face. "That sounds ominous, doesn't it?"

"I expect she might be embarrassed talking about you being gay if you're there," said Libby. "Thank you for suggesting it, anyway, even if it doesn't get us anywhere." She sighed. "I expect it will be a case of the police plodding away and getting a result in the end. They usually do."

"Do they?" said Cy.

"In every case I've been involved with, yes," said Libby. "They get a bit of help, from my friend Fran, sometimes, who's psychic."

"Is she?" Cy's eyes brightened. "Perhaps she . . .?"

"Maybe, if there's no progress from the police I'll bring her over." Libby smiled. "Harry didn't want to involve her, I think."

"Doesn't he like her?"

"Oh, yes. In fact he let the flat over the restaurant to her when she first moved down here. My son Adam's got it now."

"We must come down after Christmas," said Cy, as he helped her on with her cape. "Treat you to a meal at Harry's — or are you sick of his food?"

"Oh, no, I love it," said Libby. "Especially his Mexican stuff." She opened the front door. "Now, which one's Sheila's?"

Cy pointed across the road at an identical bungalow to his own, with rather less vegetation surrounding it. It looked slightly less friendly.

"Do you want me to pop back in here after I've seen her?"

"No, it might look as though I was getting you to spy on her or something," said Cy. "She can be a bit touchy sometimes. Not quite in step with the modern world, if you know what I mean."

"Really?" Libby was curious. "Yet she's quite happy with your relationship?"

Cy shrugged. "I think she ignores it. You must know a lot of elderly women who — well, who —"

"Who are fag hags?" grinned Libby. "Yeah — me, for one!"

Cy laughed and winced. "Still takes me unawares a bit," he explained breathlessly. "Go on, off you go, or you'll get caught in the snow." He bent and kissed her cheek. "Give me a ring."

"I will," said Libby, and set off across the road, thinking that she really must buy herself a proper winter coat if the winter was going to carry on like this.

Sheila's front door was painted a faded red, and was either a replacement, or had been hardboarded over. The chrome letter box and doorbell were pitted, and the house in general had an unloved and uncared-for appearance. Libby rang the bell.

"Come in." The door opened as Libby took her finger off the bell push.

"Thank you," said Libby, and followed her slightly unwilling hostess into the room on her right.

A three-piece suite in what Libby believed was called 'uncut moquette' sat formally in front of a gas fire mounted in a mock stone fireplace. A table covered in two cloths, one chenille and one lace, stood in the window, surmounted by a vase of dead twigs. A large glass-fronted china cabinet against the back wall contained — well, china. Libby waited to see where she should sit.

Sheila took the armchair facing the window and waved a hand in the general direction of the sofa. Libby sat, carefully.

"What do you want to ask me?" said Sheila, smoothing her brown skirt over her knees and straightening her back.

"I think Cy told you," began Libby nervously.

"He thinks I might know something from years ago about his family and Paddy Stephens's family." Sheila's voice was unemotional, but Libby thought she could sense something behind the words. Sheila did know something.

"Only because you were all families who came down hopping," said Libby. Sheila looked surprised.

"Whatever gave you that idea?" she said. "I'm local."

CHAPTER
FOURTEEN

"Local?" Echoed Libby. "But Cy said —"

"Cy don't know everything." Sheila looked amused. "Here, do you want a cuppa? I was going to have one just before Cy phoned. Thought I'd wait. Kettle's boiled."

Thankful at the sudden thaw in the emotional temperature, Libby agreed, despite the fact that Cy's coffee was still sloshing around inside her.

"Right." Sheila stood up. "Won't be a minute then."

"Um," said Libby, also standing up. "I suppose I couldn't use your loo, could I? I should have asked Cy, but —"

"I know, love," said Sheila, positively oozing camaraderie now. "Difficult with men, isn't it? Just through there, see?"

The bathroom hadn't been updated for a good thirty years, Libby thought, and had that smell peculiar to old bathrooms where no modern products were used, either cosmetic or cleansing. As if to confirm her thoughts, she noticed a large container of Vim powder under the sink. She rinsed her hands, hesitating to dry them on the rather threadbare towel hanging underneath the wall heater, and went back to the sitting

125

room, where Sheila was pouring tea from a flowered china teapot into matching cups. Libby smiled involuntarily.

"Oh, lovely," she said. "Proper tea."

"Don't hold with teabags," said Sheila comfortably, handing Libby a cup and indicating that she should sit down again. "Now, I know you want to get back before the weather closes in, so I'm not going to keep you long. I'll just tell you about the families." She sat down in her armchair and crossed her feet at the ankles. "Well, now. Cy's mum was adopted. You know that."

"Yes, and she had her original birth certificate with her mother's name on it?"

"Did she?" Sheila looked interested. "I never knew that. What was the name?"

"Rather a strange one. Cliona Masters. Cliona. Have you ever heard of that before?"

Sheila shook her head. "Sounds a bit Irish, to me."

"So it does!" said Libby. "Or Scottish, maybe?"

Sheila nodded. "Could be. Anyway. Young Josephine was adopted."

"Fostered, actually, Cy said." Sheila looked annoyed at the interruption. "Well, you see, there were no formal adoption papers. Would there have been an organisation that dealt with fostering, or adoption around that time? The end of the war?"

"Oh, yes." Mollified by the question, Sheila sat back in her chair. "Well, the Red Cross, of course. They had their little place, then there was the Sally Army, and the medical missions. And every garden had a vicar visiting.

There'd be plenty to organise something for a little —"
she stopped. "Well, for a baby."

"So is that what Josephine was?" asked Libby.
"That's what she thought she was."

Sheila looked mysterious. "She didn't come from a
hop garden, didn't Josephine. Local family, the word
was."

"Oh, I see!" Libby put her cup and saucer down.
"Her mother was a good girl, then?"

"I don't know about that," said Sheila, with a sniff,
"but not exactly a hopping baby."

"And you knew her? As a girl?"

"I knew of her," said Sheila. "She didn't live round
here, then."

"How did you know her, then?"

"Word gets round," said Sheila gnomically.

Libby frowned. "You mean, there was talk about
some family? Whose daughter might be this Cliona?"

Sheila shook her head. "It was Josephine's parents.
We all knew them."

"So they had been around then? But where did you
all live in those days? Near the hop gardens?"

"In the village," said Sheila. "Josephine's parents,
they lived there, too, but after they got Josephine, they
moved away. Then blow me down if I don't end up
living opposite her. Course, I didn't say anything to
her."

"Didn't you?" Libby was surprised. "Why ever not?"

"It was a shameful thing in those days," said Sheila.

"But it's never the baby's fault."

"Maybe not, but no point in bringing it up. Anyway, she wouldn't have known me. She was a baby when she was — er — given away."

"Did you pick?"

"Sometimes." Sheila looked away. "My dad — he wasn't too keen on the hoppers."

Libby had a vision of the young Sheila sneaking away from home to play with the rowdy hoppers.

"So what about Paddy's family? Were they local, too?"

"No, they came down from London. Hoxton, I think it was. Funny, it's fashionable now, Hoxton, isn't it? But they were bombed out while they were down here, so they never went back. Farmer found them a little place to rent. Hovel, it were, really, but they were grateful."

"So who was in the family then? Paddy and Lisa's mother?"

"No, only young Dolly. It was just Paddy's grandma and Dolly. Paddy's mum and his Uncle Bertie were born after the war, after their dad had come back." Sheila looked sadly down at her cup. "It's such a shame. Margaret only lost her husband last year, and now she's lost Paddy. I feel really bad about that."

Libby was respectfully quiet for a moment.

"So there's nothing in any of this to make us think there might be something that links the two men? Cy and Patrick?" she said eventually.

Sheila looked up and Libby was surprised to see her eyes full of tears. "Nothing," she said.

"I'm really sorry if I've upset you," said Libby awkwardly. "I certainly didn't mean too."

"No." Sheila cleared her throat. "No, it's all right. I'm just being silly. It's the waste, you see. After all those boys during the war — it's another young life wasted."

"Did you know many who were killed in the war?" asked Libby.

"Not personally," said Sheila, "but you heard of them, all the time. It was the girls . . ."

"The girls?" prompted Libby after a moment.

"Who were left behind. And the babies."

"Ah. Did you see many of those? Were they pickers?"

"Poor girls. Taken advantage of. Little b—" she looked up quickly. "Well, you know."

"I know. But you said there were people there to help them?"

"Oh, yes. I told you, the Red Cross. Dreadful things happened, though. People took advantage."

"Did they?" Libby didn't know quite where they were going now.

"Oh, yes." Sheila nodded vigorously. "Wicked advantage. Course, it was everywhere during the war. Women, as well as men."

"Right," said Libby. "You knew some of those, as well?"

"Yes." Sheila's mouth shut like a rat trap and Libby decided to get away from the subject.

"Do you know what was in Patrick's letters?" she asked, more for the want of something to say than anything else.

"Insults." She shrugged. "About his being queer. Same as Cy. Stupid."

"I just wondered," said Libby, "because there's quite a bit of similarity in their backgrounds. Both sons of mothers who were born at the end of the war in the same area."

"So were a lot of others," said Sheila.

"So no one you can think of would have had anything against either of them apart from being — er — queer."

"Both nice boys. Can't see what anyone would have against either of them."

Libby sensed a return to the rather buttoned-up Sheila who had met her at the door. She wondered what had prompted it.

"Well, thank you, Sheila." She stood up. "I should go now, before I get stuck in the snow."

Sheila nodded and stood up, smoothing down her skirt again. Libby had turned towards the door when a framed photograph on top of the china cabinet caught her eye.

"Is that you?" she asked.

"Yes," said Sheila.

"And is that your brother? And your father?"

"Yes. And my father." Sheila went past her and pulled the door open. Libby took the hint. At the front door she turned back.

"I'm so grateful, Sheila, really. And Cy will be, too. It's sad that he didn't know any of this before his mother died."

"Just as well, perhaps." Sheila shrugged. "And if you're thinking I should have told her, well, how was I to know she didn't know her background?"

"That's very true." Libby nodded appeasingly.

"Anyway, glad to help Cy. Been a good boy, he has." She looked down at her hands. "And that Paddy. So sorry about him."

"Yes," said Libby. "Well, thank you again. 'Bye."

"Bye, dear," said Sheila surprisingly. "I expect I'll see you again."

Libby thought she saw Cy behind a net curtain in his sitting room, and half lifted a hand. She couldn't wait to tell him what Sheila had said, but respected his view that Sheila wouldn't appreciate seeing Libby dive back in to report. Although, she thought, pulling away from the kerb, surely it was only to be expected?

The forecast snow had still not fallen by the time Libby got back to Steeple Martin, and when she checked the weather site on her computer before phoning Cy, she saw that it was now forecast for Thursday. Even nearer to Christmas. She sighed and went into the kitchen to put the kettle on, then changed her mind. Lunch was called for, not tea.

But before lunch, she must call Cy.

He was duly surprised at what Sheila had said, and equally as surprised as Libby that she had never said anything, either to Josephine or himself.

"She said it was because it wasn't done in her day, or words to that effect," said Libby. "No need to bring it up, I think was what she said. But if your mother knew she'd been adopted, fostered or whatever, surely she would have been pleased to know who her real parents were?"

"I would have thought so," said Cy. "It's odd. Mind you, Sheila's a bit odd normally."

"Is she? She was a bit wary at first, but after that she was fine."

"No problems, then?"

"She did get a bit tearful at the end, though."

"Tears?"

"When she spoke about Paddy. His death really seemed to upset her."

"Oh, yes. Well, it would. She knows the family. Was she friends with their Aunt — Polly, was it?"

"Dolly? She mentioned a Dolly."

"I think so. She and Sheila would have been about the same age and went way back. I suppose that's why I thought she'd been a hopper."

"She didn't mention being friends with the family back then. Apparently it was only Aunt Dolly and her mother who were down there during the war. Patrick's mum and uncle were born after the war."

"Right. Well, she's never talked much about it. I supposed I just assumed."

Libby was thoughtful. "Do you suppose Lisa would talk to me about the family? About Auntie Dolly?"

"She might, but why? I thought you said we were going to leave it alone?"

"Oh, I don't know." Libby sighed. "I'm being nosy again, aren't I? Just that what Sheila said threw up more questions. But when it comes down to it, none of them have anything to do with the letters, the attack on you or Paddy's murder. So I ought to butt out and leave you and the police to it."

132

But Libby's antennae, having been switched on, were harder to switch off. All through heating soup, eating it, loading the washing machine and staring at her easel, she was thinking about Cy, Paddy and their antecedents. She was certain there was something to find out, but she didn't know what it was. And, as she'd said to Cy, it didn't appear to be anything to do with the letters or the attacks. So basically, it was nothing to do with her!

Ben arrived just as it was getting dark with the Christmas tree on a trailer behind the four by four.

"Can we leave it outside for a bit?" asked Libby. "It's too early to put it up."

"OK. Go and open the back gate for me and I'll take it round." Ben hauled the tree off the trailer and set off to the end of the terrace, from where he could gain access to the path that led to the back gardens. Libby, wrapping her arms round her against the cold, hurried through the house and into the garden. Sidney followed curiously.

Puffing somewhat, Ben stood the tree just outside the conservatory door while Libby bolted the gate.

"Have you got time for a cuppa?" she asked, giving him a quick kiss on the cheek as a thank-you.

"As long as the car isn't blocking anyone's way in the lane, yes," said Ben, following her into the kitchen, "but I'll be home soon anyway. Only got to take the car back."

"Up to you, then," said Libby.

"What?" said Ben, leaning his bottom on the kitchen table and folding his arms.

"What what?" Libby countered.

"There's something you want to talk about, isn't there?"

Libby shrugged. "It can wait."

"You went to see Cy this morning, didn't you? Is that what it's about?"

"Sort of." Libby warmed the teapot, then spooned in tea leaves.

"Go on, then. As you're already making the tea, you might as well tell me."

Libby lifted the heavy kettle, which had been chuckling quietly to itself on the Rayburn, and poured water into the pot. "Well," she said, "I did see Cy."

While she got out mugs and milk, she told him about what Cy had said, and then what Sheila had said.

"And so," she finished, "there's no point in me doing anything more, is there? Unless Cy can think of anything else he's forgotten."

"So that's the end of it, then?" Ben said. "All for nothing?"

"Looks like it," said Libby, pouring tea.

"Poor Lisa." He took his mug and stirred the tea thoughtfully.

"Well, there's nothing we can do for her," said Libby. "She didn't ask us to look into her brother's death."

"Do you think the police will question all the members of the Players?"

"I should think they already have. Those that knew Paddy well, anyway."

"And do you think it's someone connected with them?"

"If the attacks are linked, then I suppose it must be. There's no other connection between Cy and Paddy, or their families." She sighed. "It's a shame, because it was just getting interesting. There's a whole part of Josephine's story hidden somewhere."

Ben sipped his tea. "What about our home-grown mystery? Are you not pursuing that, either?"

"No, I told you. Amy might have relatives in the area still, and I'm not going to write a play about it, so there's no reason for me to carry on." She sighed again. "So that's that. No mysteries, no investigations, so I shall be able to concentrate on the panto, and Christmas, of course."

"I wonder," said Ben.

CHAPTER
FIFTEEN

The snow came on Thursday. Trains were cancelled, people all over the country were stranded, gritter lorry drivers looked as though they'd gritted their own eyes and shops were running out of food as people stocked up needlessly. Libby and Ben went to the pub for dinner before panto rehearsal and found a very gloomy Harry and Peter at the bar.

"What are you doing here?" said Libby.

"Booked for a firm's do tonight and they can't get here," said Harry. "I'm drowning my sorrows."

"No chance of passing trade, either, I suppose?" said Ben.

"Pete wouldn't like it, duckie," said Harry, with a leer and a wink.

"Fool," said Libby. "We would have come if we'd known. We're having a quick bite here."

"In public? That's even worse than passing trade," said Harry.

"What's up with him tonight?" Libby asked Peter.

"An empty till. Always takes him this way," said Peter.

"Anyway, as it happens, we're eating here, too. You may share our table," said Harry, "and then I shall attend your rehearsal with my swain here."

Libby made a resigned face at Peter and followed them into the dining section of the pub.

"So what's the story on Cy?" asked Peter after they had given their order.

"I'm not following it up," said Libby, and explained. "And I'm not going to do anything with the Burton and Taylor story, either. Amy, at least, might still have relatives round here and it would seem — well — disrespectful. I mean, when we did *The Hop Pickers*, you'd written it and you were one of the family, with the family's permission. So that's that." She turned to Harry. "I know you wanted me to help, but now the police are involved there's nothing I can do. I've tried to look into other reasons for the attack and the letters, but I can't find any, so it seems it is some homophobic nutter, possibly connected with the theatre group."

Harry nodded. "I know, petal. And I know you weren't keen to get involved in the first place, so thank you." He patted her hand. "So now you can concentrate on your accident-prone pantomime cow and arthritic chorus."

"They're not arthritic this year," said Peter, digging him in the ribs. "They're all young and nubile."

"No, really?" Harry looked from one face to another. "Ooh, I bet you're enjoying that, Ben."

Ben grinned. "Oh, sure. I just wish they'd stop chattering. Like a flock of birds, they are, and they get louder and louder until Libby shouts at them to shut up. Then they stop for five minutes, then you hear this little buzz starting again. Nightmare."

137

"Much better dancers, though," said Libby, smiling up at the waitress who had brought their food. "This is one of them."

The waitress giggled and retreated swiftly. "She not rehearsing tonight, then?" said Harry.

"Principals only tonight, if any of them can get here," said Libby. "If you're coming, you may have to read in."

"Oooh, how jolly," said Harry. "I shall enjoy that."

"That's what I'm worried about," said Peter, and attacked his steak and ale pie.

As most people in the cast lived in or very close to Steeple Martin, there weren't too many absentees, but one or two were London commuters who just hadn't made it home, so Harry was given the task of reading in for the Queen of Hearts and one of the evil henchmen. Luckily, the Queen of Hearts always appeared with her opposite number, Old King Cole, and the henchman with his counterpart, so Harry could be pushed into position fairly easily and couldn't get into as much trouble as Peter had feared, although he did give the Queen of Hearts a whole new meaning.

It was after Buttercup the cow had fallen over Moussaka the lamb for the third time that Libby decided to call it a day. The musical director, who was reluctantly doubling as rehearsal pianist due to that reliable body also being snowbound, threw up his hands in horror and glared at the poor cow, who took off its head and glared back.

The relieved cast made a dash for coats, scarves and the pub. Ben and Peter checked the building and Harry

138

checked his phone. Libby stared blankly at the stage and wondered if the panto would ever get any better and if she was mad.

"Lib." Harry came up behind her.

"Mmm?" She turned round. In the gloom of the auditorium his face looked pale.

"Cy. He's been attacked again."

"What happened then?"

The four of them were seated round the log fire in the pub. They had tacitly agreed to leave the story until they could all hear it properly.

Harry, still looking pale, took a large swig of his lager. "Bastard was in his back garden," he said.

"Wha —?" said Libby.

"How?" said Peter.

"When?" said Ben.

"Earlier this evening. He thought he heard something out there, and thinking it might be animal, a cat trapped or hurt or something, he went out. He was hit over the head."

"Who called you?" asked Libby.

"Sheila. Apparently, Cy's next door neighbour also heard the noise and went out to investigate. He saw Cy over the fence, climbed over to see if he could help, while the wife phoned the ambulance and then went across to tell Sheila because she knew they were friends. Sheila's at the hospital with him. She took his mobile with her, sensible woman, so she could get hold of people. Hasn't been able to contact Colin yet, though."

"Bloody hell," said Ben.

"How bad is he?" asked Peter.

"Don't know yet. I don't think it's life-threatening. The police are there, too, Sheila said, but they haven't been able to talk to him yet. They've sent someone to talk to the neighbour."

"Good job Sheila was there," said Libby, "otherwise, if the neighbour didn't know any of Cy's other friends no one would have known."

"I expect the police would have contacted Colin, somehow." Harry took another swallow and practically finished his pint. "Anyone ready for another, yet?"

"No, but I'll get you one," said Ben, standing up. "Anyone else?"

"Do you think the neighbour disturbed the attacker?" asked Libby. "Do you think he would have stayed to finish him off?"

Harry shrugged. "Look, I don't know, do I? I only know what Sheila told me, and you have to admit she's not the most forthcoming woman in the world."

"No," conceded Libby, "but she was all right with me the other day. Perhaps if I call her in the morning?"

"Have you got her phone number?"

"Oh." Libby's face fell. "No."

"Let's wait until we hear more from either her or Cy himself," soothed Peter. "Or even Colin, if he can get home. None of us are likely to be able to get over there to see him in this weather, so you'll both have to possess your souls in patience, won't you?"

"I'll call the hospital in the morning," said Harry, as Ben came back with his drink.

"They won't tell you anything if you're not next of kin," said Libby.

"I'll say I'm his brother, then," said Harry, scowling at her.

"Just saying," said Libby, and Peter patted her arm.

"Leave him alone, dear heart," he said. "You know what he's like."

Ben looked from one to another of them. "So," he said, "does this make a difference to your decision not to investigate any further?"

Harry shrugged, still scowling.

"I don't see what I could do," said Libby. "The police will be knocking on doors all night, now, and will be convinced that Patrick and Harry's attacks are linked. They'll pull out all the stops. I'd be superfluous. Fact is," she said with a sigh, "I always was."

Ben nodded and Peter patted her arm again. "Not to us, you old trout," he said.

"Why will the police be convinced that Patrick's attack is linked because of this?" Harry asked suddenly.

"I don't know." Libby sighed. "I hadn't thought it through. I suppose actually it makes it less likely, doesn't it?"

Nothing much more was said until Ben and Libby rose to go home. Harry suddenly stood up and gave Libby a hug. "Sorry I was grumpy, petal," he muttered. "It's so close to home, somehow."

"I know, Hal," she said, patting him on the back. "Let me know if you hear anything, won't you?"

The high street was quiet. More cars than usual were either parked or stranded along its sides, and the snow was thick enough to come over the top of Libby's short boots. Ben frowned at his feet as they scrunched their way towards Allhallow's Lane.

"You know," he said, as they arrived at the front door of number 17 and stamped snow off their feet, "there's one similarity between Cy's story and our Burton and Taylor saga."

"There is?" Libby tripped down the step and Sidney shot out of the door into a snowdrift. Surprised, he swore, and darted back in through Ben's legs.

"Yes." Ben shut the door and took off his coat. Libby took off his spare waxed jacket and went to poke up the fire.

"So what is it?" she said.

"Adoption," said Ben going towards the drinks tray. "Scotch?"

"Yes, please. Adoption?" She thought for a moment. "Or fostering. But I'd already said that. Josephine was fostered, and as far as I can make out she was a hopping baby, even if her mother was a local girl, and Amy's was, too. So are you thinking the same organisation might have been involved with both of them?"

"Well, maybe, if there was such an organisation," said Ben, handing her a glass.

"Even if there was," said Libby, taking a sip, "I don't see how the two cases could be linked, any more than we could link Patrick's and Cy's families. You said that, remember? And why would we want to?"

142

Ben shrugged. "Just interest," he said, sitting down opposite her. "That's what you say when you get involved with things, isn't it?"

Libby laughed. "So now you're interested, is that it?"

"Well, I've seen a bit more of this one than I have any of the others apart from our first little local problem. And," he said, suddenly serious, "I saw what an effect it had on people."

"You mean Lisa."

He nodded.

"And now Harry's all upset," said Libby. "In fact, if I was a superstitious person, I might think being friends with Harry could bring bad luck. After all, look what happened to his friend who worked at Anderson Place."

"That was nothing to do with Harry, though, that was you and Fran getting involved with that Bella."

"Well," said Libby, with a shudder, "it was a horrible time, and I'm glad it didn't put me off Anderson Place."

"Good job it didn't put Harry off, either," said Ben, "seeing that he and Pete got hitched there."

"True. But still, he seems to be much fonder of Cy, and know him better, than he did the other bloke."

"He'd only met him through someone else, hadn't he?" said Ben. "That makes a difference. I get the impression he's known Cy a lot longer."

"I never asked him," said Libby. "I wonder why? One of the London friends, he said. From those clubs he used to go to?"

Ben nodded. "Guess so."

"I might ask him when he calls tomorrow."

"If he calls. He might have no news."

"Oh, of course he will. He'll manage to find out somehow. You know Harry." Libby stood up. "I'm for bed. It's been a tiring day."

"I'm just going to check my emails, if you don't mind," said Ben, collecting the laptop from the table by the sofa. "I won't be a minute."

Libby turned at the door. "Check your emails? You never check your emails," she said.

He looked up and grinned. "All right. I'm looking something up. Can't fool you, can I?"

"But what? Why lie about it?"

"Well, it could be something to do with Christmas, of course, couldn't it?"

"Ah!" Libby smiled. "I shall leave you to it, then. Don't be long."

"OK," said Ben, bending once more to the screen, where he was typing into a search engine 'Illegitimate babies born during hop picking in Kent.'

CHAPTER
SIXTEEN

"So what were you doing all that time last night?" Libby put a mug down on the bedside table. Ben opened his eyes with a struggle.

"Wha —?"

"On the computer. I didn't even hear you come to bed." Libby sat down beside him. "You weren't doing all your Christmas shopping without consulting me, were you?"

Ben pushed himself up to a sitting position and picked up the mug, taking a grateful sip before answering.

"No, I wasn't." He looked her in the eye and said carefully "I was seeing what I could find out about babies born during hop-picking."

"Oh?" Libby looked interested. "And what *did* you find out?"

"Very little, actually. All I could find were little bits about the Hoppers' Hospitals and the Salvation Army, most of which I knew anyway. I thought there must be some kind of social workers, but there wasn't anything except something called the Hop-Pickers' Medical Treatment Board, but I couldn't find anything else about it."

"Never heard of it." Libby narrowed her eyes at him. "And why were you looking? If the positions were reversed, you'd be getting cross with me. Oh, and by the way, the village is snowed in. No buses, no nothing."

"Really?" Ben swung his legs out of bed and went to the window. "Good God. I'm going to say a cliché."

"It's beautiful, isn't?" said Libby, joining him. "But we'd better make sure your mum and dad are all right — and Flo and Lenny, I suppose."

"Oh, they'll be fine. There are all sorts of security arrangements in place for the residents in Maltby Close, and the doctor's on the corner, don't forget."

"That's Flo and Lenny, yes, but what about your mum and dad?"

"There's a huge stock of logs for the Aga, so they'll be warm if nothing else."

"They won't be if the electricity goes off," warned Libby. "The heating pump's electric, even if the Aga runs on wood. And who's going to get the logs in? Greg can't, and you can't expect Hetty to do it."

Ben heaved a sigh. "All right, all right," he said. "Did you imagine I wasn't going to try and get up there this morning? I go every day, don't I? I'll have to check everything anyway. Thank God we haven't got any animals any more."

"What about Tom Barton? All his sheep will be pregnant, won't they? Will they be all right?"

Ben smiled and put an arm round her. "Tom Barton is a tenant farmer and much more experienced than I

146

am. If he wants help he knows he can ask. Stop worrying."

"OK." Libby leant her head on his shoulder. "I wonder what's happening with Cy, though? Do you think Harry will be able to find out? And will Colin get home?"

"Oh, Libby! Stop taking the world's troubles on your shoulders. If you want to worry about anything, start with your blessed son."

"Why?" Libby turned to face him in alarm. "What's the matter? Do you mean Adam? Or Dominic?"

"Oh, calm down! I meant poor old Adam who hasn't been able to work since he hurt his leg, and won't be getting any extra work from Harry if people can't get to the caff."

"Oh, I see what you mean. No money." Libby moved away towards the door. "I'll give him a ring later. Not that I can do much and he doesn't like me offering him money. It makes him feel like a kid again."

"He is to us," said Ben, sliding his arms into his dressing-gown. Libby smiled ruefully. "They all are," she said. "Are you going in the bathroom first? I'll go and cook a traditional hearty breakfast if you like."

Over bacon, eggs and wicked fried bread fifteen minutes later, Libby eyed Ben thoughtfully.

"Why are you so interested *really* in these babies?" she asked, stirring tea.

He didn't answer for a moment, then sat back and gazed at the wall.

"I suppose it's because it's so close to home," he said finally. "After all, the same thing happened to my mum, didn't it?"

"Yes, it did, but she came back and Greg — sorry, your father — married her."

"But look at the fuss it all caused. You should know as well as anybody."

"Yes." Libby thought back to the Oast House Theatre's first production, written by Peter about the family story. Murder, suicide and mental breakdown had not added up to an entirely happy production. "But the real outcome, for the family, was very positive, wasn't it? You and Susan both grew up happy here, so did Millie, for the most part."

"Yes, and that's what makes it worse, somehow." Ben looked down at his plate and pushed the knife and fork together carefully. "It could have ended happily for Amy and — what's her name? — Josephine's mother."

"Cliona Masters. But we don't know that it didn't for her, do we? Except that Josephine was adopted, or fostered, as we now know. But she could have got together afterwards with the father and lived happily ever after."

"But it didn't end happily for poor Amy Taylor, did it? Poor woman remained a spinster and committed suicide at — what? Forty-five? Fifty?"

"No." Libby sighed. "And you even remember it. I should have realised how you would feel about it."

Ben smiled. "No, you shouldn't. But it has given me an insight to how you feel when you take up your causes. It was seeing Lisa, I've told you that, and realising how much of an effect these things have on a family. On everyone. And then hearing about those babies — well. I know it hasn't got anything to do with Cy's attack or Patrick's murder. I just want to know."

Libby smiled back and nodded. "I know the feeling. And as we can't do anything to help poor Cy any more, you might as well go on trying to find out, just for interest's sake, as long as we don't step on any toes."

"We?" repeated Ben.

"All right, I expect I'll join in." Libby stood up and laughed. "How complicated we make things, don't we?"

"Do we?" Ben frowned up at her.

"Well, I do. I'm not at all sure how I ended up with the whole Burton and Taylor saga, but it was basically nosiness. If I admitted that to myself and didn't try to justify things, life would be a lot less complicated."

Ten minutes later Ben, wrapped up for arctic conditions, stomped off through the snow to get to the Manor. On the phone Hetty had been her usual self, assuring him that she and Greg were fine, the electricity hadn't gone off and there was plenty in the larder, but nevertheless he wanted to check on them, and see if there were any problems with the estate, what there was left of it.

Libby called Flo Carpenter and learned that she and Lenny were also fine, and that there was a special lunch being prepared in the community building in Maltby Close.

"And Doctor Anderson's coming to check on everyone," she added. "Nice young bloke, he is."

149

"I've never met him," said Libby. "I'm so disgustingly healthy."

"Don't you boast about it, gal," warned Flo. "Another few years and you'll have all the aches and pains. If not worse," she added darkly.

"Gee, thanks, Flo, you know how to cheer a girl up."

"Girl — gawd, that's a laugh," said Flo with a wheezing cackle.

"Yeah, yeah, all right," said Libby. "Listen, Flo, you remember telling me about Amy Taylor the other day?"

"Yeah, you was asking about anonymous letters."

"That's right. Well, Ben's got interested in her."

"Ben?" Flo sounded incredulous.

"Yes, well, we came across this other person who had been fostered and who seemed to have come from a picking background, and it sort of rung a bell with Ben."

"It weren't him Het got up the duff with," said Flo.

"No, I know, but it's part of his history, isn't it? There wouldn't be a Ben without Susan. If Hetty hadn't got pregnant with Susan she probably never would have married Greg, and then Ben wouldn't have been born. And the family wouldn't have lived here. So of course it's important to him."

"'Spose so," grunted Flo.

"Anyway, he was trying to find out what help would have been on hand if any of the girls got pregnant. Were there any sort of social services?"

"Lor love yer, no!" Flo cackled again. "Sally Army, Red Cross, them so-called Hoppers' Hospitals and a few neighbourhood busybodies, you know, like the

150

vicar's wife. And the vicar sometimes. Anyway, if a girl got herself pregnant while she was hoppin' she wouldn't know till she got home, would she? Then it'd've been born by the time she come back the next year."

"Oh, of course." Libby shook her head. "I never thought of that. I bet Ben didn't, either."

"But then, we had the odd baby born during picking," said Flo, obviously settling herself down for a nice chat. "And some of them weren't wanted, like."

"So what happened to them?"

"Dunno. But they must've been took off somewhere, mustn't they? Stands to reason."

"Would the Red Cross have done it? Taken it to an orphanage, or something?"

"Might've done. Be more likely the Sally Ann, though. They was all for spitual something or other."

"Spiritual welfare?" suggested Libby.

"That's it. Mind, they used to give us tea and stuff. And have a service on Sundays. So did the vicar, but we didn't like him much. Come to think of it," Flo said slowly, "I was wondering. Was old Amy the vicar's daughter?"

"No!" gasped Libby. "Surely not?"

"Well, see, I didn't know her at the time, this all happened early on in the war and I was only a kid. Me and Het didn't see the locals much, but I remember she used to come round with stuff for the kiddies, like. Shy, she was."

"I thought the vicar's name was Reverend Greene, like in Cluedo?"

"Cor, you ain't been listening. He was the new one her and Maud got hot under the collar for."

"Oh, yes. And you can't remember the vicar's name back in 1940?"

"Course I bloody can't! I was a kid and we didn't have anything to do with the church. Besides, it was 1939. We didn't see her the next year."

"Oh, yes. If the baby was born in 1940, it would have been 1939. She was sent away and didn't come back, then?"

"I dunno. Long before Het met Greg. Nothing to do with Ben."

"I wonder what happened to Amy? Did she get sent to a far-off relative? And what happened to babies then? Were there adoption societies?"

"Look, Libby gal, don't you go getting yourself involved," said Flo. "If Ben wants to find out, let him try. But you know what you're like. Next thing we know you'll be getting yourself hit over the head again."

"I've never been hit over the head," said Libby indignantly.

"Near enough," said Flo.

Acknowledging the truth of this, Libby didn't reply.

"Well, if that's all," said Flo, "I'm going to get meself ready for this lunch. Good of 'em, isn't it?"

Libby went and lit the stove in the conservatory, took some coal in for the living room fire and checked the oil for the Rayburn. There seemed to be plenty of everything, but as usual, not an awful lot of actual food. She sighed. Her shopping was getting worse. She always thought she'd stocked up, but frequently ended

152

up having to go out for something vital. She wondered how much the eight-til-late would have. Presumably, delivery lorries hadn't been able to get through. Still, it was worth a try. And Bob the butcher would probably have something in his cold store.

But before she could get herself ready to go out the phone rang.

"Cy's in hospital," said Harry without preamble, "and they're not going to let him go home alone. So he's coming here."

"Eh? How? Nothing can get in or out of the village, apparently."

"The ambulance will. I've just had the police on the phone. They're concerned about him. Sheila would have had him, but they think that's too close to home. So he's coming here. I can't say Pete's thrilled about it, but he agreed we don't have a lot of choice."

"Do they know what happened?"

"They haven't said," said Harry, "but someone will come with him in the ambulance, or an escort, or something, and they'll talk to me then."

"Goodness, how dramatic," said Libby. "What about Colin? Will he be able to get home?"

"I don't know. I expect Cy's tried to get in touch with him or the airline. I'll hear all about it later. Do you want to come over?"

"He won't want that, neither will the police," said Libby. "Where are you going to put him? In your spare room? Who's going to look after him? You'll be at work, and you said Pete isn't thrilled."

There was a short silence and Libby closed her eyes.

"No, Harry," she said. "You can't mean it."

"It won't be for long," said Harry persuasively. "You could just pop in and make sure he's OK. Pete will, too, but he's not exactly the best nurse in the world."

"I'll do what I can," said Libby, reluctantly, also not the best nurse in the world. "I've only just got rid of Adam, and you helped me do that."

"Well, it's a favour returned then," said Harry brightly. "I'll ring you later."

"You do that," said Libby, and switched off the phone. "And you can explain to Ben," she told the receiver. "Because he's not going to be exactly thrilled, either."

CHAPTER
SEVENTEEN

Ben was, in fact, rather cross. Libby never knew what he said to Harry, but it was a very much changed Harry who rang later in the afternoon.

"I know you're busy," he said diffidently, "but if you have time to pop in on your way to rehearsal tonight —"

"No rehearsal tonight," said Libby. "There wasn't one scheduled, and no one would have got here, anyway."

"Oh, right." Silence fell.

"So you wanted me to pop in and say hello to Cy?" prompted Libby.

"Only if you wanted to," said Harry.

Libby grinned to herself. Ben had obviously given Harry a good talking to.

"Well, I can't say I particularly want to go out again today," she said. "And I don't suppose he's in much of a mood to talk to anyone."

Harry sighed. "Well, no, but he did ask if you were coming over. I shall have to go to the restaurant this evening, even though we've had cancellations. Some of the locals might want to come in."

Ben had already suggested they ate at the caff, but Libby had braved the weather and the shops to buy food and wasn't going to have the effort wasted.

"Just tell me what happened," said Libby. "I'll struggle down to see him tomorrow."

"He heard a noise outside and went to investigate."

"Yes, you told me that," said Libby. "No more details?"

"I think he's rather hazy on the details, which is normal apparently for head injuries."

"Yes," said Libby, remembering Terry Baker's head injury eighteen months ago, also the result of an attack. "Oh, Harry, I do hope I'm not a jinx."

"Oh, come on, you silly old bat. When Cy was attacked the first time, neither of you had heard of each other. Nothing to do with you."

"But I've talked to him since," said Libby.

Harry heaved an impatient sigh. "Don't be so daft! How could talking to him have caused another attack? You weren't standing in the middle of Maidstone shouting at one another, were you? No one knows you talked to him."

"Except Sheila," said Libby. "Hey, that's a thought, Harry. Sheila was on the spot immediately after both attacks, wasn't she? And she lives right opposite, so she could have put the letters through his door."

"Sheila? Have you gone a bit soft? She's in her late seventies. Besides, what would her motive be?"

"She could have been a picker — oh, no she wasn't allowed was she. Although she went, I think, without her parents knowing. Anyway she could have known Josephine's mother. Or Patrick's family."

"And?"

"Oh, I don't know. She's just the only link between the two men that I can think of apart from the Hop Hall Players."

"And she's a member of them, too," said Harry. "Must be a master criminal."

"Oh, I know it's ridiculous, but she was there. Both times."

"She was called for after Cy's attack last night. She didn't just turn up."

"Oh, all right. I just can't think of a reason to attack Cy again. After all, he's been mugged once and Patrick's been killed. If it's a simple homophobic attack —"

"Nothing simple about those, ducky."

"No, sorry, but you see what I mean. Do they often attack someone more than once?"

"Yes, Lib, of course they do. I can give you some literature, if you like. Heard of Stonewall?"

"Jackson?"

"No, idiot, Stonewall the group. It campaigned against Section 28 and their Education for All campaign helps tackle homophobia and homophobic bullying in schools. You should look them up. They know all about homophobic attacks."

"I will," said Libby. "The things you learn. So there's no more detail on the attacks, then?"

"Not really. The police actually deigned to talk to me, as I'd offered to take Cy in, but they seem as much

157

at a loss as everyone else. They have some forensic evidence, they said, but didn't sound very happy about it."

"And what did Sheila have to say?"

"Sheila? You're not back on her again, are you?"

"No, no," said Libby hastily, "I just meant did she come with him in the ambulance, and did she tell you anything about last night."

"Of course she didn't come with him. How would she have got back? You can't hitch a ride in an ambulance. It isn't a taxi."

"The police might have taken her back."

"True. But she didn't come. I haven't spoken to her, but Cy says she was a tower of strength, as usual. I mean, she called me, didn't she?"

"I know. Did she manage to get through to Colin? Or has anybody?"

"The police contacted the airline and they're getting a message through. They're just hoping his flight will be able to land on Saturday."

"Oh, dear," said Libby. "Poor Cy. Look, tell him I'll come by in the morning, and ask if he wants anything. You know, books or something."

"Would you have anything he'd like?" said Harry, and she could hear the grin in his voice. "I mean, chick-lit isn't quite his scene, I wouldn't have thought."

"Don't scoff!" said Libby. "And don't use chick-lit as a pejorative term, either. A lot of it is really good and well written. If you had a brain I'd let you read some of mine. Anyway, I haven't only got women's fiction, I've got lots of crime, too. Oh."

"Yes, oh. Anyway, I'll ask him. Oh, and Lib"

"Yes?"

"Sorry I tried to get you to look after him earlier."

"That's all right. I'll pop in anyway, when I can."

"But you're busy. Panto and everything. And Christmas."

"Well, I haven't got to do Christmas dinner again, this year. God Bless Het. Are you going?"

"Of course," said Harry. "Let's hope Cy won't still be here!"

Libby switched off the phone and went to turn on the lights in the front room. Pushing Sidney off the sofa, she sat down and poked the fire she'd lit a couple of hours earlier. The one thing, she thought, that hadn't emerged during that conversation, was why the police had thought it would be better for Cy to be away from home. Which must mean they had some sort of evidence that the attacker was from his neighbourhood. Which tied in with the theory that it was someone from the Hop Hall Players. But who?

Harry was right of course. Although Sheila looked terribly suspicious, at least to Libby she did, she was nearly eighty and had no noticeable homophobic tendencies, in fact, quite the reverse. And neither did anyone else Libby and Ben had met at the rehearsal last week. Sighing, she stood up and went to find some books Cy might enjoy. A Simon Brett and a Judy Astley seemed to fit the bill, and she put them on the table by the window ready to take them round tomorrow.

"So," said Ben later, "you're not going to minister to the wounded soldier?"

"Don't be cruel," said Libby, putting a plate of steak and kidney pudding in front of him. "I'm not going to nurse him, no. But I'm going to pop round with some books in the morning. I really don't think he'll need more than that. The attack can't have been that serious, or they would never have let him out of hospital."

"So, how was Flo?" Ben changed the subject.

"Fine. They were having a Maltby Close lunch and the doctor was coming to see that they were all right."

"They do well down there, don't they? Perhaps we should sell up here and move in."

"Come off it. Those little cottages are smaller than this one." Libby stopped, aware that this line of conversation could lead to a further discussion about Steeple Farm. "But," she continued hastily, "she did say she thought Amy Taylor might have been the vicar's daughter."

"Really?" Ben said through a mouthful of pudding and raised his eyebrows.

"She wasn't very clear, but she thought she used to see Amy in that September the war broke out, and she wasn't there next year. I suppose she'd come back by the time your mum . . ." she faltered to a halt.

"Got pregnant," Ben finished for her with a grin.

"Well, yes. And stayed around, obviously. But I'm sure her mother left her the house she lived in — which doesn't sound like a vicar's daughter, does it? They'd have lived in the vicarage. But she wasn't living there when she committed suicide," said Libby.

"Perhaps the vicar and his wife bought a house here for their retirement?" suggested Ben. "Makes sense, doesn't it?"

Libby nodded. "Just thought you'd like to know. You still interested?"

Ben leant back in his chair and wiped his lips with a piece of kitchen roll. "Yes. As I said, it's so close to home. It could have been my mum."

"But she had a close, supportive family," said Libby. "Lillian — that was your grandmother's name, wasn't it? — and Lenny. And Flo, of course, although she wasn't family. Amy's family don't sound quite as supportive."

"Oh, I don't know," said Ben. "They sent her away, yes, but that would have been for the best in those times. But she came back, and was left the house. So fairly supportive."

"What I don't understand," said Libby, pushing her plate away, "is why, when the truth came out after she'd killed herself, other people in the village didn't remember."

"Perhaps they really didn't know. If it was given out that she'd gone away for — oh, I don't know — war work of some kind, which would be highly believable in the circumstances, nobody here would know."

"Except Maud Burton." Libby frowned as she got up to remove the plates. "Where was she when all this was going on? Do we know?"

"No idea," said Ben. "I remember her vaguely, but she wasn't involved with the Sunday School as Amy was, so I didn't know her as well."

"Would your mum know?"

"She might, but again, Flo would be a better bet. She was always up on village gossip. Frank Carpenter was more — well, shall we say — 'of the people' than my dad was, so even though my mum came from the same background as Flo, she didn't mix as much. Besides, most of the villagers resented her at first."

"Because she was a picker who'd married above her station?"

"Absolutely." Ben nodded and took his plate of fruit crumble and custard. "Are you trying to kill me off with a heart attack?"

"It's cold, and we need good solid carbohydrates to keep us going," said Libby. "I am unrepentant."

"I'm not complaining," said Ben, and picked up his spoon.

After a while, he said "Will you talk to Cy in the morning?"

"I can hardly hand over a couple of books in silence," said Libby.

"You know what I mean. Are you going to ask him any more about the attacks? Or his history?"

"No." Libby looked surprised. "I thought . . ."

"We'd agreed not to? But you said I might as well carry on looking into it, didn't you?"

"The babies, and fostering, yes." She frowned at him. "You've got the bit between your teeth, now, haven't you?"

"I told you, I can see now how you get involved. And even if Cy's background has nothing to do with the

162

attacks, I still want to know about his mum. I want to know what happened to those babies."

"We know what happened to Josephine. She appears to have had a very ordinary life."

"But what about her mother? It's all so sad." Ben scraped hopefully at his plate to gather up the last of the custard.

"More?" asked Libby.

"No, said Ben regretfully, "much as I'd like some, I think I might burst."

"Well, I can't see that we're ever going to get any further with Josephine's background," said Libby, standing up and putting her plate into the sink. "Sheila told me what she knew, which wasn't a lot, and that's about all we're going to get. We haven't any reason apart from sheer nosiness to ask any more questions of anyone."

"I can't believe I'm hearing you say that!" Ben shook his head. "Talk about pots and kettles."

"Maybe I'm learning," said Libby. "The curiosity gland has been removed."

Ben raised an eyebrow at her. "Oh, yes? I'll wait and see what happens when you see Cy tomorrow. I'm not betting on it."

CHAPTER
EIGHTEEN

Cy had aged. Libby found him the next morning sitting in her own favourite saggy chintz-covered chair in Peter and Harry's sitting room, while Peter worked at the table on his computer.

"Have you heard from Colin yet?" she asked, after dropping a careful kiss on his cheek.

"The airline rang." His voice was weak, sounding more like an old man's. "He's delayed because of the weather, but he should be home either late tonight or early tomorrow morning. They've got a message to him."

"He'll be frantic," said Libby.

Cy nodded, winced and put a hand to his bandaged head.

"So, someone came up behind you?"

"Yes. Only one blow, they said, but enough to put me out."

"They didn't hang around then? What was the point?"

"The police think they — he or she — heard Sam next door come out and it frightened them off."

"So what did the police think the attacker meant to do? Just scare you?"

"I don't know. I can't think why I was attacked again at all." Cy looked as though he was going to cry, and Libby didn't blame him. "Why are they keeping on? It can't be those kids again, can it?"

"Oh, no! I'd forgotten them," said Libby. "Of course it can't. They wouldn't have both — it was only two, wasn't it? — got into your garden, or been able to leave quietly. Perhaps it was only one. Or, it's somebody else. Goodness." She frowned. "The letter writer, then?"

"There can't be two lots of people out to get me," said Cy.

"And Patrick," Libby reminded him. "So what have the police said about this gang of youths? Did Sheila give them a description?"

"A very vague one. I don't think it was a gang. But the police don't seem to know what's going on any more than I do."

"Hmmm." Libby looked across at Peter. "What do you think, Pete?"

Peter looked over the top of his glasses. "I think it's a homophobe who, for some reason, is picking on you specifically."

"Well, that's fairly obvious," said Libby. "But why?"

"How do I know?" Irritably, Peter turned back to his screen.

"Sorry," said Libby quietly to Cy. "He can be very grumpy."

"I heard that," said Peter.

"And I've known him quite a long time, too," said Cy with a small smile. "I know what he's like."

Libby glanced back at Peter and saw him smiling.

"Well, this attack will have stepped up the police investigation, so there's nothing more that I can do," said Libby. "I brought you a couple of books."

"Thanks," said Cy, although he didn't look at them. Libby cast around for another topic of conversation.

"Ben's got terribly interested in the whole picker baby thing. Your mum set him off."

"We don't actually know she was a picker baby," said Cy, perking up a bit. "Why is he so interested?"

"Well, by accident — did I tell you? — we found out about another woman in our village who'd had a baby at the beginning of the war, and as it happens, Ben's mum is, or was, a hop picker who got into trouble with the Squire's son. He married her, though, but that's why Ben's interested. I told you that, too, surely?"

"Oh, I see. Yes, you did. Must be this bump on the head making me forgetful." Cy leant forward. "So you know a bit about it?"

"Not a lot. I did ask Sheila about it the other day, you know, and she told me about the Red Cross and so on, and my friend Flo confirmed that, but there doesn't seem to have been a formal sort of organisation. And of course, if what Sheila says is true, then Cliona wasn't a picker but a local girl. I wonder if Auntie Dolly would know?"

"Who? Oh, Lisa's aunt." Cy frowned "I don't know. Why don't you ask her? It might take her mind off Paddy's death."

"Do you think so? She *is* still alive, then?"

"Oh, yes." Cy smiled. "Not that I know her well. I thought her name was Polly."

"Yes, I remember you saying. I'll see if Sheila's got her phone number, then Ben can give her a ring."

"If she does know anything, you will tell me, won't you?" Cy said. "I'd love to know more about my mum's family."

"Of course." Libby leant across and patted his arm. "Now, is there anything else I can get you?"

A wistful expression crossed Cy's face. "Steak and kidney pie?" he said.

Peter turned round, his eyebrows raised. "Aren't we feeding you well enough?" he said sharply. Cy's colour rose in sharp contrast to the bandages.

"Of course, but I suddenly had a hankering for good old British stodge," he said. "Comfort food."

"Well, I can't do pie," said Libby, "but there's some of the pudding Ben and I had last night. "I'll bring it round later. Is that all right, Pete?"

He grinned. "Is there enough for two?"

"I forgot! You're not veggie, are you?" Libby laughed. "I'll bring it all round, and the rest of the fruit crumble, too. Just get rid of the dishes before Harry comes home!"

Half an hour later she was back with the food packed in an old trug she'd found in the conservatory.

"Have you got Sheila's number, then?" she said, unloading dishes into Harry's tiny kitchen.

"Here." Cy held out his mobile. Libby came back into the sitting room and took it, copying the number into her own phone.

"There," she said. "That'll keep Ben happy. Do you want me to heat that stuff up?"

"I'll do it," Peter stood up and stretched. "I'm looking forward to a change!"

"How disloyal," mocked Libby. "Anyway, you have an old fashioned roast at Hetty's nearly every Sunday."

"True. And I love my Hal's cooking. Just I'm a natural carnivore." He disappeared into the kitchen.

"So are you feeling any better now?" asked Libby, perching on the edge of the sofa. "Was it just your head they — or he — got?"

"Yes, but on top of the attack last week, they started getting worried about it." Cy shrugged, carefully. "But it wasn't as bad as they thought."

"Well, let's just pray that there are no more attacks to come and that the police find the oiks who did it."

Libby walked slowly home for the second time, wondering about this second attack on Cy. It was odd, really, almost as if the first attack had been something separate altogether. The poison pen letters and this second attack seemed to fit together far better, the work of just one person. The description of any youths Sheila had reported would appear to have no connection to a vicious writer of anonymous letters. And, of course, Patrick had been killed at almost the same time, which argued that it was the same attacker, but he, too, had received letters. Libby scowled at the piles of dirty snow at the roadside and wondered if the police had thought of that, too.

Of course, she knew perfectly well from her friend Ian Connell that the police usually thought of everything, usually well before the bumbling amateur, but just occasionally, as Harry had suggested after the

168

first of Cy's attacks, there was something a friend could focus on that the police would ignore. Like Cy's background, Libby had thought then, but it seemed now that his background, or Josephine's, however colourful, had nothing to do with the attack, unless — Libby stopped at the corner of Allhallow's Lane and stared up at the high wall that surrounded the vicarage — unless she was right, and the first attack had nothing to do with either the letters or the second attack.

"Now I've got a headache," she muttered to herself, and hunching her shoulders, turned the corner and crunched through rutted snow towards number 17.

She tried out her theory on Ben at lunchtime, when he suggested they should go for a drink.

"I've walked up and down to Peter and Harry's twice already this morning," she complained. "I'm not doing it again. There's beer in the conservatory if you want it, or you can go on your own."

"Charming," said Ben.

"Oh, you know what I meant. It's hard work in all this snow. And eerie. No traffic."

"All right." Ben sighed and sat down to take his boots off. "So tell me more about this theory."

When she'd finished, by which time he'd fetched and poured a bottle of beer, he looked thoughtful. "Possible," he said, "but I expect the police have thought of that."

"Yes, so do I," said Libby, "but it just seems so odd, such a coincidence."

"The nature of the attacks, too," said Ben, getting into the spirit of the thing. "The first was a vicious mugging, the second — well, almost ineffectual. Definitely seems like two different attackers."

"Or just one of the previous gang," said Libby. "On his own."

"Not so likely, is it?" said Ben. "I suppose you can't speak to your pet policeman about this, can you?"

"Of course I can't. Anyway, he's your friend, too."

"Oh, well." Ben stretched out his legs and put his glass down beside him. "If we're not going to the pub, can we have a fire?"

Libby raised her eyebrows. "You know where the coal is," she said. "You can do it."

He grunted and stood up. "Slave driver."

"Anyway," said Libby, following him into the conservatory, "I got Sheila's number for you."

"Eh? What for?"

"Cy suggested Auntie Dolly might know about the babies."

"Auntie who?"

"You know, Lisa and Patrick's aunt. I told you. Sheila said Patrick's grandmother and aunt moved down from Hoxton. Then Patrick and Lisa's mum was born after the war."

"So Dolly might know what happened to the babies? Or the mothers? I take it she's still alive?"

"Obviously, or Cy wouldn't have suggested it. What do you think?"

"He thinks Sheila would have her number?"

"Or know how to get hold of her, anyway. Although when I spoke to her she didn't say much about Auntie Dolly."

Ben sat back on his heels after building a little mound of kindling over a firelighter. "Worth a try, I suppose," he said, "although I feel a bit foolish, now. Getting worked up over illegitimate babies born over half a century ago."

Libby patted his shoulder. "Shows what a sharing, caring, person you really are," she said. "Want another beer?"

Libby, Ben and most of the backstage team for *Hey, Diddle Diddle* spent Sunday morning at the theatre. Harry arrived to tell them that Colin was finally home, and was coming to collect Cy that afternoon.

"So do we have to have him to Hetty's for lunch?" asked Ben.

"No. He says we're to go ahead. He'll be fine on his own. I brought some stuff home for the caff for him." He made a face at Libby. "To counteract the effect of meat pudding and crumble."

Libby beamed. "Bet he enjoyed it."

"He did. So did Pete." He grinned. "If only I wasn't a committed veggie!"

"So do we know any more about what the police think? Have they been in touch?" asked Libby.

Harry shook his head. "I don't think so. We might know more when Colin arrives. I think he was going to speak to them."

Libby put forward the theory Ben and she had formulated. "What do you think?"

"Possible." Harry shrugged. "But you're not supposed to be looking into it, now, remember?"

"Just interested," said Libby.

"I've heard that before," said Harry.

"Don't forget it was you who asked me into this." Libby wagged a finger at him. "Anyway, now Ben's got a bee in his bonnet about all these babies —"

"I have not got a bee in my bonnet." Ben's head appeared upside down from the lighting rig. "And it's not all those babies. Only a couple."

"It's something for him to do," said Libby with a grin. "Interesting, too. And despite everything, I'd love to know more about Amy Taylor and Maud Burton — just for interest's sake. So we'll leave Cy's problem to the police. He'll be fine now Colin's back and they can go home together."

"And that's just what they won't be doing." Peter's voice came from the back of the auditorium. "The police just called. The house has been burgled."

CHAPTER
NINETEEN

"Now what?" said Harry.

Peter had opened the theatre bar and he, Harry, Ben and Libby sat looking out at the snowy garden area with bottles of beer.

"What do they do?" said Libby. "What does Colin do? Aren't they letting him into the house, or what?"

"The police have suggested that as the house is now a crime scene, neither Colin nor Cy should stay there. I assume they will have to let them in to fetch clothes and essentials, and presumably they'll have asked Colin if anything's missing."

"So is it linked to the attack?" asked Ben.

"They didn't tell me, but it's logical to think they are linking it."

"What did they say to Cy?" asked Harry.

"Much the same as they said to me."

"But I thought," said Libby, turning to Harry, "that you said Colin was home and would come to collect Cy this afternoon."

Peter sighed heavily. "How do you think they found out that the house had been burgled? Colin got home and found it. He called the police and the police called me to see if Cy was all right. Then they spoke to Cy and said he can't go back. They're sending someone to speak to both Cy and Colin once he gets here."

"But you haven't got room for them both," said Ben. "And what about Christmas? Not to mention Cy's pantomime."

"I think the pantomime will have to look after itself," said Libby. "The first thing to do is find somewhere for Cy and Colin to stay."

"Well, it's no problem," said Ben, taking a swig at his bottle.

"Eh?"

"What?"

"Huh?"

"Steeple Farm." Ben put the bottle on the counter. "If I can get up there. Should be able to. I can use the tractor to clear the lane if it's blocked."

"Steeple Farm?" echoed three voices.

"Stands to reason. I mean, it's not quite finished, but the heating's on — I put it on in case the pipes froze — the wood burner in the lounge is in working order, and there's a working cooker, fridge and washing machine in the kitchen. And there are still beds. We'll just have to find some bed linen."

Peter, Harry and Libby all stared at him with open mouths.

"You'd do that for them?" said Libby.

"Well, what else are they supposed to do?" said Ben, sounding irritated. "It's empty, it's habitable, and they need somewhere to stay. And if the damage to their home is more than just a burglary, they'll need somewhere to stay for longer than a few nights."

174

"All my mother's old linen is at our cottage. And towels and things," said Peter. He stood up and held out his hand to Ben. "You're a bloody marvel."

"It's actually still your house," said Ben, laughing, "or your mother's anyway."

"But you've done all the work on it," said Harry, clapping Ben on the back. "Thanks, mate."

"I'm doing it for you two as much anything," said Ben. "I don't think you'd enjoy being cooped up with Cy and Colin for long."

"Come on, then," said Libby, finishing her beer. "We'd better get back and tell Cy the good news. I bet he's bricking it."

Harry looked at her admiringly. "Where do you get these expressions, dear heart?" he said. She gave him a dirty look.

Ben called Hetty and said they might be a little late for lunch, then they locked up the theatre and walked down the drive to the cottage.

Cy was on his feet by the window when they went in. He turned a haggard face in their direction.

"Col's just phoned," he said. "The place is all smashed up."

Harry went over and patted him on the shoulder. "Has he got clothes and stuff for you?"

Cy nodded, wincing. "There were some left." He let Harry lead him back to the chair.

"Well, don't worry," said Peter, "we've got somewhere for you both to stay."

"For as long as you like," added Ben.

"You have?" Cy looked between them, bewildered.

"How about a drink?" said Libby briskly. "Hal?"

"Yup. What does everyone want? Brandy for you, Cy, I think." Harry went towards the kitchen.

Peter and Ben told Cy about Steeple Farm, and Ben said he would take the tractor up there after lunch at the Manor. "By the time Colin gets here I should have the way cleared and you can drive up there."

Cy, still looking bewildered, stared at Ben. "I don't know what to say," he said.

"Look, it's empty. I put the heating on in case the pipes froze, so all that nice warmth is going to waste. Might as well use it, and we'll all be around if you need anything. I don't know quite how you'd get to work, but I guess you'd be signed off anyway at the moment."

"Yes," said Cy, "the doctor at the hospital said I shouldn't think of going back to work until after Christmas. Shock, more than anything, I suppose."

"There you are, then. When will Colin get here?"

"Not long. He's having a police escort so he can get through if there's a problem with the snow. I suppose I'll know more then."

"Right." Peter stood up. "We're going up to Ben's parents for lunch, then Ben will take the tractor to the farm and we'll come back here. There's some food Hal's left in the kitchen for you and Colin. Will you be all right?"

Hetty, unfazed as usual, welcomed them all in and told them to go straight into the kitchen, where the long table was laid, looking, as Libby said, for all the world as if the Famous Five were about to come in and ask for lashings of ginger beer.

176

Greg asked a few questions about Cy, and Hetty asked about Steeple Farm. They both nodded approval when Ben told them of the plan to let them use the farmhouse.

"Where's Ad?" said Libby suddenly. "I thought he was coming?"

Harry smote his forehead. "Shit!" he said. "Sorry, Het. I forgot. He was over at Creekmarsh and got snowed in. Lewis was down — something about a New Year's party."

"So he's not over there on his own?"

"No, Lewis and Edie are there."

Adam and his garden designer boss Mog were under contract to Lewis Osbourne-Walker, who, as his career as a television handyman had taken off, had bought nearby Creekmarsh Place, which he was gradually restoring. His current ambition was to turn it into a wedding and conference venue, but also to hold a music festival there, something that Libby was doubtful about.

"So, is it a private party or a public one?"

Harry looked puzzled. "No idea. Private, I would have thought."

"I hope it isn't a trial run for his precious music festival," said Libby.

As soon as lunch was over, Ben left to take the tractor to Steeple Farm and Libby, Peter and Harry helped Hetty to clear up as far as she would allow. Then, they slithered back down the drive to the cottage.

Cy and Colin were sitting mournfully by the fire, the remains of Harry's food on a coffee table. Colin jumped up at their entrance.

"I can't tell you how grateful we are," he began, kissing Libby and hugging Harry and Peter.

"No need," said Peter. "I'm sure Cy's told you, Steeple Farm could do with being inhabited. Now, come on, tell us what the police have said."

They all settled down round the fire and Cy took a deep breath.

"Well," he said, "the sergeant who came down questioned me again, but they seem to think someone was trying to scare me off. So it's not safe for me to go back."

"I don't understand," said Libby, frowning. "Whoever it was knows you weren't there last night. Surely, they've already scared you off."

"It's not just that," said Colin. "They've really made a mess of the place, so we wouldn't be able to stay there until it's cleaned up, anyway. And they want to do a detailed forensic examination."

"Do they think all the attacks and the letters are linked?" Harry asked. "Libby still thinks they may not be."

"Really?" Colin looked shocked. "How could they not be?"

Libby propounded her theory and watched as Cy and Colin exchanged glances.

"It's possible," said Cy. "Someone heard about the first attack and decided to take advantage of it, you mean?"

"The person who had already written the letters, yes."

"But what about Paddy? He had letters, too."

"A blind, perhaps?" suggested Libby. "Like Maud Burton!" She explained about the anonymous letters that had driven Amy Taylor to suicide. "That would explain it."

"But neither Cy nor Paddy had reported their letters. It would only make sense if they had," said Peter.

"They need to find Paddy's murderers," said Libby. "That'd sort it out."

There was a knock at the door. Harry got up to find Ben on the step.

"Right," he said, clapping his arms round himself to warm up. "The road's clear. I'd get up there as soon as possible or it'll freeze over again. I'll lead the way in the tractor."

"Shall we come?" asked Libby.

"If you do, you've got to get back again," said Ben. "I wouldn't. I can show them everything they need to know."

"You stay here, Lib," said Peter. "I'll get the sheets."

Within a few minutes, Cy and Colin had collected Cy's belongings, sheets and towels from Peter and said goodbye to Harry, Libby and Peter. Peter shut the door behind them.

"No further forward then," said Harry, sitting back down. "Does anyone want a drink?"

"Tea would be nice," said Libby. "I'm not sure whether Ben wants me to stay here then come back and get me, or if I'm supposed to go home."

"Stay," said Peter. "He'll soon ring if he can't find you."

Libby sighed. "How miserable for them," she said, "chucked out of their home just before Christmas, and in this weather, too."

Harry came out of the kitchen weaving a teapot. "Struck me the police hadn't told them everything."

"No. There's definitely more to this than Cy knows," said Peter.

"Why wouldn't they tell him?" asked Libby.

"In case he blows it," said Peter. "He might say something to the wrong person."

"Well, that's a comfort," said Libby. "That means we're not the wrong people."

"I expect," said Harry, coming out with a tray, "that they're covering their tracks. If they let Cy and Colin go back to their bungalow it's not so much that there might be another attack — after all, the police will be on the alert — but they'll disturb all the forensic evidence. And I bet they've got a line on the real attacker, whether it's one or two, so they don't want to give the game away. And if anything were to happen to Cy, or they missed some important evidence they'd be up on the carpet."

"You're right." Libby nodded. "But I wish I knew what line they'd got."

"Not your problem, old love," warned Peter. "Let's just make sure Cy and Colin stay well and out of harm's way until the police let them go back. You've got so much in the habit of ferreting about that you can't stop. Just stop it now."

180

"I know." Libby sighed and took the mug Harry handed her. "And I've mixed poor old Amy Taylor and Maud Burton up with it all and for no good reason."

"Yeah, you ought to be locked up," grinned Harry, sitting down and lifting his feet onto Peter's lap, "but at least neither of them are alive to be bothered by you."

Ben arrived back on foot nearly an hour later looking frozen.

"Why didn't you go straight home and ring me when you got there?" said Libby, pushing him into the chair by the fire.

"I took the tractor back and parked it by the Manor," he said, accepting a large glass of whisky from Peter. "I thought it might be needed if this weather goes on, so it ought to be handy. So I just walked down the drive."

"Sensible," said Peter. "Do you want a whisky, Lib?"

"Yes, please. So, Ben, did they say anything while you were with them? Are they settled in? Do they like it there?"

"Whoa!" Ben held up a hand. "Which question first?"

"Are they OK up there?" asked Harry, "that's what we need to know."

"They're fine. Most impressed. Colin was going round marvelling at everything, even when I told him it wasn't finished. The log burner's lit, and I helped Colin make up the double bed." He took a sip of whisky. "And yes, he did say something you might be interested in." He looked at the three pairs of eyes fixed on him.

"Go on," said Libby.

"Apparently, there was a message on their answerphone."

"Yes? What? Stop being annoying! Was it a threatening message?" Libby prodded him impatiently.

"No, it wasn't threatening. It was from Lisa."

"Lisa?" echoed Harry.

"Enquiring after Cy. They'd all heard about the second attack — from Sheila, I would guess — and she was calling to say how sorry she was, and how was he. Also, to tell him that her Aunt Dolly would like to talk to him when he was feeling better."

Peter and Harry looked bewildered, while Libby looked stunned.

"And weren't we saying it would be good to talk to her?" said Ben.

"Yes, but . . . good lord, this is odd." Libby shook her head, while Ben explained Aunt Dolly to Peter and Harry.

"So what did Cy have to say about that?" she asked when he'd finished.

"He said: 'Why doesn't Libby talk to her instead?'."

"Eh?"

"He doesn't feel up to it, but he thought you could be his deputy."

"She won't talk to a complete stranger," said Libby, "besides, I'm not likely to be able to get to Maidstone any time soon, not without a police escort like Colin's anyway."

"Ah," said Ben, with a certain air of triumph. "That's where the long arm of coincidence comes in."

"Oh, don't tell me Aunt Dolly lives next door to Flo in Maltby Close," groaned Libby.

"Not quite. She does, however, live in one of the New Farm bungalows."

"No!" Libby gasped. "Now, if this was in a book, you'd never believe it!"

"So, what Cy thought, was if you and Colin popped in to see her, explaining why Cy couldn't. And just have a chat. See what she wants to talk about."

"Oh, gawd'elpus," said Harry, putting a theatrical hand to his forehead. "I wish I'd never started this!"

CHAPTER
TWENTY

"Did Lisa give Colin a phone number?" asked Libby, as she and Ben walked home a little later.

"He's going to phone her to tell her what Cy's suggested and ask her. She doesn't know about the burglary yet."

"Do we know if it was a burglary?"

"No idea. Colin said he couldn't see if anything was missing, certainly the television and CD player were still there. So it doesn't look like a burglary. He said it just looked as though someone had flailed around with a baseball bat."

"Mindless vandalism, then? Like the mindless mugging?"

"Could be, but it doesn't make sense. If one of the mindless muggers was behind Cy's second attack, why draw attention to himself — or themselves — by vandalising the bungalow?"

"I've no idea." Libby let out a long breath. "Perhaps they were looking for something."

"Like?"

"Oh, I don't know. Papers. Birth certificates."

"Oh, here we go again!" said Ben. "Josephine's, you mean?"

"Maybe." Libby slid him a look. "Maybe Aunt Dolly will tell us."

"And maybe she won't." They stopped in front of number 17. "I do wonder what she wants, though. Incredible coincidence, isn't it?"

The following morning the roads to the village were just passable. The rest of the county was still suffering, and Libby thanked her lucky stars that she didn't have to go anywhere. She did worry about Belinda and Dominic, Adam's sister and brother, being able to get to Steeple Martin for Christmas, but decided that there were still four days to go, and surely things would be back to normal by then.

Ben brought the Christmas tree in and embedded it in a bucket of earth. Libby and Sidney gazed at it solemnly for a bit, then decided to decorate it. By this time, Christmas cards were hung on ribbons all over the sitting room, and the festive atmosphere was beginning to permeate Libby's brain. So involved had she been in panto preparations and Cy's attacks that it had rather crept up on her. Grateful that her present shopping had been all done online, she realised that at some point this week, preferably before Christmas Eve, she was going to have to do The Christmas Shop. If she could get out of the village.

She was just trying to find a suitable spot for a large red and gold ball that Sidney had his eye on when the phone rang.

"Libby, it's Colin. I've got Auntie Dolly's telephone number. Shall I call her? When could you go and see her if she says yes?"

"Any daytime," said Libby. "I'm pantoing in the evenings. By the way, what's happened to Cinderella?"

"They're cancelling," said Colin gloomily. "Without Cy it's all rather fallen apart. He's very upset about it. This buggering murderer doesn't know what chaos he's caused."

"What a shame," said Libby. "But I don't see how Lisa could have carried on, anyway."

"I know." Colin sighed. "Anyway, dear, shall I call Auntie Dolly?"

"Why not? She might have some answers for Cy. Does he really feel he can't go himself?"

"He's knackered, darling. Feels absolutely bloody — not just physically, but mentally, too. Very depressed."

"I can believe it," said Libby. "OK, then, let me know what's decided."

Sidney was helping remove baubles from the boxes when Libby switched off the phone. She thanked him and sent him packing. By the time the tree was finished, the visit to Aunt Dolly had been arranged for the afternoon, and Colin said he thought he could get the car down to pick Libby up. At two o'clock, Ben waved them off, and Colin's car slid bravely through the slush of Allhallow's Lane to New Barton Lane.

The New Farm bungalows were square and uncompromising, but each of them had been maintained carefully, and although the gardens were currently covered in snow, Libby could see they were well tended. Aunt Dolly had at first demurred, apparently, but had finally been convinced by Colin's (probably highly dramatic) description of the second attack and the burglary. She had also professed herself highly entertained by the coincidence of them staying in her own village, and had even heard of Libby Sarjeant.

Now, she opened the door to them and beamed a welcome. Large and still with dark hair, Libby thought she could see a likeness to Lisa. She waddled through a door on her right and waved them to a sofa before an electric log fire. Libby thought of Flo Carpenter.

"Do you know Flo Carpenter?" she said involuntarily.

Dolly's eyebrows rose. "Course I know Flo! Known her for years."

"And Hetty Wilde?"

"Yes. Not so well, o'course. Her marrying gentry and all."

"Oh, they aren't gentry," said Libby. "I'm Ben Wilde's — er —"

"Girlfriend, ducks. Yes, I know. We live in a village you know!"

"Of course," said Libby, with a wry look at Colin. "Anyway, it's very nice of you to see us, Mrs — Mrs?"

"Webley, dear, but call me Dolly. Everybody does. No, no, it's a pleasure." She drew her mouth down. "Well, not a pleasure, o'course, but I could see poor Cyril couldn't come after all this other business." She shook her head. "Poor bugger. Don't seem fair."

"Much worse for Patrick, though," said Libby. "We were so sorry about him."

Dolly sighed gustily. "Thank you, dear. He was a good boy. Funny sort of job he was in, but each to his own, I say. Can't say I knew him all that well since he grew up. Lisa, now, she stayed at home more, and she and Margaret used to come down to visit. Came for a couple of weeks last year after Margaret's Roy died. Poor souls."

"It's really tragic," agreed Libby.

"Patrick was a lovely boy," said Colin. "Cy and I knew him."

"I know you did, dear. Not that I know you." She peered at him. "Colin, isn't it?"

"Yes." Colin blushed a little under her scrutiny. "I'm sorry Cy couldn't come."

"That's all right dear, I said. So I'll tell you my little story instead. Would you like some tea?"

"No, I'm fine, thank you," said Libby, not wanting to delay the start of Dolly's little story. Colin shook his head and murmured something and Dolly settled back in her armchair.

"Well," she began, "after I heard about Patrick and then that Cyril had been attacked the same way, I remembered that Larry Barkiss."

Libby and Colin exchanged looks.

"Larry Barkiss?" repeated Colin. "Don't know him, I'm afraid."

"No? Went to school with Cyril."

"Oh. I don't know much about his schooldays."

"Well, Larry Barkiss went to school with Cyril. And Paddy went to the same school. Quite a bit after, o'course. But this Larry was still there and he started bullying Paddy. Course, Paddy was only a kid and he wasn't — well —" Dolly stopped and looked at Colin, an apology in her eyes.

188

"Gay, you mean," said Colin. "Don't worry about it. I don't."

"All right, dear," said Dolly. "Gay then. Not then, anyhow. Anyway, somehow Cyril found out, knowing the family, you see, and he took it on himself to have a go at Larry."

"He beat him up, you mean?" Colin's eyes were round with surprise. "I never would have thought it."

"Yes, dear. Mind, we all thought he was a hero, but he got into trouble for it. And then, o'course, this Larry would have it little Paddy was qu — gay, that they both were." Dolly's lips thinned. "Nasty piece o' work, he was. Not," she said quickly, "that there's anything wrong with it, but not what he was suggesting."

"I should think so," said Colin, his face red with indignation. "As if Cy would have tried it on with a kid! It's disgraceful."

"Have you told the police about this?" asked Libby.

"Well, no, dear. I mean, I'm nothing to do with any of it, so I haven't seen them. That's why I thought I ought to tell Cyril. Especially now."

"This Larry," said Colin, leaning forward. "Does he still live in Maidstone?"

"I don't know dear. I've lived down here for sixty years. My Webley, he worked at the farm, and Mr Boncastle let us buy this place for next to nothing, so no call to go back, was there?"

"Would Margaret or Lisa know?" said Libby.

"Margaret might," said Dolly slowly, "but Lisa wouldn't. Shouldn't think so, anyway."

"Worth asking?" said Colin to Libby.

"Oh, I think so. I think, too, we ought to tell the police. It's another suspect and a very good one, too. Although," she said, frowning, "I can't see quite what his motive would have been, do you?"

"Holding a grudge? Especially as both Cy and Paddy *did* turn out to be gay."

"Yes, he might feel he was being vindicated," said Libby, nodding, "and angry because no one believed him way back then."

"Because it wasn't true way back then," said Colin. "At least, not the way he thought."

Dolly's eyes had been going anxiously from one to the other. "Don't you let on as it was me that told you, though," she said. "I don't want him coming after me next!"

"Cy can pretend he remembered it himself," soothed Libby. "In fact, I'm surprised he didn't."

Colin looked at her sharply. "So am I," he said. "Especially after all the fuss you've made about his background."

"I haven't been making a fuss," said Libby indignantly. "Just trying to find out about Josephine."

"Poor little beggar," said Dolly unexpectedly.

"Who?" Libby and Colin said together.

"Josephine, o'course." Dolly looked surprised.

"You knew Josephine?" said Libby.

"Course I did. She was Cyril's ma."

"But you said poor little beggar. As though you knew her when she was a child."

"I did. Well, not to say, knew, but I knew all about her."

"All about —" Libby paused. "All about her adoption, you mean?"

"She weren't adopted, dear. That couple took her away at the dead o'night. Fostered you'd call it."

"Yes, we knew that," said Colin. "And Cy's got Josephine's birth certificate. It says her mother was Cliona Masters. Did you know her?"

Dolly snorted. "Oh, we all got to know about her," she said. "Look, I want a cuppa, so I'll go and put the kettle on, then I'll tell you another little story." She heaved herself out of her chair and waved Colin back as he stood to help. "I'm fine love. Tea do you both? It's all set out in the kitchen. Won't be a mo."

"Well!" said Libby, when she'd gone. "What do you make of all this?"

"I don't know what to make of it," said Colin, frowning. "Why has it suddenly turned up now? Why haven't we heard about this bloke before?"

"No reason to, if you think about it," said Libby. "After all, would you necessarily remember someone who'd annoyed you fifteen years ago, or whatever it was?"

"I suppose it was only one incident," agreed Colin. "You wouldn't think it could have any bearing on anything today, would you?"

"Not that sort of thing, no," said Libby. "I must admit, when I said was there anything in Cy's background, or Patrick's, I was thinking of something a bit bigger."

"Like murder?" suggested Colin, his eyes bright.

"Not necessarily, although that does seem to be the one thing that drives people to even more unreasonable crimes."

"More unreasonable than murder?" Colin looked startled.

"Well, no." Libby made a face. "You know what I mean, though." She turned as Dolly pushed open the door carrying a tin tray with three mugs on it.

"Here you are," she said. "I put milk in and the sugar's there." She put the tray on a pouffe between them and took a mug for herself.

"Now, where was I?" she said. "Oh, yes, Cliona Masters." She gave another snort. "Or, what we found out later, Norma Cherry."

CHAPTER
TWENTY-ONE

"Norma Cherry?" repeated Libby.

"Norma Cherry." Dolly's dark eyes darted between them. "Never heard of her? No, I suppose you wouldn't. But she was famous in her day."

"Famous? For what?" said Colin.

"Murder," said Dolly.

Libby and Colin stared at her with their mouths open.

"Murder?" squeaked Libby eventually. "Cy's grandmother was a murderer?"

Dolly, looking delighted with the effect she had produced, nodded and took a large sip of tea. "Want to hear the whole story?"

"Yes, please," said Libby, "but I can't understand how Cy didn't know this. Or Sheila, come to that. She knew a bit about Josephine being fostered, but she didn't say anything about this — this Norma Cherry."

Dolly shrugged. "Sheila wasn't a picker. I never knew her during the war."

"She knew all about you and your family, though," said Libby. "She was the first person who told me about you. And Margaret and Bertie being born after the war."

"I knew she was local, but I didn't meet her until she joined the Players. She might have been around when we was working on the farm, but I didn't know many of the locals, then."

"But I thought you were a local by then? Didn't you come down after you got bombed out?"

"Oh, yes, but we always felt they didn't like us much. The old farmer, he was all right, gave us the cottage and that, but, of course, he weren't never the same after it all happened."

"All *what* happened? And what's the farmer got to do with Cliona? I mean, Norma?"

"She came down, see, picking. She was with a group of them, and we thought she was family. Turned out after, she wasn't, she'd just picked up with them and said she'd been bombed out, lost everything, so they said to come down with them. She bunked in with one of the women and a couple of kids. Then she started disappearing while she was supposed to be picking."

"Ah!" said Libby. "The farmer."

"Right," said Dolly. "So next we knew, she was still there at the end of the season, and moved in with the farmer and his little boy."

"No mother?" asked Colin.

"No, she died, ages before. So anyway, there she was, and old farmer, he was like a dog with two tails. And then, next spring, she was pregnant. Course, she'd been pregnant all through winter, too, but we didn't know anything of her then."

"Josephine?" Libby almost didn't want to ask.

194

"Josephine." Dolly nodded. "But then, right about her time, the police come round. Not to us, they didn't, but to the farm. And first of all they didn't go in. Or they did, but came out again sharpish, because she'd gone into labour."

"Blimey!" said Colin in hushed tones. "What a masterpiece."

"Anyway, my mum sent me for one of the old Red Cross workers who used to run the Hoppers' Hospitals. I fetched her, and she went in to help. And later that night, or morning, I s'pose it was, this old couple from the village come up, the Red Cross woman came out and handed over a bundle, and that was the last we saw of Josephine."

"Blimey!" said Colin again.

"I didn't see any of that, o'course, but it was all round the village in the morning, and then the police came and took Cliona away. Word was, the farmer wouldn't keep the baby, and no one wanted it being born in prison, so this Red Cross woman found someone to take it. And most people knew who, although they moved away straight away. That day, they moved. Did a bit of a moonlight, you could say, although they paid up their rent and everything. Went the other side of Maidstone."

"And did the police not want to know about the baby?" asked Libby.

"I don't know. If they did, I never heard. Perhaps they thought it died. Anyway, then it turns out Cliona is really Norma Cherry, and she's been murdering men in London and taking their savings. I expect that's what

195

she thought to do with the farmer, only she got caught out."

"Pregnant, you mean?"

"Yes. She wouldn't have planned on that. See, it was easy in the war. Especially in London. It wasn't just the Blitz, you know. It went on all the way through, the bombing. There was those awful V things, and the fire bombs." She shuddered. "So it was easy to kill someone and make it look like a bomb. Only she kept taking their money and papers and things, and someone, somewhere, cottoned on, and they started to look for her."

"I can't think how they did that. It really must have been like looking for a needle in a haystack," said Libby. "I mean they didn't have the technology they've got nowadays. And with all the chaos of the war . . ." she shook her head. "Incredible."

"Ah, well," said Dolly, finishing her tea and putting her mug back on the tray, "not as incredible as all that. See, what we heard, it was in the papers, they was acting on 'Information Received'. Someone had shopped her."

"Who?" asked Colin.

"They never said. Stands to reason. Anyway, they got her, and she hung."

"Oh, God," said Libby.

"So how did you know who Josephine was when she was grown up?" asked Colin. "You still haven't told us."

"My mum knew. She knew the couple, see. So we used to go and visit sometimes. And it was fine. Josephine grew up not knowing anything about her real

196

mother, or her father, come to that, but then the old couple died when she was in her teens and she went a little bit wild. She came back in the seventies with this baby — Cyril, of course." Dolly paused. "Never could work out what made her call him Cyril. Not a name you heard much in the seventies, was it? Anyway, she bought the bungalow — must have made money somewhere, and then she married Cy's dad. And that's it."

A short silence fell.

"So what happened to the farmer?" asked Libby eventually. "You said he was never the same — mind you, I can understand why."

"Oh, he stopped seeing anyone. And then he did something dreadful." Dolly was staring into the glowing logs, and into the past.

"What?" prompted Colin after a moment.

Dolly let out a gusty sigh. "He let that poor little boy go off to Australia," she said.

"Oh, no!" Libby's hand flew to her mouth. "Not the child migration scheme?"

Dolly nodded sadly. "I don't like to think of it, even now," she said.

Colin raised an interrogative eyebrow at Libby.

"Don't you know about it?" she said. "But you must do. The Australian Prime Minister made a public apology about it a few years ago, and ours did it in February 2009. It was an absolute disgrace."

"But what did they do?" asked Colin.

"They took children from their parents and homes and sent them to Australia. They told them lies, said their parents were dead, all sorts of things. And when they got there, they were put to work in the most dreadful conditions and often abused."

"Who was doing this?" asked Colin. "It's illegal, surely?"

"Would you believe the government?" Libby half smiled at his disbelieving expression. "All true. Look it up on the web, if you can face it."

Colin looked sick. "I don't think I can."

"So that poor little boy was another of Cliona's victims?" said Libby. "And yet Josephine was lucky. She had a good life with her foster parents and then with Cy and his dad. Good job that little boy didn't know."

Colin looked up. "But what if he did?" he said.

"There," said Dolly. "That's another to add to your list. Suppose he came back?"

"Oh, gracious," said Libby. "But how would he find out anything about Josephine — or Cy, for that matter?"

"Depends when he came back," said Colin. "I'm going to look it all up later on. Is there a website about it?"

"Oh, yes. Some woman set up an association for them."

"There you are, then," said Colin. "I bet you could find out anything through that. I suppose they do help people find their families?"

Libby nodded. "And help people here find people who were sent out, too. It was on the radio a lot earlier in the year."

"I wonder how they came to take this boy?" Colin was frowning.

"Who would know more about it, Dolly?" Libby asked.

"I don't know." She shook her head. "See after Norma was gone and the farmer lost interest in everything, we looked for other work and somewhere else to live. We was lucky, because Dad came home and then Margaret and Bertie was born and we got a nice little place in Maidstone and hooked up with the Players again. I don't know anyone who stayed around there."

"The Red Cross woman would be dead, by now, wouldn't she?" mused Libby. "She would have been — what? Middle-aged? At the end of the war."

"Long gone, I should think," said Colin.

"She was a bit of cow, anyway," said Dolly. "Want any more tea?"

"No thanks," said Libby and Colin together.

"Yes, she was a case." Dolly folded her hands over her stomach. "Always preaching, she was. And heavy-handed! Gawd. Have her bandage you up, or make you swallow your medicine, you knew about it all right. Butcher Burton, we used to call her."

CHAPTER
TWENTY-TWO

Ignoring Libby's gasp of astonishment, Dolly went on.

"She came here, you know. I didn't know her, because she'd gone when Webley and I moved to New Farm. But she'd been as spiteful here as she was back in our old village. Drove some poor soul to suicide, they said."

"Yes," said Libby, "she did. Her name was Maud Burton, and she sent anonymous letters to people in the village. The one she sent to Amy Taylor made her drown herself."

"Ah," said Dolly, nodding. "Old Grimes lived in the cottages along there," she pointed, "and he got one. He was the churchwarden, see. He told us all about it. Course, we didn't know any of the people, although we met some of them later."

"So you knew Maud Burton before, then? Did you know anything about her at all?" asked Colin.

"No, nothing. She'd been doing Red Cross work all through the war, but folk said it was because she didn't want to do nothing like proper work. You know, working on the farms, or in munitions or something."

"Did she think it was beneath her?" asked Libby.

"Maybe she did." Dolly shrugged, massively. "She talked quite posh. Don't think she was local. I wasn't much more'n a kid, though. I wouldn't have known."

"So she was the one who arranged Josephine's adoption," said Libby slowly. "I wonder if earlier in the war she'd arranged Amy's, and that was how she knew?"

"That doesn't work," said Colin, shaking his head. "Amy would have known her, then, and known Maud knew. She'd know who'd written the anonymous letter."

"Not necessarily," said Libby. "Amy could have been behind the scenes."

"Did you know them?" Dolly asked Libby.

"No, but my partner, Ben, did. Hetty's son, you know."

"Course he would've done. But he was only a boy, then, wasn't he?"

"Oh, yes. He went to Sunday School and Amy Taylor ran it." Libby turned to Colin. "I can't believe what a coincidence this is. Two coincidences. Dolly living here, and now Maud Burton. What's happening that I'm not seeing?"

"Eh? What do you mean?" Colin looked puzzled.

Dolly chuckled. "You want to get your mate onto it, love," she said.

"My mate?" Colin said.

"No, hers. Libby's." Dolly pointed. "Her mate what helps the police."

"How do you know?" asked Libby.

"I read the papers, don't I? Told you I knew who you was."

"What are you talking about?" asked Colin.

"My friend Fran," said Libby. "She's a bit of a — well, a psychic. She's helped the police a couple of times."

"Couldn't she —" Colin began, but Libby cut him off.

"When I told Cy about her, he said the same thing, but she'd have to see all the people, and where things happened. The snow's put paid to that."

"Oh." Colin subsided.

"Do you remember what Josephine's foster parents' name was?" Libby turned back to Dolly, who frowned.

"Harrison?" she said. "No, not Harrison. Something like that."

"Did you call them 'aunt' and 'uncle'? People used to in those days," said Libby.

"No, I didn't call them anything."

"Don't you remember your mother saying 'We're going to see the somebodies', anything like that?"

"No. We're going to see little Josie, that was about it." Dolly shrugged again. "Sorry about that."

Libby sighed. "That's all right." She stood up. "We'd better get back before it gets dark and starts snowing again." She bent over and kissed Dolly's cheek. "Thank you so much, and it was lovely to meet you. I'll tell Flo I've seen you."

Dolly beamed. "And I'm coming to your panto," she said, struggling to get out of her chair. "Tell Flo I'll come and have a drink with her."

"Well, what about that?" said Colin, as he took the car carefully on to New Barton Lane. The sky was indeed darkening over the snow-covered fields, and in the distance bare trees stood like cut out silhouettes.

Libby shook her head. "It's all too pat," she said. "Too many coincidences."

"Do you think she's lying, then?" Colin was leaning forward, concentrating on the road. "A nice old girl like that?"

"No, I don't, and I can truly see that her living where I do is a perfectly believable coincidence. It's just that now you're here, too. Or rather, Cy is."

"There's nothing in it, you know, dear," said Colin. "I doubt if she's covering up for the murderer."

Libby looked at him quickly. "So you still think that Paddy's murderer and Cy's attacker were one and the same?"

"Well, of course. Don't you?"

"I just don't know," said Libby. "Shall we see what Cy thinks? Anyway, we'll have to inform the police now, won't we? About this Larry Barkiss."

"And ask Sheila if she remembers him," said Colin.

"And if she remembers anything about this Cliona and Norma thing. Can't believe she didn't."

Colin dropped Libby off at Allhallow's Lane.

"I suppose you couldn't come round tonight for a council of war?" he said, as she opened the door.

"Rehearsing, sorry," she said, turning back to him. "That is, if anyone comes. Bloody snow. If the lane from Steeple Farm wasn't so dodgy I'd say meet us in the pub for a drink, but even so, Cy's probably not feeling up to that, is he?"

"Not in public," sighed Colin.

"They can use the lane from the farm to the Manor." Ben appeared behind Libby's shoulder and gave her a kiss on the cheek. "Then we can have a drink in the theatre bar."

"Would Cy be up for that?" asked Libby. "Or do you think he's still a bit too fragile?"

"I'll see when I get back," said Colin, putting the car in gear. "I'll ring you."

"So what happened?" said Ben, as Libby followed him into the sitting room, where the lights on the Christmas tree joined the orange glow from the fire and created a welcoming, seasonal picture.

"You'll never guess what we found out," said Libby, peeling herself out of Ben's old anorak. "Just you wait!"

"I will," said Ben. "I'll make some tea."

"Strong stuff, please," said Libby. "I just had to drink a mug of hot water and milk. You'd think someone of Dolly's vintage would produce something a bit stronger, wouldn't you?"

"Come on, then," said Ben, passing her a mug a couple of minutes later. "Tell all."

So Libby did. Ben didn't interrupt, but his expression grew more and more stunned as she went on. Eventually, when she'd finished, he shook his head and blew out a long breath.

"Coincidence doesn't come into it," he said.

"No, I know." Libby finished off her tea. "There's something I'm not seeing. Colin wanted to know what I meant by that, but you know, don't you?"

Ben wrinkled his brow. "That there's something logical that's linking these two stories that we haven't seen?"

"Yes. Except that the logical thing is anonymous letters and Maud Burton, but there's no way anyone attacking Cy or Patrick would know a) that I was going to get involved, or b) that Joe at Cattlegreen would mention Maud Burton."

"And you don't want to ask Fran?"

"Well, I don't see what she could do," said Libby. "She couldn't get over here, not in this weather, and without some kind of physical connection it just wouldn't work."

"Would it be worth just asking her?"

"I could," said Libby doubtfully, "but I'd better ask Cy first. If he agrees to come to the theatre tonight I'll ask him then."

"I'd suggest us walking from the theatre to Steeple Farm," said Ben, "but that would mean having to walk all the way back here afterwards. No fun at that time of night and in this weather."

"No. Pity the lane from Steeple Farm is so dodgy. If it wasn't so steep it'd be OK."

"Colin got down it this afternoon?"

"Yes — just hope he got back up it," said Libby. "Perhaps I'd better phone."

But she didn't have to. Within a few minutes, Cy had called her, saying he was feeling perfectly able to walk down to the village and Harry had said they could all meet in The Pink Geranium after rehearsal.

"In that case," said Ben, "why don't we see if he can keep some post-theatre supper for us? Then we needn't cook this evening."

Appealed to, Harry said he was bound to have leftovers, as he'd already had several weather-related cancellations.

"We'll pay, of course," said Ben.

"Of course you bloody will," said Harry. "I've got Adam's wages to pay, or he'll have no money to buy his mother a Christmas present."

The rehearsal that evening was scrappy. The musical director and the front half of the cow were still at loggerheads, neither the Queen nor one half of the comedy duo had made it again, and although some of the ensemble were there, it was obvious that the gaps in their ranks had thrown them completely, and as the choreographer was yet another victim of the snow, Libby gave up after an hour and told them all to go home. Ben called Harry and Cy and said they would be earlier at The Pink Geranium than they'd imagined.

"I can't wait to hear what's been going on," said Peter, winding his long scarf round his neck as he went up the spiral staircase to lock the sound and lighting box.

"It's interesting," said Libby, struggling into the anorak. "But terribly confusing."

"When are you going to buy yourself a proper coat?" Peter looked over the rail at the top of the staircase. "You look like a bag lady."

206

"You've always told me I look as though I've been dressed by Oxfam," said Libby, "so what's the difference?"

Ben arrived from doing the rounds of the theatre and they let themselves out into the frozen night.

"Do you remember Maud Burton and Amy Taylor, Pete?" Libby asked as she walked down the Manor drive between Peter and Ben.

"I'm not as ancient as my revered cousin, or you, come to that," said Peter, linking his arm with hers. "So, no, I don't."

"And I don't remember them well, either, Lib, so we're lost causes, really." Ben linked with the other arm.

"I wish I could get to the bottom of this link with the Amy Taylor case and Cy's." Libby did a gentle glide for a few feet before regaining her footing.

"You've only just found out about the link," said Ben. "Give it time."

"What link?" said Peter, steadying Libby as she slipped again. "Oh, all right. I'll contain my soul in patience."

When they arrived at the restaurant, it was to find Cy and Colin ensconced on the sofa in the window, a bottle of red wine and five glasses in front of them. Adam hobbled up to take coats and gave his mother a kiss.

"I found some money in my account today," he whispered in her ear. "How did that get there?"

Libby grinned. "Magic."

"Internet magic," said Adam, and gave her another kiss. "Thank you."

"Harry can't join us just yet," said Colin, his wispy moustache tickling Libby's other cheek as he kissed her. "Shall we start without him?"

"I want to know what's going on first," said Peter, pouring wine. "What have I missed?"

Between them, Colin and Libby gave him a précis of the afternoon's revelations. "You'll have to fill Harry in," said Libby when they'd finished. "I can't go through it all again."

"He'll pick it up as he goes along," said Peter, "he's good at that. So, where do you go from here?"

"We need to inform the police about Larry Barkiss," said Libby. "And you ought to do that, Cy. You do remember him don't you?"

"Oh, yes, I remember him," said Cy, looking uncomfortable, "but I'm not sure about telling the police."

"Why not?" asked Ben. "He had a grudge against you *and* Patrick."

"It's a long time ago," said Cy. "I'm sure he's changed now."

"Do you know where he is?" asked Peter. Cy shook his head.

"He thinks the family moved away," said Colin, shooting a nervous look at Cy, who frowned.

"Look, Cy," said Libby, "if you want to find out who did this to you, and to Patrick, then you have to tell the police everything you know. And that includes anyone who might have threatened you in the past. If you won't do it, we will and they'll come and question you anyway."

"Why can't Dolly tell them?" asked Cy. "She's the one who remembered."

"Because she's scared," said Colin bluntly. "She doesn't want him to come after her."

"Well, suppose he comes after me again?" said Cy, turning frightened eyes on his partner.

"Well, he's unlikely to find you in Steeple Martin, is he?" said Ben.

"If he's tracked down me and Paddy's family and found out I'm not in Maidstone, he could find out where Dolly lived. Then he could find me. He'd connect it up. None of you had thought of that, had you?"

CHAPTER
TWENTY-THREE

Colin, Ben, Libby and Peter looked at each other. Then Peter shook his head.

"Why on earth would he connect you and Dolly?" he said. "The only connection between you and Paddy was that you stood up for him at school. Why on earth would you go running to his auntie in time of trouble?"

"If he even knew that Dolly lived here," said Libby. "Peter's right. And besides, even though he's a viable suspect, I just don't believe it. I still think the original attack and murder are separate from the later one."

"You know," said Colin, "there were a couple of things we didn't ask this afternoon, Libby."

"What?"

"The name of the farmer." He looked at Cy and patted his hand. "The one who turns out to be Cy's granddad."

Cy made a face. "Fancy my grandmother turning out to be a murderer," he said.

"I think you've taken it very well," said Libby.

"I didn't when Col first told me," he said with wry smile. "I was all over the place. Do you think we should tell the police about that, too?

"I suppose you should," said Libby, "and Colin's right. We should find out the name of the farmer. I can't think why we didn't ask this afternoon."

"I'll call Sheila in the morning," said Colin. "See if she remembers anything more about Josephine's mother."

"I don't think she does," said Libby, "but she'll remember the farmer's name, won't she?"

"Do you think it's something to do with my grandmother?" said Cy, twirling his wineglass nervously in his fingers. "Do you think she perhaps left another child, somewhere?"

They all looked at one another again.

"I never thought of that," said Libby.

"What was it Dolly said this afternoon?" said Colin. "There's another suspect for you?"

"You see," said Harry, who had come up behind Ben, unnoticed, "this is why we have to have Loopy Libby, the Super Snout, on the trail. She has an unerring nose for sniffing out the nasty little background details."

"But I didn't," said Libby. "Colin's just thought of it."

"But you were the one who thought there might be something in the background," said Harry.

"I know," wailed Libby, "but I had nothing to do with this! It was handed to us on a plate."

"Have you come to join us, dear heart?" said Peter pushing his chair back.

"Nearly," said Harry. "I'll just go and check on the kitchen and see if all the punters have paid. What there

211

are of them," he added gloomily, looking round at the half empty restaurant. "Then I'll get Ad to bring out some food. Come with me and tell me what's been going on."

So Peter accompanied Harry back to the kitchen, Donna brought another bottle of red wine and Adam appeared with a tray of food.

"You don't think, do you," said Ben a little later, with his mouth full of *quesedillas de hongos* "that this Larry Barkiss is also one of Norma Cherry's descendants?"

There was another silence.

"Heavens," said Colin.

"It's possible," said Peter. "Far-fetched, but possible."

"It's what Cy said, she could have had other children. We don't know. And I don't suppose anyone knows," said Libby.

"Just a thought," said Harry, pulling up another chair and sitting astride it, "but have none of you looked her up yet?"

"Oh God, no!" Libby laughed. "How stupid. Did you?" she said to Colin and Cy.

"Only got the posh phone," said Colin, "no laptop."

"There's no broadband up at Steeple Farm," said Ben, "but if that's a smart phone, you can get internet on it, can't you?"

"Yes, but it's not good for looking things up, really," said Cy. "Too small."

"We'll have a look," said Libby and Harry together. "Great minds," said Harry.

"Have I already looked up Cliona Masters?" Libby asked Ben. "I don't think I have, have I?"

"Not as far as I know. You looked up Amy Taylor and Maud Burton, though."

"And how weird is that?" said Harry. "Fancy old Maudie being mixed up in Cy's case, too."

"Now I want to know if Maud had a hand in Amy's baby's adoption, too," said Libby. "Don't you, Ben?"

"Not sure," he said, wiping his mouth with a napkin. "It looks as though what Maud did with Josephine was illegal, although to be fair, it was motivated by the best possible intentions. It got the baby out of a situation where it would almost certainly have gone to an orphanage, and gave a couple who were obviously desperate for children the chance to have one."

"True," nodded Harry, "but I bet the old bitch did it for money. No one's ever had a good word to say about her here."

"I can't see what that would have to do with anything," said Peter. "You've got Burton and Taylor mixed up in this by accident. If you hadn't spoken to Joe at Cattlegreen about anonymous letters you would have never known about them, and the case has nothing whatsoever to do with Cy."

Silenced, Libby concentrated hard on her plate, feeling the heat creep up her neck. Ben patted her leg under the table.

"Cruel, love," said Harry. "Cruel, but fair. Don't mind him, petal. Have another drink."

Libby squeezed Ben's hand and smiled gratefully at Harry.

"Putting two and two together and making five again, aren't I?" she said. "Sorry Cy. That's me all over."

Cy smiled back at her, somewhat nervously. "But you didn't stir up all these new things," he said. "That was Dolly."

"Well, you phone Sheila in the morning and find out what she knows, although I think she told me everything the other day," said Libby. "Meanwhile, Harry and I will Google Norma Cherry and see if there's anything about her on the web."

"And I just hope he remembers to phone the police about Larry Barkiss," said Libby a little later as she and Ben walked home. "I don't want to be unkind, but he does seem to be a bit indecisive, doesn't he? I mean, look at what happened after the first attack. He didn't call the police and let Sheila and Colin look after him."

"It's snowing again," said Ben, turning his face to the sky. "Whatever happens, I can't see him and Colin going back to Maidstone, so you can prod him about it all as much as you like."

"Right at this moment," said Libby, with a sigh, "all I want to think about is Christmas and the panto. Do you realise it's Monday night and Christmas Day is Friday? And I've got all the food shopping to do."

"We'd better go in the 4x4 then," said Ben, "or we'll never get through the snow."

Over the next two days expeditions were made to the supermarket, to Nethergate to see Fran and Guy and into Canterbury to pick up Libby's daughter Belinda from the station. On Christmas Eve, Libby picked up vegetables from the Cattlegreen shop and Hetty's turkey from Bob the butcher. Her son Dominic arrived in the afternoon by car, and was pleased to find out he was staying with his brother Adam above The Pink Geranium instead of on the floor at number 17.

There was no rehearsal that night, but it was party night at the pub, with a local band playing. Libby and Ben strolled down with Belinda and found themselves a corner where they were joined by a few cast members from *Hey, Diddle, Diddle* and briefly, Flo and Lenny. Belinda joined Adam and Dominic nearer to the band, where she was introduced to Lewis Osbourne-Walker and his mother, Edie. Libby waved, and Lewis brought her over.

"She'd be happier with you than with that lot," said Lewis, after kissing Libby and shaking Ben's hand. "You coming to my do, by the way?"

"Is this the one Adam told us about?" asked Libby, making room for Edie on the settle.

"New Year, yeah. Fireworks and everything. Go on, you know you'd love it."

"Go on, dear," said Edie. "I need someone my age to back me up!"

"Have you asked Fran and Guy?" said Libby.

"Course. Haven't heard from them. They'll come if you do, won't they?"

"Of course we'll come," said Ben. "We'll toss up for who's driving!"

"No, you won't," said Lewis, "we've got loads of guest rooms done up now. Stay!"

Libby and Ben looked at each other.

"Oh, all right then," said Libby. "Thanks, Lewis. It'll be lovely."

Lewis beamed and set off back to the crowd of young people near the band. Suddenly, Ben nudged Libby.

"Look," he said. "Cy and Colin."

"Oh, blimey!" said Libby. "I should have remembered to invite them down here tonight. I forgot all about it."

"It's all right, I did it," said Ben, waving to the two hesitant figures by the door.

"Oh, you are good," said Libby, squeezing his arm.

Cy was looking much better although still a little drawn.

"Edie, this is Cy — he just had a bit of an accident so he's recuperating in Steeple Martin — and this is Colin. This is our friend Edie, guys." Libby waved an introductory hand.

"Here, love," said Edie. "You look a bit done-up. I'll shove up a bit."

Cy squeezed on to the end of the settle as Edie shoved up.

"Thanks," he said, "actually this is only the second time I've been out since we came down here."

"Can't be too careful in this bleedin' weather," said Edie. "What happened to you, then?"

"I'll help Ben with the drinks," said Libby, feeling she really didn't want to listen to Cy's story again. When they struggled back with drinks in each hand, Edie was telling the two men about the adventures at Creekmarsh Libby had been involved in.

"Wonder she doesn't get herself bumped over the head," said Edie, giving Libby a nudge.

216

"I've often wondered that," said Ben, handing out pints.

"How've you been?" said Libby hastily, before this theme could be developed. "Are you OK up at the farmhouse?"

"Fine thanks," said Colin. "Ben's popped in every day, and the roads are clearer now, so I've been able to get out to do the shopping. The police even let me go back to collect the Christmas presents we'd left at the bungalow."

"Really?" Libby said. "So they're still in charge?"

"Well, in a way. They've finished their forensic examination, and they said we can go back after Christmas, but we've got to be careful."

"Oh?" Ben looked at Cy. "They still think you're in danger, then?"

"They'd prefer it if I stayed away," said Cy. "I didn't tell you, did I, Libby, I called them to tell them about everything Dolly told you. And I called Sheila. She only vaguely remembered Norma Cherry, just as a name. Didn't remember Cliona Masters at all."

"No, she said that to me, too," said Libby.

"She did remember Josephine's parents' name though."

"You knew that, though, didn't you? Wasn't that Josephine's maiden name?" asked Libby.

"I never knew it," said Cy, looking rather shamefaced. "I know that sounds peculiar, but she never talked about her childhood, so I never asked."

"So wasn't it her name on your birth certificate?" said Libby.

"My dad adopted me legally. I've never seen my original birth certificate."

"So what was it, anyway?" asked Ben.

"Robinson. Fairly ordinary."

"Does that help at all?"

"Not really." Cy shrugged. "Did you find anything on the net?"

"About Norma Cherry? A bit. There were a few minor references to her, but so far not much in depth. If you went to the archives of whatever local paper was going in the war you could probably find more."

"Did it say anything at all?" asked Colin.

"Just that she was convicted of the murder of two men in London in 1944. And it was Harry who found that one."

"Well," said Colin, patting Cy's hand, "when we go back home we can do a bit of research ourselves — if you really want to."

"I suppose I do," said Cy. "It's all a bit odd, not knowing anything about my mother's background for all this time, and suddenly finding out she was the daughter of a murderer. It's got a horrible sort of fascination."

"I can imagine," said Libby. "I wish I could help, but I've got to concentrate on the panto for the next couple of weeks, so I won't have time to do anything."

Cy and Colin stayed for one more drink, Lewis came to collect Edie and Ben and Libby left when the band took a break.

Walking home, Libby looked towards the slope of the snow-covered fields behind the church. "Very nearly a white Christmas," she said. "Hope it doesn't snow any more, though."

"As long as it does it when everyone's got where they want to be," said Ben.

"Well, we have." Libby tucked her arm through his. "The children are here, Cy's safe, and all the presents are wrapped." She kissed his cheek. "Happy Christmas!"

CHAPTER
TWENTY-FOUR

Christmas Day at the Manor passed, as usual, joyfully but uneventfully. On Boxing Day Libby and Ben hosted an open day at number 17, to which Libby had remembered to invite Cy and Colin. Fran and Guy turned up with Guy's daughter Sophie, whereupon Adam turned a pretty shade of pink and grew at least half an inch.

"They've met before, though," whispered Libby to Fran, as they watched the two young people in the conservatory, where Libby had laid a buffet.

"Yes, at our wedding," said Fran. "Did they get it together then?"

"Not that I remember," said Libby. "Not likely to be much future in it, though, with Sophie still at uni."

But, it turned out later, Adam and Sophie had indeed decided they liked each other at Fran and Guy's wedding, and unbeknown to their mothers, had been keeping in touch, in the way of their kind, by text and on social networking sites. Both had been aware of their upcoming meeting here today.

"I would have seen her before, Ma," said Adam, watching Sophie's blonde head bent over a plate of chilli. "But I couldn't drive because of this leg."

"Why didn't you tell me? I would have taken you down there," said Libby.

"No, you wouldn't. You've been too busy, and anyway, it's been too difficult over the last week, with the snow."

"You could have come on Wednesday when we went to see Fran and Guy."

"Harry was too busy. Look, Ma, it doesn't matter. And don't make too much of it," he warned, limping off to replenish his beer glass.

"And that told me," she said to Fran a little later, as they loaded the dishwasher in the kitchen. "So you'd better not ask Sophie, either."

"I wouldn't," said Fran. "She's a lovely girl, but she doesn't feel in the least like a daughter to me, so any questioning would be down to Guy."

"Well, don't let him," said Libby. "You know what kids are like."

The day after Boxing Day rehearsals resumed in the evening, and Ben spent most of the day at the theatre with a few other volunteers who needed to get out of their family-stuffed homes painting the sets.

In the afternoon, Belinda and Dominic had gone to the pub where Adam was to meet them when he'd finished at the caff. There was speculation that Sophie was borrowing her father's car and coming to join them. Libby waved them off and sank back onto the sofa to watch one of her Christmas DVDs when the phone rang.

"Ian! Good heavens," said Libby. "Happy Christmas. Or what's left of it. To what do I owe this honour?"

"I'm in the village," said Detective Inspector Ian Connell. "Are you receiving?"

"Yes, of course," said Libby. "I'll see you in a minute." With a sigh she switched off the telephone and the television and went to put the kettle on.

"So why are you here?" asked Libby, after she'd settled him in the armchair and provided him with coffee. "Not work, I hope."

"Afraid so." Ian sipped his coffee warily. "Hot."

"It's supposed to be," said Libby.

Ian put the mug down and looked at her. "Your friends at Steeple Farm," he said.

"What? You've been to see them?"

"I have. How well do you know them?"

"Hardly at all," said Libby, puzzled. "Why?"

"And yet you've let them borrow Steeple Farm?"

"It was nothing to do with me," said Libby. "It was Ben's idea, and as they're friends of Harry's and Peter's, Peter didn't mind either. Anyway, it was the Maidstone Police saying they couldn't go back to their home, not their own choice."

Ian nodded. "Right."

"So why did you go and see them? Did you think they were intruders?"

"It was a courtesy thing. Maidstone told us they were on our patch."

"That makes them sound as though they're criminals. Don't you know what happened?"

"Yes, of course I know what happened. Now I want you to tell me what *you* think happened."

"Eh?" Libby stared at him. Ian gazed back from under his dark brows.

"Well," he said, "you aren't going to tell me that you haven't been looking into things? You can't actually, because your guests told me you had. Come on, Libby, you must have a theory. Either you, or Fran."

"Fran's got nothing to do with it," said Libby. "When Harry asked me to go and talk to Cy it was simply about the letters and very delicate. Afterwards, I didn't think Cy would relish someone else horning in."

"Are you sure?" Ian raised one eyebrow. "They seemed to be quite pleased with your — what shall I call it —"

"Interference?" suggested Libby.

"Let's say help," said Ian. "So, come on, tell me."

"Why?" said Libby. "Just so you can have the pleasure of shooting me down or telling me to leave it alone and go away and play?"

Ian sighed. "Because sometimes you see things from a different angle. It might be helpful."

"Bugger me, I bet that hurt," said Libby.

"Libby!" Ian looked pained.

"All right, I'll tell you. But first, you've got to tell me what you know, either from the Maidstone police or from Cy and Colin."

"Right." Ian leant forward, elbows resting on knees. "First, Mr Strange was attacked one night on his way home by two youths, seen by a neighbour. Someone else, a —" Ian fished in his pocket, presumably for his notebook.

223

"Patrick Stephens," supplied Libby. Ian gave her a look.

"Yes. Patrick Stephens. His body was found close to where Mr Strange says he was attacked."

"*Says* he was attacked?"

"We only have his word for it. He didn't report it at the time," said Ian, "neither did his neighbour or his — er — partner."

"But you questioned them," said Libby. "They would have told you what happened."

"*I* didn't, Libby. Remember I'm only here at the request of the Maidstone police."

"Who obviously think Cy's making the whole thing up," said Libby. "How dare they? I can tell you, I saw him the day after the attack and before we knew anything about Paddy's death, and he was in a shocking state."

"All right, all right," said Ian. "I'm not saying that they don't believe him, just that there's a doubt there. I also know that both Mr Strange and Mr Stephens had received anonymous letters, only one of which Mr Strange had kept."

Libby nodded. "The one he received after the attack."

"One was found at Mr Stephens's home and seemed to refer to his sexuality and it seemed that Mr Strange also thought that the attack and the letters were homophobic."

"Yes. It was the obvious conclusion. And that's why he didn't report it at first, because he has this —

224

unreasonable, I'm sure — idea that the entire police force is homophobic."

Ian regarded her in silence for a moment, his head on one side. Then he leant back in the chair and looked at the ceiling.

"What's up?" asked Libby uneasily.

"Just wondering if that is actually what he said, or your interpretation of it." Ian bent his gaze once more upon Libby's indignant face.

"Of course it's what he said! And Harry will confirm it." She sat back in the sofa and picked up her cigarettes. "And now I'm going to have a cigarette, and I don't care what you think."

Ian's face creased in disapproval, but he said nothing.

"So that's all you know, is it?" said Libby, after a moment. "Or is there more that Maidstone aren't telling you? Or do you know more but you aren't telling me?"

"According to your friends, you think that the attack and the letters could be down to something in Mr Strange's background, and that the first attack was by a different perpetrator altogether?"

"Could be," said Libby warily. "It was just that the first attack on Cy was witnessed by Sheila-over-the-road and it was a couple of youths. It was vicious, too, and if it was the same two who then killed Patrick Stephens, I can't see that they would then come and hit Cy on the head in his back garden and trash his house."

"Much the same thinking as the Maidstone police, in fact," said Ian with a slight smile at Libby's astonished gasp. "They retrieved DNA from Mr Stephens's body, and, as I expect you know, it can now be processed far quicker than it used to be. And his murder points to a couple of youths who are not unknown to us, to put it mildly."

"And have they arrested them?" Libby sat forward again.

"They've been taken in for questioning this morning," said Ian. "Nasty shock for their parents."

"Really? They're that young?"

"Oh, yes. Apparently," he added in disgust, "it's a playground game, taunting gays."

"What Harry told me," said Libby. "Since it's become acceptable, and especially since civil partnerships, they're more visible in the community and therefore more likely to come under attack, particularly from people who are angry that it *has* become acceptable."

Ian nodded. "We're seeing a lot more of it. But now let's come to the letters and the second attack. What's your theory?"

Libby paused and threw her cigarette into the fire. "I don't know that it's a theory, exactly, but when I first met Cy and Colin and discovered that the letters had been sent only to Cy, I just wondered if it had more to do with him personally than his sexuality. I knew nothing about his background at that point, and I actually asked in the village who would be the sort of person who would disapprove of homosexuality. That was how I found out about Burton and Taylor."

"Who?"

Libby explained. "Actually, of course, it didn't take me anywhere, although I got really interested in the case. So did Ben, because of Amy Taylor's baby, and, of course, then finding out about Josephine."

"You'll have to explain that to me," said Ian. "I think I got lost somewhere along the road."

"I mean," said Libby sighing gustily, "Ben's mum got pregnant while she was down here hop picking (although that had a happy ending), so did Amy, and Josephine, as we think now was a product of a hop-picking liaison. It all sort of linked up. Except that it didn't of course. Apart from Maud Burton."

"Oh?" Ian's dark eyebrows, which Libby had always said reminded her of the Demon King in pantomime, shot up again.

"It turns out, we think, although this is a bit tenuous, that Maud Burton was the Red Cross woman who gave Josephine to the Robinsons."

"The —?"

"Robinsons. Didn't Cy tell the police about the Robinsons?"

"He might have done. I haven't had a full update. I know he rang them to say his grandmother had been Norma Cherry and he'd only just found out."

"Oh, you know about Norma Cherry, do you?"

"She was quite a famous murderer, Libby."

"Was she? There's not much about her on the internet."

Ian cast his eyes up to heaven. "Bloody internet," he said. "Norma Cherry was a serial murderess. Very much like Mary Ann Cotton a century or so before."

"Who?" said Libby.

"No time to tell you now," said Ian, "so look her up. Anyway, Norma Cherry, or Cliona Masters was also known as Norma Fleetwood. That ring any bells?"

Libby frowned. "Vaguely. I've heard it, but not sure where."

"It was quite a *cause célèbre* at the end of the war. She had moved around London for several years murdering men and leaving them buried in the rubble of bombed houses. She'd take their savings — she never chose anyone who had no money — and would claim she'd been bombed out and lost her ID card."

Libby nodded. "Yes, Flo was telling me about that," she said. "Apparently, criminals could get away with anything."

"It wasn't the easiest time to be policing," said Ian. "The authorities couldn't look into every case, and a lot of things were taken on trust. Eventually, she did it once too often, and the sister of the last man she killed in London had met her, and put the police on to her. It took months to trace her back, uncovering more murders on the way, including a couple of children. At last they had an anonymous tip-off that she was in Kent, living with a farmer."

"And was pregnant with Josephine, Cy's mother. Who was the tip-off from?"

"No idea. It isn't in the official reports."

"What was the farmer's name? Sheila-over-the-road didn't tell me."

"That's the neighbour, Mrs Blake?"

"I don't know her surname. Probably, yes. She remembered Josephine being born and taken by someone else. She thought she'd been adopted, but it turned out she'd only been fostered by the Robinsons."

"Right. Yes, I'm sure the farmer's name's on file. So come on, then. What do you think happened?"

"Well," said Libby, curling her legs up underneath her, "Cy was supposed to tell the police about a person called Larry Barkiss who victimised him and Patrick Stephens when they were at school. Did he?"

"They're looking into it," said Ian. "He's not known to us."

"Right, well, the other theory was that someone affected by Josephine, or her birth mother, really, was trying to damage Cy out of spite."

"Bit extreme, surely?"

"Cy thought maybe Norma whoever-she-is might have left other children who were jealous of Josephine. Suppose there was another child who wasn't fostered? Who had a very unhappy childhood?"

Ian frowned. "But to take it out on someone two generations away?"

"Well, how about this." Libby leant forward again. "Did you know about the farmer's son?"

"No." Ian's frown grew deeper.

"He had a son, John, and after Norma was arrested he took no notice of him at all, and let them take him for the Child Migration Programme."

"No, we didn't know that." Ian sat forward too. "How did you find that out"?

"Aunt Dolly. Patrick's Aunt Dolly. She lives here. Cy must have told you."

"Yes, he did, but not that bit."

"Maybe he told Maidstone and they didn't tell you."

"It's possible," said Ian. "I was only asked to check up on them and given an outline of the case."

"And was I right? Are they suspicious of him? Or of Colin?"

"I think because he didn't report the first attack. Although as that seems to have no bearing on the further attack and the letters, I can't see that it matters."

"But that final letter referred to Patrick's murder. Sort of 'Look what will happen to you' wasn't it?"

"Someone taking advantage of the murder and the attack. It certainly wasn't the two oiks who've been arrested."

"Anyway," said Libby, sitting back again, "that was the theory. Aunt Dolly thought it was Larry Barkiss and Cy and I thought it might be either another child Norma left behind or that poor John who was sent to Australia. At least, I suppose it was Australia. They sent them to other places, too, didn't they?"

"But in either case, it seems odd that Cy — Mr Strange — should be a target all these years later," said Ian, also sitting back and crossing one elegant leg over the other.

"What if," said Libby slowly, staring into the fire, "what if poor John has come home? And found out all about it?"

230

"He'd be too old, Libby. If he was a boy at the end of the war — do you know how old he was?"

"No."

"Well, even if he was only — say — five, he'd be well over seventy now. That's a bit late to start taking revenge, isn't it?"

"Someone doing it on is behalf? Like Larry Barkiss? He could be his son — or grandson, perhaps."

"And how old is Larry Barkiss?"

"About the same age as Cy. Mid thirties."

"Son, then. But Larry Barkiss is supposed have bullied both Cy and Patrick because of their homosexuality fifteen or sixteen years ago. How does that tie up?"

"Oh, I don't know." Libby scowled at him. "Getting me to do all your work for you."

"Don't you usually?" said Ian, amused. "Anyway, who do you suggest we talk to? Should we go and see Aunt Dolly?"

"And Sheila, I should think. Now Aunt Dolly's given us information she might have more to contribute."

"Mr Strange had already told her about Aunt Dolly. I don't think she had anything to add."

"I bet she has," said Libby, darkly.

"So you suspect her, do you?" Ian looked even more amused.

"She knows Cy and Colin's habits, she could easily have got round the back of the bungalow, and she knew Cy had gone away so the bungalow would be empty. And she lived in the village where Josephine was born.

I bet she knows more than she was saying. And that photograph."

"What photograph?"

"The one she said was her father and her brother. That could be the farmer and the boy John."

"Now you really are getting a bit far-fetched," said Ian, laughing. He stood up. "Well, I shall go back and make my report and unofficially suggest we interview Mrs Webley — that's Aunt Dolly, isn't it? And possibly Mrs Blake." He shook his head. "Too many old people in this case," he said. "Glad it's not mine."

"And I wish it was," said Libby as she saw him to the door.

"Do you?" He turned to look at her and she blushed.

"Well, you know. Someone we know . . ." she muttered.

"Ah. Someone you can pump, you mean." He put a finger under her chin and tilted up her face. "It's nothing to do with you, Mrs Sarjeant — again — so don't you go barging in."

"I haven't!" said Libby, indignant again. "I was asked to see if I could help Cy, and even you came here this afternoon to ask for my help. That's not barging in."

Ian dropped his finger and kissed her cheek. "Ah, but I know you, you see," he said and turned towards his car.

"Hmm," said Libby, thinking, not for the first time, that she could see quite clearly how Fran had very nearly fallen for Ian and dumped Guy.

"Oh," said Ian suddenly, his hand on the car door. "What did you say about Maud Burton?"

"Huh? Oh, she was the Red Cross woman —"

"Yes, I know. Anything else?"

"I don't think I did."

"But you know about the Burton and Taylor case?"

"Well, yes, I said —"

"I'll give you a ring. There's something you might like to know." Ian got smoothly into the car, slammed the door and was away down the dark lane.

"Well!" said Libby to Sidney, who had appeared on his favourite stair. "If that don't beat all!"

CHAPTER
TWENTY-FIVE

A gaggle of ensemble members gathered on stage in their new villager costumes, Freddy, the back half of the cow, wandered round in his oversized trousers looking, as usual, for his front half, and Libby, zipped into the unfamiliar fairy costume, glowered at anyone who walked past her and looked as though they might laugh.

"Doc Martens and stripey tights with that, dear?" asked Peter, stopping to survey her with a critical eye.

"Might as well," said Libby. "It looks hilarious enough now, when it isn't supposed to, so I think we'll just have to funny it up as much as possible."

"You've turned her into a funny character," said Peter, "so why not? Got any Doc Martens?"

"Some in wardrobe, I think," said a passing dancer. "They're a bit out now."

"Did that make sense?" said Peter, watching her drift onto the stage.

"A bit 'out'. Not fashionable any more." Libby sighed and wriggled. "Bit like me."

The musical director, now with his full complement of musicians, played a crashing chord which made them all jump.

"*Are* we ready, yet? *Please?*" he said. "We need to get on."

"All right," grumbled Libby, "give us a chance." She sidled on to the stage and was met with a scream of laughter.

"Yes, yes," she said, "just you wait till I put on the funny bit. Now —" She clapped her hands. "Beginners Act one, please." She looked sideways at the stage manager. "Can we have the tabs in, please?"

Obediently, the heavy red curtains swished across the stage, the lights went down and the overture started.

All things considered, Libby thought, it wasn't too bad after the break of five days. Now they had to spend this week putting the final touches and trying to make everyone remember their words.

Somebody leant forward from the seat behind.

"Can I bring Cy and Colin to a rehearsal one night?" whispered Harry. "They'll be gone by the time it opens."

"Won't that be rubbing it in with theirs cancelled?" Libby whispered back.

"No, I think Cy's glad to be shot of it, frankly."

"I haven't told you about Ian coming to see me this afternoon," said Libby, heaving herself out of the red plush chair. "I'll talk to you later. Why aren't you in the caff?"

"It's Monday and now Christmas is over we're back to not opening Mondays. Why did he come?"

"Tell you later. He'd been to see Cy and Colin." She clapped her hands. "OK, people, can we go back on

235

that bit, please. From 'The Prince's balls' Bob. Thank you."

The rehearsal wound its weary way to a finish, the cast put on their own clothes, Peter, Ben and Libby locked up and walked down the drive to the pub, where Harry met them.

"Come on, then," he said, "what did Ian have to say and why did he go and see Cy?"

Libby explained.

"I can't believe he asked for your theory!" said Peter.

"That's what I said." Ben was leafing through his script, having already heard the story over dinner. "Shouldn't be encouraging her."

"I'm not doing anything," said Libby, hurt. "Am I, Harry? The only involvement I've got now is that Colin and I went to see Aunt Dolly. Oh, but I did find out a bit more about Norma Cherry. She was Norma something else as well as Cliona Masters and quite a famous murderer. And Ian didn't think the police knew about the farmer's son going to Australia, so it was worth him coming to see me, wasn't't?"

"Had Cy told them about Larry Barkiss?" asked Peter.

"Yes. They're looking into it, but don't think it means anything."

"A genuine red herring," grinned Harry, "like your two spinsters."

"Ah, now!" said Libby. "Ian knows something about that. I mentioned them and he said there's something I might like to know so he's going to ring me."

"You didn't tell me that," said Ben, looking up. "Getting a bit friendly, isn't he?"

"I told him you'd got interested in the case," said Libby.

"Hmm," said Ben.

"You're not jealous, are you?" Harry hooted with laughter. "Of the old trout?"

Ben grinned ruefully. "All right, yes. I'm sure Ian's not flirting with her."

"Oh, thanks," said Libby. "Not worth it, eh?"

"No, just that Ian's an honourable man," said Ben.

"Right," said Libby, suppressing a renegade wish that Ian wasn't such an honourable man.

"So, did I miss something? Why exactly did Ian go to see Cy?" asked Peter.

"He said it was a courtesy call on behalf of the Maidstone police, which seems a bit odd, and apparently they're a bit suspicious because he didn't report the first attack or the letters until after Patrick was found."

"So they think Cy's got something to do with it?" Harry frowned. "That he hit himself over the head?"

"I don't know," said Libby. "I did ask, but he wasn't very forthcoming. Was curious as to why we'd let them stay at Steeple Farm."

"Cheek! It was virtually the police's own suggestion!" said Harry.

"I know, I know. And he still didn't tell me why it wasn't considered safe for Cy to stay at home."

"Well, that was explained by the fact that his home was ransacked after he'd moved down here."

237

"Yes, but they didn't *know* it would be," said Libby.

"They must have suspected it," said Ben.

"But why? All they said at the time was they wanted to do a thorough forensic examination."

"Perhaps," said Peter slowly, staring into space, "perhaps they thought Cy himself might try to get rid of something in the house. Perhaps they thought Cy *knew* what the attacker wanted."

The other three stared at him.

"Is that what you think?" said Harry eventually, in rather a strained voice.

"I don't, but that's what the police might have thought," said Peter.

"It makes sense, Harry," said Ben. "Of course we know it isn't true, but taken together with the fact that the letters and the first attack weren't reported until after the murder, you can see why the police might think there was something behind it — something that Cy was concealing."

Harry nodded morosely. "But he asked me for help. And when I suggested Libby, he was only too happy. He wouldn't have done that if there was anything he was trying to hide, would he?"

"No, of course not," said Libby. "As Ben says, we know it's not true, but you can see how the police, who are adept at jumping to the wrong conclusion, might. And Colin was quite keen on calling Fran in, too, so he hasn't anything to hide."

"That's a bit harsh on the police, Lib," said Peter. "You're always saying they get there first."

238

"Mostly. We do give them a bit of help, now and then, you must admit." Libby sighed and put down her glass. "Anyway, I'd better get home now and do a bit of work on the second act kitchen scene. It isn't working."

The three men groaned. "Not more words, Lib, please," said Ben, standing up to help her on with the old anorak.

"Why didn't you buy the old trout a new coat for Christmas, Ben?" said Harry. "She's been wearing that old blue cape for years, and now she's wearing a disgusting old thing of yours. Why can't you tidy her up a bit?"

Libby looked affronted. Ben gave her a squeeze.

"I like her as she is," he said. "I will buy her a new coat, the minute she says the word, but she does have a sort of bohemian style about her, you must admit."

"Am I that bad?" Libby asked, as they walked out into the cold night again. "Should I have a makeover, do you think?"

"Definitely not," said Ben, tucking her arm through his. "I fell in love with you in your floaty draperies and charity shop bargains. Why would I want to change you?"

"I'm not very glamorous," said Libby. "And I can't do anything with my hair."

"You're beautiful," said Ben. "Like a fuzzy peach."

Libby looked at him. "One that's got a bit wrinkled sitting in the fruit bowl for too long."

"Oh, stop it," said Ben, squeezing her arm. "One of the things I've always liked about you is your lack of vanity."

Libby sighed.

She was back at the theatre the following morning checking box office receipts when the phone rang.

"Oast House Theatre?" she answered. "Ian? How did you know where I was?"

"Ben told me," said Ian. "I just met him up at Steeple Farm."

"Oh," said Libby. "Yes. He goes up to check if they're all right."

"You don't sound very pleased about it."

"No, it's fine," said Libby, "Just I don't think he needs to. They're big boys. They can look after themselves, especially as Colin can get his car out now and go shopping."

"He's probably protecting his investment, Libby. Had you thought of that?"

Oh, bugger, thought Libby. How many times over the past few years had Ian pulled her up about some uncharitable thought?

"Yes, of course. I hadn't. Anyway, did you want me for something?"

"Remember I told you there was something you might want to know about the Burton and Taylor case?"

"Yes? I was telling the others last night."

"The others?"

"Ben, Peter and Harry."

"Of course," said Ian, in a resigned voice. "Well, I told Ben, too, so can I meet you at the pub in about half an hour?"

Libby looked at the clock. "About eleven? Is Ben coming?"

"Yes and yes. Eleven, then?"

"OK," said Libby and replaced the receiver, picking it up again immediately to dial Ben's number.

"What did he say to you?" she asked.

"Nothing except that you'd told him I was interested in the Burton and Taylor case and he knew a bit about it."

"Ian seems to know something about everything," said Libby. "What was he doing back at Steeple Farm?"

"I don't know, I left him there," said Ben. "So, you're coming to the pub at eleven?"

"Yes," said Libby. "I've just been checking the online bookings. It seems to have been worth that exorbitant amount of money for the system."

"I said it would be." Ben sounded smug. "See you at eleven."

The pub was empty when Libby arrived, just after they'd opened the doors. The fire was blazing nicely, so after ordering herself a hot chocolate, she sat down at the table beside it. Ben came in a few minutes later, ordered beer, and came to sit next to her.

"No Ian yet?" he said, as the long-legged ensemble member brought their drinks over.

Libby shook her head. "I wonder what he wants to tell us."

"And why," said Ben, sipping beer.

"Here he is," said Libby, as the door opened once more. "I think we're about to find out."

CHAPTER
TWENTY-SIX

"Tell me again why you were interested in the Burton and Taylor case," said Ian sipping black coffee.

Libby sighed heavily. "I told you yesterday," she said, and repeated the story.

"And you hadn't found any connection with Cy Strange or his family before then?"

Ben and Libby looked at one another. "No," said Libby, "there wasn't one. It came up completely by accident."

"But you then found a connection through Mrs Webley?"

"Who?" said Ben.

"Aunt Dolly," said Libby. "Well, yes. I said. She told us the Red Cross woman who gave Josephine away was Maud Burton."

"Hang on," said Ben. "She didn't actually say 'Maud', did she? She said 'Butcher Burton', or something like that."

"Not at first, but she knew it was the same woman. She moved here at just about the time of the scandal. So is there a connection?" asked Libby. "Apart from the one we now know about?"

"There is." Ian nodded. "I made some enquiries last night after I'd seen you because I thought I remembered something."

"How could you remember?" said Libby. "I doubt if you were even born in the fifties."

Ian cocked an eye at her. "Flattery will get you nowhere, Mrs Sarjeant," he said, and Libby blushed. "Anyway, I remembered because it's one of the open cases. They've all been reviewed recently because of the new Cold Case units. Here in Kent we're reviewing every cold case back to the sixties."

"Really? Every one?"

"Most. There are some where evidence has been kept in such a way that DNA can be recovered from it now, whereas it wouldn't have been possible in the past."

"Not at all in the fifties or early sixties, I would have thought," said Ben.

"No, but it has been possible over the last ten years," said Ian. "Except now we can get it from a much smaller sample and much quicker."

"Anyway," said Libby impatiently, "what has this to do with the Burton and Taylor case? Did Amy Taylor not commit suicide?"

"That I don't know," said Ian. "What *is* thought is that Maud Burton was murdered."

"Murdered?" said Libby and Ben.

"But how? The reports from the time simply said she moved away straight after the inquest on Amy," said Libby.

"Did it say she was thought to have a sister in the area?" asked Ian.

"Oh, yes, come to think of it."

"She was reported missing a couple of days after the inquest because a neighbour noticed her milk hadn't been taken in and couldn't get an answer at the door."

"Sad loss, the community milkman," commented Ben.

"Some people still have one," said Libby. "We've got one here, but he's so expensive, I —"

"May I go on?" said Ian.

"Oh, sorry, yes." Libby folded her hands in her lap and subsided.

"She was discovered to be missing and her house looked as though it had been ransacked. There was also a small amount of blood discovered in her sitting room. The police didn't release this information for a variety of reasons, no doubt hoping she would turn up. She did indeed have a sister, who hadn't seen her for some time, although she did provide some valuable information." Ian paused to drink more coffee.

"And what was that?" prompted Libby.

"That she had strong links with the village where Norma Fleetwood had been found."

"Well, we know she was the one who handed Josephine over," said Libby.

"We know that now. The police didn't know it then."

"So what were these links?" said Ben.

"For a start, she lived there."

"Well, that's hardly news, is it? Dolly told us she was the Red Cross woman for that hop garden, so she must have lived in the area," said Libby.

244

"No, half the family lived there. Maud Burton, her sister and their brother. Their parents lived here in Steeple Martin. Her father was in business of some kind, the brother was in the army and the sister married. According to the sister, there had been some kind of unpleasantness at the end of the war and Maud had left the village."

"Well, I expect she got into trouble about giving Josephine away," said Libby.

"There isn't any record of that, but with hindsight, yes, that's what could have happened, except that it's rather odd that she — the baby — wasn't taken back from the Robinsons if it was illegal."

"I expect it was because everything was in such chaos just after the war," said Ben.

"I doubt if we'll ever know," said Ian, "but what is interesting is that Maud came from an involvement with the Norma Fleetwood case, marginal, but an involvement, nevertheless, and then caused trouble here in Steeple Martin. And one of the things they found in her house was all her equipment for writing the letters."

"Yes, it said that in the report on the internet," said Libby.

"And a list of initials and locations. And two of the locations were her old village near Maidstone."

"Excuse me," said Ben, "but no one's ever mentioned the name of this village. Do we know it?"

"That's true," said Libby. "I don't."

"Curtishill." Ian fished out his notebook and checked. "Yes, Curtishill. Ring any bells?"

Libby and Ben shook their heads. "Should it?" asked Libby.

"I wondered if Mr Strange or Mrs Blake had mentioned it."

"No, because I doubt if Cy knew it. It's a bit odd that Sheila didn't. She mentioned 'the village' but not its name."

"We do the same," said Ben. "We talk about 'the village' because we assume everyone knows we're talking about Steeple Martin."

"Oh, yes, of-course," said Libby. "So part of the Burton family lived in Curtishill, and Maud was sending anonymous letters to people there, too, as well as here. Was it just anonymous letters, or was there blackmail involved, too?"

Ian looked surprised. "Why should you ask that?"

"Because there frequently is, isn't there? Well, in books there is. And kidnappers always get in touch anonymously."

"Confused thinking there, Lib," said Ben, with a grin.

"But actually, you're right," said Ian. "The police didn't look into it very thoroughly at the time, presumably too few clues had been left and no one, not even her sister, seemed particularly grief-stricken at her disappearance."

"You said cold cases back to the sixties, though," said Libby. "This one was fifties, surely?"

"A few have slipped through the net," said Ian, "and this is one of them. Some DNA has been picked up from the stored evidence and they're going to have a look into it, especially since you've turned up this new link."

"It isn't down to me," said Libby, perturbed. "I didn't do anything. It was Aunt Dolly who told us about Maud."

"And you reported it. Or Mr Strange did."

"Well, don't lay it at my door," said Libby. "It's nothing to do with me."

"Not curious, Libby?" Ian and Ben shared complicit grins.

"Well, of course I am," said Libby, "but not to the extent of getting involved. Anyway, you wouldn't let me."

"That's true, but I did ask for your opinion, so I'm perfectly willing to let you in on whatever comes up. As long as you don't go investigating on your own."

"Wow," said Libby. "Are you feeling quite well?"

"Probably not," said Ian. "I expect I'm having some sort of brain storm. And there might not be anything to find out, but I shall be working with the Cold Case unit on this one as I've been the one to bring in this information. One of their people will be interviewing Mrs Webley and Mrs Blake."

"Dolly won't like that," said Libby.

"We must try and see who in Curtishill Maud Burton was trying to blackmail and what about, so anyone who lived there at that time will be interviewed if they can be traced. Thanks to you, we know these two already."

"Hang on, you haven't told us how you know there was blackmail involved," said Libby.

247

"She'd written amounts beside the initials. It was like an old-fashioned accounts book."

"Like the ones you used to buy in Woolworths?" said Libby.

"I don't know," said Ian. "It's red."

"I know the sort," said Libby. "Well, try the Hop Hall Players. They were formed at the hop gardens during the war and apparently there are still a couple of founder members still alive."

Ian nodded and made a note. "Right. Anything else you remember that might help, just let me know. Has Fran had anything to do with it?"

"No. Both Colin and Cy said they wouldn't mind her coming in on it, but I didn't want to turn it into a full-scale Castle and Sarjeant adventure just before Christmas and the pantomime."

"Well, maybe you should ask her now," said Ian. "She might come up with something."

Libby looked dubious. "I haven't really got the time any more to be showing her everything and filling her in," she said.

"That's true," said Ben. "If Libby has any more to fit in I won't see her except on stage."

"OK." Ian nodded. "Another drink?"

They both declined, and Ian left.

"What about that, then?" said Ben as they left the pub.

"Bit of a turn-up for the books," said Libby. "It was all kept very quiet back in the day, wasn't it? That's surprising in a village like this. Especially then, when they relied on each other to pass along the news. I can just see all the housewives gossiping about it in the high street with their headscarves on and their baskets over their arms."

"And I wonder how she afforded a house in Lendle Lane," mused Ben. "It sounds as though she was a spinster, and the family don't sound as though they were that well off."

"That must have been the blackmail profits," said Libby. "And she wouldn't have bought the cottage, would she? They were all rented then."

"I wonder who her landlord was?" Ben was looking thoughtful. "It wasn't us, I'm pretty sure of that."

"Who else were big land or property owners back then?"

"I'm not sure," said Ben, "I'll have to ask Dad."

"Why were you wondering, though?"

"Well, it would still be difficult to afford the rent on a cottage for all that time — must have been at least ten years. She could have been putting the black on a landlord, couldn't she?"

"Joe mentioned someone," said Libby. "Sounds as though he came out of an Agatha Christie — Colonel something?"

"Colonel Feathers who lived at Old Hall. Yes, I vaguely remember him. I don't know that he owned any property in the village, though."

"That whole story's straight out of Agatha Christie, actually, isn't it?" said Libby. "Or Georgette Heyer."

"Regency romance?" Ben looked at her in surprise.

"No, she wrote some detective stories, too. A bit like her Regencies simply transported to the thirties —

although she wrote them into the fifties, I believe. All full of top-drawer caricatures and comic lower classes."

"I thought you liked Georgette Heyer," said Ben.

"I love the Regencies," said Libby, "but I'm highly critical of the detective stories. Probably wouldn't have been if I'd read them when they were written. Anyway, I still think the whole Burton and Taylor epic is just like a detective story in the fifties."

"I wonder if Ian will go and see Sheila himself?" said Ben.

"I doubt it. One of the cold case people will, I should think. He might go and see Aunt Dolly, as she's on his patch. Although he's not actually anything to do with the enquiry, is he?"

"Not on Cy's attack and Patrick's murder, no, but he said he'd be working with the Cold Case unit, didn't he?"

"Oh well, good," said Libby. "I expect he'll find out enough to keep us interested."

Later that afternoon Colin phoned.

"Sheila just called," he said. "Apparently the police have been to see her and they've been into the bungalow again."

"Were they asking about the village in the war, did she say?" asked Libby.

"That's right, they were," said Colin. "Fancy you knowing that!"

"It's an anonymous letter connection," said Libby vaguely. "She wasn't worried by it, was she?"

"No, just surprised, I think. She said she didn't know what they were talking about at first."

"I don't suppose she did," said Libby. "When I spoke to her she didn't know much about Josephine's background, except that she came from the village, although I suppose she might have known Maud Burton."

"Who?"

"We told you about Burton and Taylor," said Libby.

"I'm sure you have," said Colin, "but give us an update."

"Very bad memory you have," said Libby, and gave him a brief resume, concluding with the most recent findings.

"So you see there's a connection with Josephine," she said. "Not that it would appear to have anything to do with the attack on Cy, or the anonymous letters, but there's a cold case review going on now, so they're looking into everything and joining up the dots."

"It's very complicated," said Colin doubtfully. "What do you think they're looking for in the bungalow, now? I thought they'd finished with it."

"No idea," said Libby. "Something hidden? Something Josephine put there that Cy's never found?"

"Either that or they think Cy's hidden something there," said Colin.

"Mmm," said Libby. "I assume he hasn't?"

"Well, of course he hasn't." Colin was testy. "Look dear, do you think your nice policeman will let us go back home soon? I mean, Steeple Farm is lovely, but we would like to get back."

"I don't think it's anything to do with my nice policeman," said Libby. "He was only doing a favour for Maidstone, wasn't he? If I speak to him again I'll ask him, but I think perhaps Cy should call the Maidstone police. You must have a contact for someone there?"

"Oh, that scary woman, I suppose."

"Scary woman? Not Big Bertha?" Libby felt her heart sink.

"Who?" said Colin. "Big Bertha?"

"Sorry — Superintendent Bertram. Slim, blonde woman."

"No," said Colin and Libby let out a sigh of relief. Why, she didn't know, after all she was hardly likely to come across anyone from the Maidstone police force.

"A sergeant in the CID," said Colin. "Big woman. Do you know *all* the police in Kent?"

"No, of course not. I've just come across a few of them." Libby now felt uncomfortable.

"While solving murders?"

"Well, no. I haven't solved them. They've sort of been solved around me."

Colin tutted. "Anyway, dear, Sheila wanted me to ask you what it was all about."

"What what was all about?"

"Why they were asking her questions."

"Oh, I see. Well, I've told you now, so you can tell her," said Libby.

"I think she'd rather speak to you, dear," said Colin apologetically.

"Oh." Libby made a face at Sidney. "All right, give me her number. Oh, Harry gave it to me, didn't he? Sorry. By the way, Harry said you'd like to come to a

252

rehearsal this week before you go home. When did you want to come?"

"Oh, no, dear," said Colin. "We've booked tickets for next week! Wouldn't dream of missing it."

"Oh," said Libby, surprised. "How nice of you. But what about your work? Won't you have to go back?"

"I've taken compassionate leave." Colin sounded smug. So has Cy. We can't be expected to work in the middle of a police investigation, can we?" He giggled.

"Good — as long as you can get away with it," said Libby. "Right, now I'll go and give Sheila a ring."

CHAPTER
TWENTY-SEVEN

"Sheila? It's Libby Sarjeant. You know, Cy's friend?"

"Oh, hello." The whispery voice was back to how Libby had first heard it.

"Colin told me you'd had a visit from the police."

"Yes." Sheila cleared her throat and came back stronger. "They were asking me about where I lived during the war."

"Curtishill, is that right?"

"Yes — did I tell you that?"

"No, the police did," said Libby.

"The police? So you know what this is all about, then?"

"Yes. Colin said that was why you wanted to talk to me. But why me?"

"Because you were asking about Cyril's mother and dear Patrick's family. Then when the police came round they were, too. I wondered if you were something to do with the police. Or if you could tell me what it's about."

Libby sighed. "Well, I can tell you a little bit, but not everything. I'm nothing to do with the police, but in a way it was because of me that the police came to you."

"I see." Sheila's voice was now chilly.

"No, listen," said Libby. "I'll tell you what happened."

"Can you come over?" said Sheila. "I don't drive any more, you see."

"I'm afraid I can't," said Libby. "I've a panto rehearsal in about an hour and we open next week, so I'm busy every night, and a lot of the time during the day as well."

"Oh, yes, I remember. I hope it goes well."

"Thank you. Actually, Cy and Colin are coming to see it next week. Shall I see if I can get you a ticket, too? I'm sure they'd love to give you a lift."

"Oh, they're coming home then? I wondered, because the police were in there again today."

"Yes, I think they'll be able to go home. I don't think there's any danger to Cy now. So, do you want me to tell you about this investigation now?"

"If you've got time," said Sheila, back to being whispery.

"Remember you said the baby — Josephine — was given away? You thought adopted, but I said she'd only been fostered."

"Y-e-es."

"Well, the people who took her were also from your village, Curtishill. They were called the Robinsons. And Patrick's Aunt Dolly moved here to my village in the fifties just about the time when a local spinster turned out to be a poison pen writer who'd caused someone to kill themselves." Libby heard a gasp. "I know, horrible, isn't it? Anyway, she turned out to be the Red Cross woman who gave away the baby. And then she disappeared."

"Disappeared? She went away?" Sheila sounded puzzled.

"That's what they thought. She had a sister and brother living in Curtishill, although, actually, the police only mentioned the sister at that time. Anyway, now they think she might have been murdered."

"Murdered?" Sheila gasped again. "Oh, my goodness. Not Maud Burton?"

"Maud Burton. Did the police tell you this today?"

"Well, yes, they asked me if I remembered her, but they didn't tell me why. They wanted to know the name of Josephine's real father, too."

"And were you able to tell them?"

"I told them what I thought it was, but I'm not sure, really."

"Did they ask you anything else?" asked Libby. "About letters, for instance?"

"Well, they did. Asked if I'd ever had any anonymous letters. I thought they meant like Cyril's and Patrick's."

"And you hadn't?"

"Well — no. Not like that."

"But you had in the past?"

There was a silence.

"I see," said Libby. "You told the police no because you thought they meant letters like the recent ones, but in fact you received some — one? — some years back. Is that right? And you didn't tell the police about that?"

"No," said Sheila eventually. "I didn't connect it."

256

"But they were asking about Maud Burton. Didn't that make you think they might be talking about fifty years ago and not now?"

"No, it didn't. They didn't say anything about Maud and letters, or her being murdered. Oh, dear. Do you think I ought to tell them?"

"Yes, I do, Sheila. What was the letter about?"

"I wouldn't like to say," said Sheila, with a repressive sniff.

"The police will want to know," said Libby.

"Well, if you must know, it was about my family." Sheila cleared her throat again.

"Your family? Your father and brother?"

"How — ? Oh, yes, you saw the picture." Sheila paused. "No. About my mother."

"Oh." Libby wondered if she should go any further and decided, uncharacteristically, that she wouldn't. "Well, as I said, I think you ought to tell the police. They think Maud Burton was a wholesale poison pen writer."

"But they think she was murdered," said Sheila shakily. "I know what happens then. They think one of the people who she sent letters to murdered her."

Libby, who privately thought just that, disclaimed immediately. "I'm sure all they want to do is find out more about her," she said. "Did you know her?"

"I used to see her going about," said Sheila. "I even knew her name, but I didn't have anything to do with her. I wasn't a picker, you see."

"No, you told me. Did you know the Robinsons?"

"Not really. They weren't friends of my par — my father's. I'm not sure I knew it was them who took Josephine, anyway. I don't really remember." She sighed. "Oh, isn't this awful? Who'd have thought Cyril's accident would have brought all this out?"

Libby, feeling quite ashamed of her own part in bringing it all out, agreed. "Would you like me to tell my contact in the police what you've told me?" she offered.

"Would you? I expect they'll want to come and see me again. I hope they don't send that woman again."

"Is she a big woman? A sergeant?"

"That's the one. Do you know her?"

"No, but Colin and Cy do," said Libby. "I'll see what I can do."

"So there we are," Libby said to Ben a bit later, as she got ready to go to the theatre. "I've left a message on Ian's voicemail. I hope he can go and see her on behalf of the Cold Case unit rather than the lady sergeant, who sounds a bit scary."

"Perhaps they have to be?" suggested Ben. "Remember that Superintendent on Lewis's case?"

"Bertram. Yes I remember." Libby shuddered. "I had a horrible feeling she'd turn up on this one, but apparently not."

"So Sheila had received anonymous letters, too." Ben was thoughtful as they left number 17. "Did she know about Cy's before the mugging?"

"I don't think so. Not something they would have told her, is it?"

258

"I don't know. But she's scared now. I wonder who else Maud sent letters to?"

"Well, you're not likely to find out, are you? And if they're all as old as Sheila or older, a lot of them will be dead."

"Pity they didn't have a vicar like our Reverend Greene," said Ben. "Declaiming from the pulpit. I wonder what would have happened if he hadn't done that?"

"The police would still have found Amy's letter with her note at the bottom, so I expect it would all have come out anyway."

"Maybe," said Ben. "Oh, well, here we go. From one poor child to another." He unlocked the main theatre door.

"Eh?" said Libby.

"Josephine and Little Boy Blue," explained Ben, turning on the foyer lights and climbing the spiral staircase to the lighting box. "He sounds like a poor child, doesn't he?"

"Right," said Libby, pushing open the doors into the auditorium. The house lights came up, switched on by Ben from on high, and Libby walked down to the stage, climbing up and going to the prompt corner to switch on the worker lights, then back down to the dressing rooms to switch on the heating and light in there. By the time she'd got back to the stage, other people were starting to come in and there was the atmospheric and exciting sound of tuning up from the small orchestra.

"Josephine wasn't such a poor child," Libby said, as Ben climbed on to the stage to join her. "She had kind foster parents and no bullying step-sisters."

"And no fairy godmother," said Ben. "Hadn't you better go and squeeze yourself into that pink sausage skin?"

Buttercup only fell over once and the principal girl only went flat in her solo once, so apart from a few 'shits' when people forgot their lines, the rehearsal went well.

"OK," said Libby at the end, adjusting her costume, "today's Monday. Tuesday and Wednesday Techs acts one and two, off Thursday, Friday and Saturday, dress Sunday, first night Monday. Try not to forget anything between Wednesday and Sunday."

"Shouldn't we come in on Saturday?" said a voice from the back. "I wouldn't mind."

A ragged chorus of agreement rippled round the stage.

"I'd be very happy to," said Libby, "but I didn't like to suggest it. Who would be available? Seems a shame on your last Saturday for a fortnight, though."

As more people wanted a rehearsal on Saturday than didn't, accordingly Libby called one to a background of a few dissenting grumbles.

"If you'd prefer it in the afternoon so you have the evening free, I'm happy to do that," she said.

Eventually, the difference was split, and four o'clock set for curtain up. With relief, Libby went back to the dressing room, unzipping as she went.

"Not a bad bunch, are they?" she said to Ben, as he went round locking up.

"Very willing," said Ben. "I suppose at least we'll get most of Saturday evening together."

"Sorry. But we weren't doing anything on Saturday, were we? And we'll be off Thursday and Friday."

"But we're going to Lewis's New Year thing on Thursday and staying over, if you remember," said Ben, turning his coat collar up as they stepped outside onto the drive.

"So we are. Should we say we can't go because of the weather and the panto?"

"No. We ought to go and get away from all things panto and murder. I bet Lewis puts on a good party."

"Let's go and see if Adam's at the caff and ask him," said Libby.

The Pink Geranium was still full of diners, although the 'Closed' sign was on the door. Adam waved from behind the counter at the back, and Ben held the door for Libby.

"Bottle of red, Ma?" called Adam.

"Just wanted a word," said Libby.

"Yes please," said Ben.

"Oh, are we stopping?" said Libby, as Ben took off his coat and started to help her off with the disreputable anorak.

"Might as well," said Ben.

Harry appeared at the sofa in the window with a bottle of Libby's favourite red wine. "Did you want a word with me?" he said.

"Adam, actually," said Libby, "but you as well, if you like."

"How many glasses shall I fetch then?" said Adam, appearing behind Harry.

"Four," said Ben, "unless Donna wants to join us."

"Donna's long gone," said Harry. "She's worked like a navvy over Christmas. All we've got here now is us and one of the boys still washing up, bless him. This lot," he jerked a thumb over his shoulder, "have all paid, so we're off the hook."

"Glad that you're doing OK, after last week," said Ben.

"People re-booked," said Harry. "Otherwise we wouldn't have been. Now, what news?"

Libby recounted all the conversations she'd had over the past couple of days. "And now," she concluded, "Ben wants to know if Lewis's party on Thursday is going to be a good one."

Adam laughed. "Brilliant, of course. Harry's given me the night off."

"Look, sunshine, you only do casual for me. You take off whatever nights you want."

"I know, but I need the money." Adam lifted his glass. "Cheers."

"So, Cy's attack has sparked off a whole case, has it?" said Harry. "There's a turn-up."

"Not exactly," said Libby. "The Cold Case unit were apparently already looking at Maud Burton's disappearance, but when I inadvertently gave them the link to Josephine it all sort of linked up."

"It wasn't really you," said Harry. "It was that Paddy's Aunt Dolly. And have you heard if those wankers have been charged with the attack on Cy yet?"

"No, they haven't," said Libby.

"Why not? Can't you ask Ian?"

"I don't know how he'd take to me pestering him," said Libby.

"He did say he'd keep you in the loop," said Ben. "And I'm still interested in the whole baby aspect."

"Why don't you ask Fran about it all?" said Adam after a minute.

Libby sighed. "Everyone seems to want me to ask Fran about it."

"Well," said Harry reasonably, "she has been very helpful in the past. I bet she feels really left out of this one."

"I've hardly spoken to her about it," said Libby. "I've been so busy over here, and she's been busy with her first big family Christmas. I said to Ian that I don't think I'd have time to take her all through the whole thing, even if I could sort it out myself, which I'm not sure I can."

"You can talk to her about it at Lewis's party," said Ben. "She and Guy are going, aren't they?"

"As far as I know," said Libby.

"There you are then," said Harry. "Let her do her Mystic Meg thing on it. And ask Ian about those kids."

"And while you're at it, tell him about Sheila's phone call," said Ben.

Libby sighed again. "Any more orders?"

The following day, after a local radio interview over the phone, a conversation with the local paper and another with Jane at the *Nethergate Mercury*, Libby phoned Fran.

"Everyone wants you to have a look at this case," she said. "I tried to say you were busy, but even Ian has asked, so there you are."

"Even Ian, eh?" Fran sounded amused. "He must be desperate."

"No, he's not even officially on the case," said Libby. "He's sort of got into it by accident. There's quite a lot to it. What do you think?"

"I think I ought to come over this afternoon," said Fran, "and you ought to take time off from thinking about the panto and tell me all about it."

CHAPTER
TWENTY-EIGHT

"So, let me get this straight," said Fran, holding her hands out to the fire. "First of all Cy was attacked —"

"No, first of all he got letters. So did Patrick."

"All right. But the first you knew of it —"

"No, I knew about the letters. Harry wanted me to talk to him for some reason."

Fran blew out a sigh. "Right. Cy received letters about his sexuality —"

"Might have been, might not."

"Oh, for goodness' sake, Lib!" Fran sat back in the armchair. "Stop interrupting. Look, Cy's attacked, Patrick is killed, all on the same night and presumably by the same person. Right?"

"Right."

"And they've both received poison pen letters?"

"Right."

"Then Cy is attacked again and his house is ransacked. Meanwhile you find out —" Libby opened her mouth but Fran ploughed on "— that Cy's mother was the illegitimate daughter of a murderess and that her father then sent his son away on the Children's Migration Programme. Right so far?"

Libby nodded.

"OK, so then we come to the tale of Burton and Taylor." Fran pushed her heavy dark hair behind one ear and put her head on one side. "And how this came into the equation I simply can't understand. Is it just the well known Sarjeant curiosity?"

"It was mentioned by someone else —"

"You told me, Joe at Cattlegreen Nurseries."

"And I was interested," Libby finished lamely. "That's really all there is to it."

"And then, lo and behold, Maud Burton turns up connected to Cy's mother."

"And is now the subject of a cold case review."

"In which Ian is concerned."

"Only because — well, because of me, actually."

Fran sighed. "I don't know how you do it, Libby."

"Neither do I," said Libby. "Especially as I specifically told Harry right at the beginning I didn't want to get involved in anything, not with having to take on the fairy and all."

"But you still did."

"I could hardly help it after everything began to escalate, could I?"

"Well, you could, but you probably wouldn't. Is there any more tea?"

Libby got up and collected mugs to take into the kitchen.

"So what do you think so far, then?" she called back as she moved the heavy kettle forward from its simmering position.

"I don't honestly know," said Fran. "I've got no handle on it and I don't know the people. Is there anywhere I could go that might give me a sense of it all?"

"Only Cy's bungalow," said Libby, putting fresh teabags into the rinsed mugs. "And that's a bit out of bounds at the moment."

"When's Cy being allowed back in?"

"When they've finished the forensic tests and the searches, I assume. When they first moved him out it was at least partially for his safety, which, I suppose was confirmed when the place was ransacked."

"Was anything taken?"

"Colin says he doesn't think so. I expect the police will have Cy go through everything when he gets back."

Fran frowned as Libby came back with the full mugs. "So, the theory is that Maud Burton was the woman who organised the Robinsons' adoption —"

"Fostering."

Fran sent her a fulminating look. "Fostering, then, of Josephine. She then gets into some sort of trouble in — what was the village called?"

"Curtishill."

"In Curtishill and leaves. She ends up here and starts her little career plan of blackmailing people in her old village by sending them anonymous letters."

"That's Ian's speculation. And Sheila confirmed that when she told me she'd received one."

"Did she know who it was from?" asked Fran.

Libby's eyes opened wide. "Do you know, I never asked her! I don't think she can have done, because she said she didn't connect anything of what they were asking her together — if you see what I mean."

"Was she blackmailed?"

"Oh, I don't know that, either." Libby made a face. "Useless, aren't I?"

"Anyway, as far as you know, she didn't turn her attention to Steeple Martin until she and Amy fell for the vicar. Then she was found out and promptly disappeared. Which makes sense."

"But when they broke into her cottage a few days later, the place was a wreck and there were blood traces. Or splatters. So they looked for her, but she was never found."

"And they think it was murder."

"They've managed to get DNA from preserved material," said Libby.

"Has there been any suggestion that she was sending letters to Josephine?"

"No, but at that time Josephine would still have been a child."

"Oh, yes." Fran frowned down into her mug. "Her foster parents, then?"

"I don't know. That's why the police wanted to talk to Sheila and Aunt Dolly, to see if they could give them any information about her victims."

"It's very unlikely now," said Fran. "Most of them will be dead, surely?"

"That's what I thought," said Libby.

"So who are the police actually looking for?"

"The second attacker, the letter writer and Maud Burton's murderer."

"And are they all the same person?"

"Good heavens, no!" Libby looked at her in surprise. "How could they be?"

"Well, you've managed to link the two cases."

"Just because I have, that doesn't mean that they really are."

"What would be the motives for Maud Burton's murder?"

"To stop her blackmailing."

"Yes, and another?"

Libby shook her head.

"To stop something coming out," said Fran. "If Maud really held something over someone, it would be because that person didn't want it to be known, obviously."

"Obviously," said Libby. "But why at that particular moment? Had the victim just stopped paying, or what?"

"I think I see," said Fran slowly, gazing into the fire. "Think about it. Maud has just been exposed as an anonymous letter writer. Her belongings have been turned over. Possibly material has been confiscated. She wasn't charged with anything after Amy's inquest, was she?"

"No, although the coroner told her off, I think."

"But this would have been public knowledge?"

"Yes. Coroner's inquests were a popular form of entertainment in the fifties."

Fran laughed. "Only in a rural community," she said. "I think you're thinking of the twenties and thirties."

"Whatever," said Libby, "the Burton and Taylor case was reported locally."

"So, if there was someone in Curtishill who had done something reprehensible back in the days when Maud lived there and who was being blackmailed by her, and they read about the Amy Taylor case, they might get scared."

"Oh!" said Libby, seeing the light. "Of course. They would think there would be more investigation into Maud Burton and their peccadilloes would come out."

"Except," said Fran, "that if Maud had kept evidence, just killing her wouldn't be enough. It would have to be destroyed."

"And that's why her cottage was ransacked."

"Exactly. Does that make sense?"

"It does to me." Libby was on her feet. "Shall we tell Ian?"

"If you like. Weren't you supposed to be talking to him anyway?"

"I left a message on his voicemail, but he hasn't got back to me. Shall I try him again?"

"Why not?" said Fran.

This time, Libby got through.

"Sorry I haven't got back to you," Ian said. "Bit busy here."

"Sorry to bother you, then, but you said you wanted to know if there was anything I found out that you didn't know."

"And there is?" Ian's voice sharpened.

"Well, yes," said Libby going to close the curtains over the dark windows, and she told him about her conversation with Sheila, and then with Fran.

"Oh, and Cy and Colin want to know when they can go back home," she concluded. "Police were in there again yesterday, Sheila said."

"I gather they've tidied up a bit," said Ian. "I'll make enquiries. Meanwhile, I need to speak to Mrs Blake and Mrs Webley again."

"Will you speak to them yourself? Can you do that? If you aren't officially on the case?"

"I told you, I'm working with the Cold Case unit, now, and this information is to do with the Maud Burton investigation, so yes, I probably can. Is Fran there? Can I have a word?"

Libby held out her phone. "He wants you," she said, noticing that Fran's cheeks got a little pinker as she took it.

Fran's end of the conversation gave nothing away. Libby sat on the sofa and waited impatiently.

"He wants me to go with him to talk to those women," Fran said, handing the phone back.

"What?" Libby scowled. "That's not fair. Why can't he take me?"

"You said you didn't want to get involved," said Fran, with a grin. "You told me."

"That was before," said Libby.

"It's to see if I pick up anything. And I think it would look odd if you came too. You've already talked to both of them."

271

"I suppose so," said Libby. "But how frustrating. When are you going?"

"Tomorrow, if he can get in touch with them both. And he says to tell you he'll sort out Cy and Colin going back home."

"Right. Well, you'll let me know what happens, won't you?"

"Of course I will. And we'll see you on Thursday night, anyway."

When Libby and Ben arrived home after rehearsal that night, there were two messages on the answerphone. The first was from Colin.

"We can go home!" he said. "Wanted to thank you so much for having put us up here. Hope we'll see you in the morning before we go."

The second was from Fran. "Going to see Aunt Dolly first in the morning and then on to Sheila Blake. I'll call you when I get home."

"That's why you didn't want Fran involved," said Ben shrewdly, when she relayed these to him. "You do all the groundwork and Fran comes in for the glory."

Libby sighed. "I'm such a bad person."

"No, you're not." Ben gave her a hug. "And you're a very good director. Now come to bed."

The following day, Ben drove Libby up to Steeple Farm in the four by four. Colin and Cy were packed and ready to go.

"We've given the place a good spring clean," said Colin, "and I put the sheets in the washing machine."

272

"That was good of you," said Libby. "Are you sure you're all right to go back?"

"Your nice policeman phoned us," said Colin.

"Inspector Connell," said Cy. "I must say, he was an improvement on the ones who dealt with us before."

"He can be quite scary," said Libby, "but I'm glad he was nice to you. Did he tell you about going to see Sheila again?"

"Yes. She isn't happy. She phoned up just now. Apparently he's taking someone with him."

Libby nodded. "My friend Fran," she said. "I told you about her."

"The psychic one?" said Colin. "Oooh! How exciting! I said you should have asked her in before."

"Well, she's here now," said Libby. "They might pop over and see you after they've finished with Sheila."

"Oooh, I hope so," said Colin.

"We'll see," said Cy firmly. "Come on, we mustn't hold Libby and Ben up." He held a hand out to Ben, who shook it warmly, and gave Libby a hug. "Thanks for all you've done," he said.

Libby's mobile rang in her pocket. "Excuse me," she said and went outside.

"Lib? It's me. Look, do you think you could possibly come with us to see these women? They both asked why you weren't coming." Fran sounded faintly exasperated. "They seem to have taken to you."

Libby couldn't stop a self-satisfied grin spreading over her face. "Well," she said, "at the moment I'm at Steeple Farm —"

"Are Colin and Cy leaving, then? Oh, good, we can go and see them when we've seen Sheila. Ian says he'll pick you up on the way to Mrs Webley's."

"When, though? I told you, I'm not at home."

There was a muffled conversation. "Half an hour?" suggested Fran.

"So I'll see you later," said Libby a moment later after explaining to Ben, Cy and Colin her rearranged plans for the day.

"Good," said Cy. "Sheila will be much happier if you're there."

"I can't think why," said Libby, "but if she is, that's good. Come on, Ben."

"Got your own way, then," he said, as they drove back towards Allhallow's Lane.

"Not my own way," said Libby, "just not excluded, that's all."

"They ought to know better than to try and exclude you," said Ben, with a sideways grin.

"And now they do," said Libby.

CHAPTER
TWENTY-NINE

"So where does this Mrs Webley live?" Ian peered over his steering wheel.

"Just down here on the right," said Libby, pointing over his shoulder. "There, see? The first bungalow."

Ian grunted and pulled the car off on to the dirty-snow covered verge. Fran opened the passenger door and grimaced as she looked down.

"That," said Libby, as she climbed out of the back of the car, "is what you get for wearing unsensible shoes in a rural area."

"Is there such a word?" said Fran, treading carefully across the rutted surface. "Anyway, these are boots, not shoes."

"Not practical boots," said Libby, looking down with favour on her new present-from-Belinda floral wellingtons.

"You'll have to take those off inside," warned Fran.

"I know that," said Libby. "I did last time. I'm not stupid."

"Come on," said Ian impatiently. "We're not here for a fashion parade."

Aunt Dolly welcomed them cautiously, looking relieved to see Libby.

"I don't know that I can tell you any more than I told Libby here," she said, seating herself in the same chair beside the electric fire. Libby, Fran and Ian distributed themselves over the remaining seats.

"We just want to make sure we've got all the facts, Mrs Webley," said Ian, using his best dark chocolate voice. Fran and Libby exchanged glances.

"Well, all right then," said Aunt Dolly, smoothing her skirt over large knees. "I'll do me best."

Ian took her through everything she had told Libby previously up to the point where she and her husband had moved to Steeple Martin.

"And your family were still living in Curtishill then?" he asked, when she finally ran down.

"No, dear, Maidstone. I told Libby. We moved. That was how Cy and young Paddy came to be at the same school."

"Of course." Ian looked down at his notes. "And Larry Barkiss? Where did he live?"

Aunt Dolly looked surprised. "Maidstone somewhere, same as us, I suppose."

"And you never knew anything more about him?"

"Well, I was already living here when all that happened," she said, "Our Margaret told me. Very upset she and Roy were, and our Mum, I can tell you."

"What about your brother?" asked Ian.

"Bertie? Oh, he's dead, God bless him. No, he took no notice. He wasn't that interested in the family. Went off up north somewhere, Manchester, was it? Anyway, he didn't know much about it. Margaret told me, and I think the name come up a coupla times after, you know, people asking about other people at get-togethers and such."

"So, you never heard what happened to Larry Barkiss, or where he might be living?"

"No, dear, sorry." Aunt Dolly shook her head.

"And you had nothing to do with the farmer and his family after you moved from the cottage he rented you?"

"We didn't have much to do with him, then," said Dolly. "I told Libby. I couldn't even remember the names of young Josie's parents."

"The Robinsons," supplied Libby.

"Ah! That's it," said Aunt Dolly, pleased. "I knew it was something like Harrison."

"But you knew it was Maud Burton who arranged for them to take Josephine?"

"Not really, dear," said Aunt Dolly.

Libby, Ian and Fran stared at her.

"But you said —" said Libby.

"We knew she handed her over, but I don't know that she arranged it."

"Oh."

"She would have done, though," said Fran, breaking her silence for the first time. "She worked for the Red Cross. Someone would have asked her to help."

Everyone looked at Fran.

"Well, if she was involved in the Hoppers' Hospital she would have been the person to come and help with the birth," said Fran reasonably.

"What about a doctor?" asked Ian.

"Not in them days, dear," laughed Aunt Dolly. "Not unless there was something wrong. Specially during the war. They made shift, like everything else."

"Made shift?" mouthed Ian to Libby.

"Made do," she whispered back.

"Made do, dear, that's right," said Aunt Dolly comfortably, and Ian's neck turned pink.

"So there's nothing more you can add to what you told Mrs Sarjeant?" he said.

"Not really, dear. Only I did think about the gossip — you know, all the talk that goes on in places like that."

"No?" Ian, Fran and Libby all leant forward.

"The pickers?" asked Libby.

"And in the village. See, the year before, they reckoned this Cliona, as she called herself, had another baby."

"Another one?" Libby echoed.

"By a pole puller. Or someone. No one knew what happened to that one."

"Maud Burton again?" Ian looked at Fran, who was frowning.

"Could that be Larry Barkiss's parent?" suggested Libby. "Could he have been that resentful?"

Aunt Dolly looked doubtful. "I don't know, dear. It was only gossip."

"Would Mrs Blake know?" asked Ian.

"Who?" Aunt Dolly looked puzzled.

"Sheila," said Libby. "We're going to see her, too."

"You can ask her, but I never knew her when we lived in the village. Must have seen her, I suppose, but she never registered, if you know what I mean." She turned to Libby. "I told you that, dear."

"Yes, you did," said Libby, suddenly thoughtful.

"Any thoughts?" Ian asked Fran, as they made their way back to the car.

"A few," said Fran. "Let me think them first."

"I had one," said Libby, climbing into the back seat.

"Really?" Ian didn't look at her, merely switched on the ignition.

"That's twice Aunt Dolly has said she never knew Sheila during the war, even though they lived in the same village. Don't you think that's peculiar?"

"She also told you the villagers didn't like her family much. They didn't mix."

"Hmm." Libby settled back into the leather luxury of Ian's car.

"Don't get fixated on Sheila Blake," said Ian. "For a start, she's been nothing but a help to Cy and Colin and for another thing, she's almost eighty years old. I really can't see her attacking either of those young men, and even less killing one of them."

Although the snow was still proving a problem for transport, Ian made it to Maidstone in only forty minutes, despite slow going on Detling Hill. Libby directed him to Sheila's bungalow, eliciting an exasperated sigh.

"The satnav's quite capable, Libby."

"Oh, I didn't know you had one," said Libby, innocently. "I can't hear it."

"The sound's turned off." Ian switched off the engine, detached the satnav from its housing and waved it at her. "There. And now it goes in my brief case."

"You look more like a businessman than a cop with that," she said, climbing out of the car.

"Less alarming," said Ian. "Go on. Ring the bell."

But once again, Libby didn't have to. The door swung open and Sheila stood there, upright and prim in beige and brown.

"Sheila — how good of you to see us," said Libby, a little gushingly. "This is Inspector Connell."

"Is this about Cy's letters? Or that Maud Burton?" asked Sheila, without moving.

"Both, really, Mrs Blake," said Ian smoothly, turning on the dark chocolate again. "You're one of the few people who can remember anything about those days."

Sheila stepped aside grudgingly and they all trooped into the tiny hall.

"In there," she said, and Libby led the way.

"By those days," she said, when they were all seated, "you mean the war. I was only a child, you know."

"Yes, of course," said Ian. "But you knew about Josephine being fostered, didn't you?"

"I thought she'd been adopted." Sheila shrugged. "That's why, when I ended up living opposite her, I didn't say anything. She might not have known."

"How did you know who she was, Mrs Blake?" Fran broke in. Sheila looked at her in affronted surprise.

"Oh, sorry, Sheila. This is our — er — colleague, Mrs Castle."

280

"Wolfe," corrected Ian.

"Sorry. Mrs Wolfe." Libby was beginning to feel heated. "Yes, how did you know? Did you tell me?"

"I told you that I didn't really know the people who adopted her. But I'd seen her sometimes."

"I thought they moved away from the village?"

"Not far," said Sheila. "And I moved too, a few years later. When I was old enough."

"You moved away from home?" asked Fran.

"When I married." Sheila's mouth was more rattrap like than ever. It was clear she resented the questioning. Libby sent Ian a pleading look.

"I'm sorry, Mrs Blake," he said, all dark chocolate again. "You're the only person, apart from Mrs Webley who can tell us anything about those days. I'm sorry if we appear intrusive."

Sheila looked slightly mollified. "And who's Mrs Webley?" she said.

"Aunt Dolly," said Libby. "Margaret's sister."

Sheila nodded. "I never really knew her in the village," she said. "I knew the farmer gave them somewhere to live, that's about all. I got to know Ada after the war."

"Ada?" said Ian.

"Ada Weston. Margaret's mother."

"Oh, I see." Ian frowned. Libby guessed that he was getting a little flustered by all these families and names. "But you knew Maud Burton?"

"I knew *of* her."

"You said you knew the Red Cross people," said Libby.

"We all did. I didn't know her personally."

"And you know nothing about Cliona Masters?" said Ian.

Sheila looked bewildered. "That's Josephine's mother Libby told me about?"

"Yes."

"No. But the other policewoman asked me about someone else." Sheila looked from one to another. "Who was she?"

"Norma Cherry?" said Libby.

"Norma Fleetwood?" said Ian.

Sheila looked even more confused. "I — I — I'm not sure. Cherry?"

Ian nodded. "Don't worry about it. Now, the only other thing was the farmer's name. I believe you weren't sure of that, either."

"I said to that policewoman I thought it was Palmer, but I'm not sure. It's a long time ago." Sheila was now frowning herself.

"Can I make you a cup of tea, Sheila?" Libby asked, getting to her feet. "This has all been rather a shock, hasn't it?"

"Yes, please dear." Sheila looked up at her. "Will you find everything?"

"If you don't mind me looking," said Libby cheerfully, and went off to find the kitchen.

This, she discovered, was much the same vintage as the bathroom. She found everything she wanted, loaded a tray and took it back to the sitting room. Nothing seemed to have progressed while she was away, except that Fran was looking at the picture of Sheila's father and brother.

"Now," said Libby, after pouring tea, "you said to me there was something you didn't quite understand when the policewoman talked to you. When she asked you if you'd received any letters, you said no, because you thought she meant at the same time as Cy, but she meant years ago."

"Oh, yes." Sheila looked down at her cup. "I did receive a letter."

"When was that, Mrs Blake?" asked Ian gently.

"Must have been, oh, fifty years ago? I was just about to get married."

"And what did you do?" asked Fran.

A hint of colour came into Sheila's cheeks. "I burnt it. It was disgusting."

"And you got no more?"

"No. I'd ignored it, you see, and I'd moved. So whoever it was could just go on writing and asking for money. They weren't getting any."

"Was the writer threatening you?"

"Oh, yes. Threatened to tell my fiancé about — well, what the letter was about. Unless I paid up."

"How much were they asking for, Mrs Blake?" asked Ian.

"A pound a week for a year. That was a lot in those days."

"And may we ask what the letter was about?" Ian's voice was soft, cajoling.

Sheila lifted her chin. "My mother."

Fran's eyes flew to Libby's.

"That's fine," said Ian, replacing his cup and saucer on the tray. "I don't think there's anything else at the moment. It was very kind of you to see us."

Libby and Fran hurriedly finished their tea and Libby carried the tray back into the kitchen. She returned to find Fran holding the photograph and talking to Sheila about it. Ian used her return to detach Fran and make their farewells.

"So what were you so interested in?" asked Libby, once they were back in the car.

"Her father and brother," said Fran, "and her mother. Remember, she said the letter was about her mother."

"But she's never said anything about her mother," said Libby.

"No, and that's significant," said Ian. "In fact she's said very little about anything."

Libby frowned. "I suppose so." She looked up as Ian switched on the engine. "I thought we were going to see Cy and Colin?"

"With Mrs Blake watching us from behind her net curtain?" said Ian. "I don't think so. They'll keep."

CHAPTER
THIRTY

"Do you want to come back to mine?" asked Libby.

"I've got to drop Fran back in Nethergate," said Ian.

"That's all right," said Fran. "I'll get Guy to come and get me." She turned to Libby. "Perhaps we could go to Harry's for a meal, the four of us?"

"Rehearsing," said Libby. "Last one until Saturday. We go up on Monday."

"Oh, I forgot. Still, wouldn't Harry do an early meal for us? To save you cooking?"

"I seem to have eaten in Harry's a lot recently," said Libby. "He might be fed up with me."

"Oh, well, if you don't want to," said Fran, turning back to face front.

"Oh, no, I'd love to. Shall I call Ben and ask him to arrange it?"

Fran turned back with a smile. "Yes, and I'll call Guy."

"And meanwhile, ladies, if you don't mind, could I have your reactions to our two conversations?" Ian sounded exasperated. He often did in his dealings with them, thought Libby.

Fran looked at him for a long moment. "When I've called Guy," she said eventually.

Meanwhile, Libby had called Ben and asked him to arrange an early supper with Harry.

"Well," said Fran, switching off her phone and replacing it in her bag. "Mrs Webley knows no more than she told us, but Mrs Blake knows considerably more."

"There, see?" said Libby with satisfaction. "I knew it."

"For some reason, she's scared, and it's got something to do with her family."

"What about this other baby Norma's supposed to have had?" asked Ian. "Get anything there?"

"No," said Fran, sounding irritated. "I can't pick things up to order, Ian. You ought to know that by now."

Ian made a sound that just might have been an apology, and concentrated on driving.

"I'll have to think about it," said Fran in a more conciliatory tone. "There was no immediate atmosphere in either place. The only thing I felt at all was an uneasiness about the photograph."

Libby made a sharp sound and Fran turned to look at her. "You've got it, haven't you?" she said.

"Got what?" It was Ian's turn to sound irritated.

"Go on, Lib. What do you think?" Fran said.

"Is it —" Libby hesitated, "is it a photograph of the farmer and the little boy he sent away?"

"What?" Ian looked away from the road towards Fran. Both women shouted at him.

"I think Libby's right," said Fran, as he turned his attention back to the road.

"Which means —" Libby began.

"That Sheila Blake is Josephine's half-sister," finished Ian.

Nobody spoke. Eventually, Fran heaved a sigh.

"And Sheila has never been mentioned, by Aunt Dolly or anyone else. Did no one know there was a sister as well as a brother?"

"We haven't been able to find anyone else," said Ian. "The only reports we've got are from the internet. A lot of the police records from that time were destroyed."

"So who else would know?" asked Libby.

"How did Aunt Dolly know about the boy being sent to Australia?" asked Ian.

"And do we believe Sheila when she said that she thought the name of the farmer was Palmer?" said Fran.

"Exactly," said Libby. "If she's trying to prevent us from finding out who she is, she wouldn't give away her real surname. We would look her up immediately."

"The farmer's name will be on file somewhere," said Ian. "I can find that."

"I think Aunt Dolly knew about the boy the same way as she said she knew about the other baby — just gossip," said Libby.

"Hmm," said Ian, and they fell silent again.

When Ian pulled up outside Libby's cottage, he refused to come in for tea.

"I've got a report to make," he said, "although I doubt I shall mention much about your contribution."

"We haven't made any yet," said Fran.

"You have. Sheila's identity."

"I might be wrong."

"I think you're right," said Libby. "Come on, it's cold out here."

Ian drove off and Libby switched on the lights as she went through to the kitchen to switch the electric kettle on.

"I don't know why you keep that big old cast iron kettle," said Fran, following her. "You seem to use the electric one most of the time."

"When I'm at home I keep the Rayburn one on the simmer all day, but I can't leave it like that if I'm out," said Libby, fetching mugs from a cupboard.

The phone rang as they carried their tea through to the sitting room.

"Why didn't you come in?" asked Colin, somewhat querulously. "We saw you leaving Sheila's."

"Ian said we couldn't because Sheila was watching through the curtains," said Libby. "I was going to ring you. We've only just got home."

"And what did your friend think? Nice-looking, I thought."

"Yes, she is." Libby turned and grinned at Fran, who lifted her eyebrows. "And nothing much has come out yet. I'll let you know if anything does."

"Yes I am what?" asked Fran, as Libby switched off the phone.

"Good-looking." Libby grinned again. "Don't know why he commented today — he saw you at our open house, didn't he?"

"I don't think we coincided," said Fran. "Nice of him, anyway."

288

"I didn't tell him what we think about Sheila." Libby knelt by the fireplace and began to build a fire. "We don't know for sure, and it might harm Ian's investigation."

"I'm still not sure how Ian's come into this," said Fran, frowning. "It's not his area."

"I told you, he's been asked to help the Cold Case Review Unit about Maud's death, and he was asked by Maidstone to visit Cy while he was here, just as a sort of courtesy, I think." Libby watched as the kindling caught and sent yellow flames shooting up the chimney.

"And the link between the two cases is you. And just tell me again why we're looking into the case of Norma Cherry, or Fleetwood, or whoever she is?"

Libby heaved a sigh and sat on the sofa. "Looking into Cy's background to see if there was anything there that might have given rise to the attack or the anonymous letters. I've explained all this."

"Just recapping," said Fran. "And you needed to establish a connection between Cy and Patrick why, exactly?"

"Because they both received letters and they were both attacked on the same night. Only Patrick was killed."

Fran sat frowning for a while, sipping her tea.

"And you say you think the attackers are not the people — or person — who sent the letters or attacked Cy the second time?"

"It just doesn't seem the same," said Libby. "Different entirely."

"But they aren't," said Fran.

"Aren't what? Different?"

"Of course," said Fran.

CHAPTER
THIRTY-ONE

Libby stared, her mouth open.

"Of course?" she said eventually.

"I think so." Fran looked up. "I'd like to know more about Sheila's brother and about the other baby."

"If there was one," reminded Libby.

"Oh, I'm sure there was. I want to know who the father was."

"How will that help us?"

"The police are trying to find Cy's attacker and Patrick's killer. You were right in trying to find a connection between their histories. I think that's where the answer lies. But I also think you were right, in a way, in that the second attack wasn't by the same person."

"Or persons?"

"Only one, I think."

"But Sheila said she saw two youths attacking Cy," said Libby.

"Perhaps she was lying?"

"But why?"

"We know she's been lying about her past," said Fran, "and you said you suspected her."

"Of the attacks, yes, but now — well, I can't see it. If she really is Josephine's half sister, then I feel sorry for her. She sort of lost everything to Josephine, didn't she? It doesn't seem as though her father had any interest in her, and then she lost her little brother. She has every reason to hate Josephine."

"But I don't think she attacked Cy or killed Patrick," said Fran. "She's not strong enough, and she's far too old."

"What about the brother? Might he have come back?"

"He wouldn't be much younger than Sheila," said Fran.

"He might have children."

"Would they know anything about his history, though?"

"I'm sure they would," said Libby. "You'd tell your kids about your history, wouldn't you?"

Fran turned down her mouth. "If they'd listen. The only thing my daughters are interested in is money, you know that."

"How is Chrissie?" asked Libby, diverted for a moment. "Have they resolved the children issue?"

"She told me they were trying," said Fran. "For a baby, that is. How Brucie baby is taking it I'm not sure. He seemed very quiet at Christmas — for him, that is."

"Oh, well, as long as they don't expect you to babysit all the time," said Libby. "Not like you did in London for Lucy."

"You should hear her on the subject," said Fran with a short laugh. "She still blames me for moving down here. She has no life, apparently."

"That's what happens when you have children," said Libby. "And when your husband gets fed up with having a wife who can't go out because of the children, they go off with someone who can."

"Your husband didn't go off until your children were older," said Fran. "And I was the worst mother in the world, as we know. I was always leaving my children. No wonder they grew up as they did."

"Stop blaming yourself," said Libby. "And let's get back to the problem at hand. Someone who connects Patrick and Cy."

"Yes." Fran was frowning again. "That's the problem. The only person so far is this Larry Barkiss. There's no connection with Josephine or Sheila. And he doesn't appear to have any connection to a previous generation."

"He might have. Aunt Dolly didn't know anything about him, but she said, didn't she, she wasn't living here, I mean, there, then. Margaret, Lisa and Patrick's mother, told her all about it."

"Suppose there is a link," said Fran slowly, "what would it be?"

"Obvious," said Libby, sitting back and looking smug. "He's the son of the Australian brother who's come home."

Fran raised her eyebrows. "Possible," she said. "How do we find out?"

"Ian's already looked him up, hasn't he, so he hasn't got a criminal record. How on earth do you go about finding someone?"

"DVLC?" suggested Fran. "Except you couldn't unless you were the police, I suppose. Credit reference?"

"I think it's impossible if you're a private citizen," said Libby. "We'll just have to rely on Ian."

"Do you think he'll look him up?" said Fran. "I think he's been diverted now, into finding out about Sheila."

"Did you actually get something from that photograph, or was it guesswork?" asked Libby.

"No." Fran shook her head. "It was just a feeling. You know." She looked up at Libby. "I can't explain it."

"What did Sheila say when you asked her?"

"She said they were both dead. Then Ian hustled us away."

"I expect they are both dead, then. Even though the brother was obviously younger than she is, if he was treated badly on the Migrant Programme he could have died quite young."

"I wish I could talk to her about him." Fran sighed. "I'm sure it would help her, and it might help Cy."

"If it's a connection of hers that attacked Cy she won't want to help." Libby put her mug on the hearth. "And that's why she's kept the connection quiet, because if it was known, she knew she'd become a suspect."

"Not for the attacks," said Fran. "As we keep saying, she's too old and fragile."

"Oh, it's all so complicated," Libby sighed. "And what about that other baby? And Maud Burton?"

"I've got a theory about that," said Fran.

"About the other baby?"

"No, about Maud Burton. You said she was writing anonymous letters to people in Curtishill before she started on her Amy Taylor campaign."

"So Ian said. But they don't know who to. They were initials."

"Wouldn't they be likely to be people who asked her to get rid of unwanted children?"

"Of course they would!" Libby sat up straight. "Shall we tell Ian?"

"I imagine he's thought of it by now," said Fran. "What needs to be done is to check those initials and see if they mean anything to Aunt Dolly. She's the only one we know who was around at the time."

"But she says she hardly knew anybody in the village."

"Then how did she pick up gossip?"

"Oh. Yes." Libby thought for a moment. "Well, from other hop pickers. When they came down in September."

"When during the war were they bombed out? When did they come and live in Curtishill permanently?"

"No idea." Libby looked surprised. "I suppose that makes a difference, doesn't it?"

"If it wasn't until 1945 she's hardly likely to know anything at all. It must have been earlier."

"Do you suppose he'd let us look at that exercise book?" asked Libby.

"Of course he wouldn't. It's the cold case people's evidence. They could have got the DNA from it."

"No, they couldn't." Libby shook her head. "If Maud Burton's killer had found that book, he'd have destroyed it. So he won't have left DNA on it."

"Perhaps he didn't realise what it was?"

"I shouldn't have thought so." Libby sighed and got to her feet. "I think we're up a gum tree as usual. And this seems even more complicated than usual. More tea? Ben'll be here soon."

Ben arrived, and, shortly afterwards, Guy. Harry had kindly agreed to serve them dinner at six, so they had the Pink Geranium to themselves. After serving them, Donna went to put her feet up with a magazine and Adam and Harry joined them at their table. Libby filled them in on the afternoon's events.

"I really can't imagine your mate Sheila as a ravening killer," said Harry when she had finished.

"No, but she's kept a lot of things quiet," said Ben.

"Well, they can't charge her for that," said Harry.

"It looks to me," said Guy, wiping his small beard with his napkin, "as if you'll never get to the bottom of this. It's too far back. The only hope you'd have is if someone had kept old letters or something of that nature. And given that all the events, even Amy Taylor's pregnancy, were in the war years —"

"Except Maud's death and the attacks," put in Libby.

295

"The roots were all in the war years," continued Guy firmly, "when documentation for anything but the military was scrappy to say the least, I doubt if there's anything left to investigate."

Fran and Libby looked at each other.

"So even if I can pick up something," said Fran, "there'll be no one alive to confirm it, and no material evidence either."

"That's right," said Guy, and patted her hand. "Cheer up, love. There'll be another one along in a minute."

Ben, Harry and Adam laughed.

"I don't know what you mean," said Libby huffily.

"Investigation, mother dear," said Adam.

"Come on, Madam Director," said Ben, pushing back his chair. "Time to go." He got out his wallet and handed over his credit card. "My treat," he said.

Fran and Guy protested but Ben was firm. Libby asked if they would like to come and watch the rehearsal, but Fran said as they were all going to be together again the following night at Lewis Osbourne-Walker's New Year party, she and Guy would go home and get an early night.

The rehearsal went as well as could be expected, and Libby stood everyone a drink at the theatre bar afterwards and wished them happy New Year. Peter, who had joined them, and Ben went round locking up while Libby checked the bar stock.

"Er — Libby."

She looked up and saw Freddy, the back half of the cow, hovering by the door.

"Yes, Freddy? Got a problem?" Libby came out from behind the bar and turned the light off. "How can I help?"

"No, it's nothing like that," said Freddy, with a grin, as he came forward. "It's just that my Aunt Dolly was telling me —"

"*Your* Aunt Dolly?" Libby stared at him. "Dolly Webley?"

"Yes." Freddy looked surprised. "She was married to my uncle. Well, great-uncle really — my grandma's brother. They never had any children, so they were more like grandparents to us."

"Well, I never!" said Libby, sitting down with a thump that nearly turned the little white chair over. "So you know her family? Margaret? And Lisa?"

"And Paddy, yes." Freddy looked solemn.

"Oh, goodness." Libby shook her head to clear it. "I can't believe this. What a coincidence."

"Yeah — well." Freddy shifted from one foot to the other and Libby told him to sit down.

"Well, Aunt Dolly said you'd been by with a policeman today, and you'd been to see her before Christmas with someone else."

"That's right. It's part of the investigation into Patrick's death. But your Auntie didn't tell me about you! She said she knew all about me, and Flo Carpenter, but didn't mention you."

"No reason she should, I suppose," said Freddy. "But she said you were asking about Maud Burton. Aunt Dolly never knew her, not really."

"She'd heard of her back in Curtishill, though," said Libby, wondering what was coming next.

"Yes, but she didn't really know her. But see, Maud Burton lived here before she went to Curtishill."

Libby stared. "Really? How do you know?"

"My grandma knew her. And the other one — Amy Taylor."

Libby looked at him for a moment, then put her head in her hands.

"I'm sorry," faltered Freddy. "Have I said something wrong?"

Libby lifted her head. "No, of course not." Ben came through the door from the auditorium as Peter came down from the sound and lighting box. "Come here and listen to this, you two," she said.

Freddy repeated his story and Peter burst out laughing.

"All you needed to do was put a sign on the dressing room door, after all!" he said. "You ought to have known someone in the village would know all about it."

"That's actually why we were being discreet," said Libby. "We didn't want anyone upset in case there were relatives still alive."

"Very laudable," said Peter. "But you're not going to write the play now, anyway, so why the interest?"

"Because it links up with Cy's attack and Patrick's death," said Libby, patting Freddy's hand. "He was Freddy's cousin." She looked at him. "Or second cousin. Or something."

"Actually no relation," said Freddy. "Aunt Dolly's an aunt by marriage."

"Well, a connection, anyway," said Libby. "Freddy, I hate to ask this, but —"

"Yes, Gran would love to talk to you," Freddy pre-empted. "She loves a good gossip about the old days."

Ben shook his head. "I don't know," he said. "You've got the luck of the devil."

"Actually, Libby, there was something else," said Freddy, as Libby stood up.

"Yes?"

"Aunt Dolly was talking about Mr Strange, too."

"Mr — oh, Cy. Yes. Do you know him?"

"Well," said Freddy, shuffling his feet and looking much younger than his twenty-five years, "you'll say this is another coincidence, but it isn't really."

"What is? said Libby. "Come on, Freddy, spit it out."

"Well," said Freddy again, "not to say knew, exactly, but his firm supplies our water coolers and top-ups. And when he used to work out of the Maidstone depot, he used to come and see our MD."

"So you met him?"

Freddy blushed and Libby's mind clicked. She sat down again. "It's OK, Freddy," she said. "You and he didn't — um —"

"Oh, no." Freddy was redder than ever. "I mean, I thought he was very — well — cool. But I knew he was in a relationship. Or rather, I found out he was."

"Libby? Are you coming?" Ben was by the big double doors.

"Yes," Libby called back. She stood up, took Freddy's arm and walked him out of the building. "Now then," she said. "Carry on."

CHAPTER
THIRTY-TWO

"Nothing much to say," said Freddy, allowing himself to be marched down the drive. "He always talked to me when he came round, every couple of months just to check everything was OK, you know? And I . . . oh, well, I started to think maybe he was . . . you know . . ."

"Interested?" suggested Libby.

"But then he started talking about his friend."

"Colin?"

"Was that his name? Yes. Who he lived with. You see," said Freddy, turning to face Libby, "I didn't know he was gay. I don't think anyone did. But when I thought he was getting interested in me I got a bit worried. And I think he could see that. So he told me about — Colin, was it?"

"So you got to know him quite well?"

"Not really. But then there was this business at the depot and he moved to London. I thought he'd moved right away — like, you know, house."

"What business at the depot?"

"About him being gay," said Freddy. "It was all gossip, you know, but someone told someone else and they told someone in our company."

"What was it though? Just that he was gay?"

"No, someone was writing things — I don't know — on walls, maybe. It all sounded a bit, you know, nasty."

Libby was looking thoughtful. "And did you ever see Cy after you heard the gossip?"

"No. Next we heard he'd moved to the head office. No one actually said, and then I asked the boss. He said not to talk about it."

"Did he?" Libby raised her eyebrows. "I wonder why?"

"So when I said that to Aunt Dolly, she said I should tell you. She said it was important."

"It is, Freddy." Libby gave his arm a squeeze. "Very important. I'm so pleased you told me, and please thank Aunt Dolly for me, too, will you? She's been a great help in all sorts of ways."

"What I don't understand," said Libby to Ben, as they walked home, "is why Cy didn't tell us anything about this."

"Did you know he'd worked in Maidstone?"

"Yes. The first time I met them, Colin explained that they'd moved into the bungalow when the previous tenant's lease had expired and then they saw the job in Maidstone advertised. The only thing they said about London was that Cy'd had promotion."

"To what?"

"Colin said sales director, Cy said sales manager. But Freddy said he used to come round every couple of months to check that everything was OK, so it sounds as though he was in a good sort of position there."

"So it sounds, from what Freddy said, that he was moved to London because of some kind of homophobic trouble?"

"Yes, but I actually *asked* if that had happened. Asked if it was that sort of place. You'd have thought they would have said," Libby complained. "And it's annoyed me. I shall tell Ian about it tomorrow and then wash my hands of it all."

"What if Ian still wants your help?"

"He doesn't," said Libby. "He wants Fran's help."

Ben gave her a wry smile. "And you've sworn off the investigation before. What's the betting you'll be nosing around again by the weekend?"

"I won't have the time," said Libby. "From Saturday it'll be panto, panto all the way."

"You'll still be curious," said Ben, unlocking the door of number 17. "And the panto's only on for a fortnight."

"Oh, it'll all be over by then," said Libby. "Patrick's murder was so long ago now that it'll go on the back-burner for good."

"And what about Burton and Taylor?"

"That's in the hands of the Cold Case unit. I shouldn't think they'll get much on that, either."

"Freddy's gran?"

Libby wavered, whisky bottle in hand.

"Thought so," said Ben, removing it and unscrewing the top.

"Freddy said his gran would love to talk to me," defended Libby, selecting two glasses. "Old ladies love talking about the past, don't they?"

"The one I live with does, anyway," said Ben, ducking.

The last day of the old year was cold. Libby spent the morning changing the bed, dusting and hoovering in order to start the new year with a clean and tidy house. Not that it would stay like it for long, but she always tried. She looked up Freddy's number in her cast list over a lunchtime bowl of soup and called him.

"Where does your gran live?" she asked. "And when could I go and see her?"

"I'll give her a call," said Freddy, "then I'll call you back."

An hour later Libby, in a knitted hat, wellingtons and Ben's old anorak again, was walking up the lane past Steeple Farm on her way to see Freddy's gran. She crested the brow of the hill and turned to look back on her village. Steeple Lane itself wound down between steep banks, but at the foot of the hill where it joined the high street and the Nethergate road the village lay spread out. And suddenly, to her right, Libby caught the sparkle of water.

The dewpond. Libby looked to see if there was a way down to it, but a hedge and wire fencing prevented access. Perhaps to stop people like Amy Taylor drowning themselves in it. Someone had broken a hole in the ice, possibly for the sake of any fish lurking in the depths, which was why Libby had seen water. She stood looking at it for some minutes. The little river Wytch dribbled in at one end and presumably stopped, as she couldn't see it reappearing. Trees stood round one side of the pond, and what looked like a path led across frosty shrubland between them until it was lost to sight over another rise in the land. Was it from here, Libby wondered, that the man — Elliott, was his name? — walked his dog and found poor Amy that Easter Sunday morning? She shivered and turned back to the lane, picking up her pace as she gained the flat.

The row of cottages where Freddy's gran lived was a little further on. It looked to have been built around the same time as Libby's cottage, and of the same red brick, but these had what would, in the summer, be pretty front gardens. Libby went to the green door at the end of the row and knocked.

Freddy's gran was a surprise. A beautifully groomed, slim woman with silver hair pulled back into a fashionable upswept style, much younger than Libby had anticipated.

"No," she said laughing, as she shook Libby's hand. "I'm a neighbour. This is Una."

This was more like it. A little woman with curly white hair, a knitted jumper, thick stockings and comfy slippers.

"Hello, dear," she said, getting to her feet. "I'm so glad you came. You don't mind Sandra being here, do you? Only she might have something to tell you, too. That is, if you wanted to ask me about little Amy Taylor."

"Oh — oh, no of course not," said Libby, feeling slightly bewildered. "Um — do you mind if I take my boots off?"

"Just leave them by the door, duck," said Una. "Sandra's got the kettle on the boil. Tea?"

I must have drunk gallons of tea in people's houses since I got into this investigating lark, Libby thought, as she took the seat by the fire which was offered.

"So, duck, you wanted to know about Amy, young Freddy said?"

"Well," said Libby, "it was just that her name came up in connection with an investigation I was helping with." No need to say how, thought Libby.

"Ah." Una nodded. "With that Maud Burton, I'll be bound."

"Yes. Freddy said you knew them both."

Una nodded. "That I did, dear. Look, here comes Sandra with the tea. Let's get that poured first."

It was another version of Sheila's proper tea tray, but classier, thought Libby. Proper cups and saucers, teapot, milk jug and sugar bowl. Sandra poured out three cups and sat back in her own chair. "Right, off you go, Una," she said.

"How much do you know about Amy Taylor and Maud Burton?" Una sipped her tea.

Libby repeated all she knew and had learnt over the past weeks.

"Well, that's right, duck. Except that Maud Burton was here when young Amy got into her bit of trouble."

"Was she?" Libby frowned. "But in that case, Amy knew that Maud knew, why would she be upset by the letter?"

"I doubt she knew who the letter was from — that's what those letters are like, aren't they? Leastways, the other I saw was. And they being so close as thieves, young Amy wouldn't have thought her best friend would tell anyone."

"That's true," agreed Libby. "But did Maud help Amy at the time? When she had the baby?"

"No, duck, Amy went away. See, the family thought no one in the village knew, but a few of us did. Including Maud Burton."

"So who were they both? Did their families live here?"

"Oh, yes. Amy was the vicar's daughter. Didn't you know?"

"Oh!" Libby smacked a hand on the arm of her chair. "Yes. Flo thought she might have been."

"Flo Carpenter? She's a good sort," said Una, putting her cup and saucer down.

"You know Flo?"

"Of course, me duck. All us oldies know one another. Me and Dolly Webley go down to Maltby Close for the bingo some weeks."

"Oh," said Libby. "I didn't know."

"No cause for you to know. Anyway, young Amy was Vicar Taylor's girl, and she'd been a bit sheltered, like. Wasn't that young, neither, in her thirties, I think. Maud Burton was the shopkeeper's daughter. We just had the one little shop then, where the post office is now. Well, it was a post office then, too, but not so posh as it is now."

"So what happened? Was it a picker?"

"Pole puller, it were. Handsome chap. Course, Amy and Maud weren't allowed to mix with the pickers. This was before the war. Once the war came, things got a bit different."

"Yes," said Libby, remembering the story of Ben's parents.

"You'd know, duck, wouldn't you?" said Una shrewdly, watching her with surprisingly bright eyes.

"Yes," said Libby turning faintly pink and remembering how the whole village would, of course, know the story, especially after Libby herself had produced the play telling it at the Oast House Theatre.

"Anyway, Amy, as the vicar's daughter, would go round with tea and bits and pieces for the families in the gardens sometimes. Sometimes she'd go with her dad when he did services over there on a Sunday. And she met this young chap. Well, not so much met. She knew him already."

"She did?"

"He were her cousin," said Una.

Libby gasped. "Her *cousin?*"

"There!" said Una, sitting back and looking smug. "I said you wouldn't know that."

"No, I certainly didn't!"

"Her cousin — what was his name, Sandra?"

"Julian," said Sandra.

"Yes, Julian, that's right, he was much younger than Amy was, but she was allowed to mix with him, see. So he'd take her for a drink, or for walks. Anyway, the upshot is, when he goes off to university, she finds herself in the family way, so the family pack her off somewhere, I don't know where, and say she's gone off doing war work, cause that was 1939, see."

"What about Julian?"

"Ah." Una shook her head. "He was killed at Dunkirk. Barely got to university, then he was off to join up. We knew about that cause Vicar told us in church. My nephew, Julian — what was his name, Sandra? French, it was."

"Sorry, Una, I don't know," said Sandra.

Libby was wracking her brain to come up with the name of the relative she'd read about on the internet.

"Brissac!" she blurted out.

Sandra and Una looked at her in surprise.

"Brissac! That's it," said Una. "How did you know?"

"A report I found on the internet," said Libby. "It mentioned a Mrs Stephanie Brissac as being a living relative at the time of Amy's death."

"Well, I never!" said Una, looking at her admiringly.

"Anyway," said Libby, keen to get back to the story, "what happened to the child?"

"Don't know that, dear, but Maud did."

"Did she? How?"

"Amy told her, of course. And kept in touch somehow, with the babe. And Maud helped."

"How do you know that?"

"Used to drop hints, did Maud. We were a farming family, but we were local, so Maud and me got a bit friendly, like. After the war, this was, because she went off to do her voluntary work after Amy came back here."

"So Maud didn't do Red Cross work here? At the Manor gardens?"

"No, duck. And I don't know why, neither. That was a bit of a puzzle."

"Then she came back?"

"Amy come back in 1940. Maud went off then, and Amy talked to me a bit. That was how I knew about Julian. Then Maud come back — oh, must've been 1946? Her parents were dead and the shop was sold, but she had their little house in Lendle Lane."

So that explained that, thought Libby.

"And they became friends again?"

"Well, duck, neither of 'em had married. The rest of us had husbands and kiddies by then, so they was more or less on their own. So they palled up. Ran everything between them. Amy lived at the vicarage until her dad died, then she and her mum bought their little place on the Nethergate road. Leastways, I s'pose they bought it. Could've rented it, I suppose. Then her mum died, and there she was on her own. And then that there new vicar comes along." Una tutted and shook her head. "And Sandra was here by then, weren't you, duck?"

Sandra nodded and turned to Libby. "My husband and I bought the other three cottages in this row and turned them into one house. Well, just two of them, at first, until the one next door to Una became available."

Una chuckled. "I always say she'll push me under a bus one day just to get her hands on my place."

Sandra smiled, a little sadly. "Not any more, Una. I don't need the space, do I?"

Una patted her arm. "Just joking, duck. Want any more tea?"

Sandra and Libby both declined.

"So you were saying," prompted Libby, "the new vicar came along. Mr Greene, wasn't it?"

"Like Cluedo, yes," said Sandra, "although no one knew that, then."

"And Sandra's hubby was one of the churchwardens," said Una, "so he saw a lot of what went on."

Libby looked at Sandra, who shook her head. "Not a lot, really," she said. "But it's a hazard vicars have to put up with. Single women of — shall we say mature years. And poor Mike Greene was single, which was even worse! So they took him meals, offered to darn his socks, Maud even asked him to hear her confession!"

"Goodness!" said Libby.

"And Amy already ran the Sunday school, so she was in a privileged position, in a way. Which of course is why Mike asked her to play at one of his musical evenings. We were there, actually."

"And that's what started it all off," said Una, with some relish. "Cor! It was war, it was."

"Then the letters started," said Libby.

"They did." Una nodded. "And when Vicar got one — well! He does this sermon about it and holds a meeting for anyone who got one to come along. And everyone who got one went. Even Maud."

"Then they stopped?"

"And then," said Sandra, "my husband found Amy's body."

CHAPTER
THIRTY-THREE

"You're Mrs Elliott?"

"Mrs Brown," corrected Sandra. "My husband was Elliott Brown. Did you find that on the internet, too?"

"It was in the report on the coroner's inquiry," said Libby. "Sorry I got it wrong."

Sandra smiled. "It doesn't matter. Elliott's a better surname than Brown, anyway."

"So that's why he went to the vicarage — because the vicar knew Amy and because Mr Brown was a churchwarden?"

"No, he sent the police to the vicarage. He ran back here to telephone — luckily, we had one — then went back to the body. Jack actually found it."

"Jack?"

"Our dog. A black Labrador. Elliott didn't normally go near the pond because Jack used to try and go in. But that day Jack insisted. And you know how insistent Labradors can be."

"Mmm." Libby had never actually had a dog, but had been made aware of some of their baser behaviour by those belonging to friends. "So then the police went to Amy's house and found her letter?"

"That they did, me duck," said Una. "And there's Maud Burton carrying on something terrible about her best friend being dead, weeping and wailing all over the vicar."

"So how did they come to find out it was Maud who wrote the letters? In the internet report it merely said she had been found in possession of materials. Not exactly helpful."

"I don't know any of those details, I'm afraid," said Sandra, "but as far as we can make out, the police went to question Maud about the accusation in the letter."

"And o'course, she had to tell 'em she knew all about it, 'cause I'd already told 'em." Una had the smug expression back on her face. "They come to see me, see, when they came to talk to Elliott, and he said I knew them both from before the war."

"So did they search her house just because she knew about the baby?"

"Don't know, duck." Una shrugged. "But she got a telling off from the coroner and then she disappeared, like. Ashamed, I reckon. Couldn't face any of us."

Libby wondered whether to tell them that it was now almost certain that Maud had been murdered and decided not to.

"Do you think," she said instead, "that Maud could have been frightened of anyone after that? Someone who was really angry about the letters? Or Amy's suicide?"

Sandra and Una looked at one another.

"Frightened her enough for her to run away?" asked Sandra. "I can't think of anybody."

"No, duck. I reckon she was just ashamed," said Una. "Specially with the vicar and all. Going on like that when she's driven her best friend to do herself in."

"Do you think she admitted that to herself?" asked Libby. "Would she have thought it was her fault?"

"Didn't matter if she did or she didn't," said Una. "Everybody else did."

"But what was so awful about it?" Libby persisted. "She'd only had a baby, for goodness sake. And you said several people knew anyway."

"It was different in them days," said Una. "Shocking. And the letter called her some names and was going to tell everyone, it said. Amy couldn't have stood that. Specially when she was so gone on the vicar."

"It *was* different." Sandra spoke softly. "It seems incredible that only half a century ago living together was still called living in sin, girls were still sent away when they were pregnant and forced to have their babies adopted and homosexuality was not only illegal, but thought by some to be a disease of which you could be cured."

"I know." Libby shook her head. "I've thought about it a lot. And it was all going on right up to the sixties, wasn't it?"

Sandra nodded.

"I remember watching a documentary about the forced adoptions and the homes," Libby went on, "a few years ago with my daughter Belinda. She was horrified. It was almost as if she was blaming me for it all because I was actually alive when it was still happening."

314

"Well, there you are, duck," said Una. "Young Amy Taylor was ashamed and killed herself, and Maud Burton was ashamed of herself and ran away. So there you are."

"Yes," said Libby, wondering if she'd actually learnt anything new, or useful for Ian. "Thank you for talking to me."

"So you said it was to do with another investigation?" said Sandra. "May we ask what it is and how you're involved? Oh —" she held up a hand "— we know you and your friend have been involved in things before. We read about them, don't we Una?"

"Well." Libby squirmed a bit and stared at the fire. "It was another set of anonymous letters actually. Recent ones."

"Not from Maud," said Una with a chuckle. "She'd be dead by now. Older than me, she was. They both was."

"No," said Libby, "but Maud was involved with some of the victims." Not quite true, thought Libby, but she had sent at least one letter to Sheila.

"So she went on doing it?" said Sandra. "But why? Was she asking for money?"

"I'm not sure, although I think she probably was. She'd been doing it before she ever started sending them here," said Libby, wondering how far she ought to go.

"Now there's wicked," said Una. "I never liked her, mind."

"Has it helped?" asked Sandra, seeing that Libby was readying herself to leave.

"It's told me quite a lot I didn't know," said Libby, "and I'm very glad to have met you both. Are you celebrating tonight?"

"Not me, duck," said Una. "I shall have hot chocolate and go to bed at me normal time."

"I'm going to a dinner party," said Sandra. "Very small affair, but good friends. Are you?"

"A friend's having a party over towards Nethergate," said Libby. "I think it might be quite a big one. We're staying overnight."

"Well, have a good time, duck," said Una, getting up and coming to the door. "And if you want to drop in for another chat, you can come any time."

It was almost dark as Libby started back down Steeple Lane. The village sparkled below her like a Christmas tree and she could barely make out the pond now, but shivered as she looked over to it. As the lane plunged between its high banks, she looked to her left to make out the looming, thatched bulk of Steeple Farm and shivered again.

What was it about that house? She'd had the creeps about it ever since her first visit, with Peter's mother, mad Millicent. And even with Lewis Osbourne-Walker's approval of the venture, he being something of an expert in renovation, and all Ben's hard work, she still didn't like it. And Ben still did.

They drove over to Creekmarsh at half past seven. Lewis had the drive lit with garden flares, presumably from the stock he was laying in for when the house become a bona fide 'venue' for conferences and weddings. Libby had to admit it looked spectacular. In the grand hall there was a huge log fire and a large bowl of mulled wine on a side table. Edie, resplendent in black and sequins, took their coats and handed them to a young woman dressed in traditional black and white looking a little over-excited.

Lewis came leaping down the impressive staircase to greet them.

"Got yer mulled wine yet? Come on, then. Up to my room. We're going to eat up there, it's warmer. Come on, Mum. You can leave it to little Charlene here to show people in."

Charlene, eyes shining, nodded vigorously.

Lewis's 'room' was the solar, a beautiful room with huge windows, still uncurtained.

"I like to look out at it all, even at night," he said. "And look. You can see the church now the trees are bare."

The little church on the other side of the lane that led to Creekmarsh was spotlit.

"They'll be ringing the bells at midnight," said Lewis. "Now, come and meet some people."

Libby and Ben were introduced to a few of Lewis's London friends, who were all, apparently staying overnight. Fran and Guy arrived a few moments later, and Edie scurried off to make sure the food preparations were underway.

"It's a lot of work for Edie," said Libby, when Lewis approached with a bottle of red wine to top up their glasses.

"She loves it," said Lewis. "And we've got the caterers in. And they'll be leaving breakfasts all ready before they go."

"What about the bedrooms?" Libby looked round the room. "There must be ten couples here."

"So? We've got twenty bedrooms," said Lewis. "And Edie's moved into Katie's bit of the house, so she's quite separate."

"Did she want to go down there?" asked Fran. "I thought it might be a painful for her."

Lewis shrugged. "No, she seems to like it." He nudged Fran. "Hasn't got the power like you!"

Dinner was beautiful. Simple food, well cooked and presented, with nothing and nobody left out. There was a vegetarian alternative for each course — "I took old Hal's advice on that," said Lewis — and different wines to accompany them. Libby was enchanted.

To Ben's horror, Lewis proposed party games after dinner, but in the end even he joined in with Charades and made a fool of himself along with everybody else. Just before midnight, Lewis made them stand at the solar windows, which he opened, so they could hear the bells, then after a quick chorus of 'Auld Lang Syne', he dashed off down the stairs and reappeared to supervise the fireworks. Capering about in the dark with rockets going off behind him, he seemed like a figure from a fairy tale.

"But definitely a Grimm fairy tale," said Fran, looking down on him with a smile.

It was two o'clock before Libby was able to drag Ben away to their allotted bedroom.

"Nice," she said, approving the boutique-style bedroom and adjoining en-suite. "I could get used to this."

Ben came up behind her and kissed her neck. "We could do something like it at Steeple Farm," he murmured into her shoulder.

Libby closed her eyes and swore inside her head. Out loud, she said, "But that would spoil it. It's only fun if it's a treat." She turned and put her arms round him. "Happy New Year, Ben," she said. "And now, let's get some sleep!"

He smiled. "And to you, my love," he said. "I hope all our dreams come true this year."

And that, thought Libby with foreboding as she undressed, wasn't exactly what she wanted to hear.

CHAPTER
THIRTY-FOUR

Over breakfast in Lewis's kitchen on New Year's morning Libby told Fran and Guy about her meeting with Una and Sandra.

"So I don't see it gets anyone any further," she said, "but I suppose I ought to tell Ian. Not today, though. He wouldn't thank me for disturbing him today."

"I don't think policemen get New Year's Day off," said Guy. "You could give him a quick ring on his mobile, surely? Leave a message?"

"Is it important enough, though?" said Libby.

"Well," said Fran, "there's the Brissac connection. The fact that Amy's baby's father was her cousin and Maud knew about it."

"But I'm not sure that would be counted as a murder motive," said Libby, "and it has nothing to do with Patrick's murder."

"It can wait, can't it?" said Ben. "After all, it is our only day off until Sunday week."

"Day off?" Lewis came into the kitchen after seeing some of his other guests off the premises. "What are you doing then?"

"Panto," said Libby. "You know all about it. You've booked a ticket with Adam."

"Oh, yes. Not real work, though is it?" Lewis swung a chair round and sat astride it.

"You want to try it," said Ben.

"It's not paid work, no," said Fran, "but believe me, as one who has been in one of Libby's pantomimes, it's *very* hard work."

"And today we're having drinks with my parents and Pete and Harry, if you remember," said Ben, "so let's leave murder and all its works out of the picture for at least one day."

Libby leant over and kissed him on the cheek. "Very good idea," she said.

Messages left on Ian's mobile phone, however, had other ideas, and in the middle of the small, but convivial drinks party at Peter and Harry's cottage later that day, Libby's phone rang. She went into the kitchen to answer it among the shelves crammed with mismatched china.

"Go on then," said Ian. "Tell me what you've ferreted out this time."

"I didn't ferret," said Libby indignantly. "It came to me. Honestly. And I was so cross about one thing that I almost didn't want to tell you."

"There are things you've not told me in the past," said Ian.

"I know, but not like this." She proceeded to tell him about Freddy's report of trouble at Cy's Maidstone job.

"Why hasn't he said anything about this?" Ian sounded as irritated as Libby had been. "God save me from people who think things aren't relevant."

"Then there's a couple of bits and pieces I picked up yesterday afternoon," she went on. "Again, volunteered by Freddy's gran."

"Not Aunt Dolly? Confusion reigns."

"No, listen," said Libby and reported the afternoon's conversation with Una and Sandra. "So I'm just telling you in case there's anything there you can use. And now Ben'll be furious because he wanted today off from 'murder and all its works' as he put it."

Ian laughed. "Right, you can now go back to him, and I won't bother you again today. Tomorrow, I might."

"I'll only be available until about three."

"Panto, is it? OK, if I need to I'll call in the morning. Oh — and happy New Year."

"Don't tell me," said Ben, as she walked back into the sitting room. "Ian."

"Yes, but that's it. He doesn't want to ask me any more questions. Not that I've got any more answers."

Hetty tutted from her place on the sofa beside Greg. "I don't know how you get mixed up in all these things, gal."

Harry came and sat on the arm of the sofa. "It was my fault this time, Het," he said. "Sorry."

"Nothing to do with me, love," said Hetty, patting his leg. "Just don't want no one to get hurt."

Peter adroitly changed the subject to the pantomime and the chances that the ticket sales might be down because of the weather and Ben gave him a grateful grin.

322

A few hours later, feet up in front of the fire catching up on some of the television programmes they'd recorded over Christmas, Ben and Libby were disturbed by the ringing of the landline.

"Let the answerphone take it," said Ben, and Libby agreed. Who wanted to get into a conversation at this time of the evening? But they listened as the caller left his message. And, unsurprisingly, it was Colin.

"We've just had the police onto us again," he said, a suspicion of a whine in his voice. "And I don't know where they think they got this information from. I expect it was you, but if it was, how did you find out? Ring me back — please."

The please was added very much as an afterthought. Libby immediately reached for her mobile and switched that off.

"Just in case he tries," she said to Ben. "He hasn't got your number, has he?"

"Yes, because of Steeple Farm, but I'd already switched mine off." He put an arm round Libby. "I didn't want to be disturbed."

She smiled and picked up her drink. "Then we won't be," she said.

But the next morning, Colin was on the phone again.

"Why didn't you ring me back?" he said. "I left messages on both your phones."

"Because, Colin, it was New Year's Day and Ben and I were celebrating. I haven't even turned my mobile on yet, and neither has Ben."

"You heard your landline message, though?"

"Yes," sighed Libby, "and I really can't help you."

"Where did the police find out about the trouble at the depot?"

"Why didn't either of you tell me about it when you were asking for my advice?" Libby countered. "I asked you specifically if there had been any trouble."

"We didn't think it was important." Colin sounded sulky.

"I remember when I asked — you looked at each other. You knew something then, didn't you?" Libby made a sound of exasperation. "Honestly, Colin. You only make things worse by withholding things, I don't mean from me, although that makes me mad, seeing that you wanted my help, but from the police. I've no patience with it."

There was silence at the other end of the phone line, but Libby knew Colin was still there.

"And another thing," she said. "Why are you making this call and not Cy?"

"He said not to bother you," said Colin eventually. "He's more forgiving than me."

Libby exploded. "FORGIVING? Forgiving me? For fuck's sake, Colin, get a grip. My friends and I have done more for you than anyone else — giving you somewhere to stay — oh, all sorts of things. And now you have the *cheek* to say —" she stopped, took a deep breath. "Goodbye."

As she switched off the phone, she realised she was shaking. Ben, coming down the stairs, put an arm round her shoulders. "What was all that about?" he said, pushing her into a chair. "You don't normally swear."

324

Libby told him. "I was *furious*," she said.

"I could tell," said Ben with a grin. "I doubt he'll try again, though. You can, as you said the other day, now wash your hands of the whole business."

Although the rehearsal wasn't called until four o'clock, Libby and Ben went to the theatre at two, partly to get out of the house in case the phone rang again, Libby admitted to Peter, when he arrived to help out with lighting.

"Harry's mortified," he said. "Colin phoned us to see where you were this morning. He sounded very grumpy, but didn't say what he wanted. Ben called me and told me what had happened."

"Did he? He didn't tell me." Libby looked across at her significant other messing about on stage with bits of rope, and smiled. "Protecting me, was he?"

"As usual," said Peter. "And now Harry's given Cy a piece of his mind, too, although to be fair, I think it was Colin going off the deep end rather than Cy."

"Yes, he actually said Cy didn't want to bother me."

"So why did he?"

"That was where I lost it," said Libby. "He said Cy was more forgiving than he was."

Peter threw back his head and roared with laughter. When he'd recovered, wiping tears from his eyes, he patted her shoulder and said brokenly, "I'm surprised he's still alive."

"If he'd been there in the flesh he wouldn't have been," said Ben, coming up behind them. "You should have heard her."

"Mouth like a navvy," said Peter.

"Or a stoker on a coaling ship from Belfast, as my gran used to say," said Ben.

"When you've quite finished," said Libby. "It wasn't funny."

"I know, my dear old trout," said Peter, giving her a quick hug. "So now you can leave it entirely alone and concentrate on being a good fairy."

Not only the cast but several of the backstage and sound and lighting crew members had turned up, to Libby's surprise, no doubt surfeited with food and drink, so she was able to hold a full technical rehearsal, which would speed up the process tomorrow.

At eight thirty they were able to lock the theatre and repair to the pub for a drink. Libby was tired but pleased, and careful not to say anything about good rehearsals making for bad first nights. Peter went next door but one to The Pink Geranium to see how Harry was and came back to report that the restaurant was full, but Harry might be able to join them for a drink if he could get away in half an hour.

"And Fran and Guy are in there," said Peter, sitting down opposite Libby. "They're coming in, too."

"Really?" Libby frowned. "They didn't say they were coming."

"She doesn't have to tell you everything she does," said Ben, amused.

"No, but she always says if she's coming to the village."

"Perhaps it was a spur of the moment thing and you would have had your phone switched off at rehearsal?" suggested Peter.

And so it proved. Libby switched on her phone, which had been off all day, and not only found the message from Fran, but several others, including two from Colin from the previous day.

"I notice he hasn't called to apologise," said Libby, putting the phone away.

"Probably too scared," said Ben.

It was obvious to Libby when Fran and Guy arrived, that Fran had something on her mind. She felt an immediately sinking of the spirits, as she sensed that washing her hands of the Cy situation was not going to be possible after all.

"No, listen to me," said Fran, after Libby had expressed her desire to have nothing to do with it. "I feel sure there's a link, here."

"What, with the business at the Maidstone depot? What are you talking about?"

"I got to thinking about it," said Fran, "and the behaviour struck me as rather childish. Which reminded me of the other story about Cy and Patrick."

"Do you mean Larry Barkiss? But Cy would have told me, surely, if he'd been around at Maidstone? And anyway, we're not sure what sort of behaviour it was. Young Freddy thought graffiti."

"Cy didn't tell you about the business at all," said Fran. "How do you know that he didn't keep it quiet on purpose?"

"What?" Libby was amazed. "But why? When I first saw him he was looking for answers."

"And hadn't called in the police," said Fran.

"No, but he did after Patrick's death."

"Because he knew — or they knew — that either you or Sheila would if he didn't. He couldn't keep it quiet."

"But — but . . ." Libby stopped and scowled at her drink. "I don't know what you're saying. You're saying he deliberately kept quiet about the business at Maidstone because he thought it was the same person writing the letters? And knew who it was? Then why did he ask for my help?"

"But did he?" said Fran. "Or did Harry offer your services?"

Libby opened her mouth but didn't speak.

"That was what happened, wasn't it?" said Fran, and Libby felt incredibly foolish.

"But after that," she said, finding her voice, "they asked for quite a lot of help. And wanted me to go over to rehearsal and everything."

"Because you'd suggested another line of enquiry," said Fran, "which would lay their original suspicions to rest."

"Josephine." Libby nodded. "Oh, dear. I've been a bit of a fool, haven't I?"

"Not in the least," said Fran. "It was just me looking at it with fresh eyes, and seeing the whole picture, whereas you've only been able to see it bit by bit as it built up."

"I suppose so." Libby looked up from her drink. "Will you tell Ian? I told him everything I'd found out yesterday, so he's had all the info."

"I'll make the suggestion, if he'll listen to me," said Fran. "But there's something else, as well."

"What?" Libby eyed her friend suspiciously.

"Amy Taylor. I want to find out about her son."

CHAPTER
THIRTY-FIVE

"How do you know it was a son?"

Fran frowned. "I'm sure you said — or somebody said 'he'. Otherwise, I suppose it's just my brain. Again."

"I think actually I assumed it was a son, too." Libby stared into space trying to remember. "Anyway, why?"

"Where did he go? Who organised his adoption? Was it when Amy was away, and if so where was she?"

"Blimey, I don't know. And Freddy's gran Una is about the only one left alive who might know and she didn't."

"What was the sister's name?"

"Stephanie Brissac."

"Have you looked her up?"

"I think we intended to look up the name in the telephone directory but never did it. That was at the point that I decided not to have anything to do with the Burton and Taylor business."

"And how many times have you decided that over the last few weeks?" asked Fran.

"Loads," grinned Libby, "including yesterday and just now! And I haven't told you about my phone call from Colin, yet, either." She related the story and the subsequent events. "So Harry's off them, now, too."

"I should think so," said Fran. "Anyway, nothing to do with Cy or Colin, I'm going to look the Brissacs up online. And I want to know more about that book the police found at Maud Burton's house." Fran nodded decisively. "I've got some ideas."

"Yes?" said Libby after a moment. "What ideas?"

"You're too busy," said Fran with an innocent smile. "And you're washing your hands of the whole business."

"Oh, crap," said Libby. "Don't be such a pain. Tell me."

"What time's your dress tomorrow?" asked Fran.

"Two o'clock, so they get the evening off," said Libby. "Why?"

"If you've got time in the morning, I'll call you. Will you be free during the day on Monday?"

"As long as everything goes well tomorrow and the set hasn't fallen down or anything, yes. Why? What are we going to do?"

"I don't know yet. Maybe nothing."

"Stop being mysterious," said Libby. "It's not fair."

"I'm not — not on purpose. I just don't know what's going on at the moment." Fran gazed into her drink as though it held all the answers. "Don't forget I'm only just catching up with all this. And I don't know if I'm actually receiving information or making it up." She looked up at Libby. "You know what I'm like."

Libby nodded. "OK. I'll contain my soul in patience until tomorrow at least." She finished her drink and tapped Ben on the arm. "I think I need to go home now," she said. "Or I won't be fit for tomorrow."

On the way home, she told Ben what Fran had said. He sighed.

"So we're still on the case then?"

"Well, you wanted to find out about Patrick's death, didn't you? You were sorry for Lisa."

"I still am," said Ben. "Not sure I'm sorry for Cy and Colin any more, though."

Fran phoned while Libby was preparing a scratch lunch for herself and Ben the following morning.

"We've just been to church," she said.

"Church? You?" Libby raised her eyes at the breadbin.

"It felt right. Guy and Sophie and me. Oh, and Adam."

"*Adam?*" Libby almost choked. "What on earth . . .?"

"Because, as far as I know, he stayed overnight in the flat."

"I assume you're not talking about his own flat?"

"No, of course not, chump. Guy's flat over the shop."

"With Sophie, then."

"That would seem to be the case."

"Right," said Libby, feeling a slight pang that Adam hadn't told her about this development in his relationship.

"Come on, Libby, they're both old enough," said Fran.

"I know, I know. I would have liked to know, that's all."

"The only reason I know is that Sophie came to church with him."

"Still can't understand why you went, but still."

"Anyway, that's not why I'm ringing. I looked up Brissac in the online directory and there are none."

"I expect the police would have looked them up, don't you? When she committed suicide? Well, we know they did. It was in the coroner's report."

"But have you given that name to Ian or the Cold Case Unit?"

"I'm sure I told Ian," said Libby, frowning in effort to remember.

"Well, the other thing is to look up Julian. The father of the baby. Actually, I've already found one reference. Una said he died at Dunkirk, didn't she?"

"Yes, but I don't suppose that's set in stone. It has to be the result of gossip."

"But you said she talked to Amy after Amy came back to the village?"

"Yes, I think so. You're muddling me."

"Julian didn't die at Dunkirk. He committed suicide, too."

"Bloody hell," said Libby. "When?"

"Oh, at about that time. End of April, beginning of May."

"So the same time that Amy's baby was born."

"And the next thing will be to find the birth certificate of that baby."

"How?" said Libby. "You have to pay for access to them, and you don't even have all the details."

"Free genealogy sites," said Fran triumphantly. "Census record, and all that stuff. I've got Amy's name and the date, more or less, of the birth. Shouldn't be too difficult."

"As long as our hearsay facts are just that, facts."

"Don't be a wet blanket. I'll see what I can find and report in the morning. Have a good dress."

The dress rehearsal, though slow, went reasonably well, and Libby told the cast at the end all they needed was an audience.

"Panto is notoriously dependent on audience reaction, as well as participation. Once there are people out there you'll be fantastic." She beamed round at them. "No nerves, now!"

Freddy wandered up still in his back-legs-of-Buttercup trousers.

"Gran says you went to see her," he said.

"Yes, I did, and very helpful she was, too. I can't get over the coincidence of you having Aunt Dolly on one side of your family and Una on the other. You've been the missing link." Libby gave him a quick hug. "Now go along and have a nice quiet night before tomorrow."

"Going for a drink with some of the others," said Freddy. "Are you and Ben coming down?"

"I've left a casserole in the oven," said Libby, "but we might pop in just for one."

"We definitely will," said Ben, appearing at Freddy's shoulder. "As soon as I shoehorn madam here out of her chrysalis."

"Is that what it looks like?" asked Libby, turning her back to be unzipped.

"It does rather. But a pretty one." Ben patted her behind. "There you go. And hurry up. I'm gasping for a pint."

Most of the cast had gathered at the pub, and, to her surprise, Libby spotted Flo and Lenny in the corner by the fire.

"That's twice I've found you in here," said Libby. "Christmas Eve and tonight."

"We only live across the road," said Lenny. "And I do like my pint. We often come in here, don't we, Flo? Just at different times to you."

"We don't stay up as late as you any more," said Flo. "How's the panto going? You been rehearsing?"

Libby gave them a brief summary of the panto progress so far, and then said "I didn't know you knew our Freddy's gran Una."

"Una and Dolly," said Flo. "They come for the bingo in the Close. Funny how those two old biddies have brought you round to Dolly and Una, isn't it. Could'a saved you time in the first place, couldn't I?"

"Not really," laughed Libby. "Neither you nor I knew how they would be involved."

"So what do you reckon?" Flo moved up the bench as Ben squeezed in beside her. "That Maud Burton. Did they all know her?"

"Yes. It's incredible, but they're all linked, and this was long before Dolly moved here with her Webley."

"And that Amy Taylor?" asked Flo.

"Yes. Una told me all about her. And the father of her baby."

Flo eyebrows shot up. "She knew?"

"Oh, yes. I gather several people did. And you were right. She was the vicar's daughter. And the father was her cousin, Julian Brissac."

Flo and Lenny were agog. "I thought he were a picker — or a pole puller," said Flo.

"He was," said Libby, "working until he went up to university, apparently. Poor bloke didn't manage to do much, though. He committed suicide, too, a few months later."

Flo shook her head. "Poor bugger. What was it? His parents?"

Taking this to mean the reason for Julian's suicide, Libby said, "I don't know. Una thought he was killed at Dunkirk, but Fran's discovered — and don't ask me how because I don't know — that he killed himself. She's looking into it."

"That Fran'll get 'erself into trouble one o' these days," Flo warned. "If you don't get 'er into trouble first."

"I don't think we're going to get ourselves into trouble with people who are all dead," said Libby.

"But there are people still alive," said Flo. "There must be. That there baby, for one."

"But it was adopted. And no one knows where Amy went to have it."

"Hmm." Flo picked up her wine glass. "Bet you someone knows."

"But they're nearly all dead, now, Flo. There's only Una in the village."

"What about your dad?" Flo turned to Ben. "He was here."

Ben looked surprised. "So he was. But he'd have been too young to know anything about it, surely?"

"What, thirteen? Fourteen? In 1939?"

"I suppose so." Ben was frowning. "I could ask him."

"We didn't ask your mum about Burton and Taylor in case it upset her," said Libby, "so why should we ask your dad?"

"You know it's filtered through to them," said Ben, "especially after Cy and Colin coming to Steeple Farm. I'll see."

"You watch it, Libby, gal," said Flo. "You be careful, stirring up hornet's nests."

"Remember last time," said Lenny darkly, wiping a foam moustache from his neat real one.

"Yes, all right," said Libby. "But it's not me, now, it's everybody else. It seems to have spread, this story, so that everyone's looking into it."

"To be fair," said Ben, "Lib was asked to talk to Harry's friend by Harry, and it's just snowballed. Especially once there was a murder."

"Yeah, we saw about that, didn't we Len," said Flo. "Guessed it were your one."

"It's not my one," said Libby. "But it was Dolly's great nephew. Did you know that?"

"Yeah. Met him once, when Margaret brought him and Lisa down." Flo shook her head again. "Terrible for that family. Lost Margaret's Roy, too."

"Lisa and Patrick's dad? Yes. Awful." Libby paused. "Did you ever meet Ada? Dolly's mum?"

"No. I didn't marry my Frank until a few years after the war, did I? After Het had come back. Didn't know anybody but Het for a bit."

Libby sighed. "It's just so weird that it's all linked up. And all because I asked Joe up at Cattlegreen about anonymous letters."

"See? I told you, stirred up a hornet's nest, gal, that's what you've done," said Flo.

Libby glowered and Ben laughed. "And she should be relaxing and getting in the mood for panto tomorrow," he said, "so I shall take her home and take her mind off everything else."

Flo cackled and Lenny guffawed.

"And you two have got dirty minds," said Libby, standing up. "I'm ashamed of you."

CHAPTER
THIRTY-SIX

"So Maud Burton went off to stay with her sister and do Red Cross work in Curtishill," said Libby the following morning. "Which means she's got links with both villages."

"Yes," said Fran on the other end of the phone. "We've already worked that one out. What else we need to know is what secrets she knew that were worth blackmailing people for."

"Nothing real here in Steeple Martin except for poor Amy," said Libby. "What did you manage to find out about her baby?"

"I got a free trial on one of the genealogy sites and looked her up in the Births Marriages and Deaths, but I didn't have the baby's Christian name. However, there was one surprise — the birth was registered in Maidstone. There's no baptismal record, but that's not surprising as the baby was illegitimate."

"And was it a boy?"

"Oh yes. And registered as Brissac. Both parents on the certificate."

"So, she didn't go far." Libby thought for a moment. "You don't think she actually went to her aunt — Julian's mother?"

"She could have done, although it would have been a rather uncomfortable situation."

"No more uncomfortable than going miles away to live with someone you didn't know. And there wasn't as much traffic between the towns and villages in those days, was there? Especially once the war started. And Stephanie might have felt quite protective of the baby, belonging to her son."

"I would have thought she'd be scared of it spoiling his chances," said Fran.

"But he died. I wonder what drove him to it?" mused Libby. "Then it would be all she had left of him."

"So do you think Stephanie Brissac adopted him? Brought him up as her own?"

"She could have done. When the police tried to get in touch after Amy's death, the report said she wouldn't talk about it. The child would have been — what? Late teens, by then." Libby sighed. "Poor woman."

"Who was it said Amy kept in touch with the boy? Sent cards for his birthday? It would explain that, wouldn't it? If it had been a legal adoption she wouldn't have known where he was."

"And that," said Libby, "is another link to Maud Burton."

"Hmm?"

"Arranging illegal adoptions. Perhaps she arranged it all!" Libby was getting excited now. "She had a sister and brother living in Curtishill, who she probably stayed with during the war, so she would have known the Brissacs."

340

"But didn't your friend Una say that Maud went away after Amy came back?"

"Yes, but that doesn't mean to say she wasn't instrumental in the whole adoption process, and helping keep Amy out of the way during her pregnancy. And then maybe," said Libby warming to her subject, "that's what gave her the idea of helping other people hide things."

"Babies?" Fran sounded sceptical.

"There were hopping babies," said Libby, "except that they were usually born nine months later, like Amy's. A few were born during hopping."

"Or miscarried while hopping," said Fran slowly.

"Ooh, yes," said Libby, "except she wouldn't be able to blackmail hoppers. She wouldn't know where they lived."

"We're building bricks of straw, here," said Fran. "I think I've forgotten the whole point of the thing now."

"Yes, I keep feeling like that. I mean, I only really agreed to look into Cy's poison pen letters. That's where it all started."

"Well," said Fran with a sigh, "at least we're a little further forward. Shall I tell Ian?"

"I suppose so," said Libby. "If he can make any sense of it. Or pass it on to his mates at Maidstone nick."

It was several hours later, mid-afternoon, as it began to get dark, that Libby had a brainwave. Switching on the computer, she entered '1951 census' into the search engine. It took some time to track down what she wanted, but eventually, she found it. 'Mrs Stephanie Brissac, 68 and Julian Brissac, 11.' At an address in

Curtishill. Libby sat back, feeling smug. So Amy had named her baby after his father. And Stephanie had kept him.

Then she went to the next census, 1961, and neither of them were there. She frowned. Stephanie could be dead, of course, she would have been 78, and Julian could possibly have been called up. How would you find that out? Army records? She picked up the phone.

"Would someone aged 21 in 1961 have been called up?" she asked a surprised Greg.

Ben's father laughed. "Are you at it again, young woman?"

"Yes." She giggled. "I'm sorry, Greg. It's actually only nosiness now. All the investigation into the murder and the attack on Harry's friend is firmly in the hands of the police, but there were a couple of points that Fran and I were interested in."

"So Fran's in it with you now? Oh, dear. When you two get together . . ."

"I know. We egg each other on. Anyway, do you know?"

"About call up? What age did you say?"

"21 in 1961."

"Oh, yes. He'd have been called up anywhere between 1957 and 1960, depending on his circumstances. It all ended in December 1960, but he could well still have been serving in 61. The last conscripts were demobbed in 1963, I believe."

"Thank you, Greg. I knew you'd know."

"I'm not sure I should be encouraging you," he said with another laugh, "but good luck with it, anyway. Will you come and tell me all about it when you've got all the answers?"

"I will," promised Libby.

The first night of *Hey, Diddle, Diddle* and the Oast House Theatre was lit up from the tip of its white cone to its huge double doors, which now stood open. Libby approached with a strange feeling somewhere around her solar plexus and a distinct and almost unquellable urge to flee. Peter watched from the lighting gallery as she pushed open the inner glass doors.

"Cheer up, petal," he said. "They don't shoot directors these days."

Libby gave him a tremulous smile and went into the auditorium, where she surveyed the empty stage, set outside Mother Hubbard's huge shoe-house. The theatre was coming to life.

An hour later and the opening chorus raised the roof. As Libby had predicted, the presence of a live audience, warm and welcoming, had a tonic effect on the performers, and the Oast House Theatre's good pantomime reputation soared higher.

In the bar afterwards, Libby was surrounded by friends and relations of her cast, all telling her how good their daughter/son/husband/wife was. She agreed with them all. Amy, Maud, Cy and Patrick seemed a long way away.

But the next morning, they crashed back into her world — or rather, one of them did — when the phone rang.

"Julian Brissac," said Fran without ceremony.

"Junior?" asked Libby, wiping egg from her chin.

"Junior. Was called up."

"I guessed that, too," said Libby. "I checked with Greg."

"It was difficult to track him down," said Fran, "because he'd changed his name."

"Oh?"

"But I did." Fran couldn't keep the note of triumph from her voice. "Because I had a light bulb moment."

"Ah."

"I thought about the name —"

"Barkiss," said Libby.

"How did you know?" Fran sounded almost explosive.

"Sorry," said Libby. "As soon as you said changed his name it came to me. The similarity. I wouldn't have thought of it without you, though."

"Hmm," said Fran, obviously not completely mollified.

"So why did he do that?"

"Julian Brissac sounds rather highbrow, doesn't it? Perhaps he didn't want to get beaten up by his fellow squaddies."

"Good point," said Libby. "So presumably, Larry is his son?"

"Indeed he is," said Fran, "and now living not a million miles from here."

"Here? Nethergate?"

"Near both of us. Steeple Cross."

"No!" Libby sat down at the kitchen table and idly ran her finger around her egg cup to catch stray yolk.

"Not another one of those awful neo-Georgian places where Monica lived?"

"I don't know, but he's got an address in Steeple Cross. Should we pay him a visit?"

"No!" yelped Libby. "Don't be daft, Fran. On what excuse? For goodness' sake, we've never met the man, and anyway, Ian would be furious."

"I've told Ian already," said Fran. "He's going to see him later today."

"So leave it to him. Honestly, Fran, how do you imagine we would get away with going to see him?"

"I'd have thought of something."

"So how had Ian not found him before now?" asked Libby.

"He would have done, but I don't think he was trying very hard. Or rather the Maidstone police weren't. They were still trying to pin the murder and the attack on Cy on to those youths."

"But Ian told us they didn't do it."

"Doesn't stop them trying, though, does it?"

"I would have thought someone with a connection to both victims was a much better bet," said Libby.

"Exactly, which was why Ian's been listening to us, and in this instance with good results. I found Larry through the census again."

"What about Julian? His father?"

"No mention. I expect he's dead."

"He wouldn't have been very old, only 70," said Libby. "Every chance he'd still be alive."

"Old people's home?" suggested Fran.

"Not at 70, not unless he has Alzheimer's or something similar."

"So if we can't visit, how about a trip out to Steeple Cross? We could just have a look at what sort of house he lives in. And have a drink or something. Is there a pub there?"

"You're worse than I am these days," grumbled Libby. "All right. Give me an hour or so to get myself sorted."

"Oh, sorry," said Fran. "I forgot. How did last night go?"

"Great, thanks," said Libby. "No prompts and good audience reaction. Bob and Baz were the stars of the show again."

"Of course they were," said Fran. "Anyway, I'll pick you up in an hour, OK?"

Libby trailed upstairs to shower and dress. What was she thinking of, she asked herself? Going off on a wild goose chase to gawk at someone's house. It was like stalking.

But it didn't stop her experiencing a slight thrill at the thought of some action. The snow had curtailed most activities since before Christmas, although to be fair, in this particular adventure there hadn't been much adventuring to do. The odd visit to the suburbs of Maidstone was about it.

The lane to Steeple Cross was only just passable, snow piled up either side against the banks, the poles and wires of the bare hop gardens towering above them. The strange deep cut lanes of this part of Kent were almost claustrophobic, and could be quite frightening to visitors who occasionally got lost in them. Libby preferred the longer way round to get to Steeple Cross, which led through lanes at least wide enough to allow two cars to pass.

At last they came out on to the ridge below which a cluster of houses huddled round a church. Hop gardens lay to one side, while snow-covered fields lay to the other, a wood topping the rise on the other side of the shallow valley. After negotiating the crossroads at the bottom of the slope, they passed the house they had both visited the previous summer and went on into what could be called the village centre. This was merely the lane bending round the church to accommodate a couple of large old houses which looked as though they might at any moment fall into the middle of the road. A few smaller cottages were scattered around the church, one of which turned out to be a pub.

"Do you think it's open?" said Libby, peering out of the side window.

"Is it past eleven o'clock?" asked Fran, steering into the open space in front of the building.

"Yes. Shall we try?"

"Might as well, now we're here. See if they serve coffee."

The door opened into a dark, uninhabited space. A single, red-shaded light burned behind the small bar.

"Marie Celeste," whispered Libby.

"Hello, ladies." The voice came from behind them. Libby lurched sideways in alarm and knocked over a small table.

The man who smiled at them wore a collarless shirt over what looked like a grubby white T-shirt. Both were stretched over a burgeoning beer belly.

"We were wondering if the pub was open for coffee?" said Fran, recovering first.

"I can do that," said the man going forward and lifting a flap on the bar. "Got the Kardomah machine all switched on ready."

Who for? wondered Libby, as they followed him to the bar.

"Is it worth opening at lunchtime mid-week?" she asked aloud.

"Libby!" said a shocked Fran, giving her a nudge.

The man, however, didn't appear offended. He merely shrugged and said "We get a few people in. Passers-by like yourselves. Few regulars." He held up two cups. "White?"

"Yes, please," they said together.

"Now," he said, while his back was turned, "this isn't a day for a sight-seeing trip, so what are you two ladies doing in a place like this?" He turned round with the two filled cups. "Visiting, are you?"

"Yes," said Libby, ignoring a warning look from Fran. "Well, sort of. We're looking for Larry Barkiss."

Fran made a sound between a hiss and a tut.

"Larry?" The landlord raised his eyebrows. "You sure?"

"You know him then?" said Libby.

"I should say so." The landlord accepted Fran's proffered money. "He'll be in about — oh, ten minutes?" He put the money in the till. "But what the

348

— I mean — can't see you two ladies having anything to do with Larry."

"Oh?" said Fran.

The landlord looked from one to the other. "You don't know him, do you?"

"No."

He sighed. "Well, good luck is all I can say. I'll point him out when he comes in."

Libby and Fran took their coffees to one of the small round tables, dark and much polished, and the landlord switched on the small red-shaded wall lights around the low-ceilinged room.

"This wasn't a good idea," whispered Fran. "What possessed you to say we were looking for him?"

"Well, we've more or less found him; haven't we?" said Libby.

"But what will we say to him?"

But there, Libby had to admit she came unstuck. "It was your idea to visit him in the first place," she said in defence. "I said it was a daft idea. Then you said let's come over here and scout round. I still said it was daft. And now you're complaining because we've found him."

Fran sighed. "I know. I'm sorry. I think I must be getting a bit bored."

Libby eyed her friend with sympathy and a certain degree of schadenfreude. "I said so."

"Said so? To who?"

"Ben. Some time ago. I know you've been busy this Christmas, but let's face it, happily married, settled in Nethergate — what is there to do?"

"I thought I might do that creative writing course I thought about before — do you remember?"

"Or, on the other hand, we could ferret out some more mysteries," said Libby. "When the weather gets better."

"You change like the wind," said Fran. "You weren't going to have anything to do with any more murders or mysteries, and you were only saying that to me the other day. Do be consistent."

It was Libby's turn to sigh. "I know. I think the problem for both of us is that we're incurably inquisitive —"

"Nosy," corrected Fran.

"And now we've got a taste for it. And life feels boring if there's nothing to get our teeth into."

"You've got the theatre," said Fran. "I haven't."

"You could have. You're an actress."

"It's hardly round the corner from me, is it?" Fran stopped and looked round as the door was pushed open. "Is this him, do you think?"

A tall, well-dressed man had come in toting a large brief case.

"Tony," said the landlord, putting down his newspaper.

"Morning, Gary," said Tony. "Brought the new range in to show you."

"Rep," muttered Libby, turning back to her coffee.

A few other people drifted in over the next fifteen minutes, but none of them were Larry Barkiss.

"He's not coming," said Fran. "We might as well go."

"No, hang on," said Libby. "Look, the landlord's signalling to us." She rose and went to the bar.

"Larry's in the back," he said.

Libby was surprised. "How did he manage that?" she said. "We've been keeping an eye on the door."

"He often comes round to the back door," said the landlord with a resigned sigh. "Particular if he's a bit — well — under the weather."

"Drunk? At this time in the morning?"

"Hungover. If he comes round the back I give him a big black coffee."

"Can't he get that at home?"

The landlord looked at her pityingly. "You nip round the back and see him," he said. "But don't blame me."

Libby collected Fran and they went round the side of the pub to where the back door, set into a built-out porch, stood open. The porch contained the various detritus of a rural pub and the door to the kitchen.

Which was a dream of stainless steel. Although the saloon bar had given no sign of it, the pub obviously produced good food. Harry would have given a month's takings for a kitchen like this, Libby thought, gazing round until her eyes lit on the figure in the corner.

At first it was hard to tell it was a figure, rather than a collection of old clothes. But there was movement as a hand reached out to pick up the thick white china mug in the counter, and a pair of eyes met Libby's. At least, she thought they did, but the brows were so heavy it was difficult to tell.

"Are you Larry Barkiss?" Fran spoke gently as she moved towards him.

Libby expected the standard 'Who wants to know?' answer, but the figure nodded what appeared to be its head.

"We're sorry to disturb you, but we wanted to know if you knew, or remembered, someone called Cy Strange?"

The figure didn't move for so long Libby began to get worried. Then it shifted position and turned its head to look at both of them.

"Used to." The voice was harsh and sounded unused. "Knew that little bugger Paddy Stephens, too."

Libby wanted to protest at this, but Fran shook her head slightly and Larry Barkiss straightened up on his stool. His head emerged from the thick scarf wound round his neck like a tortoise and he coughed explosively. Libby and Fran drew back.

"Not my fault what happened, you know," he said.

"What happened when?" asked Libby. "When you were at school?"

"Don't be daft. What happened before Christmas. Paddy murdered."

"Oh, you know about that?" said Libby.

Barkiss's eyes moved slightly to the right. "Course," he said. Then peered at them both again. "How'd you find me?"

Libby opened her mouth, but Fran said quickly, "Following enquiries from the police." Which was true in a way.

352

"Police?" He frowned. "Ain't got nothing to do with me. Should have asked John."

"John?" said Libby and Fran together.

"John Feltham."

"Perhaps they have?" suggested Fran.

Barkiss shook his head. "Have a job. He's dead."

"You knew him? He was a friend of yours?"

Barkiss shrugged. "Met him in the hostel."

"What hostel?" asked Libby.

"In Canterbury."

Fran looked at Libby and gave a quick nod. "For the homeless?" she said.

Barkiss shrugged again. "Want to find that grandson of his."

"Grandson?" echoed Fran and Libby.

Barkiss nodded. "From Australia," he said.

CHAPTER
THIRTY-SEVEN

"Are you thinking what I'm thinking?" murmured Libby.

Fran nodded and turned back to Barkiss, who was noisily slurping his coffee.

"Did you know John for long?"

Another shrug. "Years back."

"Do you know his grandson?" asked Libby.

"No." Larry Barkiss returned to noisily slurping his coffee.

After a couple more attempts to get him to talk, Fran and Libby gave up and returned to the bar.

"I see what you mean," Libby said to the landlord as she hoisted herself onto a bar stool. "In a state, isn't he? How did he get like that?"

"And what's he doing here?" asked Fran.

"He lives here," said the landlord.

"Here?" said Libby in surprise.

"Up the road. Croft House. The Barkisses done well for themselves."

"So what happened to get Larry like this?"

"Well," said the landlord, leaning folded arms on the bar, "I don't know the ins and outs of it, but his dad had come into money and bought this place in the sixties. Larry wasn't born until ten years later."

354

"But he went to school in Maidstone," said Libby.

"Oh," said the landlord, frowning at her. "So you do know him."

"Of him," said Libby. "We know someone he was at school with."

The landlord's brow cleared. "Right. He got into trouble at school in Canterbury and they sent him to live with an aunt or something in Maidstone. I don't know much, as I said, but I managed to pick that much up. He got in trouble there, too, and I reckon he did a spell inside."

"In jail? What for?" said Libby.

"I told you, I don't know. Then he turns up back here. Ooh, this would have been a few years ago, now. Old man's dead. And he brought this bloke with him. Much older than him. Never came in here. Then he was carted off to hospital and I never saw him again."

"John?" said Libby to Fran.

"I don't remember his name, but Larry went to see him in Canterbury now and then. There was something a bit odd about him, if you know what I mean."

"And where did he live in Canterbury?" said Libby. "I think we need to know that, too."

The landlord's eyes narrowed. "Here," he said, "what's all this about? I've told you what I know about Larry, but I'm not giving out any more information. Not unless you're police, and I'm bloody sure you're not."

Fran gave him a calm, sweet smile. "No, but we are, in fact, working with them," she said. Libby marvelled at the composed way she spoke.

"Yeah?" said the landlord, still not believing.

"You've read about the murder of Patrick Stephens?" said Fran. "Seen it on the TV?"

"Yes." The landlord frowned. "You're not saying Larry had something to do with that? Gawd in heaven, look at him! He couldn't bash the skin off a rice pudden."

"No, we can see that," said Libby. "But he was a lead which needed to be followed up." And what Ian will say when he hears what we've been doing, gawd in heaven knows.

"Right," said the landlord. "And did it help?"

"Yes," said Fran, "it did."

The landlord shrugged and turned away to serve a customer. "Not sure exactly where the old boy lived," he said over his shoulder, "but I always dropped Larry near St Augustine's, if that's any help."

"You used to give him a lift?" said Libby.

"If I was going in to the cash'n'carry. Saved him the bus."

"Well," said Fran, "thank you so much for your help. It's been invaluable, it really has."

The landlord brightened up. "Really?" he said. "Well, fancy that. I'll go and tell old Larry."

"I doubt if he'll be pleased," said Libby, "but thank him anyway."

"So what do we think?" she said as they climbed into Fran's car. "John was Sheila's brother, and the

356

grandson is from Australia, so presumably, John didn't come back until after he'd got married and had a son?"

"Or a daughter. The grandson could be son of a daughter," said Fran, reversing into the village street.

"So where is he?"

"Don't know. We don't even know if he's in the country. Just because Larry Barkiss said we ought to speak to his grandson doesn't mean to say he's here. He could be still in Australia."

"But you don't really think that."

"No," said Fran. "I think he's here."

"Sheila will know, surely," said Libby. "And you'd better tell Ian."

"Is that necessary?" asked Fran.

"Oh no, of course," said Libby, her eyes wide. "Ian will probably find out all this information when he goes to see Larry later, won't he?"

"What I'm wondering," said Libby a little later, as Fran negotiated the lanes back to Steeple Martin, "is what Larry meant when he said he'd known him years ago."

"Also," said Fran, "it seems rather a coincidence — again, this case is so full of coincidences you wouldn't believe it in a book — that Larry Barkiss should be friendly with John Feltham."

"It is, isn't it?" said Libby. "So Feltham was the farmer's name and Sheila's maiden name. I suppose Ian's found that now. And there's another thing."

"What?" said Fran.

"The landlord said he thought Larry had done a spell inside. Yet Ian had looked him up and said he hadn't got a criminal record."

"The landlord could be wrong."

"Or he changed his name," said Libby. "Anyway, I suppose Ian will find out."

When they got back to Libby's cottage, she invited Fran in for a scratch lunch, which she went to prepare while Fran called Ian.

"I left a message," she said, as Libby brought in a plate of bread, cheese and ham.

"Will he get it before he goes to see Larry?" asked Libby.

"I've said it's urgent. Left a message with the desk sergeant and on his mobile, so we'll have to wait and see."

In fact, they didn't have to wait long. Ian called back just as they were finishing the last of the bread.

"Libby?"

"Yes, hello, Ian."

"It was Fran who left the message, but from your phone. She's still there, is she?"

"Yes, did you want to talk to her?"

"No, you'll do."

Libby rolled her eyes. "Gee, thanks."

"You both paid Larry Barkiss a visit this morning. Is that right?"

"Well, yes, but we didn't do it on purpose."

There was an explosive sound at the other end of the line.

"No, what I mean is, we went to Steeple Cross just to see — well — where he lived. And we stopped for a coffee at the pub."

"On the off-chance?" said Ian. "Of course?"

"Yes. And he came in."

"And you spoke to him."

"Yes. The landlord sent us round the back —"

"The landlord? So you told him all about it, too, did you?"

"Not exactly," said Libby, looking across at Fran and making a face. "I just asked if he ever went into the pub."

"And he does, and you saw him."

"Yes."

"And what did he tell you?"

Libby told him.

"So what's your explanation?" asked Ian. "Don't tell me you haven't got one."

"We don't have an explanation exactly," said Libby, "but we assume this John Feltham was Sheila's brother John who went to Australia."

"Yes. Feltham was the family name."

"So how did he and Larry hook up? And what about this grandson? Where does he come in?"

"I shall no doubt find out this afternoon," said Ian.

"Is there anything we can do?" said Libby.

"Apart from conducting the rest of the investigation?"

Libby sighed.

"Yes, there is, if you feel able," said Ian. "You could talk to Sheila Blake. Ask her what she knows about his grandson — her great nephew?"

"Shouldn't you do that?" asked Libby nervously.

She heard Ian sigh. "I thought you wanted to be involved?"

"Well, yes."

"There you are, then. A chance."

"Right," said Libby, "I'll talk to Fran about it."

"You're supposed to talk to Sheila Blake about it."

"All right, all right. Oh, and Ian. What about that book of Maud Burton's? The initials of people in Curtishill. Could we see them?"

Ian laughed. "I wondered when you'd ask. We've managed — we think — to track those down."

"Really? Who were they?"

"Sheila Blake and Ada Weston."

"Ada? You mean young Patrick's grandmother?"

"I do."

Libby gaped at Fran, who was looking increasingly impatient.

"But that's the link!" Libby found her voice. "The letters!"

"The link? Not between Cy Strange and Patrick Stephens."

"Oh, no." Deflated, Libby shook her head. "But it does confirm the link between the two cases."

"It does. I don't know how you came up with it, but it's been very helpful to the Cold Case Unit."

"Glad to have been of help."

"Go on, then," said Ian. "Go and talk to Sheila."

"So what was all that about?" asked Fran. Libby told her.

"So Maud was blackmailing Sheila and Ada. Why Ada? And why Sheila, come to that. We still don't know." Fran stared at her lap. "I wish I could get some kind of guidance on this."

"Guidance?" Libby wrinkled her brow. "Like spirit guidance, you mean?"

"No — just some kind of feeling." Fran shook her head. "Doesn't seem to be working, though."

"You haven't been close enough. You said that yourself."

"Perhaps if I went and talked to Sheila as Ian suggested?"

"On your own?"

"Well, you said you didn't want to do anything this afternoon because of the pantomime. You can't have it both ways."

"All right." Libby moved the lunch plates out of the way and sat down. "Let's work out what we want to know."

"When John came back to this country. What does she know about the grandson."

"Is the grandson important?"

"Oh, yes." Fran looked at her in surprise.

"Why?"

Fran looked confused. "I'm not completely sure, but he is."

Libby looked at her steadily for a long moment. "You're not speculating, are you?"

"What?"

"Well, I can see exactly why John's grandson is important. Or could be."

They stared at each other. "You mean . . ." said Fran.

"That he killed Patrick, yes."

Fran nodded. "Maybe it was speculation, but that must be why he's important."

"But why would he? Or attack Cy? I assume he did that too?"

"I'd better try and find out if he's actually in the country first," said Fran, with a short laugh. She stood up. "Shall I just turn up on her doorstep? Rather than warn her first?"

"She might not be in," said Libby. "Then you'll have a wasted journey."

"Better than her putting the phone down on me and refusing to see me."

"Be careful. Keep your mobile switched on. Supposing the grandson's there, too?"

Fran looked uncertain. "Ring my mobile in about an hour. Just to check."

When she'd gone, Libby called Ian again and told him that Fran had gone to see Sheila, and their worries about the grandson.

"Thanks, Libby," he said, for once sounding neither ironic nor irritated. "I'm just off to see Barkiss now. Let me know if you've heard from her in a couple of hours will you?"

Libby prowled round the sitting room. Sidney watched disapprovingly.

"What," she asked him, "can I do now? I can't go anywhere or I might not be back to be a fairy later. And I can't think what other questions there are to answer."

She stopped and stared at the computer. "Oh, yes I can!" she said suddenly.

Ada. Why had Maud Burton been sending poison pen or blackmailing letters to Ada Weston? Libby sat down with the laptop and went to the online telephone book. Now — what had Margaret's late husband been called? Pity she didn't know the address. Stephens was rather a common name, and there were a lot of them in Maidstone.

Eventually, her memory threw up the name — Roy. There were still quite a number of R Stephenses, so, trying another tack, Libby went back to the news reports of Patrick's death. Sure enough, after trawling through various different sites, she found one reporting 'Patrick Stephens, of Belleview Terrace . . .' and within seconds had found the telephone number.

"Is that Lisa?" she asked when a female voice answered.

"No, this is Margaret. Who's calling, please?"

"I'm really sorry to bother you," said Libby, her stomach sinking as she realised just what she was doing. "But I met your daughter just before Christmas at a pantomime rehearsal. My name's Libby Sarjeant. With a J," she added unnecessarily.

"Oh, yes, she mentioned you." Margaret's voice sounded tired. "Weren't you trying to help Cy?"

Not sure what Margaret thought she was supposed to be helping Cy with, Libby returned a non-committal answer.

"So, how can I help you?" Margaret went on.

"Um," said Libby, "it's a bit difficult."

She heard a sigh. "It wouldn't be about anonymous letters, would it?"

CHAPTER
THIRTY-EIGHT

"Well, yes, in a way," said Libby, after a moment.

"Paddy got some, you know. The police weren't happy that they'd been destroyed."

"Ah," said Libby, and wondered how to go on. "Um, it wasn't exactly Paddy's letters I wanted to know about."

"Oh?" Margaret's voice was much warier now.

"Yes. I'm really sorry to be so intrusive," Libby rushed on before she lost her nerve, "but it was letters to your mother I was thinking about."

"To my *mother*?" Now it was surprise in Margaret's voice. "My *mother*?"

"Yes. We — the police, that is — have reason to believe she was sent at least one back in the early fifties, or maybe late forties."

There was a long silence that Libby didn't dare to break.

"I don't know about my mother," Margaret finally continued, "but it's possible. I was too young to know then. I started getting them in the seventies."

Libby sat down hard. "*You* did?" But this was all wrong. Maud Burton was dead by then. Or disappeared, at least.

"Yes." A sigh. "Not that I'd done anything, but they just talked about my background."

"Your background? How do you mean?"

There was another silence and Libby decided she'd better back off. "I'm sorry, Mrs Stephens. I shouldn't have asked."

"No, no, it's all right," said Margaret. "I should have told the police at the time, but the letters weren't threatening, and didn't ask for money. They were just — nasty."

"How long did it go on?' asked Libby. "And did you never find out who was writing them?"

"I got them every now and then for quite a few years, then they stopped. After a year or two I realised no more were coming. I thought perhaps whoever was writing them had died. They must have been quite old."

"Why do you say that?"

"Because they were talking about my mother," said Margaret. "That was what it was all about, wasn't it?"

"Was it?" Libby was now completely lost.

"Well, of course," said Margaret. "Josie and I worked that out."

"Josie?"

"Josephine — Cy's mother."

"You knew Josephine?"

"Well, of course. We were nearly the same age. She was a bit older."

"Right," said Libby, frowning in concentration.

"And her letters were even worse than mine."

"H-her letters?" Libby squeaked.

"Didn't Cy tell you? I thought he knew."

"But what did they say? Was it about Josephine's mother?"

"Yes. But that's probably why Josie didn't tell Cy. She wasn't proud of the fact that her mother was a murderer."

"Well," said Libby, hesitantly, "yours couldn't have been about the same thing. Ada was your mother."

"But, according to the writer, my father wasn't my father."

"Ah."

"So that's why I think the writer must have been old — to have known, or thought that they knew, about that."

"Would Josephine have kept the letters, do you think?" asked Libby.

"I don't know. She showed me some, but I can't think she would have kept them."

"But someone might have thought she had," said Libby.

"Are you thinking about that second attack on Cy?" said Margaret. "Someone could have been looking for those letters?"

"Yes," said Libby slowly. "But it's interesting. Cy knew nothing about his grandmother, and I got the impression that Josephine didn't know anything about her, either."

"Oh, but she did," said Margaret. "I can understand her saying that to Cy — or to anybody else for that matter. I told you, she wasn't very proud of Cliona Masters, or whatever her name was."

"You can see why," said Libby.

"Anyway," said Margaret, "I don't see what all this has to do with my Paddy." Her voice wobbled.

"Neither do I," said Libby. "And I'm very sorry to have bothered you. I really shouldn't have."

"No, it's all right." Margaret cleared her throat. "I know you're only trying to help. Dolly said you'd been to see her, too."

"Yes," said Libby, glad of the change of subject. "She wanted to tell us about Larry Barkiss."

"And has that helped?"

"Oh, yes. I saw him this morning. The police are seeing him this afternoon."

"Really?" There was a gasp in Margaret's voice. A gasp and hope.

"I don't think he was involved, though," warned Libby, "but if he was the police will prove it."

"Will they tell me?"

"I will, if you like," said Libby, hoping Ian would share his information with her and Fran.

"Thank you," said Margaret, appearing not to question the fact that Libby would have privileged information.

Libby rang off and berated herself for intruding on someone with so recent a tragedy in their life.

"How insensitive can you get?" she asked Sidney, who twitched his ears but declined to answer. She looked at her watch and decided it wasn't yet time to call Fran, so she put the kettle on.

★ ★ ★

Fran had been received very coldly by Sheila Blake.

"I don't know what you want," she said in her whispery voice. "You're not the police."

"No," said Fran, "but you know I'm working with them."

"What do the police want with fortune tellers?"

Fran sighed and was glad Libby wasn't with her. Libby would have fired up immediately, but Fran was as dubious about her strange 'moments' as many other people and had learnt not to take offence.

"I don't see the future, Mrs Blake," she said now. "I simply see odd things from the past occasionally. Sometimes it helps the police."

Sheila made a disparaging sound, but turned and led the way into the sitting room. Fran sat opposite her where she could see the photograph, still displayed on top of the china cabinet.

"Your brother came back to this country, didn't he?" she said without preamble.

Sheila's mouth opened, but no sound came out. Fran noticed her hands gripping her brown skirt so tightly the knuckles were white.

"Larry Barkiss told us," Fran went on. "We saw him this morning. The police will be visiting him this afternoon."

Now Sheila's face was as white as her knuckles and Fran wondered if she'd gone too far, but reflected that Ian would be coming to speak to her about the same thing, so better that if anything were to happen, at least a woman would be here. Not, Fran hoped, that anything would happen.

"Will you tell me about it?" she asked gently.

Sheila shook her head. Jerkily, like a robot.

"But why be so secretive about it? It must have been wonderful to find him again."

"Why should I tell you anything?" Sheila's voice came out in an almost guttural rush. "What's anything got to do with my brother?"

"Your father let him go to Australia with the Child Migration Programme. This was a direct result of his association with Norma Cherry, wasn't it?"

Sheila didn't answer.

"And is his grandson over here?"

This time Fran really thought Sheila would faint. She felt the symptoms herself, the heavy thump of the heart, the tingling of adrenalin under the skin and the draining of consciousness from the head. But Fran wasn't the one suffering, and quickly she rose and pushed Sheila's head between her knees, then knelt at her side as her breathing became more normal and she sat up. Shakily, but she sat up.

"Would you like some tea?" Fran asked.

Sheila focussed her eyes on Fran and nodded vaguely.

"Will you be all right while I go into the kitchen?"

Sheila nodded again, beginning to look slightly better. Fran left her, unwilling, however, to leave her for long, so popped back until the kettle had boiled, and then as quickly as possible, made the tea and took it back to the sitting room. Sheila didn't appear to have moved.

"Tell me about your great-nephew," said Fran, placing a cup and saucer by Sheila's side.

"How do you know about him?" Sheila's voice was back to whispery again.

"I'm afraid Larry Barkiss mentioned him."

"Him." Sheila spat the word.

"You know him?"

"Course I know him. And his so-called mother."

"Amy?" Fran frowned.

"Stephanie, she called herself." Sheila looked down at the tea, but didn't pick it up. "*Mother*. Grandmother, more like."

"Yes, she was," said Fran.

Sheila looked up quickly. "How do you know all this?"

"The police investigation," said Fran. "And now they're looking into Maud Burton's death, as well. You know that."

"Stephanie got letters, too."

"The same as you did? And was that about Norma Cherry, or your real mother?"

"My real mother had been dead years. No, Stephanie got letters same as I did. Mine said — well, said about Norma Cherry. Cliona." She looked as though she had mud in her mouth.

"But it wasn't you that was affected, was it? There was no shame attached to you?"

"Wouldn't have wanted it known." Sheila's mouth snapped shut.

"So Stephanie got letters — about Julian not being her son?"

"Yes."

"And now, Sheila, tell me about John and his grandson."

"He was sent away. I don't know why I wasn't."

"Perhaps because you were older. Didn't anyone protest?"

Sheila shrugged. "How do I know? I was kept out of it all. Who told you, anyway?"

"Dolly Webley."

Sheila sniffed. "Ada Weston's oldest. I told that Libby about them in the war."

"Yes, I know. What was wrong with Ada Weston?"

Sheila's eyes slid away and Fran made a leap in the dark.

"Your father found them somewhere to live after they were bombed out of Hoxton, didn't he? You told Libby that, only you didn't say it was your father."

Sheila gave a brief nod.

"And what? He had an affair with Ada?"

Sheila's colour was fluctuating and Fran watched her anxiously.

"It wasn't like that." Sheila finally picked up her cup with a shaky hand and took a sip.

"So what was it like? Was your father also the father of one of Ada's children?"

"Margaret." Sheila put the cup down. "After that woman was arrested."

"He turned to Ada after Norma Cherry was arrested?"

Sheila was now bright red and her breathing had become shallow. Her eyes went from side to side.

372

Fran took another leap in the dark. "He raped her?"

Sheila seemed to sag with relief and her colour faded. Fran guessed she just hadn't been able to put it into words.

"That's terrible." Fran spoke softly. "You must have felt terrible, seeing Margaret grow up and knowing your own brother had been sent away."

Sheila gave another small nod.

"And you started receiving anonymous letters. There were more than one, weren't there? What were they actually about?"

"Norma Cherry and my father."

"And about John?"

"And Margaret. She knew everything."

"She?"

"Maud Burton. It was her."

"Didn't you report it?"

"Told you. Wouldn't want it known."

Fran thought for a moment. "So you let it go. Did you speak to Ada Weston about it?"

"They moved to Maidstone. I stayed in the village until I could leave home."

"What about John? Did you try to find him?"

Sheila shook her head. "Didn't know how. He just turned up one day."

"Really? When was that? And how did you know it was really him?"

Sheila looked over at the picture. "He had that with him. And his teddy."

"I thought all their belongings were taken from them?" said Fran.

"Not always. Anyway, he hadn't had too bad a time. And he'd married and had two children. His wife died, so he came over here to find me." She swallowed and lowered her eyes. "And he found me."

"And now his grandson's here?"

"I don't know, do I?"

Fran stared at her, leaning forward. "Oh, I think you do. He's been here, hasn't he?"

Sheila's hands were now gripping the sides of her chair. "I'm not going to answer any more questions."

Fran sat back. "All right. Tell me how you and John felt about Norma Cherry. And Josephine."

"She ruined our lives," said Sheila. "And that Josephine and Margaret, they both had better lives than we did."

Fran wondered if she would get anything more, and decided she probably wouldn't and had already upset Sheila enough.

"It was good of you to see me," she said, standing up, "and I'm sorry if I upset you. Can I get you anything else? More tea?"

Sheila shook her head. "You can see yourself out."

Fran did just that, sparing a glance at the photograph on her way. Outside, she took a deep breath and glanced across the road to the bungalow she knew was Cy's and Colin's. A curtain twitched at the front. She ignored it. She had some thinking to do.

CHAPTER
THIRTY-NINE

Libby got no reply from Fran's mobile. She waited another quarter of an hour and rang again. Still no reply. She looked at the clock and wondered if Ian's two hours were up. It was dark now and she was getting anxious.

It was nearly half past four when the phone rang and a knock at the door happened simultaneously. She picked up the phone on the way to the door.

"Fran!" she said.

"No, it's Ian. Have you heard from her yet?"

"She's in front of me on the doorstep. Do you want to talk to her?"

She handed the phone over to Fran and went to put the kettle on, listening to Fran relating her interview with Sheila to Ian, then watching Fran's face while she listened to Ian.

"So? I heard what happened at Sheila's, but what happened with Ian?" She handed Fran a mug of tea.

"The amount of tea we drink," said Fran. "I never seem to go anywhere without being offered a cup."

"Did you get one at Sheila's?"

"I made one after she nearly suffered a heart attack, poor thing."

"So what did you think?"

"Of Sheila? I'm still working on it, but you wanted to know what Ian said?"

"Of course!"

"Well." Fran put down her mug and took off her coat before sitting down. "Larry met him because John went looking for Julian after he'd found Sheila. They'd have been a similar age and both lived in Curtishill. How he found out about the name change I don't know."

"I bet it was Sheila. She's kept tabs on everybody, even if she won't admit it."

Fran nodded. "And she knew who was sending the letters. And it wasn't only her and Ada Weston that got them, it was Stephanie Brissac, too."

"Really? Gosh, what a busy woman. I wonder which one of them bumped her off?"

"It wasn't Stephanie. She was questioned by the police at the time of Amy's suicide, so they would have been bound to have connected her with Maud's disappearance."

"So what did Ian find out about the boy?"

"Nothing, as far as I can tell. But he did find that Larry Barkiss had been behind the trouble at Cy's work in Maidstone. He was daubing the walls with graffiti. Ian thinks because Cy had got a good job and he — Larry — had turned into a loser."

"So why didn't Cy tell us that?" said Libby.

"No idea. Perhaps we should ask him."

"Anyway, go on."

"That's all, really. Not much to tell."

376

"Well, I have," said Libby. "Listen to this." And she repeated her telephone conversation with Margaret.

"See how they all link up?" she said when she'd finished. "Maud Burton's friends with Amy and knows where baby Julian's gone, and what his background is. She goes to Curtishill and helps out there. She knows all about Norma Cherry and baby Josephine and where she went. She knows about John being sent abroad and about Farmer Feltham raping Ada Weston. She knows Margaret is his daughter. So when she comes back to Steeple Martin she starts blackmailing them."

"Or just sending them nasty letters," said Fran. "Sheila was the only one who said she was asking for money."

"Well, what about the letters that Margaret and Josephine got?" said Libby. "They can't have been from Maud, she was dead by then."

They looked at each other.

"And why didn't Cy know about Josephine's letters?" said Libby.

"I think Margaret was right. She wasn't proud of her parentage, so she didn't tell him."

"So there's actually three generations of letters, then?" Libby stood up and went to draw the curtains. "First, Sheila, Ada and Stephanie, then Margaret and Josephine and now Patrick and Cy."

"Well, it's obviously not the same writer each time," said Fran. "So someone is copying the first writer."

They looked at each other in silence for a moment. Then Libby said "I think you'd better call Ian."

"I think I want to call Cy," said Fran.

"About Josephine's letters? But he didn't know anything about them," said Libby.

"We assume he didn't."

"He said he knew nothing about his mother's background. He was gobsmacked when he found out about Norma/Cliona."

"Well, let's find out. I'll do it, after your last bout with Colin." Fran asked for Colin's mobile number and keyed it in.

"Cy?" she said, when a voice answered. "It's Libby's friend Fran. How are you?"

"Much better, thanks," said Cy cautiously. "How's Libby?

"Libby?" said Fran in surprise. "She's fine. Why?"

"I'm afraid Colin rather upset her the other day." Fran heard a protest somewhere in the background. "He's become very protective of me recently."

"I can understand that," said Fran. "Look, Cy, this is probably going to sound intrusive, but I wonder if I could ask you a couple of questions?"

"Go ahead." Cy sounded as though he was settling himself into a chair. "I saw you at Sheila's earlier. Was that a grandson she had with her? I didn't think she'd had any children, let alone grandchildren."

Fran went cold. "Grandson? When? I mean, where?"

"He came out just after you did," said Cy. "Young bloke in a baseball cap. Didn't she introduce you?"

"I didn't see anybody but Sheila," said Fran. "Look, Cy, can I hand you over to Libby? She knows what we wanted to ask."

378

"Sure." Cy sounded perplexed, reflecting the look on Libby's face as she took Fran's phone.

"The grandson's just left Sheila's," whispered Fran, picking up Libby's landline phone and dialling Ian's number.

"Cy." Libby cleared her throat. "Sorry about that. How are you?"

"I'm better, thanks, Libby, but what's going on?"

"Fran had to call — er — someone," said Libby, "but what we actually wanted to know was, have you found any letters of your mother's? In your loft, or anywhere?"

"There are some old boxes up there," said Cy, still sounding bewildered. "We found all the necessary stuff, like insurance documents and bills and things in the bureau down here. I've never gone through the old boxes. I didn't like to. Besides, she always said she knew nothing about her background. There wouldn't be any clues there."

"Well," said Libby, clearing her throat again, "you see, Cy, according to Margaret Stephens, she *did* know."

There was a short silence. "She *what?*"

"Yes. I'm so sorry, but she obviously thought she was protecting you."

"And Patrick's mother knew?"

"Yes. They were both in the same boat, you see. They were both getting anonymous letters."

"*They were?*"

"Yes." Libby sighed. "About their mothers. It's a long story. Look, Cy, when you're up to it, see if you can find anything that might relate to those letters. I don't suppose she kept them, after all, you didn't keep yours, did you?"

"No." Cy sounded as though he was being strangled. "If I find anything, what shall I do with it?"

"Let us know. And the police, I suppose." She looked across at Fran, who was waving violently at her. "I'll ask our policeman when I speak to him. And now I'll have to go. Tell Colin I forgive him."

She switched off the phone. "What?"

"Ian's on his way. He said he's alerted Ben and Peter, too."

"What? Why?"

"Because —" began Fran, but she was interrupted by her mobile ringing. She took it out of Libby's hand. "Hello?"

"Is that Libby?"

"No, Cy, it's Fran. What's up?"

His voice was shaking. "There are two police cars and an ambulance outside Sheila's. What's happening?"

Fran closed her eyes. "I don't know," she said. "I'd just stay put with the doors locked unless a policeman comes knocking. We'll ring you later."

"It looks as though the grandson's on the rampage," she said to Libby.

"What's going on, for goodness' sake?" said Libby. "Why did I have to take over the phone call. Why did you ring Ian? Why is he on his way?"

"Cy saw a young man coming out of Sheila's house just after I left. He thought I must have met him."

Libby's mouth was open. "The grandson?"

380

"Looks like it. So I called Ian. And now the police and an ambulance have turned up outside Sheila's. That was Cy telling me. He's very shaken."

"Oh, God," whispered Libby. "This is our fault. We shouldn't have gone to see her."

"I went to see her, not you," said Fran.

"But why is Ian coming? And Ben?"

"Ian thinks the boy might have followed me."

Libby's insides rolled. Then she shook her head. "No. He'd be here by now, if he had. And why would he, anyway?" She cocked her head. "See? That's a knock. That'll be Ian." She went to the door.

The next she knew was she was being pushed back inside the living room by a huge shape in black.

"You bloody nosy cows," said the face behind the balaclava. "You upsetting everything."

Libby, heart pounding, took in the empty hands and prayed there was no weapon. She'd also noted the slight antipodean accent.

"You're John's grandson," she said, although not sure how she could speak.

He pushed her hard and she almost fell into the fire. Fran caught her and steadied her.

"You're gonna pay," he shouted, pushing them both indiscriminately. "What you made me do."

Fran was on her knees and Libby inelegantly on the sofa, shielding her head with her arms. The landline began to ring. The boy looked round and spotted it, yanked it away from the wall and threw it at the fire. Following it with her eyes, Libby noticed what she hadn't before — on the small table by the fire, Fran's mobile, still open from where she'd been calling Ian.

Then the rest of the noise started. There were thumps on the wall. Libby's neighbour obviously protesting. The cars arriving outside. The crash of the front door being shoved open. Then the shouting.

Libby shuffled to the end of the sofa and Fran, ducking the flailing bodies, crawled up beside her. They could now see Ben and, of all people, Peter, desperately trying to subdue their attacker. And then the sirens. And all of a sudden, it was over.

Uniformed police hustled the boy outside and paramedics came in and asked who was hurt.

"All of them, I should think," said a calm voice, and Ian strolled in.

"What — how?" Libby was in Ben's arms and Peter was sitting beside Fran, who, although milk-white, appeared calmer than anyone else.

"Have you checked on Sheila Blake?" she asked Ian.

He looked down, then up again and nodded. "She's still alive," he said, "but only just." Fran let out a breath.

The paramedics insisted on checking everyone over, but amazingly, no one was hurt. Ian sat down at the table in the window and surveyed them all.

"What I want to know," said Libby, "is how Pete came to be here?"

"Ian called me," said Ben. "But I was already on my way. I called Pete."

"Why were you?" said Libby

382

"He —" Ben jerked his head "— came to Steeple. Farm asking for you. The guy who's doing the loft was just leaving and told him where you were."

"And Maidstone?" said Fran.

"Sent a patrol there as soon as I heard from you. It looks as though he was there all the time you were, Fran."

Fran put her head in her hands.

"Why didn't he attack Fran while she was there?" asked Libby.

"I don't suppose he could hear properly. I expect Sheila told him after she'd gone."

"But why?" said Ben, who'd been following this with difficulty.

"I don't know," said Ian. "We might find out after we question him, but it doesn't look as if it'll be easy."

"What's his name?" asked Fran. "Did Larry tell you?"

"No, so we don't even know that yet."

"And now we might never know about Sheila," said Libby.

"What about her?" asked Ian.

"If she wrote the letters to Margaret and Josephine," said Fran. "That's why we were ringing you."

"It all added up," said Libby.

"And now we'll never know," said Fran.

"Oh," said Ian, "I think we will."

CHAPTER
FORTY

Somehow, Libby went on as the fairy. Guy drove over to collect Fran and Harry provided everybody with supper on the house, Fran and Guy before they went home and Ben and Libby after the show.

"So what do we still need to know?" Harry asked, as he and Adam joined them at the table in the window.

"The boy's name, why he did it — presumably he was the one who killed Patrick and attacked Cy — and if he was behind the second attack. If Sheila wrote the letters."

"And why," said Ben. "I must say, this has been one of the most complicated of all your — I don't know — cases, shall we call them? All those names! I got thoroughly confused at times."

Libby looked at him. "And you didn't even tell me off after we were attacked."

"No." Ben squeezed her hand. "I really don't think you put your head in a lion's mouth this time. And, by the way, how did he know where to go after he left Sheila's?"

"That's a point," said Libby. "How did he? He can't have followed Fran or he'd have been here ages before."

"Tomorrow," said Harry, standing up. "You'll find out all about it tomorrow. And I've already spoken to Cy. He said the police came over to them almost as soon as he'd spoken to you, and that you were right."

"Right?"

"That's all he said. He couldn't believe you'd gone on in the panto tonight, but said he'd speak to you in the morning."

"Josephine's letters," said Libby to Ben, as they walked home. "He must have found them."

"Stop worrying about it," said Ben. "It's over." He put an arm round her shoulders and hugged her. "Thank God."

But it was several days before Ian suggested they all might like to get together to hear the full story. A baby-faced detective had come to take statements from Ben and Libby, and someone had done the same for Fran, Cy and Colin. Cy had kept very quiet about what he'd found, as he'd passed whatever it was over to the Maidstone police. However, when Ian suggested that Sunday, being Libby and Ben's day off from the pantomime, would be a good time to meet up, Cy had agreed. He and Colin came to see *Hey, Diddle, Diddle* on Saturday night and stayed at Steeple Farm, so Ian suggested they all meet there, if Ben didn't mind. Ben didn't.

Libby, apart from once-a-day speculative phone calls with Fran, put the whole matter to one side and relaxed into performer mode. Freddy asked a few questions, and when Aunt Dolly, Una and Sandra came together to see the panto, they also were curious, but nodded sagely when Libby said she was unable to tell them anything and fell to criticising the front end of the cow.

On Sunday morning, Libby was touched to see Cy and Colin had gone to a lot of trouble to prepare for their faux-guests. There was cake — two sorts, proper coffee and tea in a teapot. Ian's face wore a typically sardonic expression, but Fran and Guy both looked delighted.

"So," said Libby, when they'd all been served with their brew of choice, "first of all, how's Sheila? And what actually happened that afternoon?"

"Mr Strange —"

"Call me Cy."

"Cy, then," said Ian, "told you about seeing a young man coming out of Mrs Blake's house. You told me and I sent a patrol car round. They found her in the sitting room bleeding from a head wound. She briefly regained consciousness, but not enough to be questioned."

"And how is she now?"

"Better, but the doctors don't want us questioning her too much yet. She's not going anywhere."

"So what about the boy?" asked Fran.

"His name is Kyle Holmes, and he's the son of John Feltham's daughter. We've been in touch with his mother, who has refused to come to the UK, but was able to provide us with some of the back story."

"Which is?" prompted Libby.

Ian sighed and took a sip of coffee. "Give me a break, Libby. I've been working on this all week."

"Sorry," muttered Libby.

"So, Mrs Holmes tells us that her father wasn't treated too badly, not like some in the Child Migration programme, he married her mother and produced her and another daughter. Her mother had died, and she and her father decided it would be a good idea to try and trace his English relatives, although he was deeply prejudiced against his father, whom he only dimly remembered."

"Did he remember his sister?" asked Fran.

"Yes, better than his father. He remembered a woman, too, but he didn't see either her or his father very much, certainly in the last year of his life here."

"Norma. I bet he didn't," said Libby.

"Mrs Holmes says he used to tell stories about England to her children, Kyle, of course, and his sister. And eventually he left for England."

"When was this?." asked Ben.

"Some years ago. He went looking for his sister, but, of course, she'd left. Then he searched for Julian, Amy Taylor's son, whom he remembered as a playmate. All the time he was writing to his daughter and she was feeding the information, naturally, to her children."

"So how old was Kyle by this time?" asked Libby.

"She thinks twelve or thirteen. Anyway, eventually it appeared that John had tracked down Larry Barkiss, who was living under an assumed name —"

"That was why he didn't have a record!" said Libby triumphantly.

"Yes, Libby." Ian gave her a hard stare.

"Sorry," she said.

"And finally, his sister Sheila. And discovered that his father's other children, Josephine and Margaret, had stayed in the bosom of their families and lived a perfectly happy and contented life while he was shipped off to Australia."

"Bloody hell," said Guy.

"Yes. According to Mrs Holmes, he was philosophical about it, but she gathered that his sister wasn't."

"Sheila, we're talking about?" said Colin. "But she was always so nice. Do you mean to say she resented Cy's mum all that time?"

"You've seen the letter," said Ian.

"What letter?" asked Fran. "This is what you found, Cy, is it?"

Cy nodded. "I gave it to the Cold Case Unit. They said not to speak about it."

"But you can now?" said Libby, looking at Ian.

"Yes. It was the last letter, I think, that Josephine received. Margaret Stephens got one, too. Neither of them knew who'd written them."

"What did it say?" asked Fran.

"Cy?" Ian nodded to him.

"Right." Cy shifted in his chair. "Basically, it just said she — my mother — came from bad stock, and there was a lot of bad language, and that if my mother didn't want it to come out then she should keep quiet. The writer had already killed once and would kill her if she said anything to anyone."

"And the writer?" asked Guy.

"Sheila," said Libby and Fran together.

"And had she? Killed before?" asked Ben.

"Maud Burton?" Libby asked Ian.

He nodded. A collective sigh went round the room.

"DNA was conclusive. As it was when we could match up what we found in your house, Cy. Sheila and Kyle together."

"It was Sheila and Kyle who knocked Cy over the head? And searched the house?" said Colin.

"Kyle hit him. Not hard, apparently. He didn't want to kill again. Sheila wanted to search the house, so they wanted Cy out of the way."

"How did Sheila get back to her house so quickly, then?" asked Libby.

Ian sighed. "No, Libby, she wasn't with Kyle when he hit Cy. She was clever enough to realise that someone might come looking for her, so she sent Kyle over on his own to make a noise in the garden and hit Cy when he came out."

"But they didn't find anyone in the garden," said Harry.

"No, because he ran. Not back to Sheila's though," said Ian. "He stayed out of the way in case the police came. Which they did. It was later, when Sheila came back from the hospital, that they went back. Sheila had a key, you see."

"I didn't know that," said Libby, with an accusing look at Cy.

"She'd always been a good neighbour," said Cy. "How was I to know?"

"Neither of us knew, love," said Colin, patting his arm.

"And what were they looking for? The letter you found?" asked Harry.

"It seems so," said Ian. "According to Kyle, she thought if Cy found it — and she was pretty sure he hadn't already, knowing him for years — the whole story would come out. She was, incidentally, furious with Kyle for killing Patrick and attacking Cy. That was not, apparently, what she meant by making their lives a misery."

"No," Libby said. "She was upset about Patrick."

"And not about me," Cy said.

"I expect she was," said Fran. "She was fond of you, in spite of herself."

"So how did Sheila kill Maud?" Libby wanted to know. "And how did she know it was Maud?"

"Maud made no secret of it. And she had a hold over Sheila."

"Well, yes, she must have done if she was writing nasty letters," said Libby, "but just because her dad had slept with a murderer?"

"And because Sheila was the one who tipped off the police."

"No! But she was only about ten!"

"And hated Norma with a passion. The Cold Case unit finally found the information, but Sheila never appeared in the case because she was so young."

"I suppose," said Guy, "that these days the family of a convicted murderer could go into the witness protection programme. Even if we don't think it's so terrible, back then things were different."

"So I keep being told," said Libby. "Illegitimate children, living in sin, all practically hanging offences as far as I can see."

"Not to mention homosexuality," said Cy. "Poor old Sheila. To see my mother and Margaret grow up happy, and then see me and Col living openly together — it must have freaked her out."

"But her brother, John, was perfectly happy about it," said Ian, "according to his daughter. And then one day after John had died, Kyle suddenly gets it into his head that there could be a lot of money in the English family and he wasn't getting his share. She says he'd already been in trouble with the police, abo-bashing, she said, which follows."

"Abo-bashing?" said Colin.

"Aborigines instead of gays," said Cy.

"Oh," said Colin.

"And of course he knew where his great-aunt Sheila lived," said Fran.

"So he came over and they egged each other on." Libby made a face. "Horrible."

"Exactly," said Ian, "except that Sheila didn't mean to kill anyone. She just wanted them upset. 'Make their lives a misery', is what Kyle said she told him to do."

"So she knew all about it? The attack on me?" said Cy.

"No. Kyle says about that that he'd been drinking. And he was in the Aird Memorial Hall that evening. He formed some kind of obsession for Lisa. And she'd left with someone else. He followed her out and Patrick followed him."

"Ah!" said Fran and Libby.

"Now it makes sense," said Libby.

"Yes, well, Patrick tried to stop Kyle, who 'lost it' he says. He's quite forthcoming, now, especially since when briefly questioned, his great-aunt confirmed that he's guilty."

"And so she didn't see a gang of youths?" said Colin.

"No, she saw her great-nephew kicking one of her victims. She came out of the Memorial Hall and followed him because he was running. She didn't realise he'd killed Patrick at that point."

Cy put his head in his hands. "Sheila," he said. "But she helped us. She patched me up."

"And didn't let you go to the police or to hospital," said Libby. "Remember?"

"So it was Sheila writing to me?" said Cy. "And my mother?"

"And Patrick, and Margaret," said Fran.

"And Maud was writing to Ada, Stephanie and Sheila," said Libby. "And now I want to know why she killed Maud and how."

"You said it yourself, weeks ago," said Ben. "When she heard about the Amy Taylor case and Maud's part in it, she guessed that there would be an investigation."

"Which, actually, there wasn't," said Ian.

"But she thought there would be and her secret would come out, so she killed her. But how? You said there was no trace of Maud to be seen."

"We can only speculate," said Ian, "but we think she must have had transport. And I'm afraid we're having to dig up the garden of her previous home."

"Oh." Libby felt a bit green about the gills, and noticed that Colin and Fran were also looking a trifle wan.

"Did Lisa realise Kyle was after her?" asked Ben. "And why didn't anyone comment on his presence?"

"I saw him," said Libby, "remember? I asked about Lisa's boyfriend? He was right there in the hall. Sheila ignored him."

"Well, she would. Kyle used to follow her down and stay out of the way. I expect it was one of those situations where everyone thought he was with someone else." Ian put down his cup. "So there we are. An unpleasant business all round." He turned to Libby. "But without you looking into the Burton and Taylor story, Libby, I doubt if we'd have got there."

"Oh, I think you would. After all, you got the DNA," said Libby.

"Yes, and we were already suspicious of Sheila," said Ian, "but we couldn't see her killing Patrick or attacking Cy. She's almost eighty."

"Kyle must have seemed like a godsend to her," said Fran. "Someone to manipulate, to do her dirty work for her."

"But, as is so often the case, the manipulated turns manipulator," said Ian and stood up. "Now, is there anything more you want to know?"

"I want to know why you didn't tell us about the trouble at the Maidstone depot," said Libby to Cy and Colin. Ian sat down again.

"So do I, said Harry. "You were so keen for Libby to look into the attack, and she even asked you about if there'd been any trouble there."

Cy looked at Colin, who had gone an unbecoming shade of red.

"My fault," he said in a strangled voice. "I got into a state about the graffiti at the time and caused a bit of a fuss at the depot. That was really why Cy moved on. All my fault."

No one spoke. Eventually, Cy looked round at the others.

"I forgave him. And I don't see how it would have helped anyway."

Ian's expression suggested that it might have done.

"And why did Kyle attack Sheila? Ben asked.

"He came in through the back door while Fran was there. He didn't hear everything, so when Fran had gone he asked what she'd said. Neither he nor Sheila have told us exactly what happened, he just says it made him angry and she shouldn't have done it."

"In those words?" asked Peter with a grin.

"Not exactly."

In the following silence, Ian stood again and looked round t the thoughtful faces in front of him.

"Anything else?" he asked.

"Yes," said Libby. They all turned to her. "Are you coming to the pantomime?" she said.